THE
ABSOLUTES

ALSO BY MOLLY DEKTAR

The Ash Family

THE
ABSOLUTES

A Novel

MOLLY DEKTAR

MARINER BOOKS
New York   Boston

THE ABSOLUTES. Copyright © 2023 by Molly Dektar. All rights reserved. Printed in the United States of America. No part of this book may be used or reproduced in any manner whatsoever without written permission except in the case of brief quotations embodied in critical articles and reviews. For information, address HarperCollins Publishers, 195 Broadway, New York, NY 10007.

HarperCollins books may be purchased for educational, business, or sales promotional use. For information, please email the Special Markets Department at SPsales@harpercollins.com.

FIRST EDITION

Designed by Renata DiBiase

Library of Congress Cataloging-in-Publication Data has been applied for.

ISBN 978-0-06-328270-4

23 24 25 26 27 LBC 5 4 3 2 1

For only in praising is my heart still mine, so violently do I know the world.

—Rainer Maria Rilke, "Fragment of an Elegy"

PART I

CHAPTER 1

We left for the bobsled race in the afternoon. At one p.m. it was beginning to get cloudy, although in places the sky was still blue. We wore our matching red Welcome Team uniforms, which were the wrong choice, because they were barely insulated. We boarded a bus to Cesana. There, we took a fully enclosed gondola lift, which Federica called an *ovovia,* up over the bobsled course, a mass of silvery tubing. In the *ovovia,* there were two benches facing each other. I sat with my back against the peak of the mountain and watched the course tumble out below her. Federica had wide shoulders and narrow hips. She wore her hair in a low ponytail; she never wore a hat. She had a long straight nose with no dip where it met her forehead, like Augustus Caesar's profile on coins, and angry eyes that were archaically large, too large for her face.

We got out at the bobsled course, but it was deserted, so we got into another *ovovia* and made it up over the *sci di fondo* course to the top of the mountain. Back at Cesana Pariol we built a snowman and I couldn't tell what language the children were speaking.

We entered the course and walked all around to try to warm ourselves before settling into a spot near the starting line, where the track went vertical and the five rings were printed in blue below the ice. We sat on a platform built for a TV camera, and I chatted with an Alpino in a feathered cap.

Federica ignored me for a long while, as usual, though there was nothing to do but talk to me. Then she made me reach under her red uniform jacket and take her phone out of her right pocket because her hands were frozen.

The best part of the race was the noise, a low rumble that shot from one ear to the other like a stereo. The bobs were very shiny. We stayed for one heat. It was just too cold. We got back in the *ovovia* and went up the mountain again. The air was so charged with misty snow we couldn't even see the car ahead of us.

This was how I met Nicola. He got in our gondola at the top of the mountain.

THE GROUND FELL away. We slid among the evergreen steeples, and the snow shushed against the rounded windows. I scanned the rubber seal around the doors. The ride back was going to take so long, and there was no way to exit. I felt the first twinklings of panic. I didn't know how to adjust to the intrusion of this boy into our space. The height would have been manageable if he weren't there. I clenched and unclenched my numb toes.

He's (she found the word I didn't know) a nobleman. She whispered it to me, while he watched, smiling. *È nobile.* He was a bit older than us. Nineteen. His coat was all the way buttoned up.

The snow brought the sunset close; it was in the frost on the window and in the hazy trough of mist between our descending gondola and the ascending gondola across the way. No conductor visible anywhere. We were caught in a scheme of disembodied, geometric power. Like solar system or vortex street. Carried along by hidden power with hidden motives.

Federica and I sat on the bench on one side, and he sat on the other side. He had an intelligent face, baroque, used beauty. There was something examined about his face, adored. I had the sense lots of people looked at him. It was an agile, active face, or it was carrion, picked over, it seemed to me, even in those first moments. The face showed that everyone wanted to know what he thought all the time. He had smoking green eyes.

"Ciao, Fede," he said. She later explained she'd met him at a few parties. He was famous around Turin and good with names.

"Ciao, Nicola," she shot back, with a note of contention in her voice.

Down we floated in our white globe, glass circle in the white world. The gondola was even farther from the trees; we'd drifted over a crevasse. The poles holding the wires were as tall as skyscrapers. We rocked back and forth as we parted the snow. The sun was bristly between the flakes. I was worried I was having trouble breathing; my heart was beating arrhythmically. I watched her for clues about how to behave. I reached for her hand. He smiled at that; he kept his eyes on my hand when he said, in Italian, "And your friend, who's she?"

I was terrified of him and what he might see about me and Federica. He could tell I depended on her. I tried to tell myself, Don't worry, he can't look into your mind. I didn't know whether he was good—responsible, sincere. I later learned that many people found him arrogant, he was so knowing.

Federica took my hand off hers. I wanted to grab it back, but I was afraid I'd fall apart if she refused me. My shame ricocheted within me, getting stronger. My ears rang, and hot queasiness squeezed at me from the inside. Meantime, the gondola went falling at increasing speed through the air. I was worried I would throw up. I couldn't breathe. I put my hand under my coat and pinched my waist trying to ground myself, but my body was disobedient. Stop it, stop it, I either thought or said; I was rocking and grimacing, and I had to do whatever was necessary to stay alive. Silence rolled over me, my pulse was overflowing and escaping. My heart hastily counted down. I was aware that I could keep breathing, but my heart was going to stop and there was nothing I could do about that. Could I do my own chest compressions? We were so far from a hospital. I never found out how Federica answered "Who's she?"

"Are you afraid of heights?" he said. His voice was far off. He spoke to me in English with a formal, old-fashioned American accent. I couldn't lift my head. "We'll be down soon." It was like hearing a painting speak.

He stood, crossed the flying space in one step, and knelt in front of me. He put his leather-gloved hand on my shoulder and neck. His touch was a shock. In the black midst of my panic, it thrilled me. No one had ever touched me there or in that manner.

I tilted my head back against the window and felt the cold glass. I was pinned there against the window by his tense hand while the pink atmosphere continued, in slow motion, to shatter all around us.

Fede didn't like that. "She's being silly," she said, in Italian. Fede didn't want me to have the attentiveness and gentleness from the nobleman.

I wondered if he could feel my whipping heart. I couldn't look at his face, so I just looked at the dark curls on his temple. I'd dreamed of being saved, but I'd never felt it. He was part of it, the dawn on the Po and the long purple cypress shadows, the scent of the evergreen boughs broken by snow, the exaltation—and now I felt something so consuming I was worthy of it—that fine cold glove, that knowing compress on my neck. An ultraviolet feeling.

The gondola was a shuddering fantasyland, the sun emerged, and the snow was an endless cascade of gems. He looked out from the window of this little flying room into the winter room of next year, the year after that. He swapped my panic for wonder.

What is the purpose of art? *To classify certain things as types of things,* my high school art teacher said. *To classify certain things as types of things.*

In a certain sense that day stood still forever. No day ever passed since then. Some mornings I woke up in midair in the snow, kissing the air that fluttered out of Nicola's mouth.

CHAPTER 2

I had arrived in Turin five months earlier, in August, at the station called Porta Nuova. The other station, Porta Susa, was under renovation for the Winter Olympics. Carla, the mother, carried a sign that said "*Benvenuta* Nora." She had fluffy blond-dyed hair and stringy, convex bangs. Later I realized it was the kind of hairstyle that was popular in the eighties. Gianni was long-limbed with a gray curly head and a stubbly face. He held the leash of Rosa, the purebred German shepherd, and pointed out the police dogs. "Good husbands for Rosa," he said, with a crooked smile.

I didn't like Federica at first, as we walked down the platform and out into the sunshine on the grand baroque city. She was terrible at English and skeptical of me. I wanted to begin a sisterhood right away. At home in the US, I wasn't close to anyone. I couldn't imagine confiding in a sister, didn't even think about what secrets I could confide; I just wanted to experience life alongside a friend, life not so arid and shut away.

My parents had sent me to live with these distant relatives because I'd been self-harming at home. It was my tenth-grade year and I was glad to get out of Florida. We lived in the old people part, on the Gulf Coast.

I liked to put myself in situations and see how they felt; I was the scientist and the rat. That was why I cut myself, which was the behavior that sent me to Italy. I thought it was silly and dramatic to cut my arms, so I cut my thighs. I didn't want my actions to be interpreted as a "cry for help." I did it because I wanted to see how everything felt and I wanted to be an artist and I didn't know what to do with my energy. My parents had given me a Swiss Army knife with a silver emblem so smoothly embedded in its red plastic case that I could barely feel the difference in the two materials. Secreted within its rounded body were its multitude of skills: the beige toothpick, the tweezers, the tiny scissors, the nail file, and then that knife with its nail grip like a long slitted eye. I wondered, Am I capable of this? It seemed to work for some people, like meditation or exercise, and I wanted to call myself brave. In my shower, standing on the knobby pink nonslip mat, I tried a dozen times. I wanted to feel myself gather into a bolt of energy, but the results were not promising, and I didn't want to take a shortcut with a bigger, sharper knife or something less painful, like a bunch of pills. Where would I have gone if no one had stopped me? Maybe I could have pressed my distress back into my body, like the knife back into its slot of darkness, and tried another way of being.

But then, to my surprise, there were external consequences. The pediatrician told my father, and his crying immediately made my behavior serious. Serious enough to earn me a plane ticket across the ocean. Serious enough to find me stretching my legs at five a.m. in the soft plane corridor as the ocean turned cold red. The sun came over the horizon in a hot blade. First my hair and hands, then the ocean became lustrous copper. Cold air leaked in around the oval window.

They asked me why I did it, and I couldn't say much but apologies, and they decided that I needed a change, and they were right about that, though their love made me squirm.

It was hard to comprehend the cause and effect, how pushing at my thigh with a Swiss Army knife in the shower had produced this. On the plane, I had the first coffee of my life.

IN THE END of summer and the fall, as Turin prepared for the Olympics, Federica and I walked together by the Po. We walked down the white stone quays, where sometimes she made me light her cigarette. Orange enamel streetcars slid over the arched bridge and vanished into the cypress-heavy hillside. Boys in long boats dipped their oars. We walked up the stairway and into Piazza Vittorio. Streetcar wires criss-crossed overhead like a zodiac ceiling. The piazza started broad and narrowed into Via Po. Turin was more north than you'd expect, as far north as Minneapolis. Once, Hannibal marched over the mountains and into town with his elephants. You could still see the red brick gate the Romans built. Like everything else in Turin, the Roman gate was unremarked upon, unfenced, and there for the taking. In Turin nothing was barred off. It was like an old tomb no one had discovered.

Federica and I walked along Via Po with the evening light cutting at us along the arcades. We walked along Via Roma, buffeted by the crowds. Early on, when I didn't speak Italian, Turin felt void of conversation. People could be talking loudly and the effect was still one of silence, nothing for my thoughts to grip. People passed like shades of the underworld.

We walked from the fascist arcades of blocky, polished granite to the eighteenth-century arcades. She showed me Libreria Luxemburg, which had an upstairs room of English books, and there I bought Rilke and Primo Levi. Turin smelled like laundry, cigarettes, diesel fuel, and lemon balm.

For the Olympics, we were too young to be full volunteers, so we were going to work for the "Welcome Team." We attended trainings and received cheap red jackets and padded pants.

Part of my function in Italy was to teach English to Federica, but she was a terrible student, restless and forgetful and angry. And I didn't know how English worked. I was supposed to teach her the difference between "I'm going to" and "I will." One of them signified a planned future and the other a spur-of-the-moment future and I never found out which was which. While we worked, she would take an entire liter water bottle—no one drank tap water—and slowly crush it down to the table with her teeth, gulping up the water as it escaped.

Her eyes would be pleading for rescue while she cursed me for drilling her on prepositions. But I couldn't explain why "get" is so different in get together, get over, get up, get down, get in. I pretended that it wasn't fun for me either.

In reality, it was fun, extremely fun. I loved how Federica would cheat off my tests at school. I loved being patient with her. I loved her helpless, enraged gratitude. At school, someone told me she only liked dogs. I took this as advice. I looked for ways to be her dog.

She did have a dog, Rosa, the German shepherd, and at fifteen she was already something I've never become, which was the kind of person who could train a dog. She was able to be strict. She was able to subject others to her will, even if they protested. She had something to prove.

On one of those early days, Federica and I took Rosa out to the Parco del Valentino so that Federica could teach her tricks. Competitive walkers swished past on the royal paths. The orange tram eased over grassy tracks. Boys in red caps sculled on the steely Po. A blushy sky and Rosa's black gums. Federica held biscuits in her hands for Rosa. She told me, "If a dog likes treats, it doesn't mean the dog is stupid. The best dogs love treats. The best dogs will do anything for a treat."

Desire didn't make me stupid. Desire made me sharp, and good.

CHAPTER 3

School was Liceo Classico Massimo D'Azeglio. The building had once been a monastery. After that, it had been Primo Levi's school. It was a cold building, like a cellar. We all wore our coats in class. In the marble bathrooms, there were no toilets, just porcelain holes in the floor.

Here, I never thought about cutting myself. I knew who I was suddenly: the American girl. And the distance I'd felt from my life in Florida was now enforced by the language barrier, and every day I fought to express myself, and that was exciting, because it was friction animated by hope. Besides, I had learned not to count on privacy. There wasn't even a word for privacy in Italian. People just said the English word.

Fall in Turin turned to winter. The men leaned long ladders all the way up to the arcades, scraping down and repainting the arches. Already you could buy Olympics key chains with little rubber mascots, Neve and Gliz, who represented snow and ice. It was cold, and on clear days you could see the snowy Alps on the horizon at the end of the streets.

Everyone had a fountain pen with a thick nib and transparent blue ink. Everyone was reading *I Promessi Sposi* that year. I could not take Italian, Greek, or Latin, which were all at too high a level for me, though I helped Federica memorize the conclusion to Ovid's "Pyramus and Thisbe": *"nam color in pomo est, ubi permatuit, ater"*—mulberries are dark from lovers' blood. In Florida, I'd loved to paint, but there was no studio art class I could take here. I took several art history classes. I studied Guarini's domes and Etruscan art, the muted Etruscans, known only from their tombs. I wrote a short essay on halos and aureolas. An aureola is the kind of halo that surrounds your whole body with gold.

We had to stand up when the teachers entered the room. After my first oral exam, everyone applauded.

I took several PE classes. In the beautiful old-fashioned wooden gym, we carried out nonscientific exercises—walking around the room raising and lowering our arms—and played all different kinds of handball.

A *caffè* vendor came at the breaks and sold brioches in the hall. I liked the brioche with apricot jam and the brioche with custard. I liked that classes usually ended at one p.m., and then all the boys would go down to Bar Big Apple and drink coffee and wrap their kaffiyehs around their necks and spread out over the city on their motorcycles.

AS OUR SCHOOLWORK piled up, Federica and I spent less time walking together. But one Saturday in November, Federica took me to the disco. I hated the music and the strobing lights. I watched her kiss three different boys. I was enraged by how much attention she paid them, and how little she paid me.

I sat on a leather couch and watched people touch each other under their clothes. I liked watching this and no one minded me. I'd never gotten drunk, and I refused to drink now.

Outside, Federica blew smoke at the side of my face, which I loved. I thought about how in Hamlet the poison goes in through the ear. "You don't need to be so scared," she said. But I was waiting for someone to take control of my better nature. Someone to say: *Drink this right now.*

Finally, at dawn, we took a streetcar home from the disco. The streetcar's interior was a shiny gray enamel which kept flooding down its length with the sharpening shadows of empty trees and tall palazzi. It was cold and I could barely hear. Federica and I sat on the round wooden seats in the back. She smiled at me. "You hated that," she said.

I nodded. "You weren't nice."

"It's good for you," she said. I realized she'd been ignoring me to bother me, to make me jealous. Mania began to grow in me. She'd been trying to bother me: She was thinking of me. Even among all those kisses from boys.

The sun was rising. It caught in the arcs of dried soap that the window washer had left whenever he washed. He'd washed quickly. The sun turned his haste electric pink. The stale cigarette smell of our clothes lost itself in the soapy smell of the morning; the tram jingled. There were just a few shutters opened by the earliest risers, green against the yellow walls. Bright ice melting in the gutters. The whole city rang like a bell. Turin that morning was a very thin veil behind which reality glowed. It wasn't only that the city was different, though it was: it was in its tautest, most lavender state. But that morning, I was also different. Maybe I could scrub off my layers of anxiety and habit, and all the adjustments I made to feel consistent, all the choices constrained by previous choices, the part of me that ran straight for solitude, that didn't really believe that the most important things could be shared. A hope for discontinuity was what I felt. Federica had been thinking of me. How was it possible? Each view of the streets—the arcades, the towering palazzi with enormous open doors into courtyard gardens—lifted me into exaltation.

We passed the bull's head fountains under the arcades, decorative fountains that were also drinking fountains that never turned off, pouring out fresh water that gravity pulled down from the Alps. In fact, the entire city was a fountain, perforated and trickling. The birds, the berries, the fat light and blue shade; dogs, breaths, Alps linked in white. "You don't need to be so scared," Federica had said. This morning was ours. I wanted to seize her hand. I turned to her, about to speak.

"*Cazzo*," she said. Then "*Cazzo, cazzo.*" She liked the sound of her voice on that grown-up word. She'd chosen the wrong tram. We'd end up far from home. She was angry. We exited in Piazza Vittorio Veneto. She could not revel in the morning, which we hadn't been sharing at all.

She asked me to light her cigarette while she cupped it against the wind. I couldn't get the clicking wheel to turn, and she laughed at me.

All this was before the Olympics and the gondola lift and Nicola. Later, Nicola gave me a way to think about the different kinds of power. Federica's was just one way. In history class we learned about the Franks and the Saracens during the crusades. The Franks were unbeatable, for a time; they covered themselves and their horses with armor and mail and ploughed into their enemies like tanks. But then they encountered the Saracens. The tank-line of the Franks was useless. The Saracens were light and fast and centerless. They scattered and shot arrows from their horses.

The shadows of the cypresses were long and blue. The morning air was lilac; on the way home, we bought blood oranges from a street stand and they were impossible to peel. Federica gave me two euros, and I drank a latte macchiato in a tall glass. Foamed milk with just a tiny bit of espresso. The Po was slow and green.

*

I WAS HELPFUL and quiet, "good" in that innocent friendly way that was so important to me, and I knew she disliked my success at school and at home, and I kept it fraught for her: I'd glance at her when Carla complimented me. I was full of fake humility when permitting her to copy my work. I told her how to adjust her answers so they weren't quite mine, and I dominated her with speed and intelligence. The point of being helpful and quiet was making it charged with her. It was all for her. *Let me light your cigarettes, Federica. Tell me what to do.*

A rivalry makes more sense if you're fighting over something of common value, but we were only fighting over each other, and so we kept sliding around, toward and away; there were no places to measure.

One afternoon I came with her to the DVD rental store and picked out *Star Wars: A New Hope*. I wanted her to see the scene when Darth Vader comes with the shiny round torture droid to torture Princess Leia. This was my favorite scene in any movie when I was growing up; I could spend hours thinking about it.

We sat on the couch. She had her Onitsuka Tiger shoes up on the coffee table. I held the DVD box and rubbed its pebbled plastic cover across my face.

The droid floated toward Leia, and we could hear Darth Vader breathing. *E ora, Altezza, discuteremo l'ubicazione della vostra base ribella segreta.* The dubbing made Darth Vader seem debonair and self-conscious. I knew his words well. *And now, your highness, we will discuss the location of your hidden rebel base.* The camera zoomed in on the syringe, containing some disabling injection that Leia would not be able to escape.

"Awful," I said to Federica, watching her face. "I hate this scene."

"Why are we watching it?" she said. Neither of us moved

to turn it off. "Because you were talking, I couldn't hear," she said. She rewound, and we once again watched the droid approach, calibrated to keep Leia alive while forcing her to submit.

AS WINTER ARRIVED, she was searching for a reason to be angry with me. One day she found one: a boy named Marco bought me a croissant at break. She left school without me, and when I got home, she was frying chestnuts and shaking with rage. I knew she was going to punish me somehow. "Ciao, Fede," I said. She hit her pots so hard against the sink that Rosa started whining.

I went to work in our shared bedroom. I was jumpy and excessively kind to Carla and Gianni at dinner. I took a shower and thought about what I'd done, letting Marco buy me that croissant. I washed myself with the family's bodywash from Dì per Dì. We all used the same bodywash that smelled like fragrant olive flowers, a smell that long afterward made me cry. The bathroom was white with steam. Steam velvety on the shower door. Falling in long drops. I stepped out onto the mat and heard the door unlatch. I had just turned to see the source of the sound—and she busted her way in.

"Why didn't you lock it," she said. She stared at my naked body.

The air was condensing, and there was a cold draft from the open door.

She must have heard the water, and heard me shutting off the water. She knew I was in there. She picked that moment. She meant to invade. She meant to make me ashamed.

But I was, strangely, not ashamed. This was a surprise to me. Despite all my interest in being good—waiting on the edge at the disco, being humble when praised—I liked her looking at me. I liked that she didn't ask permission. I liked that I was guiltless. I liked that I was exposed. I was patchy red with heat, small-breasted; my hair was pulled into one long dripping tail. I didn't move to cover myself. And because of that, I noted with a thrill, she became the one who was ashamed. She blushed and withdrew. No one had seen me naked at this age but the doctor who had inspected me for cutting.

"What happened to you?" she said.

"You know you have to knock," I said, in a high voice. Though I didn't feel panicked then, because I hadn't understood her question.

She turned and went. "Lock the fucking door," she said from the hall.

AFTER THAT, SHE increased her campaign of ignoring me. She was punishing me, I thought, for not being cowed by her invasion. For transforming what she'd intended to be her moment of power into mine. Or, beyond that, for acting as though I wanted her to see me, and thereby calling up in her a desire she did not want to face. Maybe she felt she'd edged up too close on it; she had to introduce distance; she was afraid.

And then I realized: *What happened to you?* She meant, *How did you get those scars?* She thought I was weird, inhuman. She pitied me. Something had gone too far, it was too much, what I had revealed was too extreme. Then I thought, hopefully, she felt she had to protect me.

The air was mostly purple in the winter. The days of the swallow, Carla called them, black and cold as soot. Our clothes out on the balcony froze stiff as cardboard and we shifted them inside. The snow on the roofs was the finest, purest lavender.

I bought a down coat, a *giubotto*. A jagged clock in Piazza Castello counted down the days to the Olympics.

On Christmas, we ate *agnolotti* and rabbit *all'arnois* and *bunet* and then we went to the midnight mass. We sat so close I could smell her hot licorice odor. She was only pretending to be bored. She fidgeted slightly.

I imagined tutoring her in English again and making her angry. She was chaotic inside and evil, and her giant eyes looked dull only because of the candlelight and the way they were set in her heavy brow. She was a genius of disaffection, her eyes staring straight back into the thirteenth century, when she would have been put to death. I was certain that no one knew how to appreciate her except for me.

SOMETIMES WE HAD a good weekend, though, when we drove the terrifying chasm-paralleling roads to Sestriere. In preparation for the Olympics, vivid webbing blocked off tracts of snow. Already the risers were being constructed at the foot of the massive downhill slope, the floodlights raised, by coatless workers from eastern Europe.

In the Alps, Federica would relax her strictures. She loved to ski. She had a red Kappa jacket with an eagle on it, a fascist-looking eagle, I thought, and signatures from famous racers all over the sleeves in permanent marker, and her skiing trophies were above the kitchen cabinets. She was a graceful, expert skier. She loved to exhaust herself in the Via Lattea. If I was dominant at school and increasingly dominant in the family, she could still dominate in the mountains. She would barely speak to me, but she'd ski with me until she got tired of the easy slopes.

She'd push me onto the path for the ski lift. I was always so frightened that the swinging chair would knock me over, or that I'd get a ski caught and break my leg. But she'd put me in place with her strong grip, and up would rush the chair, and suddenly we'd be swung out over the white hills, over flags and moguls and quick gaudy skiers, over pine-filled chasms and bivouacs entombed in snow. The glitter would fall from the tops of our skis. Silence, and my face reflected in her red goggles, and my ankles protesting the heavy attachments. Sometimes she would let herself whoop with delight, and I wanted to tell her that we were the same.

Then onto the snow, which some days squeaked, some days shuddered away under the skis and ridged like a seashell, some days flew up in flashy clouds of dust.

I had to V-shape on each turn, but she kept her skis closely parallel; she skied on a different substrate from the sticky chaotic stuff that kept knocking me down. She was nonchalant and show-offy like a dolphin. "Brava, Nora," she'd shout as I made my nervous way.

Sometimes in the evening we'd ski until the sun set. The snow easily took on any color and became a vast field of gold or trunk-striped lilac. Then we'd find our way to a *baita* restaurant she liked, a mountain inn with tearful windows and a pungent woodsmoke smell. We always came upon it from a different angle. I could never find it on my own and I never learned what it was called.

We'd thrust our skis vertically into the snow, then walk with loud ski-boot swagger to the table and eat chestnut soup and melted cheese and melted chocolate, among a few rich Europeans but mostly old locals who all knew each other. Sometimes they sang. The Alps had been full of resistance fighters. I wondered if any of them had been partisans, captured like Primo Levi in the mountains. If they'd carried out stealth attacks against the Nazis with whatever weapons they could scrounge. Or if they'd thrown their lot in with the fascists, with the Republic of Salò.

All these things were available to me, exactly as they had once been, and how could I understand them? How could I break through to all the reality and knowledge that had preceded me here? Others' lives, and the past, even communicated at specific length, were sealed. But sitting in the *baita* with Federica, losing track of time and picking up more and more Italian, gave me fluorescing hope for a shared subjectivity. These men knew of encounters that had never been recorded, they knew of wickedness and heroism that had not been formalized in writing, so their value was still determined personally, and the personal was always higher stakes, to me. Could I join the resistance? I wondered.

Federica drank the homemade wine from the large green bottles. She was comfortable and assured in this world. She was the grandchild of men like these; I knew her peasant grandparents had not fought for the resistance, but I didn't know what they had done in those years instead.

In my memory, we were always at the *baita*. In reality, it may have been only twice.

When we left, the moon would lie on the snow. We'd fall silently through the slopes, sinking fast on the liquid snow, with no anchors, weightless in a weightless world. We skied past tilted farms where we could hear the cowbells ringing inside the stables.

The best was when we reached flatter parts of the snow: she'd fly out in front of me and hold her pole back to me, and I'd grip it and she'd launch me forward, and I'd crouch and surpass her in speed, then I'd pull her forward with the pole, then she, then I, then she, then I.

* * *

THE OLYMPICS ARRIVED. As volunteers, we attended the dress rehearsal of the opening ceremony: Opera, anvil, fireworks, commedia dell'arte puppets and sloppily executed human formations. The next day we drove up to Sestriere and held a green, black, and blue ribbon tight across the entry of the new Olympics lounge, and the mayor snipped it. Sestriere filled with languages, enamel pins, and beautiful tan people; the athletes weren't guarded like celebrities, rather they walked among us in their national uniforms. In the evening, we went to a party at the communal pool, and members of the Savoy family, Italy's ejected royals, were there, drinking in the lit-up chlorinated steam.

After the first night of the games in Sestriere, when we all looked out of the window of the apartment with binoculars to see the downhill races, Carla and Gianni returned to Turin. Federica and I had one week alone. The first five days, we sat in the Olympics lounge and played card games and watched the bartender boys practice their tricks with the tumblers. We watched curling.

Then one of the many aimless journalists gave us tickets to a bobsled race. This was the only event I attended of the Olympics.

And it was the end of one life and the start of the next.

CHAPTER 4

We disembarked and said goodbye to Nicola. He disappeared into the snow. But the feeling stayed. I was filled with ferocious joy. My longings had snapped into line. I'd felt myself collapse into total embarrassment and there I found tenderness instead of punishment. And Nicola had disrupted something in Federica; she became possessive and competitive, a rougher surface for me to grip. I felt capable of making the world what I wanted. This was borne out first thing by Federica steadying me as I reeled down the path away from the gondola. Her arm around me was tight and insistent.

That evening, Federica and I went to a party. L'Irish was clamorous and jammed. The gold medalist from the day's downhill skiing was there, her skiing onesie unzipped and a medal around her neck. Bode Miller was there. He signed a napkin for me. Two cross-country skiers talked to us, but when they asked our ages—fifteen—they laughed and left us. "We don't want to get arrested." I felt embarrassed by this; clearly I'd made a mistake.

I got drunk for the first time. I started with limoncello, which went down hot and seemed to pool in my ears, then vodka with pear juice chasers. Then every blink made the bar bounce. The lights became squiggling wires.

Federica and I could barely get home. We held on to the railings as we walked up the sloping central square. The cobblestones had a fluid look. They bulged and streamed. I felt I was walking parallel to the two of us on the morning after the disco, when it hadn't been possible to connect. Now it was different. We reached our apartment. Fede turned on the overhead light, which bounced chaotically off the walls. *No!* I cried, and turned it off. I felt a strange intensity. Intensity headed toward wrath with the stereo roar of the bobsleds.

When I tore off my scarf, I could feel Nicola's cold hand on my neck. I'd lost it in the *ovovia,* my obsessively indirect and sensible behavior. I wanted to see if I could get her angry enough to hit me. That was the challenge her kind of anger proposed. Why not try, I thought.

I touched my neck, trying to feel what he felt. To Federica, I said, "Why are you so mean to me?" Being drunk made it easier to speak Italian, I noticed. I'd learned so much since the summer. I felt hard hilarious clarity.

"I'm always looking out for you," she said quickly. She was unsurprised by my question, which reinforced my courage. I wondered whether she'd planned a conversation like this. Her chin was high; her face, transparently lit by the streetlights bouncing off the snow, was strict. However, I could not be intimidated, because I was aiming for her to hit me. I was amazed at the surging energy I felt from running toward the thing I had always tried to flee.

"Why don't you talk with me anymore? Why don't you go out with me?"

"You're my little sister," she said. "I do what's good for you." I could tell she was drunk and ready to fight.

"You wanted to see me naked," I said.

The effect was even more extreme than I had intended. She blanched and looked away.

"You came in on purpose," I said. I was dizzy and inel-oquent, but I felt surgical in my degree of control over her emotions. "Why did you want to see me?" I said, overly gently.

Now she was fidgeting. She stepped from one foot to the other, and kept smoothing her hair and tightening her pony-tail.

I stepped closer to her. My heart was exploding. I heard the *chug chug chug* in my ears. Take it out on me, Federica. "What's wrong," I murmured.

She was looking to the side. I stepped a little closer. "Don't be angry with me," I said. I reached my hand out to her face, but did not touch her. I held my hand close to her cheek, then dropped it. I wanted to say, *You love me.* "You wanted to see me," I whispered.

Finally, she moved. She lunged at me, and too fast to think, she'd pushed me onto the floor. I felt the hard heat of the floor's impact and not the fall itself. I looked up at her electric face. She was so angry her brown eyes looked almost green. She was so angry her face looked almost wise. I grabbed her arm, pulled her down. She fell without a sound.

With both hands, I brought her face into mine and in-haled her alcoholic breath. She leaned forward and pressed her nose to my neck. Up spun Nicola's hand, a phantom ac-celerant. My whole body caught in my throat, like I had been beheaded, and then below I was a wash of air.

She'd kissed boys at the disco before, but she was also innocent.

I don't know how long we kissed, I was drunk and breath-less. I was helpless and empty of shame. I kissed her mouth. When her lips were closed, their soft tautness was like a persimmon; when her lips were open her mouth was wet-giving and fleet and changeable. Ghostly. I experienced the chalk sweetness of her deodorant, the alternating heat and sourness of her body, her humid breath. We didn't touch each other under our clothes, but she reached for my breast and felt its shape and pressed on it.

THAT NIGHT I slept on the couch. In the morning, the sunlight on the trophies daggered my eyes, my head felt kicked in, and the ice-covered road to the square was rainbow-white like an opal. In the *caffè,* my cappuccino and *brioche alla marmellata* were so sweet and warm I thought Federica and I would carry on like that every night, and be married, and live forever.

I read *La Stampa.* I knew Italian now. I read that when they flew the lions home in the cargo airplane, they arranged the cages so that friends faced friends.

CHAPTER 5

No more did we pull each other on skis, or walk together on Via Po. She began to tell her parents that she hated me and that I was mean to her. At first they didn't believe it. But she kept repeating it. She had something to prove.

As spring arrived, I mostly stopped eating, which made me miserable but gave me something to focus on, a new definition. I walked in endless circuits around Turin. My body grew fine hair all over it. I couldn't sleep at night because I was so hungry. My legs were always cramping. Even during hot midday, I shivered. I wore many layers of clothing. Like the cutting, I did not want this to be a "cry for help." I thought I was completely in control.

Every day I thought about the gondola lift. I couldn't think about the drunk evening that followed—just about the gondola lift, where I'd made such electrifying contact with helplessness.

Why had I become desperate? I'd been fine on the way up. Was it because of the enclosure, or the weather, or the boy, Nicola? He knew everything. He knew that in the shower and the school and the church and the long vaulted passages of Turin, I wished that Federica would take what was hers. He knew that I had a power, leading her as I did on my leash.

*

THE PART OF the Quadrilatero Romano where the massive obelisk appeared, suddenly, as one came around the corner. The church down Via Mazzini with a two-story copper door, green as the Statue of Liberty, covered with the jutting heads of saints. I navigated by spires, following my feet to the point of transcendence. On my walks, I was always wondering: Can I find Nicola here? Can I find Nicola here? Under his influence, not only could I interact with Federica, I could control her. Now, after meeting him, I was more isolated than I'd ever been. I was so fluid I couldn't tell who I was. I wanted the phrase or image into which I could pour my personality, like water into a cup. I could not remember what I used to be like. I could not remember feeling excited about schoolwork, or the times when Federica and I walked together. Were we peaceful and silent together? And just a blink before then, I had gotten excited all week to eat Saturday fries with my father on the wharf and listen to him talk about the Rolling Stones, and just before then I had believed my teddy bear could talk. All these states were dead and gone. If I had known how completely the past would fall from me, would I still have wanted to meet Nicola? I blamed him for the kiss.

In one of my art history classes we were up to Caravaggio, and I dwelled on Caravaggio's *Saint John the Baptist in the Wilderness,* the one in Kansas City, reproduced on a full page in the textbook, because it reminded me of Nicola. The page was glossy with ink, and I turned so often to it that the blackest parts became scaly. It had a special scent, like a cassette tape. *See how his sensitivity isolates him,* the teacher said. *See the intensity of the burden that only he can carry.* I brought him up once to Federica: "How did you know that boy in the *ovovia,* again?" She explained that she'd met him at a few parties, that he knew everyone, and was famous.

I asked why he was famous.

She said, "His family is evil. His father is bad."

"Because they're nobility?" I said. She refused to answer me. I didn't ask her again. It was too painful to feel how much she liked to deny me.

Federica's claim did not scare me. I thought I could judge for myself, with my own secret values, whether or not he was bad.

I wondered what Nicola would do if he saw me. I wondered where he lived when he wasn't at university—in a palazzo, in a castle in the hills. If he saw me, he'd say, "What happened to you?" He'd take me to eat. I imagined sitting at a long table in some immense salon in his noble lodging, or sitting with him in the *baita* with the raclette, or sitting with him at Platti, in a stiff banquette of oxblood velvet. He'd try to tempt me, and I would refuse. And then he would force me, I imagined. He'd hold my head still. I imagined his fingers bracing against the back of my head. I imagined him holding my nose until I had to open my mouth.

I WAS TRYING to eat eight hundred calories a day. I fantasized about cool, fatty, creamy things. *Semifreddo. Primo sale,* somehow blander than milk, though made only from milk. *Sfogliatelle* with their ricotta hearts, southern pastries which unspooled like ribbon from a clown's mouth. In the back rooms of Fiorio, I ate a lump of sugar that had been bathed in pure alcohol. It was supposed to be set on fire, but it burned my throat instead.

I bought cookbooks and fantasized about sticky sweet desserts—rice pudding, bread pudding, cassata, ricotta with honey. I watched Gianni crush persimmons into his mouth. Carla started to weigh me. I used to drink a lot of water before the weighings, which made no difference.

My stomach rumbled at the ancient dates and bread from mummy tombs in the Egyptian Museum.

Because Turin was a forgotten city, it was generous. Its emptiness meant it was willing to be claimed. The trade-off for this generosity was its incommunicability. What was the value of the rain settling on Palazzo Carignano, on an empty afternoon when everyone was inside? What did it mean to me, to me alone? Likewise, where would I want to live if everyone else in the world died? I wouldn't want a mansion, I'd want a small dark room with blankets.

As in-control as I felt, I could tell there was something wrong with me. I was lost, really lost, like I'd never been in my life. And I knew he'd know how to save me. *Are you afraid of heights?* asked in English. *We'll be down soon.*

NOT LONG BEFORE the end—but I always told my mother in Sarasota that I was fine, terrified of being found out, as though I could avoid it forever—I used to wander through the Quadrilatero Romano until I found the Consolata church, a big rococo flourishing mess, and I'd go in to look at the ex-votos.

The hand-illustrated scenes filled several incense-fogged rooms, reaching all the way to the ceiling: Here were Mary and Jesus, watching peacefully as a baby crawled precariously near a wood oven. Here they were again, contemplating a woman escaping from under a tram. And the pair in different outfits, taking care of a man eating a big piece of steak. There were saints watching soldiers parachute out of planes, watching people crash their 1930s cars. This was the type of faith that made sense to me. Personal faith, the watchful all-knowing saint, myself as the unlucky desperate exhibitionist, the one to be taken care of.

I wanted Federica to pay attention to me, but I was

already past her. Nicola showed me there was an ending coming for us. That I would have to keep looking. I could not grow and change with Federica. She was through with me, and so, for self-preservation, I wrapped her up tight in my mind and put her away. I wanted to keep her as a memory of perfect passion, an accomplishment. I was afraid that talking would disarm that night we'd been together, and reveal it to be an accident to which she had given no thought. I couldn't let her destroy my vision.

I stayed quiet with Federica. I only thought about jumping off the unbelievably ornate balcony of the Galleria Subalpina, breaking some bones, Fede visiting me in the hospital. There she would laugh saintlike down at me on my cot.

AROUND THIS TIME, Carla and Gianni called me into the living room and said that, because of some changes with their budget and some difficulties in the family, they'd been in touch with my parents, and I'd be going home after the school year ended, in May. I felt nauseated with failure and shame, but I reacted impassively, muted by my hunger. It was hard to understand that time would ever pass, and bear me toward consequences.

THE LAST THING the family and I did together was attend a wedding. This was two days before I left Italy. Carla drove us hours into the wet green hills to a tiny, molding stone chapel. The air in the church felt soapy before I realized it was raining. We filed to the front to toss rice, but the bride and groom thought it would be funny to exit out a side door. They ducked and laughed in the slanting green rain. We threw the rice anyway and some of it stuck in Federica's ponytail.

All my time was used up. All my doors were closed. I was

so sad at that wedding that I did wish to die. I was sixteen and all of life seemed like a process of detachment.

It was freezing in the rainy hills. At the dinner, everyone was speaking Piemontese. There was a huge block of *grana padano* and we broke little pieces off of it with a silver trowel. We ate raw beef and porcini mushrooms and juniper berries and boar. Forest meat with forest herbs. I cut everything into tiny grain-size pieces, and mostly I drank water, till I was bloated, which was almost like being full. Everyone drank a lot of wine. Carla and Gianni were purple with food or wine. We all talked about the Olympics, and I asked the couple next to me about Nicola Gonfalon. "Wicked, wicked," the girl said, smiling. Federica was looking away. "Did you know his dad owns all the trains and the roads?" I tried to ask more, but the conversation became a debate about whether Italy had nobility anymore. And when it was time for the testimonials, no one could find Federica anywhere, even though she was supposed to give one. So the waiters brought out the *crostata* with fresh fruit and the *bonet delle Langhe* in shimmering brown slabs.

She had tried to escape me. I looked all around the dining room and the bathroom and the foyer and then I went out into the rain, the rain clinging to the chains that took the place of downspouts. She was hiding sopping wet behind a tree. She'd almost disappeared into the May green Piemonte rain, the green that ate away at things from the outside to the heart.

I admit that I thought of her as less than human.

CHAPTER 6

I saw him again, five years later, when I was in college. I studied painting. I just wanted to learn foundations. I wanted to draw drapery and glass. I took six-hour classes in the art studio with its huge windows overlooking rural New England, the snow, the iced-over river.

I never felt the Federica emotions anymore, and I never talked about her either. I was embarrassed by how obsessed I'd been. I was repulsed by that part of myself. I didn't want to dream of helplessness. I rejected that. Italy was fake, a time I never discussed beyond its logistics. Only the time before and after it was real—real, and innocent. I'd needed a place to put my energy, and now it went into art. My life was full of painting.

A teacher told me: *Go to museums like it is your job*.

Another teacher said: *Look at Titian's drawings, because his paintings are too perfect to learn anything from*. The teacher was near tears when he said this. Venus, her back soft and melting and pale, clings to Adonis, Adonis holds the leashes of two red-mouthed dogs, and a rainbow across the teal sky is as strong as Adonis's arm, and as temporary.

Another lesson: don't use all the colors that are available to you; pick a set of colors you like, and mix those. Cerulean, indigo, cadmium red deep, each with its own opacity and weight. The zinc white was heavy in the tube, the alizarin crimson was not.

To what extent does the artist's intention matter? This question was important to us, the students, but not important to the teachers, who seemed so immersed in their careers they'd forgotten about the time of life when *plans* mattered so much.

I DIDN'T FALL in love. I had a few kisses, some blue-gold walks by the river, one trip to the Cape, and a silly fumbling half hour in the stacks of the library. And these experiences were enough for me. I was amazed that they had happened at all. I had a rule that I needed three invitations before I would agree to attend something. I was sure everyone was better off without me, and was inviting me out of duty. But I didn't want to ask for reassurances, which would be self-centered. Besides, I never knew what to say, and was always making terrible mistakes. This rule, meant to spare people from the burden of talking to me unless they *really* wanted to, was not beneficial for my social life.

At that point, I had an optimistic view of people. I believed that everyone had something to offer. I believed that everyone on earth was living rightly by some definition. I also believed that people eventually returned to their baseline mood, after lottery wins or partner deaths: the line dropped or rose back to normal. I strongly believed this, and it had been true in my own life. Nothing external had too much effect on me. My decisions mattered more than anything, and even those were overrun by the strange violence of my shifting moods, which corresponded to nothing.

THE WINTER AFTERNOONS were all glare of mauve sunlight, finishing in cobalt black sparkling and the rushing feeling of the passage of time.

The results of painting were often less beautiful than the process: the sink with its spontaneous color, the colors melting in solvent on the glass taboret, the brushy sketch halfway fleshed. Afterward, rubbing soap on my oily brushes, I got to know the paradox feel of the soap trying to mix with solvent and oil. The solvent thinner than water, vaporous. The slick roughness of the volcano soap on my paint-covered hands.

Models in their robes; I always felt an intense need to be kind to them, to thank them. Models with little heaters pointed at their feet. Some easily reassumed the pose. Others didn't and you had to redraw their faces. None of them seemed nervous. Just standing there, naked, without speech, presenting a challenge, mirroring us back. *Where does your mind go?* They reminded me of myself in the shower when Federica had come to see me. Standing there, not moving or speaking, I forwent the power to shape her judgment.

On cold snowy nights I sometimes slept in the studio; you were allowed to, but if you left, at a certain point the doors would lock and you couldn't get back in. It was like camping.

Le mystère Picasso was the most instructive film about art I ever saw. Picasso was all right destroying a beautiful painting and making a weird failure instead.

I liked watery red under landscapes. Ruin the canvas first, touch every part of it. Take a previous painting you don't quite like and paint over it.

My landscapes and sunlight studies didn't clearly connect to anything that was happening in my life. While painting, I was directed by thousands of longings, reflexes, and needs, which contained me like the golden threads of an aureola-type halo.

The rich students were the messiest. The rich ones bought six-foot-by-six-foot pre-stretched canvases. The rich ones ended up as artists. I went for writing afterward because it was logistically simpler. You don't need a certain space and toxic materials. The first short story I ever wrote was about a boy who wanted to eat his watercolors.

In the rare-books library, I opened Hemingway's Finca Vigia envelopes and read the letters he wrote his editor about boxing. I looked at his drafts with his wide downsloping scrawl. I couldn't help liking him. He wrote so beautifully about skiing in the Alps.

The second half of my third year, a girl from my art class told me to try out for the literary magazine. The literary magazine had seemed unapproachable and not for me, with its wealthy editors who thought of themselves as middle class. I contributed at the editorial meetings and attended to the paradoxes ("There is a paradox here," I said each time, or something synonymous), and got on. I think it helped that I appeared not to care much, which was true at the time. When I got on, though, I started to care.

For the initiations they came to my dorm room with bare faces and black clothes and stole me away through the common room of clarinetists and programmers into the building that was black and bustling with a pile of golden apples in a corner, for a ritual. The magazine was a microworld of pure potential where before judging the quality of a work of fiction or poetry or art you had to produce a real reading of it. I'd thought I read a lot. I had no idea, actually. These were people who took books with them into the shower. Why not seize all the best literature in the history of the world, these people asked. It's out there, let's take it, who else but us. As unlikely as it seemed, we were driven on by moral urgency. It was so real to us: everyone believed that literature was efficacious.

I wasn't bored by these people on the magazine. I was intimidated, which gave me energy. In meetings, I was amazed by how stupid I was, dashing off pat conclusions, then trying to backfill with insight. I knew nothing.

I attended endless late-night conversations, in which I didn't participate; I just wanted to listen. Loud radiators, blocked fireplaces, slumped sofas, where do certain books fall on the line from allegory to psychological realism? Even for the high modernists, realism is not about fidelity. You always reduce the fidelity for the sake of other things. Realism immerses you in a series of events, presented *as if* actual events and people, though everyone knows that they're not. It is just a skein of "this is what consciousness is like." It's not punctilious. What paint is to painting, noticing is to realism. The speed of fiction is the speed of noticing as it is remembered. We always wondered: to what extent does the author's intention matter? Maybe to the same degree that you can intend to notice. Coursepacks, Hans Jonas, Zora Neale Hurston, William James's "Moral Equivalent of War" on the floor. Feet and feet of snow piling outside the windows. We tossed short stories at each other's heads.

Patrick was one of the leaders; he loved to stake out a difficult argument, then go on defense. Another was Arman, with his scissoring relish and horsetail hair; he became a real editor. Ray from another country, drooping eyes, jingling chains, shining pleats. Ray disappeared after graduation, perhaps to an even smaller and more exclusive scene. The avant-garde in some countries may consist of four individuals. The head of the fiction board was named Angelica. Her father was always in the papers for his huge arms manufacturer. I couldn't tell whether she felt embarrassment about her origin or total acceptance, because she never mentioned it, the missiles and jets, and after graduation the people like her all took their places in the firmament; they were only slumming there, in a kind of mass hallucination about the importance of books.

Eventually I would leave to meet my undefined, boyfriend-type person. His name was Tad and he was an Egyptologist and the kind of boy who was popular in middle school because he was scary, a boy with a live firecracker in his watercooler, a boy who'd push you suddenly into the lake. He approached me with an effective kind of coaxing carelessness. He made me uncomfortable, which helped me grow. He was like a version of Federica, but almost everyone in college knew not to behave like her, so the only ones left acting that way lacked any grace or awareness. Finally, I lost my virginity to him, whose metal bedstead I gripped in a blaze of agony.

Patrick said, "What do you see in Tad?" which was as close as anyone came to an objection. "He likes to hang out with me," I responded. Only with the short stories, which were anonymized, would Patrick let himself be vicious.

ANOTHER LESSON, AND the most useful, it applied to everything: keep working, keep working. Patrick told me this, and after college I ended up working for him, and this was part of why. Patrick said it was a real occurrence (though I couldn't verify it), but it functioned well as a metaphor: They put some subjects in a room with clay and told them they had a period of time to make the best clay pot they could. Then they put other subjects in a room and told them they had a period of time to make *as many clay pots* as they could. The many-pot people ended up with plenty of terrible pots and some that were much better than those of the people who spent the whole time laboring over one. With that I went from the *purpose of art is to classify certain things as types of things* to *the way to be an artist is to make a lot of pots.*

THE PUBLICATION OWNED a small building with offices on the first floor and a meeting room on the second floor. There was a fireplace, bookshelves, a wood floor destroyed by alcohol and cigarettes. The building was the setting for our parties.

Everything was just beginning, then—our building swept clean, the bottles in a gleaming row, the first guests bold and loud in the hall, the first drinks and then the first dizziness and stumble, the first cold sheen of snowy air, everything beginning and beginning again. I would slip in and out. I would approach our building and look at the dim, mysterious, unified bodies against the condensed windows, then re-enter, and touch the party through its moist heat, and taste the party through its bitter vodka.

The meeting room would become dangerously crowded. There were always people I didn't know, grad students, people from New York. Angelica would pull me out to dance, kiss my cheek, her silk leaking the scent of tuberose, and the dancing would continue till four and then you could sit on a couch and talk and smoke until the sun rose and then you could walk along the river, either in the crusted snow or as the mist came off of it and the crew teams carried down their shells. There was a line from Rilke I loved: *As if all this promised you a lover.*

These were the best parties of my life, matchlessly populated by gorgeous people about whom I was endlessly curious. I could never effect a knowing posture. I was dazzled by everything.

My fourth year of college, Nicola appeared at one of these.

I WAS IN the upstairs room in the dim fractious center of the party, having my ear spoken into by the Egyptologist, my sort of boyfriend, Tad.

"Nora," came Nicola's voice. I turned. I knew exactly, exactly who he was. Finding him present in front of me was an experience of grace. I was back six years before in the snowy Alps. He'd thrown me there like a javelin. I lost my breath. The humid party moved around us—Tad's shifting face, people marooned in dance, cigarette smoke flowing like milk. Nicola considered Tad and me. He formed, I could see, a diagnosis. Then he said, "Come here," and I did, and he took my arm (I saw the flash of Tad's dislike as I turned) and led me down the stairs.

The girls coming up the stairs all looked at him and then at me. He was so luminous. I saw it occur to them too.

My whole body was his grip on my arm. I was snapping with energy. Shudders flowed up my spine. It was quieter here in the half-lit hall. The floor was sticky like a flytrap, so he could hear my restless movements.

"You interrupted my conversation," I managed to say.

He shrugged, and smiled. "Nice to see you again." I was surprised by his sober, almost melancholy voice.

"Who brought you?" I asked.

He was there with a French girl named Dominique who had graduated last year. She'd been on the magazine but too cool even to attend meetings. He didn't say how he knew her. He'd read theology at Oxford. Now he was living in New York and Switzerland.

"I remember you so clearly," he said. He let go of my arm and I flushed all over. I was drunk and wanted him to comment on how red I was.

I said, "What do you remember?" Sticking and unsticking my feet.

"Your hair," he said.

Everyone said that—I had long, tangled hair, a half-accidental statement like so much else about my self-presentation. I didn't know if I was happy that he remembered something about my appearance. I wanted him to say something he remembered about Federica. That time, I'd thought, was completely lost. Could never be confirmed. Could not, I thought then, be excavated in art or writing. It was as distant as babyhood or a dream. And he, like a psychic, had seen it.

"I remember you too. You were very friendly," I said fool-
ishly. "Thank you."

"You're welcome," he said.

"Do you remember that girl I was with?"

"Who?"

People pushed past us to the offices to do cocaine; cold,
refreshing air was coming under the broken back door.

His hair was dark, in soft curls. I didn't even know what
I was looking at, he shifted so much before my eyes. There
were few facts of the matter about his face. His much-
examined beauty, center beauty; he had an expressive,
mobile face that revealed that he knew everything. A face so
sensitive it looked perpetually on the verge of tears. If I kept
looking at it, reading it, I would understand everything—
what of our situation was important, what was forgettable,
who had power and who was following, and how our mood
connected to the rest of the world and time—for his presence
made us expansive.

There were few facts of his face: green eyes, a refined
nose, a closed mouth, a small mouth that did not show much
of his teeth. He wore a thin gray sweater—I wanted to touch
it—and under the sweater, the short standing collar of the
shirt he was wearing had a scalloped, embroidered edge,
which I found vain and mysterious around his wide neck.
The embroidered edge offset his masculinity, clarified his
confidence, which was so apparent that everyone kept looking at him. He attracted so much attention just standing in
the hall; there was something ravishing about him.

"Fede," he said, answering himself. "Yes. She controlled
you."

I underwent an instant horrible flush. Yes, maybe. But
privately. It was essential that it was private. He was so certain, reaching into my brain and wrenching it. He watched

me just long enough to see me redden. I liked in what a friendly manner he spoke.

"I don't like that guy," he said.

"Tad?" I said.

He shrugged.

"He's just surprised," I said. "Surprised we know each other."

"I see," he said. "Is being surprised the same as being mean, to you?"

I tried to formulate an answer from within the warm slippage of my drunkenness.

"See you later, Nora," he said, looking past me. The girl approaching him was Dominique. She had a black ribbon in her hair.

I KNEW THEN, like I knew when I was fifteen, that he was the pinnacle of something. It was amazing to me that he'd show up here; in fact it actually lifted the college in my eyes—that this was a place he'd visit, a party he'd attend. He was the real authority in that building. He was the real speed. I had the sense of passing the beginning, those opening notes where we had lingered for so long. He was a development.

During the party, we all talked about him. He had left a golden handprint on each person he'd conversed with. One friend called him "magnetic." Another friend said, "I just wanted to listen to everything he had to say."

Other people found him repulsive, arrogant. Flirtatious—was that what he had been doing, flirting with me? Certainly, Tad was angry.

I didn't like the people who didn't like Nicola. The people who didn't like him seemed fake to me; it was tiresome, I thought, to be pure. I didn't mention that I'd met him another year in another country, in a snowstorm, fifty feet above the ground. I drew power from the secret. It was a way to own him.

I sat for a while in the design office with friends and drank Svedka with juice and when I went back upstairs I saw him kissing a girl who was not Dominique. A girl in my year, whom I barely knew. She'd taken formal logic with me; she'd had the confidence to demonstrate truth tables on the board. I watched him put his hand around the back of her neck and I felt a shock. I only wanted to see what he would do. I wanted to see because his school was not this school, his world was not this world, his mind was unknown, his hands were unknown, but he was very, very appealing, and he knew it, and he was aware, he attracted attention and he liked the attention, he was joyous in that way.

If life were that easy for me, I thought, I'd lose the sense of limitlessness. I loved to feel that there were people who were incomprehensibly much smarter than I, people whose strangeness I could not fathom, that there were disciplines I would never encounter.

I didn't think I was good enough to get to know him in any practical way. I'd get to know him privately, like a dream. I noticed Dominique on the couch. She was watching too. She smiled at me and the smile belonged to Nicola and haunted me for years.

HE APPEARED IN my dreams frequently during my senior year of college. I dreamed about him on narrow streets, in narrow colonial rooms of masters' residences and house libraries. The campus twisted and brightened until it was Turin, and the river filled with boys in red hats on their sculls, and the riverbank beyond grew until it was the Collina. I was focused on that instant knowing ease he had, as though we were very old friends.

How did Nicola fit in with the life I'd built? He didn't;

he smashed in from the side with a totally different value proposition. Even though I had no reason to think I'd ever see him again, I could tell that what he offered was infinitely more fragile, and volatile, and intuitive. Not a good idea to pursue something like that. Not a good idea.

Federica controlled me? Did he really think that—was he teasing, hadn't he forgotten her and remembered me? Wasn't it I who controlled her? Did he think I liked being controlled? I'd think about that, about him thinking I liked being controlled. Only he had spoken aloud that part of me.

It could be that his knowledge of Federica and me in the *ovovia* meant he knew me better than any college friend. He was down at the root of first love and first transgression.

Later I'd learn Nicola was good with mystery and obsession. He was good with twenty minutes in a ski lift having an unfathomable influence. I liked this because it felt true to how life really is.

The rest of us tried hard not to influence each other. We tried to show compassion, make room. We were used to humbling ourselves. And avoiding risk and shame.

He'd appear in my dreams in chambers and on streets of irregular size and touch me and I'd wake up tormented. I never touched myself in those days, I found it boring. It never amounted to anything.

IN ADOLESCENCE, MANY people have someone like Federica, and eventually, everyone's Federica fades. When you grow up, your integral center forms: you forget what it was like to let another person define you. When you have children, maybe that is another time of consuming love. When I remember my parents' eyes when I was packing up for Italy, how they looked at me as though I was covered in blood, I can imagine how parents may be consumed by love for their children.

But that is not the same as being consumed before you have any integrity at all, when your integrity lives in some other person. No one believes in this other way because, if we lived it at all, we lived it a long time ago, when everything was irrational and liquid.

I LIVED IN a shared house. I stretched canvases. I bought a prism for my window. The lilacs bloomed for my last time in New England. The quad filled with chairs; I wanted to cry as I walked past. Banners in the trees. I unstretched my canvases, rolled them, and mailed them home. On the last morning, we walked from the college gates, and drummers led our procession. The grass was dreamy with dew. Bright robes on gentle hills. I graduated. I moved to New York.

CHAPTER 7

My first date with Leif was at a trattoria in Bedford-Stuyvesant, out in the backyard with a mosquito coil and tiny grapes on the soft-leaved vines.

He wore a five-panel hat in faded denim and maroon, and had a modest smile, as though self-conscious about his teeth.

The first oscillation in the dating dread I'd become so familiar with was when the harried waiter asked if we wanted to hear the specials, and Leif said, "We're good, actually," and the waiter sighed in relief. I liked that Leif knew what he wanted, and that what he wanted was dishes with anchovies and olives, and something with a whole clove of garlic. I myself would have felt ashamed to ask for such things.

I asked him about his work. He was a technical account manager at an app that allowed users to understand, through data visualizations and games, how various insurance policies really worked. While he spoke, the waiter delivered our wine.

"What should we toast?" I said.

"To happiness," he said.

We discovered then that the metal table was unsteady. He gripped the sides of the table and tested its wobble. I grabbed the wine-glasses but he made me put them back down—"That would be giving up." He tore off an edge of napkin and knelt on the concrete. I was glad when he was on the ground because it gave me a chance to assess how I'd done so far. It was going to be okay to hold a conversation with him for another hour, I felt. Not everyone would admit an interest in happiness. The shining, blackish, fragrant wine moved in the glasses as he stabilized the leg.

When he returned to his seat, I said, "I do like to dig into an insurance game in my free time." I was joking, but could tell from his face that I was being rude.

"I love insurance," he said. "To be honest. It's a field with a lot of realism. And a lot of decision-making on the hardest questions." He'd hidden all of his olive pits somewhere. He asked what I did for work.

My work was tutoring middle schoolers for the specialized high school tests.

"What's that like?"

"I know all about triangles," I said.

"And you like it?" he said.

I shrugged. I wasn't proud of my writing, which was just short stories here and there, but I liked how attentive he was. So I mentioned it.

"Why do you write?" he said seriously.

"I don't have a great answer," I said.

"It always seems like a shame when people spend all their time talking about things they don't care about."

I quickly drank wine, then coughed. The evening was almost misty, catching just slightly in yellow wreaths around the patio bulbs.

To find a place for all the nature awe. Flat fields (I didn't say this) of colored snow, striped by tree shadows, and the flower-shaped end of Federica's ski pole caught between my forefinger and thumb, as, with her weight, she accelerated me past her. Pelicans opening and closing their beaks, hunched on poles by Siesta Key, when my father confronted me. There were these moments when the mood and image joined in a funny coincidence that revealed the structure of things. *To classify certain things as types of things.* I told him my teacher's old saying.

"What does that mean?"

"I don't know," I said helplessly. I didn't know how to make it stand up against skepticism, and didn't want to ruin its meaning for myself.

Now he took his hat off, and revealed wavy hair, streaked with blond. It surprised me that he'd worn his hat so long, as he still had all his hair. "I think you have some idea," he said.

The other tables were noisy, but for once I didn't try to listen in. I smiled at him, with my head whirring from the wine, and the smile was enough, he let me off.

"Want to hear my story idea?"

I nodded.

"I have a lot of hiking stories." He described hiking the Appalachian Trail, how one day he saw what had seemed to him the most incredibly handsome man in the world, a star he had idolized, but then with a shock realized that he knew the man, a friend from elementary school who had moved away long ago. "What's amazing is, he's completely average-looking." The recognition made him hot.

"You should write that," I said.

He said he wanted to read more books by women in the coming year. A bit too formal, I thought, but good-natured of him.

We examined the dessert menu. There was *granita di gelsi.* "What is *gelsi,* do you think?" he said.

Gelso, mulberry. *Una requiescit in urna.* I remembered walking with Federica on warm fall evenings, turning up Via San Quintino where we lived and going north to Siculo. In my memory, we were always at Siculo. But maybe in reality only twice. At Siculo she would order a mulberry granita crushed ice. *Gelso* was the word for mulberry. She told me not to get anything. We'd share, she said. We shared the fragrant magenta grains of ice, layered with plushy whipped cream. I loved that we ate from the same spoon.

I told him I'd lived there at the age of fifteen. This year was no longer essential in my life. My friends had no idea I was fluent in Italian. I was there for the Olympics, I said. I met my first boyfriend there. Marco. I chose the name of the boy who'd once bought me a croissant. I was trying to be halfway truthful.

"Why Italy?" he said.

I shrugged. I was a little drunk.

"You don't know why?" he said.

I put my chin on my hand and just looked at him.

There were so many reasons, so many causes. Why Italy? Because it was my parents' idea for their troubled daughter. Because of the troubledness itself. "Because my distant family lived there," I said, finally.

He nodded and said, "So it's private, Nora." I looked up. My eyes were teary. "You can tell me about it sometime," he said.

I liked that he didn't try to touch me. I loathed men's exploratory touches on dates.

But not Nicola's, because he was not attainable.

We didn't order the gelso granita. We ordered a fig *panna cotta,* which the waiter recommended heartily, and it was bad, the fig pieces bland and wet in the squirming custard.

When we parted, I said, "See you around," and then I waited five days for him to text. Everything I'd said had been a variant on "I don't know."

FINALLY I TEXTED him about when we might hang out next and he wrote, "I thought 'See you around' was final."

"Oh dear!" I wrote, my heart pounding.

"You seemed to run circles around me," he wrote. "It doesn't bother you that I'm not widely read?"

But it had been apparent that he was a man with mastery of himself, a certain confidence, even to ask me that question. I could tell then that I would be able to find a level with him. Not with Federica, not with Tad, had I experienced this push toward balance.

On our second date, Leif held my necklace under the Brooklyn Bridge. I loved that. I wasn't ready to be touched, but he held my necklace and then I wanted him to hold my face. The necklace was a little silver apple on a short silver chain. I didn't wear jewelry usually, but I'd gotten dressy for him. Federica and I had bought the necklace near Piazza Statuto, where criminals used to be executed.

BEFORE WE MET, Leif had believed in independence at all costs, so he'd blocked himself from happiness. He had left Los Angeles after college because he could tell he liked it too much, so much that he didn't feel independent anymore. I made him happy, so it was a struggle to see me, he said, but either he won the struggle or he identified that the happiness I provoked in him would not thwart his independence, because he kept seeing me.

I liked his high-up apartment in Long Island City. He had a spotty back, like it was a different material from the rest of him. I liked his bony cheeks. He was two years older than I, but everyone thought much more.

He was the first person who ever made me come. I'd never even made myself come. I didn't tell him this at first. I just told him it wasn't easy to make me come, and he said, "No one's in a rush, Nora." It took four months. The wind around the horrible, bland Long Island City buildings. The torching red tulips in the lobby. The uneasy elevator to the fifteenth floor. He had few possessions; he didn't really read. He was persistent and accommodating.

After a year, we moved in together to an eighth-floor one-bedroom with modern fixtures in Clinton Hill. The decision to move in together was easy, and we lived together easily.

I tutored, then I worked at an ice cream store, writing short stories when I could, while Leif paid for almost everything, and then I heard secondhand that a friend from the literary magazine, Patrick, was looking for a research assistant to help him with some financial intelligence work someone had hired him to do. Patrick had told me about many pots and we trusted each other, though those days the productivity had more to do with work than with writing. For a while it was just the two of us. I made PowerPoints and took minutes. Over time we hired more people. Now I'd lived in New York five years. Patrick always told me, *Don't be so afraid! Don't be so afraid!* That was what he called my anxiety, and eventually, with his sponsorship, I took on an assistant of my own.

Leif was proud of me for my work. Leif loved burying himself in complex detail. He loved the seemingly drab nature of insurance, and the power and ethics underneath. We liked to say to each other that he was a man with only three moods: happy, hungry, and focused. He liked Ultimate Frisbee in Prospect Park. If I came out to surprise him in one of those internal fields, he'd walk his bicycle all the way home just to keep me company. After a depressing election, he started volunteering as an after-school tutor with elementary schoolers. He was never moved. That was my job. He could steer boats. We went out on the purple bay.

Then we were going to weddings. The best part of a wedding was wandering off, to the back room or the forest, and sitting quietly alone. He did not like how anxious I remained. I would never be truly social, we realized.

We never did talk about Federica or Italy. He let it go. I let it go. I didn't even repress it. I did not have confusing, cavorting feelings of dissolution of self. I forgot about being the scientist and the rat. My parents were happy. His father was happy. His mother didn't like obligations; she had left the family and moved to Nevada. His father lived in Los Angeles and was a lawyer. We went to Los Angeles for Christmas each year and ate satsumas with skin you could just pull off.

I carried on untroubled by Federica and Nicola and my descent into the white flailing hell, my resurrection. Untroubled by cigarettes on quays, manipulation of Federica's rage, anorexia, blood-colored ice buried beneath cool layers of cream. Nicola had watched me panic. But I was no longer in touch with the version of myself that he had seen. I had calmed down. I didn't dwell on control and power and submission. My life was not rife with omens of shattering significance. Leif and I had achieved the steady state.

It was a surprise to me how, as my twenties continued on, my body began to turn itself inside out. I was becoming an ideal artist's model. Delineated muscle and vein, a strong neck, strong hands. Each year when I unbandaged myself from my winter clothes, more veins had appeared in my inner arms. I liked to wear layers of loose clothing. When I didn't brush my long hair, it tangled into clusters like a spider plant's pups. And what was the effect of all this? Some of my male classmates and colleagues loathed me automatically. So I could be guileless, but I was aware that I could be threatening too. Leif liked how I looked. That was enough.

We kept moving. The earth was like a cookie being rolled in sugar. We rolled from forsythia to crabapples to violets, rhododendrons, azaleas. We entered and exited each phase. May: the sparkling clusters of gnats, wormy pollen piles. Rats, built for function. Summer in Prospect Park, ducks breaking a path through the algae. A partial solar eclipse. Fall in Central Park, the red maple by the Delacorte. Winter, and slipping down the icy path by the Shakespeare Garden.

New York was good for people who didn't want to forget. We all ended up with the same memories.

NICOLA EDGED BACK into my life slowly.

The night before Nicola's second reappearance, Leif and I walked in fine rain to the edge of the East River. I was twenty-eight that spring. Leif and I had been together for five years. He always wanted us to share one umbrella, but I made us each carry our own. It was all totally fine. We were aging together and it was what you would want.

All the towers of lower Manhattan faded into a gold mist that dissolved into pink near the Statue of Liberty. The light bent as if through a lens. Water taxis made milky trails in the shimmering, weightless world. The sky darkened. Fluffy waves broke on the stony beach and someone—not Leif— yelled to me, "Careful!" Leif was distracted those days. He was realizing that the app had to change its revenue model.

We walked under the Brooklyn Bridge, and at a few weak or low places in the span high above us, the rain gathered and fell in thundering columns that dented the asphalt. Later I felt that Nicola had sent it down, a sign.

THE NEXT DAY at work, Patrick came by my desk in a talk- ative mood. Because we'd known each other so long, he didn't often indulge in chatting with me; Leif said it was like the coach who's toughest on his own son.

Patrick, who grew up in New York, had a rugby build and a lot of nice suits, custom-made by a man named Mr. Guy. He'd worked in international finance before he started what we now called the boutique research firm. He knew everyone, especially in European energy, traveled constantly and attended conferences to keep all his networks hot, and connected investors to experts in the field. When he was excited, his nostrils moved, bunny-like; he retained the excitability of the boy who always rushes to head the soccer ball or flip off the diving board. But unlike so many men in the world of finance, he roved without restriction into disciplines of uncertain value. In college he'd applied this energy to philosophy and poetry. There was always a moment when new contacts would notice the other part of Patrick, and glance at each other, and then the conversation would get much faster. He liked to contemplate ultramercenary men, but he himself was not mercenary. He liked the brilliance, the stakes—because so much money was in play, people became truly ingenious and subtle. One of the clients told me at a dinner party, "It's very unsettling to see the efficiency that's possible when your favorite compensation is the uncovering of unsound reasoning."

This morning, Patrick came by my desk, sat on my easy chair, and told me that the most dashing man he knew had gotten married. "I wish I could meet his wife," Patrick said.

Oh, I knew it was Nicola right then. I asked who it was, this dashing man.

"A friend of Dominique's," Patrick said, "Did you know her? I met him once at the magazine." He leaned back in the easy chair, which was white like all of our desks and furniture. We subletted a town house floor from someone's family office, and we had a view of a narrow wedge of Central Park treetops. Patrick liked to squeeze a spring, which he was squeezing now, but when he couldn't find it, he would put anything into service without realizing, twiddling pens, opening and shutting his headphone case, putting his fists into mugs and clinking them together like gauntlets. "He's very much—well of course I'd like him—he's this Italian lord or knight of some kind. And somehow not full of shit." My heart was pounding, and I started laughing. Tears fell out onto my face. "Dominique was over in Italy for the wedding."

"Didn't Italy get rid of its nobility?" I said.

"It's that kind of family," said Patrick. "They have several popes."

"You met him just once?" I wiped my face and stood to go behind Patrick, so that I could be more privately hysterical. "But how did you stay in touch?"

"We email," said Patrick. Patrick showed me a photo on his phone—towering mountains, cypresses, a fountain, a colonnaded patio. Nicola and a thin woman in a simple dress. No veil. Nicola in a dark understated suit, looking only at the woman, his eyes focused on her, his face elegant and defined with dark lashes and brow, his mouth half-parted in a smile. Maybe he was speaking. A crowd in old-fashioned hats and white suits with their backs to the camera. "He's one of the few people I know who needs nothing from me." I was sad that his hands were hidden below the line of the crowd. It was unbelievable that he had touched me.

I wasn't even hurt to find that he was married. I was overwhelmed just to see that he was out there and alive, and that Patrick also remembered him, remembered him and had been in touch with him and recognized his appeal. All these years, Nicola and I had been brushing up against each other, through Patrick. Even if Nicola didn't know we worked together, he would have known Patrick and I had both staffed the same literary magazine in college. Sometime, he must have thought for a moment of me, whom chance had twice surfaced in his life.

Patrick and I scrutinized the enchanting photo. Urns of white flowers, petals on the ground. The stone of the patio and the columns greeny with lichen, a vine-covered tower, lilac mountains beyond. Somewhere in Piemonte. Maybe these were mountains I'd seen from Turin.

"His dad is quite a figure," Patrick said. "He runs a big industrial company that's been involved in mass-scale bribery and other garbage."

I remembered Federica saying his family was evil. At the time I thought she was just trying to upset me, or to make a political point about nobility. In truth, the idea of evil didn't worry me at all. There were all these checks on it, of romance and restraint. In such a context, evil was intriguing.

"But you know, I admire it for being productive enterprise," Patrick said. There was a saying that the stock market was no more about investment than sex is about babies. So Patrick, always running into the rough, was partial to the people trying for babies.

"Does Nicola talk to you about it?" I said.

"He knows what my job is," Patrick said. On this rare occasion, I didn't know what Patrick was implying. It would, of course, be an extremely bad idea for both parties to talk about illegal activities.

"Is Nicola going to inherit the company?" I said.

"I'd guess," Patrick said, "that he'd rather force his father out of leadership."

"Did he tell you that?" I said.

"Of course not," said Patrick. "It's just my impression that he has some kind of compunction."

I lifted up Patrick's phone and looked again at the photo. Nicola's mouth was slightly open, his expression serious. Perhaps he was reciting vows. We'd had two extremely brief interactions and exchanged a few dozen words. What would it be like to get to know him, to get more of him? It might overthrow my life. I thought of a secret messaging app Leif had made me download, though we had no major secrets—to help add crypto strength for the people who really need it, Leif said. My memories felt that way, looking at the wedding with Patrick. More powerful and more hidden.

I couldn't be sad that Nicola was married. I never thought he'd be mine.

PART II

CHAPTER 8

In August, during the regular client conference call, Patrick said, "Interesting item today. Nicola Gonfalon is coming to the United States. He's the Gonfa SpA heir apparent . . ." It was four months after his wedding.

I looked up from my notes and stared at Patrick.

One of the investors began to ask a question, and Patrick muted the conference line and said, "You just turned red."

The investor said, "Is Gonfa expanding to the US?"

Patrick unmuted. "My expectation is that Nicola will try to explore some joint ventures. Power grids." He muted and said, "I should say, I'm going to see him and his wife in a few days, would you like to come?" This conversation was so typically Patrick. He was enjoying himself.

The investor said, "But with Gonfa's blessing?"

"Good question," Patrick said. I hit unmute and he said "Good question" again. "I have a suspicion that Nicola might be looking to take Gonfa in a new direction, the direction being away from the marvelously self-enriching graft of which his father is universally, well, unacknowledged to be a master."

"I didn't quite get that," one of the investors said, during which Patrick muted and said "Well?" and I said "Why are you inviting me?" Unmuting, Patrick said, "His father is indirect and surprisingly effective, for Italian industry. Evidence of his mastery is that he's never faced any major legal action." Patrick muted and said, "He thought he'd met you. He liked you."

I could tell that Patrick was impressed. Nicola's goodwill was not exactly enjoyable, however; I didn't know why he'd be kind about me.

"And you think the son disapproves?" said the investor.

Patrick unmuted. "I do."

"Why?"

"Just a character impression," Patrick said. I heard the crackling sound of exhalations and shiftings from the various investors on the line. This kind of subjectivity made them uncomfortable, though they paid Patrick for it.

"You know him?" someone asked.

"Enough," Patrick said, which was so confident it crossed the line into showmanship. I felt a prickle of defensiveness on Nicola's behalf. Patrick added, "But if he's going to try partnerships here without his father's blessing, he will fail as soon as his father finds out. And if he's seriously trying to raise capital, he's going to hit our regulations pretty fast."

"It's going to be a ride," one of the investors said, during which Patrick muted and said, "So what do you say?"

I pressed my hands to my mouth. It was hot in the office. A memory of summer in Turin, nights without AC, the windows open, curtains lifting, scooters and drunks out on the street, their sounds hot in my ear as I bit my sweaty fingers to balance the pain from the cramps in my legs. The fan stirring the languid air, Federica in the bunk above me, hating me. Nicola brought this all up to me like a cup to a mouth— drink it.

"Sure," I said, into my hand. "Maybe."

As soon as the call was over, I stopped feigning nonchalance. I knew Patrick was interested too. I made Patrick look him up with me. There were no photos of him on Google. There were many old, bland news stories about his family, and his father, Vittorio; evidently they were not ostentatious people. Their company website had a pearl gray background. There were sections for infrastructure, construction, automation, energy, technology, over a glowing blueprint. We clicked on infrastructure: railway, shipping, water treatment, electrical grids . . . every section opened onto vagueness. They were not consumer-facing.

"Gonfa grows by eating," Patrick said. He explained they focused on automation and digitization of everything, first joint ventures, then acquisitions. In electricity, they made smart grids, so that generation and transmission naturally merged; indeed, all of Gonfa's techniques—automation, digitization, efficiency—tended to subsume formerly discrete steps into one massive intelligence.

They'd avoided news about their wrongdoing, or they'd scrubbed it. They were the pride of Italy, the resurgence of Italian manufacturing in the world. And just a few hits about Nicola, in Italian, his *nozze*.

We found his wife's name, Iris. We looked her up. In high school in Switzerland she'd invented an MRI contrast agent for brain tumors that was now in wide use. Both Patrick and I found this emotionally satisfying. It was right that Nicola married a prodigy, who was, in the one photo we could find of her, beautiful. Sleek dark hair and soft lips and Renaissance eyes. And what had she done since then? We couldn't find anything.

"You really think he's going to try to take the company away from his dad?" I said.

"I am sure that he'll try."

We looked at the image result for Iris. I imagined that Nicola must have married someone he truly respected. Someone who could be his equal. Maybe he was caught between her and his father. "Maybe the new wife put him up to it," I said.

"Could be," said Patrick. "How many ambitious heirs do you know? Most of them are decadent."

"You don't think he'll succeed?" I said.

"Yeah, that's the thing," Patrick said. "His father is rumored to be a kind of madman. Nicola's facing a lot of risk in this maneuver."

"Maybe Nicola is here working in his father's interest." I looked at Patrick steadily. "In our interactions, I never got the sense he was particularly explicable."

"It's not actually diminishing to be plainly and simply good," Patrick said.

ON THE SUBWAY ride home, I thought about Nicola saying, *She controlled you.* But Patrick surely knew him better than I did. And we weren't invested in his business. I was defending Nicola in a war I actually wasn't involved in, against an imagined foe, and the foe in this case was moral rectitude. I didn't understand my motivations. But I knew they were related to the candlelit spaces of Turin where people had wept and thought and been forgotten—I liked to feel that not only were there things in the world that I hadn't learned yet, but there were things in the world that were truly unknowable, that analysis and intelligence and speech, even, had to peter out, that certain doors opened out only onto the void of space.

CHAPTER 9

The day before I was going to meet Nicola and his wife, I knew I would not be able to sleep.

I left the office and walked through the park after a torrential rain. Now the paths held mirror puddles and the greenery was steaming. Purple coneflowers and evergreens. Turtles in the dark water. Amplified flutes and gunshots in the Shakespeare theater. Leif and I had planned to get dinner, but I said I was busy late at work. Like everything Leif-related, the lie was easy. I didn't tell Leif that I'd been thinking about how this man I'd met only twice, Nicola, was in the city again. It was too strange.

Finally I came home. All the lights were off in the apartment, except the TV, tediously flashing. Leif was quiet—angry that I hadn't eaten with him.

I rinsed the mud off my legs, and then I went to Leif. I pulled my wet hair back while the TV blinked white, blue, red. He killed the volume.

I'd never imagined Nicola while having sex with Leif. But now I did. I imagined Nicola's hand in the gondola lift. What if his hand had moved further along my neck and held my throat.

While I was with Leif, the gondola lost its windows. A slippery shell with the snow bleeding in. The gondola rocked and Nicola barred the window with his arm.

While Leif was over me I was imagining Nicola choosing me and not that other girl at the magazine party. That had been my chance. Why hadn't I flung myself at him? Why hadn't I tried? What could I learn from him? Could he make me helpless again, like I'd been in the gondola? What would it have been like to fall into helplessness, to let him control and consume me?

Leif caught some part of this. He was not a fool. He said, "What's gotten into you," and came wildly.

THE FOLLOWING DAY, Nicola was coming to Patrick's apartment after work. I wasted the work hours, then went home with Patrick, feeling intriguing as my coworkers watched us set off together. Even not yet arrived, Nicola made everything more urgent, more sparkling, a holiday feeling. We climbed the five flights to Patrick's. His apartment had a special countryside feeling because of its wood-sashed windows. Because his wife, Liana, was out, Patrick smoked cigarettes. I liked to watch him smoke. It reminded me of the literary magazine. He never smoked at work.

One hour to go. I anxiously pretended to work on my laptop, then pretended to read. I didn't want to have to talk with Patrick at a time like this.

She controlled you, Nicola had once said. Now what would he say? I planned to be quiet. I was going to be quiet and let him and Patrick talk. Just watch quietly, like Iris might, I told myself. She looked so watchful in the photo. Let the two of them talk, and see if you can figure out how he holds himself. Why did everyone at the magazine party want to look at him, and afterward, why did some people describe him as intolerably arrogant? See if he's rigid, if he lacks empathy. See if everything is of interest to him, or if he's bored. Act like you don't care if he looks at you or talks to you. If pressed, maintain ironic distance.

He was supposed to arrive at six. But he didn't appear. At eight, Leif called me. "Where are you?" Leif said. "You missing dinner again?"

"I'll be there soon," I said.

If I continued to wait for Nicola, I'd get the third encounter, and it would be like the first two, embarrassing, unsettling, and it would shift my understanding of my own desire. Maybe I'd dream about it for years or it would reveal some new way to interact with Leif or the city. Or some new way to write. If I left, I might never see him again.

I waited another hour. Leif called again. "Train trouble," I said. But didn't I like my life? Hadn't I built the life I wanted? Why should I want him to tell me who I was? I gathered my charger, backpack, book, pen, very slowly.

The train ride home was anguish. Leif was happy to see me. He asked why I was so late. "There was an investigation," I said. Poor Leif, who was happy.

NICOLA HAD SHOWN up at midnight, Patrick texted me later. His wife hadn't come after all. "What did you talk about?" I wrote.

"Everything," he wrote.

"Gonfa SpA?" I wrote.

"No," he wrote. "Theology. Especially the Cathars, whom he claims as relatives. Good and evil, sin, things like that." I hadn't been expecting this. I felt a wonderfully confused pang. It was so good to see that Patrick's "everything" with Nicola didn't include how both of them made their livings. The fundamentals, the priorities, were shifting.

There was a pause, then he continued—even Patrick was effusive under the influence of Nicola. "He's definitely taking away his dad's business, by the way."

"How do you know?"

"He's fixated on right and wrong." I kept thinking Patrick

had finished, then the dots would reappear. "The whole thing was very medieval."

"Medieval in what sense?" I wrote.

"He seems kind of tortured," Patrick wrote. "You know, it's all very real to him."

I wondered if Nicola had asked at all about me. I wondered when I would see him, or if I'd missed my chance. I silenced my phone and laid it facedown and went to give Leif, who was asleep, a kiss.

CHAPTER 10

A few days later, I got the text from the unknown number: "So sorry to have missed you." He said he was at an art gallery, which was near our office in what he called "a big town house." He wanted me to meet him. He didn't seem aware of work hours.

Patrick let me leave. "Tell me all about it later," Patrick said.

I walked north along the park. My energy overwhelmed me. I lurched along the tricky cobblestones. I hummed and laughed and watched the pigeons cavort in the pilled light from the elms. Everyone I passed smiled at me. I knew that I was headed for terrible disruption.

I had the sense that I needed to bring him a gift, but I couldn't tell what would be appropriate. I stopped at a pretzel cart with a blue and yellow umbrella and asked the man for two pretzels, although I didn't like them. "Two?" he said. He gave me four and winked.

The town house was enormous and white, with Renaissance ornamentation, dragons, crowns, putti in glazed terracotta. I stuffed the bag of pretzels into my backpack, then I rang the bell. After a long wait, I tried the door. It took me a moment to realize I could just push it open and enter. I'd been waiting for a buzz, a butler, or a guard.

The space was so large that it left the realm of romantic—it felt neutral and bureaucratic. It was like an embassy. It was silent, and no one was around. Impossible to imagine what sort of business would justify an office like this. I looked for Nicola as I walked into the atrium with a fountain at its center and five layers of balconies above. The floor was made of marble, with no cement visible; a pattern of dark green, veined stars on white, and around the fountain, vermillion points like compass marks. At the top was a skylight, which let faded sunlight down onto the marble child in the center of the fountain. The size of the space sucked away all the sound, so even right next to the fountain I couldn't hear the water. Four turtles sent arcs of water into the dish at the cherub's feet. The streams held their shape and moved dreamily, like serpents.

I came closer to the fountain and watched the ribs of water tumble from the high dish into the low one. The water seemed to flow at half speed. I leaned closer. I put my hands against the marble rim and tilted to look up at the atrium. Each floor was brighter, and then at the top, the pointed skylight, with its black sashes, geometrically diminishing, seemed like an infinite spire, like the pointed Mole in Turin. When I shifted my head one way the skylight seemed to cascade down inward toward me. But when I moved it back the point reverted up to the heavens. That sense of endless captured space, and the incomprehensible acoustics of the drifting water, gave me the feeling that the fountain was growing in size, that this space of Nicola's contained an entire ocean.

Stupefied, I held out my hand and pushed against the rope of water emanating from one of the turtle's mouths. The whole pattern of the fountain disrupted, and the sound grew far louder.

Something about the cherub reminded me of him. Maybe

he simply had an abstracted, classical face. The water in my hand had a wonderful, fresh scent. A scent almost of lavender and basil.

I did not know how to imagine sitting with Nicola, being his friend. What had transpired in the gondola lift was a result of our initial conditions, and how the world happened to be. He was perfect then. He entered, comforted me, exited; there was no drama on his side (while for me it was an eruption of fear and passion). He didn't change.

It was impossible to imagine an encounter with something truly other. All of us have radio waves shimmering through us all the time, and other forms of radiation that don't have the right shape to be absorbed, and so invisibly pass through. The world—I thought, leaning against the fountain, now letting the water fall from the dish into my hand—was full of these phenomena so alien that they left no trace. Daily life, as I experienced it, was pressure. It was student loans, health insurance, rent, the semi-exhaustion of all the artistic media I cared about. However decent Patrick was, I still had performance reviews, had to think about pleasing him for my wage. Nicola had been formed by none of these pressures. He was therefore monstrous, unsympathetic, unforgivable.

Watching the water thrust itself out through the spouts, I remembered how, as a child, someone bought me a picture book about a volcano. The book filled me with such sublime fear I couldn't even open it. Even looking at the book's spine on the shelf frightened me. The book was about the farmer in Mexico who had discovered a volcano in his cornfield. One day he was out working and the ground opened up. The volcano rose up from the cornfield and destroyed two towns. Accidentally digging up a volcano used to be one of my top fears.

At last I leaned over the marble edge far enough to put my

face in the turtle's spouting, and I let the water fall against my lips. I plunged my arms into the cool water. The weightless compression seemed to squeeze against my heart.

There he was, he caught my eye and beckoned through a doorway across the atrium. I straightened and laughed, wringing the water off my arms.

Dark hair, green eyes, dark gray suit. I was surprised that I recognized him so quickly—by his posture, as though he were a sibling of mine, even though he'd grown up since I'd seen him in college. He disappeared through a doorway, and I ran to follow him into what appeared to be an art gallery. My feet barely seemed to touch the floor. I crossed from an antechamber with a sagging silver sofa into a room filled with large landscape paintings. The smaller space was more graceful than the large, with dark paneling, marble fireplace, mirrors. It smelled like a home: coffee and must.

He sat at a table across from a man in his seventies with gray hair so neatly arranged you could see the furrows from the comb.

Nicola caught my eye and gestured at me to stay back. So I went to sit on the couch and watch. I felt silly in my clothes. I wore a floppy linen dress with a tie waist and a large cardigan with moth-holes at the wrists.

I could see Nicola's face, but not the face of his interlocutor. Yet I couldn't get a handle on his features, on what made his face so lovely. He was rarely still; he was mutable and confusing. From straight on, he looked almost about to lose his composure. He looked as though he were beginning to cry. He was tremulous, vulnerable—but when he turned his head, I could see the refinement of his nose and ear and brow, and his aspect was controlled and entirely calm.

The table held two white ceramic espresso cups, a crumpled plastic sleeve of butter cookies, and a white lily in a spherical glass vase. At one point, Nicola reached his arm out and put his hand on the other man's forearm. So Nicola had some kind of power in this situation, I understood. Nicola had a generous, conspiratorial expression, he was nodding as the silver-haired man gestured. They shared an easy understanding. Two men passed before me to join them, ignoring me completely: another in his seventies, and one in his forties or fifties in an exceptionally elegant suit, drapey with a silvery sheen. Nicola stood and kissed them each once on the cheek.

The younger man sat next to Nicola. His eyebrows each had a small gap in the center; I wondered if they were scars, or for style. The four bent their heads together. I watched as the younger tried to take the conversation over, while the older two were still looking at Nicola for endorsement. The older two admired Nicola too much, and the younger displayed a glint of envy.

Their connection looked different from family, since there was no age-related hierarchy that I could discern. They finished all the butter cookies, scattering the table with crumbs. I thought about the huge quantity of information that Patrick would have been able to gather from this, had he been here with me. Was Nicola trying to bring them on for a joint venture with his father's company, secretly or not? Was he getting advice about power infrastructure, expanding, fundraising? No—it was impossible that he was trying to make a pitch or solicit advice. Rather, *Nicola* appeared to be advising. It looked to me that perhaps someone was in trouble with debt or the law, and Nicola knew how to get rid of the trouble.

Patrick could have helped me understand, but I didn't want to text him, or take secret photos for him.

Nicola's suit was softer than Patrick's, softer in the shoulders and in the fabric, which looked, from this distance, matte like flannel and slightly rumpled. Patrick, who'd grown up in

New York, knew when to turn away, and when to use a long, attentive glance—he knew how much other men wished for affirmation, and how a man like him who withholds affirmation is immediately strong. I loved Patrick. I loved watching him do his work. But watching Nicola conduct himself was intensely mysterious. Here was the Titian-painting surface. What could I draw out of this? It was a posture of shrugging refinement. He was extremely cocky. Yet there was no mistaking the respect the other three had for him.

Nicola suddenly stood. Then I could taste the intense sweetness in my mouth, as though it was filled with sugar. My heart started its whipping way. The three men inclined their heads to him.

Nicola walked to me. I knew the three men were watching. I looked at his face for him to demonstrate how I should behave—what to do so it was clear this wasn't an affair, was my first thought. I didn't want to embarrass him, or seem confused about the fact that he could never be mine. What to do so that I looked like his writer friend. But he showed me no sign. He looked only happy to see me. I stood up. I wanted him to give me a kiss on the cheek.

"Are you all right?" he said.

I didn't know why he said that. I tried not to be embarrassed. I ducked my head, and lifted it, and attempted a new expression, calm, easygoing. Right away, he'd unbalanced me. "What on earth were you discussing?" I said. Six years since the last time we'd spoken. Eleven years since the time before.

"In truth," Nicola said, "infrastructure." His voice was warm and confiding and precise, and only the precision suggested that he hadn't grown up here. He didn't look back at the men, who were still watching. "Let's go."

I followed him back into the atrium. "In here, Nora,"

he said, and we entered another dim room, another office antechamber. He drew the door almost closed. I moved to put an appropriate distance between us. I started to try to talk to him, but he put his finger to his lips. Through the narrow aperture, we watched the three men walk past the fountain and out the front door, disappearing into a burst of light.

"Why are we in here?" I said.

"I want to go thank my friend," he said.

We returned to the room with landscapes. Now another man joined us. Nicola gave him a kiss on each cheek and introduced him as Peter, the gallerist. He introduced me only as Nora.

"Come look at the new Carracci," said Peter. They walked to one of the landscapes, brightly lit against the dim velvet wall. The painting showed a river running through a layered, hilly landscape, populated by a few journeymen or farmers. In the foreground, a boat passed over luminous water. In the distance, stony mountains massed below cream-colored clouds.

"*Bene,*" said Nicola. I loved to hear the Italian vowel.

He held his hand close to the landscape, an unsettling thing to view—his hand like the hand of God, large enough to pluck the trees and toss the people, large enough to stir up the weather, the sort of scale that, when it comes into our lives, is an abstraction. And then to my shock he touched the painting.

Peter didn't react to this violation, but I did—I flinched, and that touch in the gondola lift ignited in my mind. Nicola touched the figure.

"The browns and blacks need to be brightened," he said. "There's some kind of residue."

"Yes, yes," said Peter. "I will get that fixed."

Then the two of them stood and looked silently at the painting for long minutes. I stood a few feet behind them. I tried to look at the painting, but I mainly looked at Nicola.

He held himself strangely. There was something off about him. "Tortured," Patrick had said. I'd had a teacher in elementary school who'd seemed off in this way, some discomfort or formality, and one day her pant leg had ridden up and her sock had fallen down and I'd seen that she had a prosthetic leg. I never mentioned this to anyone. And there was a boy on the college literary magazine whom I became friends with who gave me the same feeling. Once I'd seen a rectangular shape through his shirt, pressing against his spine, and thought, Yes, there's his monitor or dial, it's tracking his whereabouts—then he took it out, it was only his cell phone. But years later he emailed me from a treatment program and told me he had dissociative identity disorder. He said that the whole time I'd known him he'd had these flashes of blankness, even while walking, or at a party, or in class. I wondered if Nicola had a big wound under his clothes, lines from surgery or fire—there was something I wanted to take care of.

I watched the changing angle of his head as he took in the landscape. He looked at a figure in the middle ground, painted in black with a sweep of red. I imagined that he was decomposing and composing the figure in his mind, but really I had no idea what he thought about anything.

"*Bene,*" he said at last, with a sigh. He took Peter's hand and kissed his cheek again. "We have to get going." Though there was no real reason to leave, that I could tell. His next appointment was just me.

CHAPTER 11

We walked into the park. I knew the park so well but I had no idea where we walked that day. The undifferentiated green moved around us.

I was noticing that he liked to enter and exit situations and states with no ado. And with me—how did we look? In the park, we attracted attention. His radiance, my eagerness. His dark gray soft-shouldered suit, his heavy, polished shoes. We walked respectfully apart, so it was impossible to smell him or brush against him.

I didn't know how long I had with him, whether I was walking him to another appointment, or whether I wouldn't be back at work the rest of the day.

"Good weather today," he said. This so affected me I could barely think.

"I liked that fountain," I said.

"The fountain and the floor were shipped from Italy," he said, with an edge in his voice. Leif had three moods; Patrick, being my boss, was filtered and slightly inhuman. Next to me, Nicola mysteriously seethed, full of trouble.

"I want to say I like things removed from their contexts," I said, "but I'm worried you'll take it the wrong way." Attempting to maintain some emotional distance, my brain had entered a nonsense mode. Even I didn't know what I meant. I was worried I'd seem to be complimenting him.

"No, no," he said. "Tell me everything. I've gotten ready."

"Ready?" I said. "How?"

He didn't answer this. I wondered if he was thinking about the ski lift, and the emergence of his black-gloved hand in our glass in the snow.

We walked through a cold tunnel. A violinist sent her music wrapping around us.

When we emerged onto the vivid lawn, I asked him if he wanted a pretzel.

"Sure," he said, and I produced the white paper bag with all the brown limbs twisted inside, crackling with salt. He tore off a small length and gave it to me. I'd imagined him feeding me but now all I felt was throbbing embarrassment.

I took it from him, then handed it back. "I don't like pretzels," I said.

"I see," he said. "So there are four for me?"

I nodded, in ecstatic misery. "What was that meeting you were having?" I expected a light repudiation, *Why are you interested* or *I can't tell you that.*

"A favor to my father," he said.

"How long have you known them?"

"Did you tell Patrick about seeing me with those men?" he said. In a different tone, this could have been accusing. Or it could have been suggesting that I was Patrick's flunky. But Nicola's voice showed that he knew that Patrick was interested in his work.

"I haven't yet," I said. Because of the tone Nicola had set, this came out suggestive, not hostile.

"I feel," he said, "that if I told you not to talk to Patrick about this, you'd obey."

I got hot and saw him seeing it. I could tell that I already wanted to be loyal to Nicola, and enter into his confidences.

"Obey?" I said hastily. The word sounded perverse. "I'm respectful. Not obedient," I said. "I think plenty of people are curious about what business you're hoping to do here."

"Anything my father wants," he said.

I could tell why Patrick was so sure Nicola was actually trying to take the business from his father. His words had an extremely compelling double valence. It was impossible to avoid the impression that he was speaking indirectly about everything. That when he said *Did you tell Patrick,* what he meant was *I know you didn't;* when he said *I feel you'd obey,* what he meant was, *You are disobedient;* when he said *Anything my father wants,* he meant *I loathe my father and would like to usurp his position.* This impression came partly from his poise and antique self-presentation, and partly from his measured, slow, precise way of talking, as though we were very intimate. He exuded a sense that talking directly about things was vulgar. He also suggested that the truth was far too complex to talk about. And yet there was an element of respect to it—as though he was giving me room to come to my own conclusions; he was allowing the conversation to be like a painting or poem, where multiple interpretations breathe in the life. Then I wondered—was it actually disrespectful that he didn't trust me to handle a straightforward statement, and that he taunted me with fake sincerity? In the end, all this just meant I had to listen with extreme attention, and I was not sure if he was being candid or not.

"I do the money world and my father does . . ."

"Does what?"

"The physical world," he said, with shivering grimness.

"You're a very dutiful son," I said.

My tone made him ask, "You don't think so?"

"Have you considered becoming decadent?" I said.

"My father would never allow that."

My view was of the side of his face, the graceful, not the

brutal. His skin had a lavender undertone. He was bluish pink, like a flower.

"If only my life were as simple as yours!" I said.

He laughed. He asked me how I was, and how work was, how Patrick was, how Leif was. Were we near the fountain, the obelisk, the Ramble, the bridge, the castle? I had no idea. The important thing was that he wasn't making motions to leave. Probably I would not be returning to work. I felt I was talking too much, but he made me feel like what I was saying was interesting.

"And Federica?" he said. "What about her?" I hadn't mentioned her—the last mention was six years before, in college. Yes, he had been paying attention. He was deliberate! And he was not going to let me get away unbothered.

"We haven't been in touch," I said. I did not like to think about Federica, to have her invoked for me this way, pulled out from behind the tree in the rain where I had left her. Nicola and I had come into a zone of entropy, passing over the backs of big boulders on the way up a green hill I had never interacted with before. Now through a grove with milky puddles in pea gravel. I wondered how I could sustain the conversation.

He asked me if I fell out of touch with my friends a lot. "You seemed cold then," he said.

"I truly just have social anxiety," I said sadly, getting more and more confused. I did like his willingness to show me that he too remembered that brief conversation in the literary magazine's marmalade hall.

He was just in the corner of my vision, an elegant darkness at the edge of the path. "Tell me about Federica," he said.

It was good to switch the topic. Now I met his eyes. His dark hair curled at the temples. I told him about how she was my host sister, and we got along, then we fought, then I went home. He asked why we fought, and kept drilling down into it until I described how she saw me in the shower. "I met you after that, didn't I?" he said. I said yes. "And so?"

I said I didn't know what he meant.

"Did you get together?" There he was with his openness, suddenly disturbing. I couldn't possibly tell him how the gondola ride had freed me. He was married. He was married, and also, I did not want him to recast that memory, did not want him to remake my life's most intense moment of help-less splendor into something casual and accidental.

"I loved her so much," I said defensively. The word "love" felt justified to me, although this was the first time I'd spoken it. There was something so special about that time, and what she taught me, even though I'd renounced the part of myself that had wanted to be at her mercy.

"I don't think you loved her that much," he said. "It sounds like you wanted to have sex with her."

I was virulently embarrassed and desperate to protest. "It was more complicated than it sounds," I said.

He touched his mouth, then dropped his hand to his side. He had long fingers and short, perhaps bitten finger-nails, but he moved his hands so much I couldn't really see. I wondered if he was embarrassed about them. His hands had mania in them. The fingers were articulate but not fluid; brittle, marionette fingers.

"I like the way you describe Leif," he said. I'd talked about how he liked to take me out in a boat sometimes and how capable he was with different kinds of water, and how he liked insurance, its heady investigation of risk and prepa-ration. "Leif is very good."

I shouldn't have cared so much what Nicola liked and disliked. But I was in his thrall. If you don't immediately run from him, you have to engage with his worldview. I felt so much pressure from this conversation. Something tactile about his words. What did it mean to be dashing? It was the glamour, the humor, the mildness. He had me thinking about courtesy. The base note of courtesy is ignoring the other's faults.

We were by the lake now, and walked through a clearing to the stony shore. Pairs of mallards and wood ducks with their appliqué heads slid toward us on long, tendrilling Vs. Without speaking he handed me the pretzels and we tore them and tossed them across the dark water. The ducks wagged their tails and dipped their bright beaks.

"Tell me about Iris," I said.

"You and Patrick really looked me up, didn't you," he said.

"It's our job," I said.

The sun was setting. Pink globes all up the eastern sky, and fractured, dreamy curves of rainbow. I wanted to stop and look at it, but he was unmoved. "Dinner?" he said. I let his decisions carry me along. We stepped out of the park and found a random Italian place.

The waiter with a silk camellia in her hair gave us wine for free and laughed her head off when he said thank you in Italian. I ate one single strand of my pasta and gave up. I remarked that it wasn't very New York of him to alight on the first available place. "I have one vice," he said, but he wouldn't say what it was. He said, "It's okay, you know, that you don't like many people."

"I know it's okay," I said.

"I like it," he said.

I felt a surge of affection. "I'm having a nice time with you," I said recklessly. As soon as I said it, I felt I'd misstepped. Now I was in the unfortunate position of having to scrutinize his face to make sure I hadn't gone too far.

He smiled. We talked about Patrick, and oral exams, and secret rituals, the objects made into gifts or challenges: special cups, flowers, golden apples. I told him about home, the circus museum with the pink walls by my house, the miniature circus with its tiny trapezes and seal pups that took a man fifty years to build. My mother and father, I told him, were quiet people. He talked about a party his father had thrown with a fortune teller who told the fortunes of all the heads of state—she was said to really know the future and she looked like a professor and was serious. She sat alone in a dark room and one by one the guests visited her. "Many people were so disturbed they had to leave immediately after," he said.

"Did you get your fortune told?" I said.

He said yes, and that she brought up things he'd never spoken to anyone. He said she moved a red glass with her mind. It tilted itself to the side and rolled along the table with its base like a wheel. And she just sat there like a professor.

"And what did she tell your father?"

He wouldn't answer. "Would you meet with her?" he said.

"No, thank you."

I didn't know what his smile meant. I did know that it wasn't often that I spent so many hours in conversation with someone, but I'd been almost free from my familiar anxiety, which had to do with interacting correctly with people, talking the right amount about the right subjects, acting interested and giving them what they wanted, which was always so difficult for me—a laugh or a repeating-back? With Nicola, I didn't have any of these normal concerns. Through stalled moments, he'd continued. An unearthly fatigue now prevented me from fretting.

Now he talked about Iris. "I'd do anything for her," he said. "She's the only person I've ever had to *work* to make friends with. She made me who I am. Before her, I was simple, it was all a dream, and nothing had any weight. Nothing but my father and me."

"And now?" I said.

"Now I'm nine layers in," he said. "It's all different." He leaned back and lifted his wine to his lips. For a moment it painted them darker.

He was so romantic I kept searching for the false note. Maybe my perception of his duality had more to do with me and my skepticism and my confined world than with him. Still, something about him defied belief. As he gesticulated about her, how he realized his life was now *for* her, there was nothing he wouldn't sacrifice about himself for her, he fell out of his chair. He laughed and picked himself up, and I saw the private emerald satin lining of his suit. This was a key to Nicola: he put his whole body into things, so he could never quite achieve the neutrality of elegance.

The waiter moved us to a booth. She loved him.

"Have you ever sacrificed any real thing about yourself for Iris, though?" I said.

"Yes," he said.

"What?"

"I can't tell you."

I didn't like this. "I can't believe you didn't care about the sunset," I said. I remembered, but did not recount, the night on the quay, the cypress shadows, the pink snow-storm through which our gondola had plunged, all the high-inducing beauty he was related to. Instead, I told him all my old paintings were formed around nature-awe. "Have you ever felt that?" I said.

"No," he said.

"I thought so," I said. "How can you be a romantic and not know that feeling?"

"I don't trust that feeling of being overtaken," he said.

He wasn't really a romantic like I was, looking to be caught up in the sublime.

He was premodern. He had a fairy-tale severity, a fairy-tale impersonality to him—grand passion, honor, irrational, primitive devotion.

I drank cold red wine, and the restaurant shimmered around us, the only still point his bright, enameled eyes. The russet tones, candles, and couples shifted and disappeared. I had to pay close attention to him. I couldn't coast. I almost wanted to lay my head on the table.

Into this dark, melting state he poured his words. "In my life, I've found that there are some people for whom the gates are always open. For those people, life is like walking through a structure with many gates with attendants in front of them. You don't know if the structure was built as a warning, or for a particular battle, or for some religious purpose by some ancient civilization—but you're allowed to pass through every gate."

I wondered if he was describing the experience I'd had of waiting for the guard at the town house where I'd met him. And finding no obstruction.

"Easy for you to say," I said. "You're a nobleman."

The word, the hierarchy I'd presented, didn't bother him at all. "I have an idea about you," he continued. "I don't think—don't think you're socially anxious. I think you're restless, you're bored. Anxiety is a sign of restlessness in the organism."

"It really doesn't feel like boredom," I said, dismayed. I didn't want him to define me, but also, I *did* want him to understand me. I wanted to confess myself to him.

"I might be wrong," he said.

I was glad when he concluded our dinner. He paid. He stood first.

HE DID NOT offer to walk me to the subway station. He hailed a cab—I loved watching how quickly he did it; still after five years in the city I found hailing a cab stressful. Then he disappeared south. I wondered whether I would ever see him again. Yes, I thought, maybe in another five years.

I sat on the yellow seat of the subway, faint with exhaustion. I leaned my head back and caught my hair in the ad frame. I let my legs fall open and I closed my eyes. I'd lived in the city long enough to feel private even in public. We went slowly through the tube under the river.

What I noticed about him was his extremity. He was too serious with the men, too focused in his questions about Federica, then too intense talking about Iris. He didn't care about the flow of the conversation. Which made me nervous in a different way, and which made me tearful on the train. Was it true that I was restless, not anxious? His comment made me feel like I'd played the victim. I didn't like that feeling. I felt more connected to the plaintive confinement of anxiety than to the roving irresponsibility of restlessness.

Maybe he liked our funny coincidental relationship. Maybe he liked that I'd changed so much. He wanted to toy with the memory of Federica and me, and see how much I'd forsaken my old self. I'd had the impression at the magazine party, and again today, that he was so commanding he might easily be evil. I couldn't tell whether he'd side with his father and self-dealing and corruption or try to make a break for a more standard, stable, aboveground sort of business. Whether he had the moral compunction that Patrick believed he had, or whether he was entirely a shape-shifter, or driven on by challenges and objectives I hadn't even begun to uncover.

But that kind of evil was abstract, and I was careless about it. What did I know? How could I judge? I was more worried about the interpersonal. He could upset me, I knew. Maybe today would prove hurtful; it was too soon to tell what meaning of Federica's he may have shattered. He acted as though he knew the truth. How confident he was. *She controlled you* was possibly mean, as was his question about whether we had gotten together. Especially because he gave me no space to dispute them.

For the first time I felt I could regard myself like a stranger would, as though the mirror had lost its sheet and I could reach through and take my own face by the cheeks and see my particular ugliness, my particular appeal. This was the real feeling of meeting a person to whose words you assign maximum credence.

I knew I was giving him power by dwelling on him. Maybe he was creating the truth and then I had to live in it; we were opposites.

But no one had tried to look at me square, as he had. In my experience, people were like suns—it was hard to look at them full on. Do you really want to know what your neighbor dreams and fears? Won't knowing create a burden to act? Won't people thereafter want to follow you and hear your insights and rely on you? It was too much to engage with people like this, but Nicola did.

CHAPTER 12

Two weeks, then he texted again. I was at work. When I got the text, I did not open it. I wasn't sure I wanted him to return so soon to my life. I wasn't done thinking through the gallery and the park and the dinner, and work had suffered and Leif had suffered. I was constantly distracted; even when I was talking to other people or writing, it felt like someone was screaming in my ear. I wanted to be entirely alone for a few more weeks and get to the bottom of it. But when I sat on the train or lay in bed with Leif sleeping beside me and tried to think only about Nicola, I felt squeamish and desolate.

I detested every part of how I'd behaved, but the target of the hatred kept switching around. Sometimes it was about how I'd complimented his facility with people, sometimes I regretted not making more claims about him and forcing him to look at himself, the same way he'd forced me about Federica. Often I wished I'd told him, *Right after I met you, I kissed her and ruined everything.* What would he do with that kind of knowledge? I imagined telling him, *After I saw you in college, I dreamed about you for years.* I knew I wasn't the only person who wanted to tell him that—which was part of why I couldn't under any circumstances actually tell him. I didn't want to be like the waitress or the girls at the magazine party, blunt about their longing.

But more than that, I didn't want to invite real intimacy. The greater the intimacy, the greater the disruption.

So when I got his text, I felt pain, then fear. Once every few years was enough. Or maybe I didn't ever want to see him again.

For two hours I didn't open his text. I considered deleting it without looking at it. I didn't delete it.

I hadn't told Patrick about the business conversation I'd seen, nor what Nicola had said about it (*a favor to my father*), reasoning that I simply didn't know enough for this information to be helpful, while knowing that the longer I went without being open with Patrick, the more intimacy I felt with Nicola, and the more devotion. I didn't have the self-control to avoid intimacy. The rumors about his family didn't mean much to me. His magnetic charge felt like goodness to me, because it felt right to get closer and closer.

I asked Patrick what to do. "Open it," Patrick said. "You want me to?"

Then, because of Patrick's envy, I couldn't stop smiling. Of course this was good. Nicola had texted me—he'd been thinking of me; he wanted to continue the interaction, if only to say goodbye. Maybe he was already back in Italy. With that in mind, so quickly it was like I was tricking myself, I opened it. He'd written, "Come over to my father's house after work."

"You should go," Patrick said.

For thirty minutes, I didn't respond. Didn't I like my life? Did I want his scrutiny again? Did I want him to wear me out and confuse me again? Did I want to give Leif some excuse again? Did I want the long comet's tail of nausea and self-doubt that would follow?

"And tell me what you find out about his dad," Patrick said.

I wrote to ask him for the address.

*

HIS FATHER'S HOUSE was a four-story brick town house in lower Manhattan. I was surprised. I'd expected something grander, like a wide white mansion near Central Park. Nicola asked me to wait outside. Then he came up behind me; he was returning from an errand, he said. Again he did not kiss me on the cheek. During our greeting, I avoided looking at his face. Why was I here? "I'm very happy to see you again," he said. He did look happy.

We entered a dark foyer. The floor was black and white squares of marble, like my old high school, Massimo D'Azeglio. The walls were dark and matte. I didn't have time to take in more than the single gray banksia in the vase before Nicola beckoned upward.

On the third floor off the stairwell, in the dim, I was staggered for a second to see a woman looking calmly at us through a small window in the wall. No—I hoped Nicola didn't catch my error—it was only a portrait of a lady wearing a lace collar, glossy web against the shadows behind her. "A relative," he said. I'd never seen such an old painting in a private home. To diminish its effect, I imagined painting it— the highlights on the lace were the brightest dry white. Yet she kept rudely disturbing me. Even though I knew she was flat, every few seconds she pulsed out and made my eyes think she was real again. In the half-light, she was watching us from the world of the dead. The painting made me wonder what was wrong with Nicola's family.

I could vaguely hear, from what sounded like an expensive stereo system in a distant room, a Renaissance choir. "I must have left the music on," he said. I followed Nicola down the charcoal-colored hall. He alternated light and dim as we passed open doors. I couldn't understand how the hall was this long; the town house we had entered was not large. It must have extended far backward from the street, I thought. The singing cut off, and then began again: the long, balancing, relentlessly changing chords of polyphonic sacred music. I didn't know what it was. Du Fay, Nicola said. I couldn't tell how many singers.

The music grew louder as we walked, and I felt I was tracking straight into the past. Time was reeling back; a new context was emerging. Nicola began to shake his head and bend back and forth to the music. Now he reminded me of myself, a bit silly against the music's cosmic seriousness. I nodded too, and leaned from side to side, and waved my arms around; I couldn't help it. My heart was beating hard. The music twisted into trouble, diminished, and then gave itself over again to those mercurial, exultant chords, which I would never be able to separate from Nicola. He was just like them.

We hadn't even reached the end of the hall when he said, "*Vieni,*" and opened a door. And inside, in the overwhelmingly bright library, a crush of golden fronds, frames, books in tall caged shelves, there was not a stereo system—I was astonished, and couldn't tell whether I heard or saw my error first—there were four singers standing up and swaying, with their mouths open, their faces distorted. I stepped forward, but he took my waist sharply and pulled me back into the hall.

One spell replaced by another. The touch detonated in me.

"My father," he whispered. I peered over his shoulder and could see the legs of a man evidently reclining—two long legs in dark suit pants, crossed at the ankle, and heavy black shoes. My mind jumped to the terror this body must have inspired in many people. I didn't want to see the rest of him.

"I'll see you out," he said.

I followed him down a few flights of stairs. I felt his grip, felt his grip, felt his grip, the beating of a drum. Those legs belonged to the same world as the woman in the painting. They, like the inhabitants of the past, were not accountable to the rules I knew. It was realer now, Federica's warning. I preferred to imagine bad people than to trespass in their houses. And we exited out of a different building than the one we'd entered. The brick town house was to the left; we'd just stepped out of a white cast-iron building. The windows weren't level. His family must have knocked down the walls and gutted both to make that long seamless hall.

"Nora," he said with finality, and nodded.

"Okay, thank you," I said coolly. My back, the base of my spine, were still trembling. "Why didn't you know he was there?"

"I thought it was my music. From earlier." He looked at me and his face contracted. "He likes to have a little concert at home."

"He wanted to trick you?"

"I guess so."

All I wanted was for him to invite me to go somewhere and talk a little longer. If I really had to go, I wanted to know if this was the last time. If it wasn't, I wanted to know when I'd see him again. How much longer he was in the country, and what he intended our friendship to be. But I knew he liked to enter and exit without ado, and I let him set the terms. If he didn't want to discuss it, I would not force it.

"I'm sorry about my father," Nicola said.

"It's okay," I said.

"He's not a human," Nicola said, his voice bitter. "It's a shame. I wanted you to meet Iris."

He texted her. "Wait," he said. "She's coming now."

We sat on the steps of the white building. At this point, I still felt only interest to meet her and thus see another part of his life. "Why isn't your father a human?" I said.

He shook his head. "It's a waste of our time to talk about it," he said. "I too much enjoy our conversations."

My face heated up. "Right," I said. I tried to let it go. "The music was good," I said. "Why do you enjoy our conversations?"

He smiled now. "Most people *respect* me much more than they *like* me," he said. "I think it's reversed with you. I find this very nice."

"I don't know," I said. "Maybe you need to work harder to be respectable." Maybe I didn't understand enough about his context to be properly respectful. I always went for the ignorantly personal—like with Turin, like with the painting. Until today I'd never seen his context, and it still wasn't his, it was his father's. I'd only seen how he slipped in and out, and didn't fit anywhere.

"You did dance with me," he said. "But you're not sure you believe what I think."

It wasn't that I didn't believe him. It was that there was clearly so much more to say. Incompleteness was a form of lying. My obsessive interest in him meant I could not be satisfied, and my hunger was a form of strength. I had to think of a response. It was an opening to press him.

"What did you sacrifice for Iris?" I said.

"Intimacy," he said without hesitation. "Of a certain kind."

"What do you mean?" I said.

"It never ends. It's different from normal life."

I looked at him. I couldn't tell if his face was obscene or gentle; it kept changing. "I wouldn't want to kiss so many people," I hazarded. "I don't want to taste so many people's mouths." This was a stand-in for the larger problem of intimacy: for how hard it was to share anything at all.

"I wasn't in it for the kissing," he said.

Then, without warning or process, I truly didn't know how to act. I had no idea what my voice normally sounded like or how to make it sound as it was supposed to. I could feel it in my teeth, and just then Iris arrived.

"This is Nora," Nicola said. I wondered if she could tell that her husband had just kissed me with words—that was how I felt. It was hilarious to try to interact with her, but I was grateful for it. I couldn't keep sinking into the well.

"Wonderful to meet you," I said. "The person Nicola would sacrifice anything for." I was foolish, trying to reassert the primacy of their relationship. I'm sure Nicola saw what I was doing, but it was a reflex.

"Ah, did he say that?" said Iris, with a slight French accent. She was elegant and withdrawn, the way I'd expected Nicola to be. She was much more like a noblewoman. She had a ponytail of dark, shiny hair and wore a stiff short jacket and pleated trousers.

"I should go," I said. Nicola stood behind Iris. I took a quick look at his face and he bestowed upon me a beautiful smile. And too soon he had taken Iris's shoulders, and they went back into the house. The singers were still going—I heard a few quick notes and imagined Nicola's inhuman father in his library, whipping them to continue.

AT HOME I put Du Fay, the random first motet that came up, on the speakers. The first song, first crumpled tears, then thinking about Nicola made the tears come rolling down my cheeks.

When the music fell into those long raw notes, it was like him touching me. I remembered the sun in Piazza Vittorio, yet I also felt caught in the rain. Elation.

What did he like? He didn't like kissing. What would he say if he spoke directly? Did he like the chase? No, he wasn't that kind of threshold person. He liked to enter all the way into the chambers of the heart. I imagined what he would make of me. He wouldn't be tentative or distant. I wanted him to mash my face and lay into me. I wanted him to take and take and take whatever I could give him.

What did he like? In the future, he would call me from a walk when he was traveling far away, and tell me:

When I look out at life, I see a great drift of gray, a great field, and, punctuating it, millions of dark vortices, knotty sinkholes, locations of great density. Those are the people. It's not that I am assessing this landscape so that I can command it. What I like is the way that people's particularity exploits them. The extremities of human emotion are heterogeneous. In the Cathar times, to which I trace my origins, people spent a lot of time trying to live up to abstractions, abstract ideas about humility, charity, nobility. Art mattered back then because the value system was so different. People wanted to live like saints in paintings. There was none of this federalism, nothing about distribution or equality. People were striving after an ideal instead. It was a world of symbols.

I love people, he would say, because everyone privately is still patterning themselves off some need, some heartache, some fantasy, that is still arcane and spiritual, in every single case. You rub off all the layers and you find the absolute diversity again. I've looked over manuscripts and found the people as they truly are: women with the hindquarters and wings of bats, furry dragons with red and blue wings, naked men stuffed into green-faced, saber-toothed hellmouths, monkeys tending to owls, men holding their own severed heads, men with lizard bodies and snail bodies, cats in cloaks, roots with faces, skeletons with crowns, long-haired women with arrows through their breasts.

He would tell me, people can't help their real urges. We live in a flattened, grayed-out world, but the extremities are still there, hidden, heroism, wrath, self-abnegation, and so on, little ladders all the way into the heavens. Sometimes I feel that I have the cheat codes for being a human. My parents forced this sensitivity on me.

CHAPTER 13

What is it?" Leif said, when I watched him silently at dinner. We'd grown up together and he had the first strands of gray in his hair. I'd paint them with a dry brush, like the highlights on reticella lace.

I told him I loved him, and he said he loved me.

No more Nicola, I decided. I sensed that I was moving from a time of pleasant fantasy to a time of pain, of dense, dark, leaden longing.

Leif was the early riser: *Joy of Cooking* waffles before work, the butter crackling on crisp edges. He cooked, I cleaned. He knew to get me fragrant flowers—in the city the scent meant more to me than the look; I knew to get him sticky rice in a lotus leaf. At a certain point all his clothes were clothes I bought him, just because I liked to buy him things. I liked him in real wool flannel. I liked him in marine blue.

He had the energy and money to rent gear and a car and all I had to do in return was love the nature that we saw. We camped in the Catskills and watched a raccoon reach its paw in the unzipped slit of our tent. We camped in the Blue Ridge Mountains in a horrific storm, and he made me sit on my pack so that the lightning couldn't get me from the ground.

When we stepped off the plane at Burbank I'd always

point out to him the citrus-smelling air, the smell of his childhood, and he'd always thank me although he couldn't tell the difference. He drove us up into the crumbling, dusty, mansion-filled hills; he drove us to the cold ferocious sea, then out to the farmstands in the plains, where we ate Gaviota strawberries and pie and sat together in silence in the fast-moving desert twilight.

He fell in the mud playing Ultimate in the park, and when I came to find him, he hugged me so I'd be muddy too, because it was a state he personally enjoyed.

I had in a box two nineteenth-century painted candles I'd bought at a flea market, a lady with ringlets in a straw hat and a bell-shaped skirt, and a gentleman with a white ponytail tied with a blue ribbon, all in molded wax. I'd been saving them. Though I loved their sweet blushing old-fashioned faces I knew I would burn them when I married Leif. I liked the idea of burning something precious to give sacrificial weight to the occasion. Leif would let me do what I wanted, I knew, and I wanted a bouquet with daisies and cornflowers, something small and informal and outdoors in a location of such total splendor that it alone would be worth the trip, the Northern California coast, maybe, so that the guests didn't need me and I could come and go as I pleased.

So many times Leif had consoled me when I'd been caught up in pain. He filled in a missing part of my brain, the part that would have reasonable reactions. And for him, I filled in reasonable interaction with his mother—my witnessing staunched her endless criticism.

We leaned on each other. We were already in drydown. We were never all over each other and never would be. I was sad, happy, sad, happy, feelings that had little to do with him. The feeling that he did own was his calm that muted my anxiety, and I loved him for it.

No more with Nicola.

No more, but nevertheless, in my dream Nicola came to me and touched me with both his hands. He didn't have sex with me in the dream, just touched me irresistibly. I woke up feeling like I had a fever but what I had was two texts from Nicola.

My first thought was, I ought to block his number, then I won't have to worry anymore. My second thought was that I'd open them later at work. Then I opened them right there lying next to Leif, keeping the phone too close to my face for him to see. Nicola said he was having a get-together over the weekend with Iris and a few of her friends. Would I like to come?

At work Patrick called to ask if he was invited—he was. This gave me permission. I texted Nicola, "Can I bring my boyfriend, Leif?" Then silence for a few hours, and horrible regret. I was clearly having a reaction to what he'd said about intimacy. And now he wouldn't say any more on that topic. No more said was *what I wanted*, of course. Of course. There must be some way to interact with him without that kind of heat.

I asked Patrick if he'd met Iris. "Not yet," he said.

I said cautiously, "It seems like Nicola used to be a bit of a rake."

"Dominique suggested that," Patrick said.

"How sad," I said, though I didn't find it sad. I found it, despite myself, extremely interesting. I was thinking about Lord Byron and Modigliani and Canova, whose Perseus brandished the Medusa head in a deep hall of the Met. What was he doing, back then, before Iris? "Does he have an open marriage now?"

"I don't know," Patrick said. Then he said, slyly, "Why do you ask?"

"I met Iris the other day," I said, showing off, because Patrick hadn't met her yet. "I don't think she'd put up with it."

Nicola soon texted "Yes, excellent!" about Leif, which shouldn't have been a letdown.

Sunday. Leif and I went to Nicola's father's house. The house that was two houses invisibly joined, just like the Palazzo Madama in Turin, which was half dark medieval castle, half white Baroque palace. This time we entered through the white cast-iron side. The interior had a resinous, toxic scent, like turpentine. A cook had made tagliatelle and fennel salad. She was just leaving when we arrived. She had a white dress shirt and a black apron. "The pasta is cold," she said to Nicola in Italian.

We came to the second floor in a living room with dark paneled walls and gold mirrored sconces with real candles burning in them. There were leather-covered chairs, inlaid tables and sideboards, and a chandelier with pear-shaped crystals. The candlelight made the gilt vivid and glowed on the folds of the olive velvet drapes. Iris had two friends over, dark-haired and trouser-clad like her. She spoke with them in what I took to be Swiss German. Candles, bel canto, ice, glass, laughter. I could hear Patrick and Nicola in the kitchen. The door was open to the hall, which was limitlessly long.

Leif was not as enchanted as I had been. Sometimes I was frustrated by his inability to enter a state of rapture, but here it was attractive. "How do you know these people again?" Leif said.

"Through Patrick," I said. "Nicola used to visit the literary magazine." I hoped the truth—Italy, as teens—would not come up.

We made spritzes. I had never been so grateful to drink. Nicola emerged. I was glad to notice that I was more preoccupied with what Leif thought of Nicola than with what Nicola thought of Leif. Maybe this was because I couldn't hide anything from Nicola, I was helpless, and therefore it made no difference to Nicola that Leif was poised and dispassionate, with a smile that did little to modify the true nature of his face, which was bony. Leif talked to Nicola about the insurance app and the issues they'd been having with revenue, and I mostly wondered whether Leif found Nicola's responses helpful or bullshit. Leif, who was not a fool, made it impossible to tell.

Patrick was trying to converse with me but I kept glancing at Leif and Nicola, trying to see what Leif would be seeing. An elegant man with uncouth enthusiasm. An elegant, green-eyed man who compelled respect; he could only be your superior or your equal; so maybe too knowing, too arrogant. A green-eyed man in worn polished shoes and a black sweater with long cuffs, his dark hair a few days too long, a man who liked to get women to yield.

No more. I drank my spritz. Cadmium red light, but translucent. A glossy solvent. Patrick said, "Nora?" I excused myself. I found the bathroom, which had a complicated panel of buttons instead of a light switch. I pressed various buttons, brightening and dimming the room. I put my spritz on the sink. The walls, ceiling, and floor were all dark panels of slate. The hand soap smelled like firewood. I stared at myself, my halfway inside-out body in my linen dress—my veiny arms, my corded neck. With the same carelessness I'd used to open his text—*oh, I barely know what I am doing*—I tipped the rest of my drink and ice onto the ground. Now I had a reason to stay in the bathroom. I cleaned it up slowly. The slate floor was heated. I pushed the ice cubes around on it and watched their trails evaporate. Patrick had taught me you can't prevent thoughts from arising but you can change how you respond to them. *Just use it as fuel. Enjoy this nauseating arousal, use it in your writing, use it in your work, use it as fuel.*

I knocked the glass down too. A bell-like noise, then a high-pitched skitter as the light-struck fragments exploded across the slate. The glass had broken into three large pieces and a thousand crystals as small as sand. I pressed them up with damp toilet paper. Then I sat for a while on the floor. I wished I could drink what I'd spilled. I needed another drink.

Finally I returned to the party. Everyone was finishing their tagliatelle but I had no appetite at all.

Nicola took Leif's dishes and washed them in the prep kitchen in the next room. I was so surprised by that. It was a sign that he was treating Leif too like he'd treated me, recognizing him as an agent.

As I made myself another vodka-heavy spritz, using up the last drops of Campari, Leif whispered to me, "I really like him. He asked such specific questions." I was safe.

I wanted to ask Leif what questions. But Nicola was approaching.

"Come with me, Nora," said Nicola. "We need to find more Campari."

I blushed. "Okay, Leif?" I said. But it was ridiculous that I was asking permission—by asking permission, I was attracting attention. "You'll be all right chatting here by yourself?" I added lamely.

"Probably," Leif said.

"I can't wait to see more of this house," I said to Nicola, as though that were the draw.

"Come on," he said.

We passed into the hall. "Thank you for being so nice to Leif," I said.

"Don't be ridiculous," he said.

I wondered which thing seemed ridiculous. I imagined most of all what would seem ridiculous to Nicola was my attempt to manage the situation of being in the dark hall with him by talking about Leif.

Nicola said, "Leif is good."

"I know," I said.

What I thought was a lighted doorway was an elevator. We descended to the "Lower Basement." Thank God I was drunk, otherwise I wouldn't have been able to handle the quiet. "I wish I'd known you better when you were in college," he said. We were in a dark hallway with arched brick doorways.

"Why?"

"We could have been friends."

"We can be friends now," I said. I was looking at his face and neck and chest and arms, I wanted him to feel that my gaze was physical, was touching his skin.

He shook his head. "Are you having a nice time?"

I nodded.

"I worry about you," he said, pushing open a door into a wine cellar. Small gold lights illuminated the dark bottles.

"I don't believe that," I said.

"Believe what you like," he said, "I don't want you to feel thrown to the wolves."

"You mean, Iris?" I said.

"Look for Campari," he directed. Then, softer: "I mean, I know I get worked up."

"Oh," I said, feeling suddenly sad. I wanted him to get worked up. And I wanted him to lack self-awareness about it.

As we stepped among the dormant bottles, the light moving like sparks over their necks, he told me more about what he'd felt when he saw me years before, at the party at the literary magazine. He'd come up the stairs and seen a man leaning whispering into my ear and he had remembered meeting me at the Olympics. He said that there is a way of living that he quite respects, which is a life lived under layers upon layers of mediation and alienation. Yet this was the opposite of my way. He seemed to be puzzling it out. There is usually a falseness to the opposite, he continued—to what is openhearted, pure, sincere, all reaction, unmediated, all response. "Anyone who truly cares about life in that way generally refuses to discuss it," he said. "Certain things are inexpressible."

Nicola said he'd been thinking about me trying to understand what he liked. I reminded him of someone he knew a long time ago, he said. His own first love. "It's your unmediated quality," he said. "That way that you want to get swallowed up."

"Have you told me this before?" I said. *There are some people for whom the gates are always open,* he had said when we'd walked in the park.

"Maybe it's that you seek it out—that's what makes it so sincere." A thought which filled me with shame that felt like terror. I'd stepped right into it. So quickly I moved from happy to offended. Yet this felt like my best and only shot at actual self-knowledge.

"Seek it out?" I stuttered.

"Don't you agree?"

I thought about him gripping me in the gondola lift. Was I just hunting for that helplessness all the time? Had I compelled him to treat me that way? "Do you think I have bad intentions?" I said. Even I had no idea.

"You mix me up," he said. He looked at me straight on and I felt caught in a klieg light. "You seem like a good person. I could use more of that in my life. You scheme about only one thing, about opening yourself to the vagaries of will-lessness. I'm working around something I cannot and will not articulate," he said. "Certain things are inexpressible," he said again.

I said nothing, praying for him to continue. What was it that he could not and would not articulate? But "you mix me up" was extremely good. I could feel the hysteria rise like the swallows that reverberated in Turin's mornings. If only I had a better sense of what to say. But lovely Nicola, he let me be my true reactions.

"Can you hold this?" he said, and passed me a bottle of Campari.

I nodded. Weighty, chilly bottle. And white energy shot up my spine, radiating tremors. My legs shook, and my back all the way up to the neck.

"You can?" he said.

I leaned against the wall. We were together in the global subterranean temperature: the cellar in which you preserve, the shelter where you wait out the hurricane, the tomb that you excavate. What would he do now? He could step closer to me. He could close the distance, and put both his hands against the wall around me. He wouldn't have to touch me, he could just come closer. No one would ever know, and there would be nothing to tell; I just wanted to feel his heat, and to receive one more clue.

He regarded me, with concern or amusement, impossible to tell. "Stay with me, Nora," he said. I barely realized he'd shifted into Italian. *Stai con me.*

He called the elevator. I wanted to scream, I wanted to fall to the floor and sob. I wanted to break every bottle of wine. I wanted to hit him and hit myself. I wanted him to hit me. It was a moment of supreme discomfort inside of my body. I was imprisoned.

Entering the elevator, I touched his back. Almost but not quite by accident. It was corded with energy. I felt his adrenaline rage.

The conversations had collapsed into one when we returned. Iris was talking about wanting kids; she wanted to have a baby sometime in the next few years. Patrick was sympathizing. He didn't mention that his wife was recently pregnant. She'd been pregnant before and it hadn't worked out. Then Iris talked about how much she loved her parents.

I felt the first pricklings of dislike for her. Oh, my heart was all awry. But who could be rich and beautiful and also love their parents? Not Nicola, even. How spoiled she was. She'd invented an MRI contrast agent in high school, but now what did she do? Maybe extreme wealth and luck had corroded her ability to work, which would effectively nullify her intelligence, or so I hoped. Of course Nicola liked her, everyone liked Eden and perfection, everyone dreamed of happiness around the familial table, happiness and support and parents and children who really enjoyed each other's company.

For a while I flirted hard with Leif, and even a little bit with Patrick. Leif had seen me in anxious states and knew how that itchy, uncomfortable feeling could drive me to excessive liveliness. I hoped he thought this flirting was due to normal social anxiety. But at every moment I was tracking where Nicola was in the room.

Finally Nicola returned to me. I got still drunker and spoke Italian with him, just talking about the house and the cook and nothing in particular. Speaking the language sent the water to turn the old waterwheel; all the creaking machinery began to move. My secret skill, Italian—neither Patrick nor Leif had ever seen me speak it before.

I shouldn't have done that. But Leif was only charmed. Good Leif. He believed the version of me he had come to know, which for a long time I'd thought was the true version.

CHAPTER 14

I didn't form memories on the trip home. Leif had already left when I woke up in the morning, which was slightly unusual, but I was grateful. Maybe he'd wanted to let me sleep off the hangover. I took painkillers with my coffee.

On the train I was hyperalert to the scent of everyone's shampoo and coffee. In our swaying, narrow room, I was confronted by the city's faces. The feeling of being embedded was often signaled by a feeling of discomfort—at times growing up I felt compelled to embed myself in the lawn in Sarasota, but lying among flowers and grass meant yellow jackets and beetles and prickling stems. The subway is like that too, you're pressed against people's moist backs, looking at their whiskers and their apps. And when your life is changing, what does it feel like? For me it didn't feel like a process, but rather a jarring period apart of hysteria and appetite loss and endless, insane, personal laughter.

At work I called Patrick to ask why Nicola hated his father. "It seems like there are many good reasons," Patrick said. "I'm traveling. I'll tell you when I know more."

"I think he loves his father," I said. He loved the wrong things, in the wrong ways, I hoped—so that he could love me.

"This isn't complicated," said Patrick.

Then I just daydreamed at work, wonderfully sick and famished.

I felt Nicola wasn't fuel, but solvent. I was dissolving into his unstable liquor.

Some outside researcher presented on batteries in the conference room, and I excused myself and lay on the floor of my office inwardly panting, feeling the breeze from the AC— everything was a turn-on, including my own breathing— thinking about *We could have been friends.*

In the night, a thick fog visited the city, and I walked along the south edge of the park. Stunning respiring August. Horses in the glinting white fuzz. The fog green then red then green. The cobblestones wet. The Plaza sending light upward and out. I had a lonely sandwich in Columbus Circle. I bought underwear to keep in my backpack, and then I walked up through the park. There was no way any human had ever been as aroused as I was in that fog that night. I walked north to the Shakespeare Garden. And in the cottage restroom, barely thinking, I squeezed my arms and legs and sighed. I was full of shimmering sensation, glitter in oil in kaleidoscope. It was incredible to think that he might find me scheming and good at the same time. I'd always thought innocence and goodness went together, and I had known since the Federica days that I wasn't innocent in my desires. Once I'd dreamed of getting sick; I didn't want to be responsible. I felt that way again. Nicola needed to step out of the shadows and put a heavy hand on me. He needed to put a heavy hand on me or I would blow up.

I walked back south under America's largest remaining stand of American elms. Elms with twisted arms. I was alone by the pond except for the ducks. Even in the city, the ducks sounded wild and peaceful. They napped on black rocks on the coppery pond and some of them flew up and across when I approached. They called with that quiet, spooky, resonant sound. By the Plaza, a carriage driver was reading to his horse.

AT HOME, LEIF was sitting in the armchair, where we almost never sat. The armchair faced the door. He had one arm bent behind his head. He said, "He told me he met you when you were a teenager."

His anger jolted me.

"Who?" I said.

"Nicola," he said, pronouncing it wrong, with the accent on the *Nic*.

"That's true," I said. I took a long look at his face, which was reptilian in the jungly light of the muted television. It didn't matter that it was an innocuous omission. I'd been late or absent so often recently.

"How did you meet?" He spoke quietly.

My heart sped up. A feeling from the Federica time. I wondered if I could escalate his anger. I needed the anger so that I could refind his vitality. "In Italy," I said.

He said, "Why didn't you tell me?" just as I said, "It's hard to talk about." Our words overlapped. He looked at me; his mouth was slightly open.

Let him ask again. The silence tightened. He said, "Is there something you need to say?"

"It was just too much to get into," I said. "You know I don't like to think about Italy."

I walked to turn off the TV. Now that I was closer to him, and the light was still, I could see that he wasn't angry. He was soft and sad. He looked at me lost.

"It was all coincidence," I said. I took his hand and sat him down on the bed. I tried to push his shoulders so he would lie down. He wouldn't move. I put my knees on either side of his lap and kissed him, but he turned away.

"I just wish you were comfortable with me," he said.

"I am," I said. I told him I loved him.

Then I went to the shower and knelt in the tub, thinking about Nicola mashing my face. I manifested and I prayed. Keep passing the plough over the pit, keep digging up the volcano in the field. It's just a fever I'm in, I thought, it'll pass, it'll pass, it'll pass.

ON FRIDAY, NICOLA texted Patrick that he'd come by and visit the office.

Patrick and I were listening to Offenbach. Nicola arrived, a bolt of energy in a soft-shouldered suit, and my throat constricted with emotion, I was choking on his glory. He swept his arms wide. "Offenbach, I could hug you!" he cried, and broke a glass all over the floor.

I leapt to clean it up. He wouldn't let me. He told me to sit down. "I mean it," he said, with real or fake heat in his voice. I sat at the table. "Take your elbows off the table," he said laughingly. I did. Yes, yes, yes, tell me.

Patrick was amused by all of this. I could see him notice that something had changed about the way Nicola and I were interacting.

Nicola put his jacket on a chair and I saw its emerald lining. He knelt to pick the pieces of glass up off the floor. I looked at the curls on the top of his head.

"Nicola, what did you mean when you said certain things are inexpressible?"

"When did I say that?"

In the cellar after you told me that you could use a little more goodness in your life, and told me that I reminded you of your own first love. "At dinner the other day," I said. I explained to him and Patrick that I'd long been troubled by those walks around Turin, that I didn't know what to do about the ancient city, didn't know what thoughts it could bridge me to. "Is that what you mean by inexpressible?"

"Yes and no," he said, still adding broken pieces to his handful.

"The devil's answer," said Patrick.

Nicola said, "We don't even understand the contexts we're in, we don't understand the literature we read, or the art we look at. We only get these pinpricks of insight." He straightened. His hand was full of broken glass. He looked directly at me and these stinging barbs of energy attached themselves to my flesh and I felt shaky all over.

"You'll cut yourself," I said.

He asked if I knew about moral luck, and I shook my head. I said encouragingly, "It always seems like a shame when people spend all their time talking about things they don't care about." Finally I stood up, on my poor weak legs, to get him a napkin—guessing he'd scold me again, but he didn't; he picked the glass sequins off his hand, one by one.

My whole body felt like the eerie, light numbness that comes when your foot falls asleep.

He said, a person might be lucky to be born to good parents, to a stable financial situation, and with certain capabilities. But most people and most conceptions of justice don't account for the fact that you are also lucky to be born *good*. Goodness is not actually an essential property. You might seem like a good person, you might think it's one of the few things that didn't come about by chance, over which you did actually have control, one of the few things that does deserve reward in a justice scheme, but it's because you were born in this context, in this world. He said, "I see no reason to think that the ability to perceive what is wrong is correlated with not committing wrong things. Presumably you could put people in enough pain that they would do anything, including murder their own children. You could put wires in their necks and watch their characters fall apart."

I couldn't look at his face. He seemed too much on the verge of tears. I looked at the little pile of glass and at his hands. I knew Patrick was hearing him talk about wrongness and wondering about whether he approved of his father's work, whether he would sustain a corrupt business or destroy it. And I was hearing him talk about wrongness and wondering about *not in it for the kissing,* and why he would say that to me, and why he would say that while undoubtedly knowing how upset it made me when I met his wife. And meantime Nicola was saying, "Life is incredibly, deeply strange, and when you try to talk about anything, you'll probably get *everything* wrong, the fundamentals and the details." And it was impossible to know what he was thinking about. Here again the duality came forward strongly. Even as he said "you'll probably get *everything* wrong" I felt that what he meant was that certain things you *can* know, that there is real truth to be found.

Patrick had been listening, reassuring and squared off in his dress shirt, screwing and unscrewing the lid of a fountain pen. Now he said, "There must be some role for knowledge in goodness."

"I only know where it's relevant by the grace of God," said Nicola. God! The name hit Patrick and me like a sonic wave. Both of us flinched.

I sat in my chair for a moment feeling vaguely humiliated and confused.

I picked up the napkin filled with glass, and on the way to the trash, squeezed it in my palm until I drew blood.

I SHOWED HIM down in the elevator. He invited Patrick and me to come over to his house the next day.

We stood on the sidewalk outside the office building.

"I'm very conflicted, Nora," he said. "I don't know what to do, and this never happens to me. I seem to be swimming in a sea . . ." He smiled, glowing, gold-pink.

I was blushing, sweat glittering in my eyes. Floating! I smiled and looked straight at Nicola, burning with want. I stroked the little cuts on my palms. I wished I would choke somehow, right on the doorstep, so he would have to compress my chest. I wished I would faint or get hit by a car. How could I otherwise get what I wanted? I would do anything for him, anything, anything, anything.

It was not a good idea to have these thoughts in front of him, because I was unmediated. I was certain he could see exactly what I was thinking. He watched me writhe. He was the saint in the ex-voto. Beautiful messiah face. He knew.

"See you tomorrow," he said. He turned away from me.

IN THE OFFICE, I gathered my belongings hurriedly. I didn't want to talk it through with Patrick because I knew I would appear too obsessed. Cut it off, Nora. "Fun to have him in the office," I said.

"I didn't like the way he treated you," Patrick said.

"What?" I said.

"Does he ever—let you do what you want?" Patrick said.

I said he did. But I didn't know. He seemed to listen to me, and to see me, and I wanted to trust him and believe that he was good, but I also knew he was not available, and that everyone fell for him, and that I was being a complete fool.

CHAPTER 15

He'd canceled on Patrick. But I only found that out later. "Patrick couldn't come," he said, when he let me into his house, with that lovely faded solvent scent, which was to me the scent of desire.

"Is your father here?" I said.

"No," he said.

"Your mother?"

"She died years ago. I thought you knew."

"Oh," I said. "I'm sorry." I couldn't believe Patrick hadn't mentioned this to me. I wondered how she died. Cancer, maybe, and he waited by her bed. Or a car wreck; I imagined him as a child called out of class by a grim-faced administrator. I wondered what their last interaction had been, and what memories of her he returned to even as she receded further and further into the past. I wondered who had comforted him, if he'd wanted to be held or had sat stonily apart. A little pause. "Is Iris here?" I said.

He laughed. He showed me to a room I hadn't seen before, on the ground floor, a high-ceilinged sitting room with striped silk walls, alternating gold and moss colors. "She is in Italy," he said. Pedestrians passed behind the sheer drapes, and their baffled shadows moved across the walls. I waited for him to talk. He wouldn't. *She is in Italy.* It bloomed over me.

My spine felt hollow, composed of feather quills, of long empty shafts, and the nervousness was like icy liquid poured up and down them. I was not comfortable.

I walked around the room. It was characterized by a general contemporary tastefulness with a few spots of troubling density. On the sideboard there was a mirrored box containing a blue satin cushion and a necklace with an enormous ornate openwork pendant, ribbons of gold, studded with rosettes, wreathing a scene of a kneeling penitent and an angel with an upright hand.

"What's this?" I said, lifting the glass lid of the box. It was a bad idea to lift the lid; it shook exaggeratedly in my hand.

"Don't touch that," he said. I reddened. "It's my father's Holy Annunciation badge," he said kindly. "For knighthood."

"Oh, let's not summon him," I said, and incompetently replaced the lid, which made some chattering chiming noises. Nicola watched me walk the rest of the perimeter of the room, along the honey floor. I drew this out, feeling him watching me, pretending I was neutral and taking a stroll and in no hurry at all.

"Satisfied?" he said.

"What should we do?" I said.

"Sit."

Thrilled by an instruction, I half sat on the arm of one of the armchairs, upholstered in silver.

"Do you play any instrument?"

"No." I could barely look at him. "I just did painting. Then writing, you know."

"Know any poetry by heart?"

The end of Ovid's Pyramus and Thisbe: *nam color in pomo est, ubi permatuit, ater*—mulberries are dark from lovers' blood. The beginning of the *Aeneid,* and Anchises's speech to his son in the underworld. Pieces of Rilke, which I had also discovered that year. *Let no one tell me I don't love life.* "Absolutely not," I said.

"You do!" he said.

"Why don't you recite something for me?" I said.

"You're my guest."

I looked at his black shoes with their old-fashioned shine. His legs in thin wool, long in front of him, crossed at the ankle, their reflection wavy across the shining floor. He reclined on the armchair, his elbow against one of its silvery arms, the other arm flung across its back. I couldn't look at his face. "I want to hear you do some poetry," he said.

"No," I said.

"Come on," he said.

I thought of Patrick's question: *Does he ever let you do what you want?* Yet I couldn't keep refusing. He wasn't giving me time to think it through, watching me coolly from the chair. I started to recite the Ovid—it was nothing special, it was elementary. I looked at the glaring floor; my voice wavered. *"Dixit, et aptato pectus mucrone sub imum . . ."* Thisbe began, in my recitation, to stab herself with the sword still warm from Pyramus's blood. I remembered teaching Federica the passage in our bunk bed room, our metal-shaded desk lamp, Rosa's fingernails clicking down the hall. I remembered the Latin teacher with her dyed red hair, the pull-down map of ancient Rome, the cold classroom. That year, all the girls liked to wear a single long earring, and the popular earrings were made of many iridescent sequins hanging from a little loop, like a fishing lure.

There was a rushing in my ears. I'd thought I would never forget the lines, but I found that I had. I stopped, uncertain.

"That's enough," he said. I felt very exposed. He told me to sit down, and I did. He put on a Palestrina mass. It poured out of the walls from hidden speakers. In an immediate wave of gratitude, all my hair stood up on end. I sat back in the chair.

We listened to the mass four times. *Again! again!* we said to each other. Inhuman, he said—ringing I said—the texture comes forward more than the melody, he said. We traveled together through the singers' delay, emphasis, repetition growing ever more complex and uneasy, reunion followed by a dark turn.

On the third round I attempted to follow the melody and immediately lost track. The music pulled and stretched and bent my body out like hot glass at the end of a glassblower's tube.

The feeling of plenitude is irrational. You hit a happiness threshold when you're happy for cause. And above it is this plenitude feeling that is not rational or transparent, which doesn't conform, and over which you have no control. It is the vast, dark, sparkling place where things take on their real forms.

Nicola had his head back. How could I normally read while listening to music, or talk while listening to music, or walk while listening to music? The colors of the room, and the ease with which I could breathe, and the length of my spine, and the way Nicola looked, now sensitive, now dead, now dangerous, all kept changing. My whole consciousness had gone effervescent.

Part of me wanted it to end so that he would talk to me, maybe criticize me or draw out more memories from the Federica time—lighting her cigarettes on the night quays, the cold, sanctified halls of our *liceo*. Part of me recognized that I might never experience music like this again in my life, so it was right to inhabit the state as long as I could. What I felt was apprehension of the real. Recovering the lost contact. We listened to all the songs until we'd finished them, and the light had changed. The gold stripes were copper-pink now, and the moss stripes looked silver.

"Would you like a drink?" he said.

"No," I said. Now we sat in silence. He stood up and walked toward me. I became extremely warm. My body was flaming. My bones were starting to melt like wax, my head to fall to the floor with the density of a white dwarf star. No, he was only going to get himself a bottle of water from the sideboard. Acqua Panna.

He walked behind my chair returning and my body had so much blood close to the surface I could feel him move. Complete attention. I felt like an animal. "Please give us something to talk about," I said. "Or else I'll start asking questions about your father."

He shook his head. "It's distracting to talk to you. I don't know—you're in my head."

"What do you mean?" I said. I had been avoiding looking at him. But in this moment, I did, which made me feel begging and emphatic.

"People like you, Nora, are on the isle of the blessed."

In fact, even looking directly at his face, I could barely see it. It didn't coalesce into anything in particular—my view was of the front of his face, that had at times looked loutish to me, but I couldn't tell what it looked like, as a unified entity, now. It set off nonvisual reactions: pounding heart, anguish. Every part of the interaction signified. His tilted head, his ease, my rigid posture and downcast eyes. Certain things are inexpressible, and when you describe anything, you're bound to get everything wrong, the particulars and the details. The words we said were not as significant as the way we occupied the space together. I felt there were stiff wires connecting me to him—like the golden wires of the aureola, the halo.

"I'm keeping up hope," I said, "because you tend to tell me everything, eventually."

I could feel him in my head, my neck, my teeth and my palms. We were so attentive to each other we had a sense of complete control—it was a spoken conversation that felt to me like nothing so much as writing, like the act of writing, because all the interpersonal anxiety of conversing was gone, and instead I was charged with portraying precisely a set of deeply felt images whose meaning and truest expression were unclear even to me. Maybe what I meant was we were setting down a body of common knowledge to which I would refer many times. Nothing was lost, not a single piece. Maybe what I meant was I had the fuel to be as attentive as life actually demands.

"I don't want to make you uncomfortable," he said.

I was laughing so hard. "Be a good utilitarian," I said. "Even if you're uncomfortable, maybe I'll be so comfortable that we'll net comfort."

"I've been thinking about why I find you attractive," he said. "I'd like to overwhelm your nervous system."

It's on, I thought. It's on! I'd wanted him for years, since the first moment I met him, and I never, never thought it would be reciprocated.

"I can't betray Iris," he said.

"I can't betray Leif," I said.

"He wouldn't understand?" said Nicola. I didn't know what he was trying to confirm. Maybe he knew Iris would under no circumstances understand, and also knew he was exceptionally good at keeping secrets, that a secret would not split and destroy his life, whereas it might destroy mine.

"We can't not do it," I said. "You have to run toward intensity. It is the *point* of life." I had never spoken in this kingly voice. As it turned out, one of the borders of the land of desperation was—authority.

"You hid it very well," he said. "I had no idea." He looked at my neck and his look made me swallow.

"Hid what?" I said.

He didn't answer. At this point I went to the bathroom to try to calm down. I didn't take a long moment to gaze at myself or touch myself or collect my thoughts—I didn't want him to change moods while I was gone. The floor in the hall had a bouncy-castle feel, springing under my feet.

Back in the silken room, the pedestrian shadows were all going in one direction, away from the subway, and their movements gave the room a dizzying, slipping feeling, like we were in a well-appointed car of an enormous train. I was completely ill. Famished. "Can you keep a secret?" he said.

"For the past discussion?" I said. "Well, isn't it late to ask now?"

"For the past and the future," he said, and beckoned me into the hall. He opened a door, behind which stone steps fell into shadow. He turned and descended into the black.

I had the feeling I was heading for my doom. I held the rough walls.

He led me not into the wine cellar but into a small side room. He pulled a chain to illuminate its shipwrecked contents: a few marble torsos and a birdbath, a pair of yellowed globes in wooden stands, a fringed rug on the stones. Yet I knew we were going to wake this quiet, dead room.

With no delay, he reached for, then touched my right arm. His hand was pure electricity, sparking with heat. He took my arm, and extended it, and then he ran his fingers up and down it, a scintillating feeling which provoked me to tears.

Up we went into the snow again, my panic playing out above the pistes, the crystals condensing and beginning the dive. As in the park—as always with Nicola—I did not know how much time I had. I didn't know whether this was the beginning or the whole. I didn't know how much he felt he could betray Iris.

He kept stroking the inside of my arm, barely. He was coaxing something from me. What was it? I began to shiver. I tried to stiffen, to stop my motion, but it only got worse. I felt extremely tense, yet my eyes were closing and my mouth opening, while he played his fingers across the crook of my arm.

He pulled me to him. I could not have prepared for this, the warmth of his body, suddenly, the soft press. *Shhhhh,* he said. With his body he ended my affliction. *Guardami,* he said, which meant *Look at me,* and so I tilted my face up. He had a focused, assessing look. How strange, strange beyond measure for Nicola to collapse into this face I could kiss, somehow awkward, even as I laughed in my head that he'd kissed hundreds and hundreds of people. Even as he quickly reached around, and put my hands, which had defaulted to open in the air, around him. Very soft skin, so broad.

He stabilized me against him and kissed me. His soft lively mouth intersected mine. I wondered what he thought of how I kissed. I was in a daze that did not permit me to have any control over my own reactions.

I didn't yet think of Leif. We were on a timescale longer than his.

"Maybe that's enough," he said. His voice was coarse.

"No, it's not," I said.

He lifted my hand to his mouth and kissed and licked between my fingers, tender and invasive.

I wanted to beg for more but I was scared he'd stop. "Please," I said finally, and pulled his face to mine with one hand—with the other I sought his body.

He shook his head, and lifted my hand away.

I truly felt that if he'd make contact with the rest of my

body, just this once, I would be satisfied for the rest of my life. I would not need any more ever if he would touch me just this one time, and then fuck me. The one fuck was all I needed, a secret composed of the kind of chemical—thermite—that once you light it burns through solid walls, burns resolutely underwater. It would be real, it would be enough, it would be the solution, if he would only fuck me once.

"Come on," he said. "We're going out."

HE CHANGED SO quickly between states. How could he?

I followed him up the stairs. It was difficult to walk. I blotted off my face in the bathroom. In the mirror, I looked flushed and insanely, wickedly beautiful.

He opened the door onto the street. The lilac evening had descended. The sun-heated cobbles were giving the heat back.

We sat at dinner—a doleful, mostly empty, white-tablecloth, expensive French restaurant, attended by an older waiter; my heart went out to him. Who knows what I ordered.

"You're really in the center right now," he said. "I hope it's not disturbing you. It's a temporary condition."

Yes, I know, Nicola, why remind me? The center, the still point around which the world turns, so quickly that it blurs and becomes abstract. The center, the dazzling circle of light that makes everything beyond it blacker than black. The center, the most crowded place, or the emptiest.

For a moment I felt destroyed by sadness. "Temporary condition" could mean that today—what we had just passed—would be all that I ever received from him. Maybe this was as unfaithful as he would allow himself to be. Maybe he'd leave and I'd never see him again. But if I did see him again, then at some point would come the day when I wouldn't hold his attention, when I would just go to work and work and leave and go home and fall asleep and

wake up. I knew this. I knew. My whole life I'd been cultivating my own garden. I knew that I could not possess him.
So why bring up that the center was temporary?

"Are you okay?" he said.

Forlornly, I said, "I feel a little dragged along by your intensity."

He said, "You could blow me off more." I shook my head.
It was dishonest, I felt, that he'd even suggest it. "Nora, I'm
warning you," he said, with his green eyes obtrusively direct,
"I want to be clear. I'm non-negotiably married."

"Yes," I said, "it'll be okay, I think it'll be okay, it'll be
okay . . ." If we ever discuss this again, I told myself, just say,
It's all good, and leave it at that.

"I don't want to mess up your life," he said. He put his
hand to his forehead, then rubbed the side of his face with
his whole hand, looking at me.

Maybe he had to emphasize that it was temporary because that was a way to make it feel less like a betrayal of
Iris. She was the permanent one, I was something else.

I started to cry. I turned away from him.

"Nora," he said. "What are you thinking?"

Now, finally, I thought of Leif, whose trust I had encour-
aged out of him over the course of many years. But I was
crying both because of Leif, and all the hope we'd bound
up in each other, and his guilelessness and support, and because of what Nicola had said about his own attention. And
it compounded; I became horrified that my tears would
cause Nicola to leave me alone. He'd realize that he was
messing up my life and decide he had a moral imperative
to step back.

"You know what I'd like?" he said. "I'd like to talk about
painting." He put an elbow on the table and leaned back. I
didn't remember when it was that I mentioned that I used to
paint. "Tell me about the colors you used."

I told him the names of the colors, cadmium yellow, cadmium red, heavy in the tube, and alizarin crimson, light. I went through the whole range. He asked me about my process. I told him about building stretcher bars and how I liked to wash my canvases in acrylic color before I began with the oils, so that they were already touched and alive all over, so all the white was ruined. I never talked about painting to anyone, but he drew it out of me, and I realized that he was calming and bringing me back to the world in which I could be independent. The conversation gave me a plunging feeling—the feeling of being taken care of.

I kept capsizing back into awareness that his attention would move on. I said, "It's hard for me to tell if this is all bad or good, it's so much."

"That's a shame," he said, "for me it is happy, just happy. I'm sorry it isn't for you." I didn't want to wear him out, and I didn't want my outburst to cause him to cancel our future engagements. It was important to be brave, I told myself, but it was difficult.

The waiter removed our plates, and Nicola asked for two cups of tea. He prepared the tea for me, a little cream, a little sugar.

He asked why I wouldn't talk, and I said I was anxious. He said I didn't seem anxious—and this made me sad because I wanted to be believed. "I am simple, but you are not," he said with warmth. It was becoming easier to look at him, at his face that was deceptively tremulous, the rims of his eyes always seeming just a moment away from filling with tears. He said, "In my work, when you're trying to make enormous changes to complicated systems, what matters most is the shape of things. Some points you can fit to a line. Some points you can't fit to any function —they're a ring shape, say. You find path dependency, inertia, stairsteps and cliffs and so on, and the snags and hatreds, or fundamental goodness. Flows structure themselves. And in determining their structure, the local matters very much. You can average out the costs or the debts, but that hides the local patterns, the shape. I admire specificity wherever it exists, that's what I like about Carracci. And what I like about you, so much."

I held my teacup up to my face and looked at him through the tongue of steam. I wanted him to say something more particular than this. He reclined, his hand on his head, the soft shoulders of his suit jacket looking particularly careless.

"Isn't everyone specific?" I said, at last. It was insane how much I needed him to affirm me.

"I saw that you cut yourself, you know," he said.

I grimaced and looked at the tablecloth, which we'd managed to soil somehow. Those scars on my thighs were so faint now that Leif had never commented on them. I'd never wanted it to be a "cry for help"—the point was the private action—but fifteen years later, it was a cry. Would he drop me for having once been that way? Would he step back, out of reasonable caution? "Only as a teen," I said.

"You have to let me know if you ever feel like doing that again," he said.

"It won't happen again," I said.

"You're in my domain now," he said. "Of responsibility."

"I don't know about that," I said.

"This must be good," he said. "What is between us must be good. Whatever else you may think, I want to be entirely moral in my private life. It is a world apart. It is where there can be real tenderness."

He took this question of goodness a bit too seriously, I thought. There was a creepy prickle behind these assertions. He had a powerful position, and I wanted him to be good in his public life too. I didn't know anyone else for whom moral decisions had public consequence. And I wanted something deeper to be right, something like his soul. "Okay, Nicola. Are you bad elsewhere?"

"Well, I work with my father," he said. "You can ask Patrick what he thinks. Everything else aside, what I really want is to make you happy. I ache for you," he said softly, "all the way into my narrow heart."

Then, below the table, he shifted his leg so it pressed against mine; I felt the swarm. I hadn't ruined our interaction. It was going to continue. I could not speak. There was nothing I could do that wasn't a signal to him. He had possessed the whole of me.

"No, it's happy," I said. "It's happy." A pause as we listened to the soft flow of the cars outside, New York's latent hum, and, in the kitchen, the hiss of water and chime of china.

I felt that he was my reward for living my life the way I did. All those books I read, and how sad I was and how I went away in high school, how independent and uncompromising (and weird and alone) I was. When all I wanted had been exactly him. But you can live your independent uncompromising life and have no reward other than your self-determination. In other words: you can live your independent uncompromising life and have no reward.

"Text me when you want to see me," he said, "all right?"

"You want *me* to text you?"

"Why not?"

"Well, you're so busy," I said. And I wanted him to want to see me. I didn't want to have to dictate the frequency myself. It was too much choice.

"I'll be around whenever you want. Text me." He made me promise.

WHEN HE SHOWED me out, he said, "I will remember your face then for the rest of my life."

"What was my face like?"

"Sad and serious, eyes closed and overwhelmed. Overcome."

That power I'd seen in him, the way he could tell people who they were and make them so, the way he could control situations, that power I'd feared in him, I'd joined him there.

CHAPTER 16

I'd told Leif on that Saturday morning that I was going to Westchester with Patrick and his wife. Patrick's parents had a mansion with a swimming pool and a gazebo and a tennis court, and on the train home from Nicola's, I imagined myself there among the hibiscus flowers and echinacea, I imagined the bats that came out in the evening. "I was in Westchester," I said aloud to myself.

Stumbling-tired opening the door, I located Leif on the couch as usual, which signaled that he was not suspicious.

When he asked how my day was, I said they'd had a friend there—a woman—Nicole, I said. I wanted to give him some partial detail, just so that he could understand something of how I was feeling. She was really into music, I said, and I'd had a transcendent experience listening to Palestrina. "Have you ever felt like you're hallucinating while listening to music?" I said. He said no, and asked so many follow-up questions I had to keep adding complexity to the lie—she was a college friend of Patrick's, but I hadn't known her then, she was a musician nowadays, in Chicago somewhere, I couldn't even keep track of what I was saying. I got angry and claimed exhaustion.

From this, I learned: It's better to be totally quiet about a lie of this magnitude. Don't give anyone any data points. Don't try to give a partial story; it'll only confuse you, and it will relieve none of the emotional burden. Let it be so totally silent that it exists in a different world.

In the evening, right before I fell asleep, Leif came into bed and kissed me on the cheek, and a bolt ran through me, the wish that Nicola would die.

I DID WHAT he said, and, after composing several possible texts and saving them in my notes, texted him first: "Hi, Nicola." But he responded so quickly I felt he'd been sitting with his phone waiting for me. I changed his text tone, a good idea; it tells your heart when to speed up. His tone was two little clinks and the haptic was two tiny movements of the phone, and when he texted me a stream, my phone had a heartbeat.

I WENT BACK to his house. As I walked from the subway, the straps of my tote bag on my hands made me want to puke. In the striped room, we sat and talked for a while. He kept asking how I was. "How is it with Leif?" he said.

"It's okay," I said.

"Just okay?"

"We've talked before about having an open relationship," I lied. "It's okay with him." In fact, we'd discussed it when one of our friends had professed to it, and Leif had said that it was inhumane and pathetic—"Just leave me if you ever want an open relationship," he'd said. "Never," I'd said. And I'd meant it. I had never been tempted. Leif had been the only one I liked.

"You told him about this?"

"Yes," I said.

"No, you didn't," Nicola said.

"I intend to." I wanted to ask him about Iris. What was his plan there? Why was he pushing me so much when he got to remain silent? But, on balance, I was more afraid to ask, because I didn't want to force him to think about it and then realize he should stop things with me.

"Don't hide from me," Nicola said. "You're not capable of it anyway."

I flushed. I was dying for him to grab me to him. I didn't know what his plan was. I didn't know if his plan was shifting. I wanted him to force me to take off my clothes.

I pointed to the tall red wineglass that stood on a round of felt on the marble-topped sideboard. The stem was decorated with twin glass seahorses. "Was this here before?" I said.

"No," he said.

"What is it?"

"A cursed goblet," he said. "Sit down, Nora."

I sat.

"We talk a lot," he said.

"I like to talk to you." I turned away from his gaze and looked to the other side of the room to the mirrored box that held his father's Holy Annunciation badge.

"Too much," he said. He approached me. I felt nausea and fear, and the violent shaking in my legs and back. And with that distant, assessing, formal look, he knelt by my chair like a prince and gripped my face. His hands were freezing cold.

My eyes shut. I had a choice—I could have shaken his hand away or told him to stop. But I turned to him and felt myself languidly relaxing. The room was as red as blood and very close in.

He pressed his palm against my face. What came to mind was something I must have read—a slippery teal river fading into lavender, trees with feather leaves half melted into the mountains behind them, a white city in the distance. The water slapping against the boat. Where had I read this? A tilting tree like a white spider, and journeymen in red, hastening toward me, their mouths opening, about to call to me. To say what? I lifted my hands to his. No, I had seen it. The painting he'd touched. "Put your hands down," he said, so I did. What he meant was *Let me take over*. His breath in my ear was better than words.

He pulled me up, and led me down to the basement again. Now on the descent I had a feeling of safety—when we re-emerged, maybe all of New York would be a firebombed ruin.

We returned to that dim storage room. "I don't know when my father will be home," he said. We kissed. I felt him and thought again about his experience. His mouth opened and occluded mine. He held my face with one hand. I didn't know what to do. He kissed me first on the lips, and then on the ear, his heat and his breath and his words curling into me. Words about whether I knew what I was doing. In this manner, he was invading me triply.

He kissed the inside of my ear with skin-crawling sweetness. My eyes were shut. I nodded. He held my neck gently between his thumb and forefinger and then he let go.

"Maybe that's enough," he said.

My blood was pounding and my skin was as sensitive as the surface of an artifact, the kind you can't touch without dissolving. I opened my eyes and shook my head. I pleaded with him.

"Be quiet," he said.

He lifted up the hem of my dress and pushed up my slip. I was against the wall. The rough cold stones made my skin prickle all at once. His shoulder was against my throat, heavy, but his hand was light. "What do you like?" He was speaking into my ear as he touched me with excessive gentleness across my belly. Now his hand was hot. "How did you want Leif to be? How did you want Federica to be?" I didn't like hearing their names at all. Especially not Leif's. I couldn't tell Nicola anything. I couldn't tell him because he'd stolen my wits, and because I wanted to oblige him.

He pressed his heavy lion head against me to keep me

still. I begged him disorderedly. The picture was slashes, the fluid color bleeding; chaos threatened if we slowed, but it all threatened to fade out too, into pure airy sweetness, that twinkling pure disappearance like gasoline. He unbuttoned the top of my dress, he felt my ribs, then reached into my bra. He was so precise; he used his whole body. He was preparing me. I was cold and hot, too firmly held in one place and held too lightly in the other, standing while too weak to stand, being treated gently while I wanted to be attacked. And as a result of all of this my body knew there was nothing that could be done. I looked at his dissolving eyes. My sharpness, my grip was gone. I entered a state of torpor. "Good," he said. For the first time I felt certain I had pleased him and some new excitement winged into the room.

"Is this what you wanted," he said, running a hand between my legs again. "Tell me." I said yes.

"Right there?" he said, and finally he touched me where I was swollen and drenched and determined. I leaned hard against the wall, my knees folding, he held me there with his body as he touched with his fingertip. My teeth were chattering and my breath felt as thick as wax. He sighed as he touched me. His beautiful calming voice, asking me over and over.

He started to lift my dress. I told him no, I took his hands off the hem. I was too modest. I was embarrassed. He told me I looked beautiful, and lowered me down. He told me to lie on my back, and I did so on the old rug, feeling suddenly the hard unforgiving floor. He pushed my skirt up and I felt the rough fibers of the rug on my skin, and he unzipped and unbuckled and pressed his thighs into mine. I opened like an unguarded door, feeling my muscles stretch away from that place of pure ashamed softness, and with a gasp, he plunged into me, a sharp ache that went straight into my veins. The room pulled away his scent and I only felt power. Being taken on the floor, I felt his full weight and no give.

He was precise, teasing, somewhat impersonal: as though it wasn't mutual. I saw the river at night, the still water, its give and float, the drag of the leaves on the surface, the blur of the moonlight. Always amazing how, when exhausted from swimming, one small hold, a branch, an inch of rope, is enough to steady, the water transforming from a dark threat just like that—the hold allows for erasure.

"You are like a fist," he said into my ear.

Too much acknowledged. I began to worry, and the worry began to loop, and I pulled away. The room reappeared, the worn rug, the stone walls, the headless statues in the corner. I turned to the side. "What's wrong," he said. "Nora, what's wrong." I couldn't tell him—but what was wrong was that it was incredibly difficult for me to come and I didn't want to fake it and I didn't want to seem ungrateful. With Leif I was more willing to *use* him—so it always felt to me—to let him go on at length, and I could relax with him. But I couldn't ask that of Nicola and I certainly couldn't manage. I couldn't.

"I can't say what's wrong," I faltered. I didn't say *never mind,* because I didn't want it to sound disingenuous, though indeed I did not want him to mind. I wanted him to let me be unmediated—while experiencing something terribly frightening and new, which I'd dreamed about so desperately. What I needed was for him to carry on. Carry on, stop noticing me, notice me just the right amount, be patient but hide it, take over but be responsive but not let me know. I had so much shame and I respected him so much and cared so profoundly about not bothering him.

He understood this; I don't know how he made the assessment. He did not let it become a disaster. He looked at me a moment. "Come here," he said. He kissed my cheek. He kissed my mouth, by degrees fiercer. His tongue tested me.

He rose over me again, and just that way it was so sweet, and it mounted, and suddenly to my shock I was coming, doused in liquor, set fire to, burned off. I seized on him and I was so so embarrassed. I pushed him off.

"Did you come on me?" he said.

I didn't inhabit it because it was so fast and physical and because I was so taken aback that it was happening. I ran off and sat in the dark wine cellar for a minute in my bra and dress, sitting on the cold dusty floor. I realized my lower back was bleeding from the friction of the rug. I touched the hot, sticky patch. My thoughts were suspended, as though held in the black glass bottles all around me. I was embarrassed for having run away and felt I should wait out a few moments so it could seem like I was collecting my thoughts, when I knew that it would in fact be impossible for me to collect my thoughts, and all I wanted was to go back to him.

When I returned he had put on his clothes. I asked him if he wanted more and he said no. I kissed him on his large heavy head. I kissed his dark hair. He had a warm lemon skin smell that I inhaled hungrily—so this was the scent of his charisma, of his brain.

We were sitting side by side against the stone wall of the basement; he was asking me how I was. "I'd love to touch you," he said. "Can I?"

"No," I said, but only because he'd said no to me. I was confused. I put on my cold underwear.

We sat in silence a moment.

He wasn't like I'd imagined. It was so much more personal.

"Come closer," he said. When I didn't, he moved closer to me. He put his hand around my ankle, which began to arouse me again. Relentlessness: a godly virtue. Baucis and Philemon realized they had gods in their house when the wine started refilling itself.

I wondered when he and Iris had gotten together. How long had it been since he'd kissed someone else?

"You've been with a lot of people," I said. I felt my nervousness begin to fall—no, not to fall, merely to take on recognizable shapes, so I could see myself and recognize Nora, my lifelong companion; I am now the same, but the wish came true, and what does it feel like? Like a slow, glowing orange happiness. This image rose up in me, I didn't choose it. I was picturing a slowly brightening fog lamp, though I knew at a certain point it would begin to hurt quite badly.

"You are not one of the types I know," he said. "I don't know what you are."

I didn't want to seem closed off or unresponsive. I had no idea how I appeared and was not able to put any effort into it. It was involuntary. And not generalizable either, I was only this person with him. I was coming in and out of this existence very rapidly.

"You have an inevitability to you that I really like," he said. He kissed me with lovely calm on the side of my head. "I'm talking about the same thing that makes me feel all the social anxiety is false."

"It's not false," I said.

"It mixes me up," he continued, and kissed me. He said if we were in a murder mystery, I would be the murderer. The last one you expect.

I wondered if he was talking about himself too—and what he was capable of.

We went upstairs. The sun had set. We returned to the striped room. It was warm and smelled like sap.

I had two missed calls from Leif. I'd told him in the morning that my aunt was in town and so I would be spending the day with her. I didn't want to ask Nicola how much longer we had, so I couldn't guess what my arrival time back home would be. I texted Leif and told him I had to stay with my aunt in her hotel because she was going through a tough time. I pictured her, soft where my mother was hard, her teal scrunchie and the swinging purse where she kept all the receipts and Hershey's Kisses with the tips broken off. Last year my cousin had gotten a DUI—I could use that again if I had to. Another lesson: when you have to lie, put as much truth as possible into it. You'll be less confused that way.

Nicola and I sat in the same chairs as before. "Is your father here?" I said.

"Not yet," he said.

I couldn't guess how much time we had. I'd been sure I only needed the one encounter, just the one. But I hadn't been able to notice anything.

He received a text. "We have twenty minutes," he said.

"Then what?"

"Then you have to go."

I was too dazed to feel sad yet. But I could feel the sadness wake up and begin to wing its way.

"Are you okay?" he said.

We both needed reassurance from me. I told him it was important to me that *we were in a fragment:* that was, though I did not use this word, adultery. A broken process was beautiful in the same way as handiwork, as seeing the window wiper's residual motion traced in soap in the tram's dawn window. I said, my teacher said, look at Titian's drawings, you can't learn from his paintings. I talked about the parts left over after all humanity has been wiped out, or the dusty fallen-over statues in the tomb that hasn't been discovered. What is the world offering to us?

I did not say that I was already dreaming about what was under the sex. What the sex was about, and how it was that he touched my wrist and his hand had gone through my wrist, gripping so the whole arm was pressure.

"You want that, don't you," he said. "You're maniacally focused on it. The 'I don't know yet, tell me everything.'"

"Right," I said, but I said it nervously, because his interpretive schemes had nothing to do with mine.

"Maybe the weather has cleared," he said. He was back to formal. He showed me out the door. "Turn right," he said. "Go quickly."

CHAPTER 17

I wanted a goodbye kiss, but I didn't get one.

And then I was on the sidewalk. I walked quickly right—east—then I turned north, and my shadow grew, shrank, doubled, and faded under the lights.

At that moment he was like a bone sticking through the skin.

I felt alienation from my body, and adrenaline suspension away from normal thought. I felt horror mixed with revelation. So this is what I'm made of, this is what has been inside me all this time. *An inevitability to you.*

A Sunday night in Tribeca in September, people drinking at sidewalk tables. It was ten p.m. I could have gone home to Leif, but I wasn't ready.

What could I do about Leif now? I couldn't stop loving him, I told myself decisively. I wouldn't stop—I would will it and be strong. Leif was good, so supportive always.

I walked north. Through Soho and into Washington Square Park, under the triumphal arch. Up Fifth, past the Flatiron building, past the stone lions. Past the luxury store windows, past Trump Tower and the pink Plaza, and finally I was in the park. I was checking on the ducks in the southeast pond. The water was calm and tar-black. Where the ducks huddled, the water rippled slowly out in bronze curves.

How could it be all right with him to love Iris that much,

and cheat on her with me? How could he be actually good and kind, if he did that to her? What were his patterns of resignation and demand? They didn't map onto anything I understood. I knew I could not truly trust him, because of his infidelity, and because of his father, whose influence I did not know.

If I explained myself to him, if he came to understand the ways in which I was simple, would he lose interest in me? Could I explain my desires to him, would they change as I explained them? Was he seeing truths about me that had been hidden from me before, or was he inventing new parts of me? How would I manage when his attention moved on? I did have the sense already that this kind of attention was unsustainable. That was part of his devastating interest to everyone too: no one got all of him, no one kept him.

I walked north, up the slope in front of the pavilion called the Dairy, then down the mall with its elms with twisted arms. I saw others in the park, far away, but I didn't pass a soul. I wasn't sure when the park closed. I'd have to go back to Leif. But I still wasn't ready.

I realized I was starving. I had barely eaten since the dinner party, when Nicola had first brought me to the basement—two weeks before.

I exited the park. I found a deli on Lexington and asked the cashier if he could reheat his griddle. I'd never bent others to my will this way. This was how Nicola behaved.

I ordered two bacon, egg, and cheese sandwiches on rolls. He spilled the yellow over the griddle; it bubbled and whitened. He folded the egg around the squares of cheese. I was famished, pressing on my forehead and temples to withstand the wait, pacing the aisles of the store and touching the products, palpating the gummies, rattling the nuts. He wrapped the rolls in foil.

As soon as I left the store I ripped a hole in the foil, rat-style, and scarfed half of one of the sandwiches. Moist, salty bacon, cushy egg and cheese, bland toasted roll. Then I vomited right there on 72nd Street, outside the entrance to the park.

I reentered the park and walked past the turtle pond, flat and shimmering. I couldn't stand the smell of my one and a half sandwiches. I threw them both in the trash. I put on my cardigan. A breeze was picking up. I walked into the Shakespeare Garden, up around its snaking paths. I walked over the Great Lawn. The sky felt loose. A crescent moon shone bloodily through the clouds.

I wasn't thinking about how Nicola had touched me. It was all too repulsively vivid. I shuddered and cringed even beginning to imagine how I had sunk down before him. My mind spared me. As for being alone in the park at this hour, I was too exhausted to be afraid. No one could possibly hurt me. And if they tried, I could easily overwhelm them with sex. The city floated around me, the towers levitating above the ground.

I continued north, past the reservoir. I could just see the ducks gathered in the center of the water, sleeping. I walked past the North Meadow's baseball diamonds. I had entered a zone of gentle hills. I was nearing Harlem.

I lay down at the top of a hill underneath an elm tree whose branches came down close to the lawn. I put my head on my tote bag, which was lumpy with wallet, phone, keys, notebook. This morning, when I'd packed these things, I'd made a one-time mistake. When I'd packed these things, I had only had sex with Leif since college. I felt tenderly toward my possessions, which had accompanied me on my crossing over.

Seed pods and roots pressed against the raw friction spot

on my back. My legs hurt. I turned to lie on one side, then the other, but lying on my back felt most stable. The earth held me, though the two of us were veering.

I heard sirens and gusting winds. No one came to bother me. Above me, the clouds were peachy from the light pollution.

As I lurched into intermittent sleep, I realized I was not going to leave Leif. Nicola was temporary, Leif was permanent. I was going to stick it out with him. I might see Nicola again, but I would be one of those people who uses infidelity to strengthen their actual relationship. I'd never believed that infidelity could be a good thing. But I could see I'd been too closed-minded. Because now I felt I loved Leif more than I ever had before. I loved his calm, his acceptance of me. I loved how he *let me be*. Nicola began to feel erratic and frustrating.

Erratic and frustrating, traits I had long ago craved. "*Anduma,*" Federica used to say, which meant "let's go" in Piemontese, the dialect her parents spoke. On my first night in Italy we took the tiny beige elevator down and walked through the russet-lit streets to the Po. The river was much louder at night, sounding like hoarse barking dogs as it slumped over the break. We walked down the staircase onto the quay. I had a very strong feeling that I might jump into the water. I soothed myself by asking: have I ever done anything so impulsive? No, I told myself, so there was no reason to expect I'd do so now. So often I returned there in my mind, I walked down the quay wondering what Federica would do next, feeling the warmth of that wondering in my ears and throat and teeth. I imagined falling over the side and catching myself against the wall by my fingertips. I imagined her looming over me. To give me a hand up. Or to step on my fingers.

Federica had a cigarette in her mouth. She handed me her lighter. *"Fiamma,"* she said. I tried the lighter again and again. She put her hand over my hand and pulled.

IT WAS ALMOST too cold to sleep. I could see a few stars. I huddled into myself and lost consciousness.

I woke up briefly when the edge of the sky was brown. Then again, moments later, when it was burned orange with a high, starry phthalo blue. Already there were bicyclists whirring on the path.

After some time, the sun woke me for good. The leaves hadn't started to turn yet. Through their green the sky was bright as stage lights. *Don't hide from me. You're not capable of it anyway.*

It was seven a.m. on a Monday. The grass was adorned with cold dew. I heard the helicopters that were inspecting the traffic. I turned and looked down the hill, where the dogs were running.

CHAPTER 18

I made my way stiffly out of the park. The day felt more like a dream than the night had.

I had transgressed but I had no sense of the consequences at all. Now my life was the tomb no one had discovered. Maybe Nicola would soon be defused. Maybe he would go back to Iris and this heavy enormous jewel would sell for pocket change.

The Met-nesting hawks circled above the North Meadow. I bought a cup of deli coffee and a banana that was extraordinarily beautiful, lime green but already covered in vivid spots. I thought of the Frank O'Hara line: *I don't know the people who will feed me*. The city was able to catch and hold me on that desperate morning. Like the insurance that Leif loved, we had a formal system for community that allowed me to be fed and carried home, which at the moment felt purely magical—the magic of the functioning of money, which allowed for this exchange between all these different categories. No one had to trust me.

Pleasant to take the rush-hour trains in the wrong direction. My phone was dead; at home I'd email in sick. I got out in Bedford-Stuyvesant to make completely sure to use up the time so that there was no chance that Leif would be home when I arrived. Even so, I whispered thanks when I opened our apartment door and he was not present.

I took a nap and woke up coming. I turned on my phone. Nicola hadn't texted. This made me sadder than I could have predicted. I had to be okay with it, I reminded myself.

Leif had texted. "How's your aunt," he'd written. "See you in the evening."

I wrote that I was spending the day at home. "Too tired." I took a shower.

I made a pot of coffee, a moka pot like Federica had taught me years ago. I'd forgotten how many of my daily habits were hers. Drying jeans on the line and changing clothes for indoors, yelling at Leif to come eat the pasta fresh. Sometimes I felt like I hid her from myself, but she lingered with me, unacknowledged. I emailed Patrick and my two junior staff that I was sick. An afternoon of liberty lay before me. I imagined telling Patrick about Nicola—I would never, ever tell him, but I imagined his fascination, and envy, and how he would think differently of me, as I'd always been so loyal and so modest and so nervous.

I wished Nicola would text me. I typed out to him, "I had a wonderful time yesterday," then I deleted it. I typed out "Come va," and then I deleted it. I typed a stream of weather and outer space emojis. I deleted them. I felt the urge to joke, but I knew jokes would seem nervous and false.

I made the bed, then I removed my nightgown and lay back down on it. I put my hands in the rainbows from the prism I'd hung in the window. I lay naked in the sunlight and looked at my body. I felt deliciously connected to myself. The sun on our jade and our spider plant and our peperomia, the construction sounds from the new condo next door, the birds, the delivery vans rushing below, all in praise. I thought about his weight on me and the slow and deliberate push. I thought about how he'd given it to me like it was good for me, like he was doing a service for me.

Then I put on the nightgown again and a belt so it would

look more like a dress and I went to a gourmet market and bought mortadella, yellow pear tomatoes, and one enormous, grotesque sunflower. I was going to make Leif a beautiful dinner.

And what could I eat? What could tempt me? I bought ricotta and honey, which I used to binge on in Italy when I was anorexic, after which I'd have to run for miles in Parco del Valentino.

I WAS NERVOUS when Leif returned, but he calmly ate my dinner, pasta with the popping sautéed tomatoes. We talked about long-form articles we'd read.

I thought everything was all right. We were in bed, we turned the lights out, I faced the window, where I could see our bland neighbors across the way in their duplex, watching TV as their beagle hopped down the stairs.

"Just don't see him again," Leif said, into the dark. "Don't go back to him. Please don't. I don't want you hanging out with him again. Is that where you were? Were you with your aunt?"

I turned to look at him. He was staring up at the ceiling. "Don't be paranoid," I said. I touched his hair.

"I don't think your aunt is in town," he said.

"Of course she is," I said. "At the Marriott."

I didn't know where Manhattan might have a Marriott. He could maybe have looked on Facebook, I realized, or even called her work—I didn't know what information he had. If he knew I was lying, then how offensively determined I must have seemed, increasingly contemptible every minute.

This knocked some of my confidence out. I waited for him to tell me I was lying, but he didn't.

"Promise me you won't go back to him," Leif said. "Promise me."

"Nothing happened with him," I said, "and nothing ever would."

"Tell me you're not going to see him again," Leif said.

"He comes by the office with Patrick sometimes."

Leif roared in exasperation. I'd never heard him make a sound like that. I did like it.

CHAPTER 19

I thought I was alone, but I felt eyes on me, and turned—there was a man on the shoreline path behind me. It was a bright, windless noon, the sky lying on the water like a blue film. A heron skimmed the lake, then landed on the reedy edge of an island. Men fished just out of interest; no one could eat those fish.

I had left work at midday. I said I had the doctor. To pass the time before meeting him, I walked in the north part of Central Park, by the Harlem Meer.

I turned past the rink into the North Woods to shake off the follower, but he turned the same way, and I wished I hadn't taken this route. This was the darkest, coldest part of the park, with squishing, wet pine-needle paths and a few black waterfalls pushing rings of foam into stagnant pools.

I began to walk more quickly. I disturbed sparrows along the path. Manhattan was invisible here, and the forest twitched, little branches creaking, squirrels or rats moving under the leaves.

At a certain point I would come out of the ravine and find the lawn opening up again, and the afternoon light, and it would be time to go on the train to Nicola.

"Excuse me?" the man called. He had an accent. I walked faster.

"Excuse me?" I looked behind me. He wore formal shoes, an overcoat. I started to jog.

"Do you know Nicola Gonfalon?" he called.

At that, I stopped. "Do I know Nicola Gonfalon?" I said, to buy myself time.

He came up close to me. He was the man with two nicks in his eyebrows. The man from the gallery.

"You look familiar," he said. He had high cheeks, a long, sculpted wedge of nose, and small, curling lips.

"No, no," I said. "I don't know that person."

"I think so," he said. He was much taller than me and close. He smelled like olive flowers. He wore a gray scarf with a fine weave.

"What's your name?" I said.

I thought he wouldn't tell me, but he said his name was Matteo Crema. He smiled at me. "Do you remember me?"

I stared at him, confused; I couldn't tell how I was acting, whether I'd told on myself. "I have to go," I said.

"I understand," he said. And I turned and just ten paces away the woods broke suddenly, in a chaos of purple asters, back into the clear light.

I TOOK THE subway to Nicola. I wondered when I would tell him about Matteo Crema. I did not want to tell him, because it might mean that he would stop seeing me: someone knew what he was doing. Maybe Matteo did simply recognize me. Or maybe he was sent by Nicola's father, *mass-scale bribery and other garbage,* the kind of man who would send his people to tail his son's friends. Or maybe Matteo was a competitor of Gonfa SpA, working with Nicola to take it away, spying on me at Nicola's orders.

Nicola opened the door, so slim and appealing in a navy suit. He had fissioning energy. I would have fallen to my knees right there. He offered me a seat in the striped room. I let myself follow his lead. "How are you?" he said.

"Busy," I said. Busy thinking about you and coming in my sleep.

"Are you all right?" he said.

"I'm only here to talk more about my painting process."

"What's your painting process?"

I looked at him confused. "We talked about it for so long last time," I said. "At the restaurant."

"Oh," he said. "I don't remember what we discussed." This hurt my feelings. I turned away from him.

We all had access to the same social tools, attention, praise, assimilation, and their opposites, but I'd never met anyone who wielded them this way. He held himself apart. Only a visitor to our planet. It made him—I felt sorry—more an object of consideration than a participant.

"Do I seem like I'm not paying attention?" He leaned on his elbow, holding his face in his stiff hand.

I shook my head.

"Come on, Nora," he said. "You have to trust me more."

"Don't be silly," I said, without much bravura.

"I think we talk too much."

"Why do you say that?" He wouldn't answer. "You can stop it, you know," I said.

The way his face tensed gave him an aspect of great pity or pain. "Let's go upstairs."

"Where's your father?"

He didn't answer. In the elevator to the fifth floor he said, "I can't think straight."

I just looked at him. I was incandescent with lust. I couldn't even smile.

The elevator door opened. "Be very quiet," he said. He told me to take off my shoes and carry them.

In the landing was a vase of white lilies.

He gestured at me to stay back. He tiptoed down another one of those long halls, checking each room, putting his ear to each door. He listened for a while at one, then opened the door. A wedge of light fell into the hall. He beckoned.

I followed him as quietly as humanly possible. When had I ever had to be so quiet? I was exercising a criminal side.

In the room was a bed with a bare wooden canopy frame. There was one small oval painting on the wall, of a man in a red cloak. The rug was white, angora or cashmere or some other animal with such fine fibers it had a mist over it. Outside, thick, hail-adjacent rain had begun to fall.

Nicola told me to wait. I imagined the saint in the ex-voto, a level above, recognizing the relation, pushing the believer down below the train tracks so the train would pass overhead. I imagined the aureola, the golden threads unfolding, growing out, reaching out for contact. He was the one who surrounded me with this gold.

Nicola locked the hall door, then opened the door to a bathroom, which let out onto the next bedroom. He locked the bathroom's second door. I was so excited it was hard to move. I felt packed in Styrofoam, in a divot of exactly my dimensions. He removed his suit jacket.

Then he was close to me. His shirt was so finely, densely woven it was almost plasticky. "Kiss me," I said, but he didn't. First he just reached out his fingers and gripped the bone at the back of my neck.

An extremized person, as absent as he was in conversation, in his castle with staircases that only descended to the clouds, he was that present now, with me, a demon, an interiority. He wrapped my hair around his wrist and gently pulled my head back. A gentle suggestion of how much more violently he could have done it.

*

HE BROUGHT ME a hand towel from the bathroom. "That is, in a way," he said, "the best I've ever had in my life."

He told me to wait behind the locked door, and he'd text me when I could go. He left the room. Soon my phone lit up. "Take the elevator," he wrote. "Go immediately." I slipped out the front door. I went around the block and sat on someone's stoop. I sat on the wet stoop for an hour with my eyes half-closed.

MAYBE HE WAS able to engineer the kinds of experiences I wanted to have, better than anyone, to a degree I didn't think possible. I didn't want him to be an illusionist and live in just one illusion he could cast. It was important that these experiences be sanctioned by his being good, and his understanding me. I wanted to admire, and wanted others to admire, how much of an actual agent he was. From there the desire flowed.

LATER, AT HOME, I texted him. I was getting used to being the one to get in touch. He was always there. He called, and I ran down the fire stairs of my building to go talk to him where Leif wouldn't surprise me when he got home from work. It was night. I sat on the stoop of a brownstone a few houses away, half-concealed behind a rush of neon roses.

He said I was missing the power positioning that he detested, the falseness of the people he associated with. He said, "Your reactions are not coherentized into specific tendencies. Your reactions are almost random. Different responses in different moments. You like to subordinate yourself to other people," he said.

"No, I don't," I said hotly.

"But you have a natural sense of superiority too," he said. "Why don't you express it?"

"You're not always right about everything," I said. I

reached through the flaking banister to touch the saw-edged rose leaves. A few bright petals dropped.

"I am," he said. I laughed. "You mix me up," he said. "Why are you so kind to me?" He said I treated him like the older brother who neglects himself in certain ways. He said I treated him like a nurse. That I was always so good to him, and made him feel like he could be good too, in this wretched world. He said I was nothing like Iris.

I laughed as he said all this. Giddy on being compared. I pressed my phone hard against my ear and my ear was sore. I felt for the first time that I might be able to offer something novel to him—that kindness and sisterly fondness. Something that Iris could not give him.

"You've turned my brain back on," he said.

"You said you'd be soft, and you weren't," I said.

"Next time will be different," he said. "I am taking you up and up and up with me. I want you to feel good. I want to make you happy."

"It makes me happy," I said.

"I really care about you," he said. "I hope," he said in a low tone, "that you believe me." There was always a duality to his words. The closer he came to sincerity, the more evasive he sounded.

I wanted to say it back. I was about to. *I care about you.*

But on the phone it was easier to voice my misgiving. "In the park, I saw a man who knows you," I said.

"What's that?" he said.

I told him about Matteo Crema calling out to me on the path. Nicola was silent.

"Do you know Matteo Crema?" I said.

"I don't."

I described his eyebrows. "Oh, I suppose I know him," Nicola said.

"I know you do," I said. "Why are you hiding?"

Nicola was silent again. "I believe you," he said.

"Do you think he's spying on you?"

"My father never looks after me," Nicola said.

"Does he work for your dad?"

"We all work for my dad," Nicola said. "Everyone works for my dad."

"Is it dangerous?"

He laughed. "No, no, Nora. You and Patrick know what we're up to. We're exploring an expansion here in the US."

"And your dad knows what you're doing?"

"I do what he fucking asks," Nicola said. It surprised me to hear him cursing. It sounded silly in his voice. I didn't say anything. The phone hissed. "Please leave it," he said. "Nora. You don't think I would put you in danger."

But my heart was pounding. My toes were numb; I tried to unclench them. His voice sounded far away. Something began to turn in my mind. It was Federica and me, walking up the hill from the club where I first got drunk. Federica with her arm around me, after the gondola lift ejected us at the foot of the mountain. And departing, Nicola, just like Caravaggio's John the Baptist. The doors sealing back up, and rising up, empty, to the white obscured peak of heaven.

He said, "I suppose Matteo was just curious about our friendship."

I didn't respond.

"Nora?" he said. "I care about you so much."

Why say it back? I knew that this time wasn't mine, and he wasn't mine, and he was not going to reshape his life for me. Did I care about him—or did I only care about what he did for me—was that as far as he would let me go? I didn't know him at all.

There are things you work for. And things that are just chance. And moral luck meant that being a good person was also, in a way, just chance. To spend time with Nicola meant that chance and the senses and that way I had of asking to be overtaken, of letting myself be constrained, were at the center of my life. But these things were supposed to be at the margins. The magical texture that life had taken on lately— had nothing to do with the substance of my life.

"Are you there?" he said. "What are you thinking?"

"I'm thinking," I said, and just when I said that tears scorched my eyes. I felt desolate, idiotic shame. I liked all the trappings of brutality but not the brutality itself. Thus we needed to inhabit a boundary condition; I required him to be self-aware, but not so much that it all felt like a game. This cheating thing we were doing was a profitable boundary condition, since there was plenty of room for romance and hurt, but nothing about it could persist. The problem was that it was going to end in real sadness. It was real brutality. Despite the feeling of game, despite the warmth and care that it gave grounds to, it was a humiliation.

Nicola loved having many fast inputs—I knew this from his conversations with Patrick—he loved testing and being tested. He was good with secrets, he liked being pulled this way and that, he liked thinking fast to hide from his father, he liked charming and dominating groups of businessmen with their own complicated desires and needs. If I stopped texting him, he'd return to his myriad duties as easily as he'd walked from the gallery to the park.

But I liked having just one thing. I was slow and extremely resolute. One project: the lifelong project of writing. One pastime: walking in parks. One person.

I had learned enough, I had changed enough. It was time to return to Leif. I didn't like Nicola's dissembling, but it was mine to profit from—I was free.

"Let's talk later," I said. I knew as I said it that these would be the last words I ever spoke to him. This was the end. My whole front, my neck, my ears were slimy with tears. The worst part, perhaps, was deceiving him.

Before he said goodbye, he said again, "There's an inevitability to you," and I felt that he believed in my life more than I did.

CHAPTER 20

I was not going to speak to him ever again. He was gone. I tried to convince myself of this. Yet people started giving me free things. Free coffee. Free brioches. Seats on the train.

Everyone, men and women, was making eye contact with me. I'd never been propositioned to buy drugs, or to join a group picnicking, or to join a group of runaways, until now. The people in the park who fed the raccoons told me all about their favorite raccoons, who had parented whom, who'd disappeared and then come back. The shrubs were full of raccoons, trundling back and forth, reaching for treats with their dexterous hands. "I get so much from them," a man told me. My eyes were always seeping tears, all hours.

He'd drawn certain dormant parts of me all the way up. Innocence and openness, actually, though I'd transgressed and become a liar. Sometimes it was hard not to text him. Three or four times a day I felt desperate for it, I'd become clumsy and my heart would pound. I calmed myself with the knowledge that if I texted him he'd be right there. I didn't delete his number. In order to be able to sustain my resolve, I needed for the option to be there, or so I told myself. It made me feel in charge, rather than rejected or walled off. I was managing. I did not write about him.

I WAS NOT going to break up with Leif. Of course not. He was always there for me. It was October now. The rose garden was worse for the wear, but the black velvet peonies were blooming. In the park I saw an intricate sunset. Pink, richly textured, mushrooming dots, then the dome overcome by peacock blue.

I bought dinner plate dahlias. I thought of him every second, so it didn't feel like *missing* him. He was present in my obsession.

I bought the sweetest dark-red-with-powdery-blue-bloom Italian plums and brought them to Patrick's fifth-floor walk-up on the Upper East Side. His wife was getting on with her pregnancy. It was increasingly likely to work out this time, and Patrick was filled with fraught optimism. I washed the plums, some with crystals over their wounds, and sat in front of Patrick's wood-sashed windows, which always reminded me of old bungalows by the beach, at home. He wore a red polo with the collar popped and athletic shorts, and white socks pulled up his calves. As we talked about babies, we looked out at the clutter of east 90s rooftops and backyard trees just beginning to turn.

Patrick said offhand that Nicola was out of town.

"Where?" I said. I'd been feeling all this time that if I really needed to, I could text Nicola and he would be there.

"I thought you two talked," said Patrick.

"Oh," I said, and my dry throat made me cough. "I guess we used to more." I paused. "So what's he doing?"

"Nicola will be meeting with the board. He'll be meeting with Italy's finance ministry in Rome, they own so much of Gonfa. I bet they'll be glad to have his dad, Vittorio, out of there. Because, you know, he spends his life on the lam. If I know about his corruption, then everyone does." He pitched his plum pits at the bin, accurate half the time.

"Does his corruption hurt anyone, actually?"

He laughed. "What's with you and your sympathies?" he said. "After the war, they focused on places with fewer resources and fewer regulations, and they laid waste while making themselves indispensable. They've destroyed people's homes and land with their dams and their power plants." A burr of emotion in his voice. "They kill and kidnap people, poison whole communities, and then elegantly apologize. I feel insane when I think about it."

"Oh," I said. I felt the irrationality of my moral reckonings, the superficiality, how easy it was for me to forget what I didn't see.

Patrick stood to collect his missed plum pits, then sat back down and tried again to hit the bin. "The truth is, our infrastructure is outdated," Patrick said, with the neutrality he used in front of his clients. "We need their stuff. If they get in, they'll do the subways, they'll do light-rail, the wires and the roads, they'll use their cranes to make hospitals filled with their imaging machines . . . So Nicola's right about that, too." Finished with the pits, he wiped his hands on his shorts and picked up a pen. "To be honest," Patrick said, "it's something of a relief to have more distance from that messed-up family. There have been many assassination attempts over the years."

I thought about the eyebrows with scars in their centers and I felt sick. "To kill the dad?"

Patrick nodded.

"Did you find out what's up with him?"

Patrick said, "I'm worried Nicola isn't the person I thought he was."

"So you're no longer sure about the break between father and son?"

"If I know one thing, I know that Nicola doesn't want to end up as Vittorio," said Patrick. He spun the pen out of his fingers so it fell onto the desk, then picked it up again, began clicking it.

I loved the idea of Nicola running stray, away from Europe, his father, Iris, away from tradition and family bonds. I loved the idea so much I felt it couldn't be true. It was too much to hope for. I said, "You heard what he's saying to investors?"

"I haven't heard a thing," Patrick said. "The level of lockdown is eerie. It's like they can get total fidelity." He wasn't looking at me now. He spoke so much faster than Nicola, and was so much more gentle. He'd played rugby, and I still felt that indomitability in him, and the desire to make a pass. "I don't think you should spend so much time with Nicola," he said.

"I don't."

"It's not safe."

"The Red Brigades are defunct," I said.

Patrick shook his head, irritated. "I might as well tell you everything."

"What have you heard?"

"I looked into it as much as I could," Patrick said, "and it's very old news, something of an open secret—Vittorio poisoned the mom."

"No," I said. A bomb of horror.

"She died when Nicola was ten. After years—a contact told me—of incapacitating illness."

I imagined Nicola as a little dark-haired boy. The back of his head as he sat in the front row at the funeral. "How can you be sure?"

"He has talked about it openly," Patrick said.

I shook my head. I felt admiration for Nicola, for making it through.

"Nicola wants revenge," Patrick said.

Now he put the pen down and started to rub the top of his head, his chestnut buzz cut, looking at me as though I had the answers.

I said, "I'm not sure Nicola has straightforward motives like that."

"Things aren't always complicated," said Patrick.

"Why would Vittorio kill his wife?"

"So many reasons," said Patrick. "Money. Raw ambition. Perhaps he only used her for a son, an heir."

"How can you be sure about it?"

"Some people in Italy seem to perceive him as a mythical monster."

I got a thrill from this. Away from the idea that Nicola's father may have hurt him, I liked to hear these terms from Patrick's mouth. It verified my sense that Nicola was beyond belief, and also, for a bleak moment, made me feel close to him again. *A mythical monster, a madman,* Patrick had called Vittorio. *Not a human,* Nicola had said. Patrick could never guess what I knew about Nicola. I'd been with the monster's son, and he'd come down on me with all his power.

Patrick had a work call. He said his farewell and started to put in his headphones.

"But you haven't heard from Nicola?" I said.

"Don't worry about Nicola," said Patrick.

"I'm not worried," I said.

"You're too kind to people who really don't need extra kindness," he said.

I THOUGHT ABOUT Nicola losing his mother. Now that I knew it might be murder, the thought would not leave me. There was something wrong with Nicola. I'd always known that.

Intimacy was what he loved.

Intimacy, and vengeance. Not mercy. Vengeance—I did not understand it. I did not have that kind of center.

That day I was glad not to be in touch with Nicola. I felt a shiver when I thought about the cold black water pooling in the North Woods, and Matteo's overcoat. For a minute, though, I had liked to imagine that I could be important enough to be a lure used by someone who wanted to catch Nicola.

I didn't want to see him again and wonder how to lie. It would be better to stay separate, and say honestly, if ever again asked, *I once knew him, but I do not know him anymore.*

THE FEELING OF our separation changed. It became less calm, less happy. That aura I'd had, that command, began to fade.

Patrick was always curious how I was. He said I seemed like I had one foot not in this world. I said I was writing, but it wasn't true. I called my mother one day, and just hearing her talk about what she was cooking and what she thought of the new rabbi and her friend Ellen's new husband and a nice cookie that my dad had brought her had me pressing my palm into my mouth so she couldn't hear me crying. My parents and I maintained this pleasant muted connection, so deeply a part of my life that I could barely perceive it. I imagined something I knew I was impossible, Nicola coming with me to Sarasota, how he could sit out on the concrete deck with my parents under the silky she-oak and look out at the inlet where the pelicans sat on poles. My mother would bring him pesto chicken and lemonade, like she did for all my friends, and with Nicola there I would be able to perceive at last the blazing import my parents and I had in each other's lives.

The cold days reminded me of the cold halls of my Italian

school, D'Aze. I remembered the coffee robot and the sugar button and the falling spoon, how all the children smelled like cigarettes, how Federica gave me euro coins for croissants. These images, which for so many years had existed in half-forgotten isolation, now united my life. There was congruity now, like the resonant voices in the Palestrina mass, of incalculable number in their clear synthetic harmony.

I didn't want to think about him, but my mind was disobedient. I thrilled myself thinking about him saying, *Is that good?* I thrilled myself thinking about him saying, *Right there?* He knew how to give me a head rush. He wanted to give me a head rush. My body would start to zoom as I thought about these things—I'd feel dollops of energy move through me, glittering, queasy, taut sensations, a body high.

Sometimes, lying in bed late at night, I'd think about him and Federica both. What if he'd come with us after the gondola lift? What if he'd been with us there the first time I got drunk? What if he'd been there watching when I made her angry? What if he'd been there the following morning, and had told her not to be afraid?

But there was a sense of loss in these imaginings of Federica and Nicola together. I was glad that at least once in my life I had had the power, I had acted alone. I imagined how it would have been if Federica, instead of shouting at me when she'd found me naked, had instead stepped into the bathroom and quietly closed the door.

Leif got a promotion to software engineer and drove me upstate to pick apples. I felt okay during the trip. He exclaimed that it was so windy going over the George Washington Bridge that he could barely keep the car straight. We drove high into a residential forest, then down to an orchard by a lake. We found trees bending under lantern-bright apples. Leif liked the ones that were almost purple, that sweet kind that often goes grainy, but these weren't grainy, instead they were so soft and juicy their flesh was almost like marshmallows. The alcoholic smell of apple rot, the bees, the wind, a tuna sandwich in a gorge, giant plate-size morning glories still wide at dusk.

When we got back to the city, I felt suddenly extremely sad, which Leif did not like. After he parked the rental car, he made me have a long difficult conversation as we sat on benches in front of Borough Hall and watched literally hundreds of rats move around under the shrubs. I was trying to explain that when I got sad I sometimes needed to be left completely alone, it came on and subsided randomly. He was dissatisfied with this answer. He said I'd seemed much more distant recently.

I was so committed to our conversation I didn't even feel like I was lying. One way to lie effectively is to forget you're lying.

I COULD BARELY eat, so I tricked myself and ate while I was walking. One evening I ate my bread roll at full speed on Canal Street and choked. Briefly I panicked, the world slow and quiet around me as I thought, I'm going to die here. Then I hacked and sputtered and spat out the wad of bread. Though I was surrounded by hundreds of people, no one noticed any of this. It was a hot, violet evening, and the tops of the buildings held the last butter-colored light, and I felt I was boneless. Transparent. A phantom.

But once I reached the bridge, three men in dark clothes seemed to follow me with their eyes. I was glad to be restored to visibility, though I felt a shiver of unease. They made me think of Nicola and the death of his mother.

Maybe the murder was only a rumor.

I tried to write and I couldn't. I tried to read and I couldn't. I didn't know why I behaved the way I did. Not being able to read or write must have been what made me feel only half-alive. Leif was out playing Frisbee and I was in our apartment alone. I had the window open, letting in the gray night, the noise of helicopters. I lay in bed scrolling through my phone. *I seem to be swimming in a sea,* he'd said to me. I ached all over. I was viciously bored. I opened my phone and searched for his name. I'd deleted all our old texts.

He was invulnerable. I wondered when he would ever open himself to me. *"I like people, all people,"* he once told me. There was a falseness to him.

Barely thinking about it, I wrote out, "What should I read?" There, this felt informal, barely romantic, a question to ask a friend; it didn't have to go too far. But if he gave me a book I could reflect on him every page and wonder what he liked about it. I wanted to be close to his mind. I sent it.

Then he seemed so close to me he was breathing inside of me. I lay back with glory pounding through me. Sweaty and overcome, I waited.

CHAPTER 21

When he responded, an hour later, he didn't ask me anything about the long break. He wrote, "Want to talk on the phone?" and I said "Yes," and he texted me a PDF of troubadour poetry. Then he called. "Read it," he said.

"Why?"

"I'm walking."

"Where?"

"Singapore." I could hear honks and birdsong. It was morning rush hour there.

He sounded so cheerful and commanding. I felt angry at him for his invulnerability.

"Patrick told me something horrible." I immediately regretted it. No, I could not bring up his mother, however confident and calm he seemed.

"Tell me," he said.

I told him about the dams and the power plants that wrecked people's land and health, and lives. I said the last cautiously, not wanting to accuse him directly of death. "I hate that that's your business." My heart pounded because I'd objected to him. I almost didn't want to be taken seriously. Even now, I wanted him to explain the world to me.

"How can I talk about this?" he said, his voice now heavy and slow. "It is hard sometimes. Here's how I think about it. There is always a trade-off, but listen, Nora. It's raised people's quality of life, income, food, education, everything, to have better infrastructure in their communities."

"Simply trade off some human rights," I said.

"Flows structure themselves," he said. "There are path dependencies, new formations that become institutions. Someone is the goose that flies first to open up the air, you know." But still I knew he was proud of his role in the world. This language was only for me.

"I've heard Gonfa's activities have led directly to—mortality," I said.

"There's friction. There's always friction," he said. "In one phase. Then we connect it all, automate it; it is as painless as a well-functioning body. That's our ethics, win-win integration, in the long term. The people are okay. This is the real world. You know how my dad answers these questions?"

"How?"

"I'll tell you what my dad says." His voice grew more lilting. "'You don't have to talk to me. Maybe you have to reckon with why you like me. You want to be in the beating heart of the world.'"

His tone was light, his whole manner sympathetic, skimming, rumpled like his suit, and touched with tremulous emotion.

"I don't know if I like your dad," I said. I felt idiotic to have burned these first moments of our reconnecting.

"Will you read me that poem I sent you?" he said.

I read to him. I didn't understand how he could find interesting this mid-level-abstract, somewhat vicious work in translation. I read him Bertran de Born.

At Toulouse
Past Montagut,
The count shall plant his gonfalon
In the county meadow near the stone
Steps. And when he shall have dressed his
Tent, we'll come and set up camp around it,
If we have to sleep there three nights without cover.

At first it was impossible to read to him because I was so self-conscious about my pacing and my voice. But he kept asking me to read to him—and after a certain point, like everything else with Nicola, my self-consciousness fell away. Reading to him was the best form of reading. My attention was entirely devoted to the words.

WITH RELIEF, I surrendered into a new period immediately. I texted him every other day and he always responded quickly, even though I had no idea where he was in the world. It was easy to understand things now. He told me to download the music he was listening to, sacred music that was like listening to math, or Romantic music led by lesser-known conductors, and even though he pressed me for my opinions and, what was more, incorporated them and referenced them later, he'd always finish three times as fast as I, and know every note, and point out motifs and key passages, while my mind wandered. I was honest with him about what I felt, but my opinions always sounded so murky compared to his, so subjective. He was too fast. He was fissioning and frustrated and hot, hot, hot. He liked being pulled in many directions, he liked many obligations and, I knew, many secrets. He overspilled and overwhelmed me.

He loved surreal tales of obsession and distress, the stories of operas or of the composers or the musicians. In every other time before the present day, he said, before, that is, capitalism and its games and mechanisms, the only way to get social groups to cohere, to move beyond their self-centered loneliness, was through some kind of appeal to the sublime, to religion or other special knowledge. Everything in his mind was fused and luminous—music, the state, his father's skills, private desire, poetry, paintings, his heretical ancestors. He loved religion but had a high tolerance for the more abstract, schematic kind of religious thought. I kept trying to meet him there, to understand. He would often get rabidly excited. This was part of his magnetism.

Part of his magnetism was his mysticism. He strongly believed that some things were just good and some things were just bad. He said, when it comes to justice, if we all most want for the others to get what they want, then we have an empty set, with no sense of the good. Nicola truly believed that there was good and he knew what the good was and not everyone could know.

And yet when I pressed him to tell me what the good was, he became evasive, and this was part of his magnetism too—he was an endlessly complexly unfolding flower. When you think all the petals have opened, there's a whole other tight core inside, which opens to reveal another tight core, and there was something nightmarish about this side of him, because he was endlessly subtle and endlessly concealing and every conversation ended too soon.

On the phone he'd ask me how I was. What I was thinking about. What I was reading. He barely talked about where he was, and never about business, his father, or Iris. He wanted to talk to me about music and history. I wished he would confide in me, but I could tell I played a specific role in his life. His family was filled in by what he left out.

Part of his magnetism was his ease at switching between states. As a result, everything was inflected. Talking about history or goodness was inflected with his carnality, his sadism. His sadism was inflected with interest in me. He made me respond much more than I wanted to. He forced me to talk about what I was reading or thinking about, but I was so intimidated and lost for words I would sometimes begin to cry.

I liked to be immersed in the fruit or the fat. He didn't need that; he liked unbalanced, astringent things.

What did the Cathars believe? I asked him. He said the key thing was that they weren't monotheists. They believed in good and they believed in evil. This was heretical and they were subject to a crusade. They believed in trying to be pure in an utterly corrupt and degraded world. At the ends of their lives they starved to death. And you had Cathars in your family? Yes, he said. And you are sympathetic to their views? To a large degree, he said.

I always wanted him to explain himself. But he fled as I pursued and kept shifting form.

I am quite aware that no one in power deserves it, he told me. To wield power effectively is to know how to make it about the world. If you want to command, command with the substance of the world. The point wasn't that he could touch the painting, as he had in the gallery in the fall. The point was what was in the painting. At least that was what he said.

And those people in the Carracci painting, what would they say, if we could talk to them? How did it feel to be them? It was his hand in the sky and me falling into their feathery meadow.

Intimacy was what he loved. He was always pushing. He'd talk about how he wanted to see me. He said, would you like it if I fucked another girl in front of you? I don't want that, I said, thinking of Dominique. He said, would you like it if I brought you with me on a business trip? I'd love that, I said. Would you like it if I gagged you? I don't talk this much for no reason, I said. I wish I could date you, he said. I wish we had more time. I wish I had a month only for you. (In my head, I was glad that he didn't have a month only for me, because I could not stand the idea of a finite period of happiness ending.)

Then always, he'd ask, do you like that? What would you like? What do you fantasize about? What was your first fantasy? I was too ashamed to answer. And I didn't want to head off possibilities, or what he might imagine me into. "I can't talk about that," I'd say—my obliging side coming into conflict with my shame side, and to my surprise, the shame won.

He'd ask, you hate the idea of being with Federica? And what about me with Federica? Or with Iris? What do you hate about it? I said I didn't want to share him. I said, "Iris doesn't know how lucky she is."

"I don't want you to make her an enemy," he said.

"Is that what I'm doing?" I said.

"You haven't yet."

This slight correction worried me. The worry was always that I would give him cause to cut our engagement off. It was such a bad idea, what we were doing.

He said, "Would it make you angry to watch me fuck another girl?" Lovely Nicola, he knew to carry on. "Wouldn't it hurt you?" he said.

"Yes," I said.

"I want to hurt you, you see," he said.

I wondered as I did so often whether he was finding me or inventing me.

He said there was a swollen sound to my voice.

I said, "Why are you taking over your father's business?"

"My father is immortal," he said.

"Would you ever conspire against him?" I said.

"I'll hang up if you ask me again." But his tone was light. Sometimes he'd tell me to touch myself, and I'd make myself come listening to his voice. We talked once about how he got people to do what he wanted. Like walking through the edifice whose purpose he didn't know, he wouldn't behave as if he knew the specific causes of someone's behavior. He said that manipulation was the application of persistent pressure and not calling your shot.

All autumn, I felt I was always having sex. Because I was taking notes about him, or reading the books he was reading, or thinking about him, sex was no longer constrained to physical contact with a person in a bed.

The closer I got to coming, the easier it was to remember him.

SOMETIMES I WAS lonely, and told him so. His calls revealed to me how often I was alone. If not at work, I was almost always alone, walking or out in the park. He said, "You live an actually uncompromised life. This is what it looks like."

I said, "There are about four things in my life, which puts each one under immense pressure." I meant, *Don't abandon me.*

When he called I would pause everything. I would leave work. I would go out in the rain. I'd put down my grocery bags and let my ice cream melt. The subway doors closed on me right as I was receiving his call, and I caught my body in them and forced them open so I could continue talking to him. If I was with Leif, I'd tell him it was my mother calling, or my father calling, or my college friend calling, and I'd leave our apartment and take the stairs eight floors down. Nicola didn't call often enough while I was with Leif to get Leif suspicious. By November, it felt pointless to maintain that vigilance, and I'd sometimes talk to Nicola in the hall outside our apartment.

I always moved swiftly to hang up on Nicola when our

conversations were drawing to a close, because I hated to hear the triple-beep of him having hung up on me.

If it had been a long conversation, when I hung up I was relieved. Now I could go back to thinking my own thoughts. He whirled me around and around. I always focused so intently during our conversations that only their end restored me to myself. Then my blood would be up, and the city would give me free things, a free gimlet, a free anemone, a free sunset.

Sometimes he disturbed me. But it was hard to understand how much.

"You're my moral luck," he said. "With you, I can be good. You counterbalance my father so well. You are open, unmediated, like my family used to be." I wondered if he meant when his mother was alive. I didn't say a thing, desperate to hear more. "You are the one who creates the unity again. Now at last I'm at peace with him. I am even proud of him. I find that I want to prove myself to him. You make me strong enough to try. You remind me a new life is possible."

"You're trying to take over the business?"

"He'd know if I was exploring a business takeover. Realistically, and I say this with no veiled meaning, the only way to get rid of him is to kill him."

"Surely you're not thinking of killing your father," I said, which didn't come out as funny as I'd intended.

He sighed. I knew I was pushing hard. "You make living with him tolerable," Nicola said. "I mean it lightly. You open up a space to imagine life without him."

"Just say you're not going to kill him."

"What do you take me for," he said. And then, as he had warned me, he said he had to go, and the line went silent.

When he was gone I got a hollow feeling and knew that I would stay hollow until I texted him again. I had come in too close.

Sometimes, hollowed, I would compulsively pull out my hair, or clench my teeth, or whisper to myself; if I stopped it felt like I was about to collapse into the sucking hole in my own chest. I had a phone note of texts I'd drafted to him but not sent. Hundreds of lines of nervous or angry follow-up or checking-in. Sometimes I'd feel like cutting myself, but I'd content myself with scratching at my hips, where no one would look, until they bled. I'd wonder whether he was losing interest in me. I'd run over our conversations in my mind and hate myself, for being hysterical or slow or inadequately responsive, or for not having read enough or written enough. I'd wonder why it was that he liked me, why it was that he called me from his luxury rooms in Beijing, in Bonne, in Brussels.

He was investigating a goodness. I was his balance, he said, a model for a life he'd lost long ago. What was it about me that that he called good? Devotion, intensity, no guards at the door. Sincerity, obsession. Maybe I was as devoted to him as he was to his father.

I imagined him in beautiful sheets, or being arranged by all the people he was used to doing things for him, the people who pressed his suit or carried his luggage or brought him coffee on a tray. These people materialized for him everywhere he went. He read me Milton. *"Did I solicit thee from darkness to promote me?"* I wondered what Milton meant to him, lying high above a city on percale sheets, compared to what it meant to me, soaking wet under a bodega awning.

CHAPTER 22

When Nicola wasn't calling, Leif proved his worth. Even when I was talking to Nicola, I found Leif generally stabilizing and kind. I was planning to marry him. At a certain point, Nicola would move, or we'd start families, something abstract like that, and then Leif would seem like the only one I had ever loved.

In November, I went to DC for an energy policy convening. It was an exhausting trip, and when I got home, after having dragged myself through Penn Station and the squalid subway, I was so happy to see Leif—he'd bought me dumplings in spicy oil—and I told him how happy I was, and how much he meant to me, and how I wanted him in my life forever.

And what surprised me was how cheery he was afterward, extra kind, almost giggling. This compounded the love I felt for him. I wanted to help him feel that way always.

ONE NIGHT SHORTLY before Thanksgiving I texted Nicola and he only called very late, around five in the morning. It was like he didn't bother to check what time it would be here in New York.

I was half-asleep and in pajamas and carried my phone out into the hall. I put in my headphones. "Just responding," he said.

"Where are you?" I said.

He told me to guess. I said Australia. He wouldn't tell me. I could hear rustling. "What are you doing?"

"I'm packing Iris's suitcase," he said.

"Why?" I said.

"She likes me to," he said.

I knew that he did things for Iris. But I'd never thought about what that meant—I could see him folding up her shirts, rolling up her pants, accompanying her, knowing her preferences. I imagined him taking care of her when she got sick: he'd smooth the blanket over her, he'd bring her tea, he might stand in the hall, talking quietly to the doctor about her. When she was away, he'd call her and tell her he missed her.

"Are you there?" he said.

"Yes," I said.

He sighed, and I could tell he was done packing; he was lying down now. "I wish I knew what you want," he said, "or what is just beyond the edges of what you want." So he was in a plotting mood.

I said, "I want you to know my favorite animal and things like that."

"I know already," he said. "You like chamois."

"What is that?"

"The goats of the Alps." He paused. "You want me to keep pressing you further and you do seem somewhat indiscriminate about the direction." I was looking at the hallway wall, the curdled surface in the yellow light. I was sitting on the hallway carpet, which was maroon with gray diamonds. But there was no space he couldn't pervade with his radiance.

"I don't know myself," I said, and tilted my head back against the wall, and let my legs fall open.

There was a dark vertical in my vision and I turned and in a roll of horror saw Leif standing there.

It was like seeing a corpse risen from the coffin. He was never awake at this hour. He was so long, and his eyes were swollen and half-shut.

"You're . . ." Nicola was saying, and for the first time ever I hung up on him mid-sentence.

"Who's that?" Leif said. A reasonable question, but I began to shiver in fear. He reached a hand down to me to help me stand, and I gratefully took it.

Since he'd offered his hand, he couldn't be that mad, I thought. I wondered what he had heard. I couldn't remember what Nicola and I had just said.

"My aunt," I said.

"Okay," he said. "Okay, Nora."

As soon as I was standing, he dropped my hand. He went back to the bed without me.

I sat on the couch in the dark for a little while. What had Leif heard? He'd heard me asking something about whether my interlocutor knew me. Why would someone say that to their aunt? I couldn't think. I looked into the neighbors' apartment. I could see the dog huddled in its bed by the TV. I knew Leif, didn't I? He was unlikely to bring it up again. If he brought it up again, that would in itself indicate that he felt a level of suspicion I would have difficulty dispelling.

I told myself to be positive and loving the next few days, and then he would let it drop, probably. But the prospect of being positive and loving now was repulsive to me. It would require such exuberant fakery, such active lies.

There were several moments where the elevator I was in with Leif had fallen a few stories. This was one of them. If we hit the ground, the relationship would be over.

I was desperate to see the neighbors' dog move, I willed it to stand, but it remained a collapsed, dark lump. I was so distraught that I'd forgotten my phone. Now I lifted it.

Nicola had texted. "Everything okay?" he said. The screen was a little lantern in the dark.

I typed, "Yeah, sorry," and deleted it without sending. It would have been an invitation for him to call again. I ought to try, for Leif's sake. I had to try. I typed, "Yeah, but Leif is a little annoyed, it's late here." I sent the message and then I felt a stab of guilt. Rereading it, it looked like a rebuke. It wasn't Nicola's fault that it was late in New York, was my first thought. But *of course it was*.

Nicola wrote, "Didn't you tell him about me?"

I typed, "No," which was the truth, and deleted it without sending. I knew Nicola was watching my dots appear then disappear.

I had to give Leif a real try. Come on, now. I drafted, "I need to work some stuff out with him, so I'll call you in a few weeks?" I looked at this text for a while before sending. I didn't want to limit myself this way. But maybe I, committing to not speaking for a while, would be able to relax into a more realistic rapport with Leif. Realistic was all I was aiming for. Real would not return until Nicola left forever or died or whatever.

He had wanted to know: *What is just beyond the edges of what you want?* Yes, that was what we had been discussing.

I sent the text. He didn't respond. And it was his nonresponse, not Leif catching me, that kept me awake those long hours.

When Leif rose I was still awake. I pretended to sleep. He likely knew I was pretending. He took off his nightshirt in a beautiful limber movement, and he stretched in front of the bureau. I watched his flexing back. It was unbelievable that we were together, that this fully formed man with his particular, circumscribed life, and his software engineering about contingency and risk, and the money with which he supported us, and his apartment and his tent and mountains, loved me. I watched him choose boxers and an undershirt. I was aware of the choice he'd made to love me. He was a person with convictions that he, too, had to work to sustain. He dismissed his doubts about me. He re-chose me each day. This man trusted me.

I felt so much guilt that it was wonder. Wonder about his own subjectivity, which had the facts so very wrong. It was like watching a man through a sniper's eyepiece. I saw the laser centered on him, and he pulled on his cotton pants. He wore an Oxford shirt today, which meant he had a meeting. He didn't know, but one of these days I could shoot him and watch him slump to the floor without a sound.

CHAPTER 23

I thought I was managing everything fine. But a week later, Leif asked to accompany me on a walk through the park, which was unusual. He said he wanted to see the mute swan cygnets which I'd been watching grow up. They were full-size but still fuzzy gray and black-beaked. As we looked at them, he said, "Maybe we should try a break."

I laughed.

"I'm not committed to the idea," he said. "I'm just bringing it up."

The cygnets and the mother swan, who was white with a red beak, all paused to flex and groom their tubular necks. I felt an urge to raise the stakes on him, to say, *Fuck you, I'll commit to a break*. But thoughts of Nicola constrained me. I couldn't be single, with Nicola non-negotiably married; I'd need to rely on him all the time, I'd clearly be ruining my chance at a self-supporting life, and then he would have to cut off the affair, out of frustration or sympathy. I needed Leif to balance out Nicola, to be there when Nicola wasn't, to make us equal, more or less, in remorse. Beyond that, I knew a break would not heal my relationship with Leif. If we took a break, how could we come back from it?

"Oh, Nor," he said. "I didn't mean to make you upset."

I felt a cut of irritation. I'd laughed. Hadn't he noticed how easy and light I was?

"I do feel upset," I said.

"It's just something to think about," he said.

"I don't even want to think about it," I said. "Don't you love me?" My voice sounded broken and vulnerable. I didn't feel I was being manipulative. I needed to save this relationship to avoid trapping myself with Nicola yearnings, and so I truly cared all the way down. The swans were now visiting here and there along the shore. The water was smoky gray. I wasn't going to ask things like "Where would I live if we took a break" or "How long would the break be" or "How much contact would we be in." Nothing practical, because I didn't want to encourage it.

"Of course, you're the love of my life," he said.

We walked over the green bridge and into the dank forested part of Prospect Park, to the hidden pond in the Vale of Cashmere, which was unmaintained and full of trash.

We gazed on the half-sunken plastic barrel, the scraggly vegetation, the fatigue-green water. He said bullshit: "I'm not being fair to you, living together with all these doubts." I disliked and disagreed with that recycled language, "not being fair." In fact he was only not being fair because he wanted to stop trying. We'd been together for five years. He was stupid, very stupid. I wanted to tell him he was too emotionally closed off, too cold and distant, to ever be loved by anyone else, and to fill him with a lifetime of doubt. But in reality I just humbled myself and, in the vale, covered his head with kisses.

He said then that he'd like to break up. I could not believe five years were over in one conversation. It should have been long and drawn out.

"You've embarrassed me," said Leif.

"In front of whom?"

"In front of myself."

We walked home under a smeared, dun-colored sunset on the Great Lawn, and we talked about other things. I thought he'd phase out of it. At home I reached tentatively for him, and he allowed me to suck him, which was ruinously comforting.

A few summers before, we'd witnessed the solar eclipse together. The crescent-moon shadows underneath all the trees, and the streets choked with observers, and the tiny bitten-out circle in my oatmeal box theater, were magic, but what stuck with me was the horrible tinny sunlight in the hour leading up to the eclipse. Leif was bathed in that sort of light now, there was a cosmic wrongness to him, which made me more frantic to feel him. And when he turned me over and made me come, I was so glad to shut my eyes and block out this dim metallic vision, the horror of light that is half-obscured but cloudless.

And then right after that, he said he was going to go stay with a friend. "Take care," he said, with a chill in his voice. "Text me if you need to."

I didn't ask which friend. I couldn't even guess; I didn't know who his best friend was, or whether he'd set it up beforehand.

I HAD A wretched, falling feeling: the feeling that I'd never known him. But who had ever been closer to him than me? I knew his breathing and the way he got sick. I knew what his footsteps meant and what his pauses meant. He had three moods: happy, hungry, focused. When he was too hungry, I knew to force him to eat, to lure him with buttered toast. When he was too happy, I knew to look away from him and stop speaking; he'd drive himself crazy trying to figure out what was wrong. There was no way to know him more deeply.

And that was all right. A relationship wasn't supposed to be an endless process of getting to know each other. That's just the first, short part. The second, long part, once you get to know each other, is journeying through life together.

Nicola would have found what was complex about him.

I opened the window. It was almost Thanksgiving but it was as warm as mid-fall, and such a gorgeous night—a gorgeous night for a dinner or a sidewalk or a drink on a roof or a walk through Fort Greene—but I did none of those things. I looked out the window. A man with an overcoat stood across the way, looking down the street. He reminded me of Matteo Crema. I wished he would do something strange, gesture to me, but after a few minutes, he walked away. I put on Beethoven's "Heiliger Dankgesang"—which I'd never listened to with Nicola, but it was kindred to our dance in the hall, and to our Palestrina afternoon, and him beckoning me and turning and descending, and it was also kindred to the painting studio, the way that oil paint takes months to dry, that sensation, that was once commonplace in my life, and now years past and gone, of adding a brighter color on top, and feeling the darker color below in your brush, viscid, and then modulating your pressure slightly to bring that color up. It was kindred to Federica skiing down toward me at the base of the slope where they did Olympic slaloms, her red jacket with the eagle, her dark ponytail, her lovely vivid face. I tried not to think about it, but I knew all this would end, I knew I would die and spend infinity in blackness.

I SAT ON the couch. I couldn't do anything but hit the back button on the "Heiliger Dankgesang." There was no one I could talk to. I wept.

I stayed up very late and very sad, hating Craigslist rooms for rent, such a dismal place. On homeware sites, I looked at sheets and furniture. A yellow chair. A floral duvet. A table-top. I looked at my bank account. It felt so real now.

THE NEXT DAY, Leif texted that he was going to visit friends in Mexico for two weeks, and by the time he came back I would need to have moved.

I called and said, "I hoped to get your help with the move." One thing I had to do now was worry about money.

He said I was selfish.

I said we ought to be in touch.

"No," he said. "I will never be your friend."

He must have known I'd been unfaithful. If he didn't know it through and through—it was possible he'd over-heard more than I knew, possible he'd seen my texts when I'd carelessly checked them in bed while I thought he was asleep—then he had intuited it.

It was hard to have an affair without a good quantity of suspension of reason. I was sure I'd change his mind when he came back from Mexico or at some abstract future point. I'd fight for the relationship and bring back to him all the times we'd shared, which at the moment were like liquid slipping out of my hands. I was as sure as I was about any-thing those days that I would get him back without too much trouble, and things would be better after that.

ON THANKSGIVING, I had nothing to do. It was winter now, a dark morning with crunchy salt spread out on the streets. The salt entered my mouth when I breathed. I was twenty-nine. I put rose-hip oil on my hands and face. The scent of woe. My mind was rushing, but I kept having the same realization over and over. I missed Leif, but especially the stability of Leif. What was I doing, knocking out my load-bearing walls? So that's why I am sad. An hour later: so that's why I am sad. An hour later: so that's why I am sad.

Before the sunset, I walked through Central Park. It was a perfectly still, milky evening. I met a leashed long-haired cat with giant golden eyes, which looked so placid until it noticed a squirrel and thrashed violently against its rope. I saw the ducks and geese on the lake, the mirror of water below Bow Bridge, a hawk that made all the ducks quack and move when it settled in a tree.

The next day, I walked all over lower Manhattan, and I accidentally found the Earth Room and went up. I was all alone looking at that pristine large white apartment filled almost two feet deep with rich dark tilled soil. I touched a clod; it wasn't dry and crumbly, but moist. How did they keep it from sprouting, or did it sprout?

It had been eight days since I'd told Nicola that I'd wait a few weeks before calling him again. Still, whenever I felt my books shift in my bag or the subways move or the wind against my dress, I thought it might be him texting or calling. For my part, I didn't call or text him. I considered it many times, but I was too afraid.

CHAPTER 24

Federica joined Facebook, and Facebook recommended her to me. In a jolt, I remembered asking Federica why Nicola, the boy in the *ovovia*, was famous. And she said, *His family is evil. His father is bad.*

I clicked to her profile. Her photo showed her kissing a man, backlit by a pale blue sea. It surprised me to see her kissing a man. I thought she'd be alone or with a woman. It was uncomfortable to feel my own expectation that I could have shaped her life, my arrogance to feel that I should have. But we hadn't kept up. She had become a symbol to me just like the cutting, a daring escapade of transgressive feeling. And what was I to her—maybe even less than that. The truth was that there was a complication to Federica that I could never have with Nicola. The complication was the lack of adultery. Potentially we could have been together. We could have acted in each other's lives. I owed something to her (or I had, once) because I had had the power to shape her or hurt her. In contrast, being with Nicola was like dancing with a statue.

I added her as a friend and attempted a message in Italian: "Hello, my dear sister! Message me back! I'd love to talk!"

I imagined her opening it. She hated me, last time I saw her. But maybe she had forgotten. Maybe my message would be enough to reframe the past. If she responded, I would ask her for a call. Maybe there would be something there to connect on, a way to pick back up the conversation we'd broached and lost on the day of the bobsled race. I could tell that what I wanted most was to tilt the conversation to Nicola. And I would say, *Why is he evil?* And I would press—as in a dream, I would beg, I would scream, and I would cry until she told me.

THE FIRST APARTMENT I saw was the second floor of a half-width, filthy three-story house. Two film students lived on the top floor. When I encountered the bedroom, I thought it was a kitchen, because the floor was covered in battered, shiny, beige linoleum. But there were two south-facing windows. And my budget was different now, without Leif. "As soon as tomorrow," they said, and I took them up on it.

I cried to see all my things packed up. Leif called from Mexico, and he also cried.

I unpacked on adrenaline, not hungry, not tired. I put my bride and groom candles in the back of the closet. I rolled out a floral rug. I plugged in my lamps and filled up my desk drawers and hung up my clothes. I pinned floral sheets on the walls. I put rose-patterned sheets on the bed. The room looked like a floral tent; this was apparently who I was without Leif.

I'd bought the cheapest bed frame and the cheapest mattress. The mattress was six inches thick and I could feel the slats of the bed frame. And yet I was so satisfied with all this I could barely stand to turn out the light.

I'D TOLD NICOLA "a few weeks," but two weeks came and went. I did not want to text him. He ascribed a lot of power to me. I wasn't sure I deserved it, or wanted it. Hadn't he seduced me? That's what I wanted. I wanted him to be in charge. Was he quelling his own guilt? Had *I* made this happen?

He wanted our relationship to be a bubble of goodness outside of life and time—his father, his marriage, his mother, her death—just he and I up and down in the gondola lift perpetrating our dualist heresy, that we could be good together, and bad apart, without all the snow bleeding in. I felt a little used and I felt a little angry because for me the inside and outside were muddling; here I was losing Leif, and being trailed by men I didn't know.

All the anemones were done. The wind came ripping off the flapping blue reservoir. I'd been living in a dream world. I couldn't do it anymore.

After I decided not to text him, each day of December was a fading. I'd been sick the whole time he was gone, and worn out, and I'd ruined my relationship, and still I knew that, if I got in touch, at some point afterward his attention would move on. If I got in touch, I'd be setting myself down a path whose ending was already so stupidly visible.

I never lost sight of the fact that he could destroy my life.

Knowing he could destroy my life made him terrifying. *Mercy, mercy, mercy,* I wanted to beg. I gave him everything. In some moods, I'd recommend it. I'd recommend giving everything to someone.

I don't want to consume your life, he'd said.

This is the *point of life,* I'd said.

Do you know what I mean? Would you have done it?

To what extent does the author's intention matter? Pulled this way and that by a thousand threads. We don't even understand the contexts we're in, we don't understand the literature we read, the friends whose personalities influence us; we only get these pinpricks of insight.

There's an inevitability to you.

*

I LIVED IN my flower room in a daze. The pain of Leif was centered around the loss of hope—the candles in the box, and the citrus in the windy car on the California coast, had been lit from within by hope. And now that he was gone, I had these useless dark husks instead; I found no refuge at all in the moments we had shared, which were most of the moments of my adulthood.

As in my loneliest times in Turin, I made contact with the city. I walked across the Brooklyn Bridge completely alone in a howling gale, then I warmed myself in the nearest open building, the Surrogate's Court, discovering the resplendent zodiac ceiling, its golden mosaic tiles gleaming in the shadows. In the Museum of Natural History I stood before the case of passenger pigeons in a dimly lit hall of rodent skins, a group of eight pigeons with bright red eyes and orange throats with a purple shine, among oak leaves. If all of New York were to liquefy and begin to spin like bathwater, that glass case would be the drain where it all funneled to vanish.

At home, the snow fell outside my windows, and the radiator heat shimmied up my floral walls. At last I had enough time to think about him. So strange that, if I wanted, I could just text him. It was as though I could resurrect a dead loved one.

I'd dream of him and his mouth, hands, voice, and I'd steep myself in desire for him. This was a glittering high-energy time, running on empty—I was frayed, dazzled by my strange capacity to keep moving. I dreamed about Federica too. I dreamed about her brown hair, the long gait she had in common with the German shepherd, the way she looked out on the quay of the Po, her face lit pink by the cigarette. All the evidence in my life just showed how hard it was to connect to anyone. With Nicola I had wanted to be controlled, and I could lose myself without responsibility.

With Federica, I had deliberately made her angry. Maybe our severest personality traits come in pairs—we get both the thing and its opposite.

We were not in touch at all. Patrick gave me, for the holidays, *Remarks on Colour* by Wittgenstein and a gift certificate to a paint store. Wittgenstein wrote: "Why can't we imagine a grey-hot? Why can't we think of it as a lesser degree of white-hot?" Patrick said that he'd discussed the book and the paints with Nicola. "Recently?" I said.

"A while ago," said Patrick. "But you came up in that discussion." He said these were gifts from both of them.

The store, which I had never heard of, sold historic pigments to art conservators, and lapis lazuli blue. When I went, I could tell that it was a Nicola place. It was the only manufacturer of lapis lazuli blue left in the world. It sold ground-up diamonds and rubies and booklets of gold leaf. It sold magenta made from the secretions of magenta snails, Tyrian purple made from the secretions of rock snails, bluish green earth from the Cypress highlands, and the exact kind of poisonous lead yellow used in the thirteenth century. I lingered among the watercolor pans, touching the tiny solid bricks of dear pure color. I tested opaque blue and glittering pink. With Nicola's money I bought a white tin of eight colors. I would never use them. They were so precious that they were abstract.

I WENT HOME to Florida for the holidays. I was never expecting to be single at twenty-nine. At twenty-nine my mother had had me. My parents were good. They were so good that Alice Miller's *The Drama of the Gifted Child,* a book of supreme import to many of my friends, was meaningless to me. I didn't want to tell them about Leif, but finally, when I did, they were only kind.

On Christmas, we lit the menorah, though Hanukkah was past. I was entirely outside of the moment; I was entirely in the past and future. It wouldn't be long now. It wouldn't be long now. If I wanted, at any moment I could write to him and resurrect the dead.

CHAPTER 25

I was back in New York by La Befana, the January holiday when the witch comes to visit all the children in Italy. I guessed he was there or Switzerland.

I saw the Carracci in the *New York Times,* so dear to me I could tell how I would feel if he were to die, and realized I had been extremely dishonest with myself. There was no point in living this way, in treating as dead a person who was alive.

"When can I see you again?" I texted. There were no words for the blown-out energy I felt. I was high and manic.

He responded in a half hour. "Tonight?" I read the word and felt a good hard hit. How long had he been in the city? It was as though he'd been waiting for me.

He told me to meet him at a restaurant.

I was so early, alone on the train, all carefully cleaned, in a black silk dress and stockings, my long hair back in two silver clips.

Tribeca was blessed to me, blessed because these sidewalks had felt his feet. The streets were icy, the sun had set, I was as light as a water strider. I kept laughing. The gold before seeing him. The piled snow, the penetrating wind— not hungry but queasy, heart scrambling. It was a scurrying, surging kind of happiness, and I felt like my body couldn't contain me.

Forget the lonely moment in the Duane Reade to get out of the cold, looking at the discounted Christmas candy and thinking about Leif spending the holidays with the mother who hated him. Forget how I began wondering whether Nicola would sleep with me, even whether he'd still be attracted to me.

Remember going out to the street again, the pine fragrance, woodsmoke fragrance straight out of Sestriere, and crispy sand and salt, the light on the Hudson River, on the Po. Remember how I was laid out by desire.

When I told the maître d' the reservation name, his posture changed, he welcomed me like a friend, and I thought, If Nicola doesn't put a heavy hand on me the instant he arrives, I will explode.

He came in the door, in an icy gust. I blushed all over. I was beside myself. The maître d', winking at me, took Nicola's loden coat. Nicola wore a suit. His hair was longer; I yearned to touch it and feel the cold night in it.

We sat in a green leather booth. I was much more afraid of him than I remembered being. And the tension in my back, the shakes in my spine, were more than I remembered. At first, he was distant and intimidating. I wanted comfort and familiarity. Then he ordered wildly expensive wine, and I knew everything was okay.

He also ordered some kind of food, which I did not eat. I only remember the crème fraîche on top of the tarte tatin, just because it was good and sour on the cold spoon. The table was a landscape of candles and shining silver and glass, all vaguely bothersome to me, like bees and grasshoppers in a meadow. I couldn't wait to be rid of them and alone with him in a bare room. This must have been the way he always felt—his luxurious world with its refined obstacles to his seething intensity. He'd pushed aside the flatware and the small plate and the water glass to make room for his forearm and cuff-linked wrist.

We talked but I barely knew what about. Like that time he'd talked to me but only to see my anxiety diminish, now I talked to him but only to use up the time until I could have him. I was laughing and laughing and the wine sank into me.

We talked about how he was exhausted by the work he had to do—so why do you do it, I asked, and he said he had obligations to Iris and his family. He said he felt often that there was too large a sense of possibility in his life. It was vertiginous, he said, that each day he had to reckon again with what he was doing, and with what he should be doing, knowing that he could do anything. "The ultimate questions are too vivid," he said. "I feel too much awareness. The awareness follows me around and won't let me go."

The world was easy for him, and he had no respect for almost any of it, for the academy, contemporary culture and art, politics . . . Only those obligations to Iris and his father, as painful as they might be, felt real. The riptide of his noble family. Of his father, he said, "It's sort of him or me, except I'm younger." I thought he must be talking about who would win. In the end, his father would get feeble and die first. Maybe Nicola was relying on the simple advantage of time to become his own person, eventually.

He asked me about my writing. I mostly remember my pounding heart, and his green eyes, his refined head. Of all the people I knew, he took my writing most seriously. I felt nervous about this level of seriousness, because I didn't feel I could live up to it. He'd never read my short stories and I would never permit him to. He didn't like contemporary literature. But he liked that I was single-minded about it. I couldn't tell him about Leif, but I told him I'd been very sad in the winter, and he said, "You need to write. It's foremost in your life."

"It's too soon."

"It'll make you feel better."

"Therapeutic writing is uninteresting," I protested. Limited and self-indulgent.

"Why? People build their kindness in complicated ways. Likewise with their art."

Nicola was imperious, presumptuous, exuberant. Only Nicola told me what I should do, told me what I believed. Leif wouldn't have dared. I should have resented it, but I needed it now. I was lost. I needed a vessel to pour my personality into. So soothing to speak to him.

What is the feeling of something being better than you remembered? Something quite a lot better than you remembered doesn't feel like the same thing but somehow improved, like, for example, an apple but 10 percent sweeter. Instead it feels like a new thing. Like you thought you were holding an apple, but you bit into a nectarine. Alien, unresolved, toxic maybe.

"Why did you text me today?" he said.

I felt like I couldn't live without him. That was the truth. "I liked the paints."

"I thought I'd lost you," he said.

I shook my head. He made everything alive; the figures in paintings, the very statues moved. Also my past and my writing. He was the weather in the spirit world.

He hadn't yet touched me. He hadn't touched my hand, hadn't put his knee to mine under the table.

The waiter was very interested in Nicola. She brought us dessert wine for free.

It must have been around this time that he reached over behind my hair and gripped the back of my neck.

I felt total joy. The best touch of my life.

My body was crazed for him. I excused myself and tried to pee and couldn't. In the restroom, I changed my underwear.

Returning to the table, I felt I would vomit with nervousness. "I need you now," he said. "Drink your wine."

He marched me down the sidewalk. He held my neck. The touch was so profound. It made my heart desperate. I sensed his coat swinging out behind him, and the people looking at us.

HE FELL BACK onto the silver seat in his sitting room on the ground floor. Quiet for a while, I was half-asleep, stupefied and wine-drunk. The people passed outside, making soft shapes against the curtains.

I want it to feel close, he said. This made me laugh.

Does it feel close?

Yes, I said. "But—I have to tell you something."

"Tell me."

"I'm worried about what you'll say."

"You can trust me completely."

"Don't—" I started. It was difficult to speak, suddenly my throat was clotted. "Don't stop seeing me even if I tell you this."

"You're in the center," he said.

"Leif and I broke up," I said. "A month ago."

"Oh, Nora," he said. "I'm sorry."

His tone made me tear up. "It's okay."

"Are you sad about it?"

I thought for a moment. "I am more nervous," I said. I turned to look at him. He was lying back on the couch. He had glowingly pale skin, his hair sweaty at the temples. I couldn't believe this was my life. I never thought I would hurt people or let myself be carried away. "Do you understand why I'm nervous?"

"Don't be nervous on my account," he said accurately. I looked at his long eyelashes and his crushed-looking green eyes. "I feel all this tenderness I did not expect."

He angled my head toward him, again making me available to him, and kissed me. "I like what we're doing," he said. "I don't know what to make of it."

I broke away and moved down the couch. I felt completely at peace. I listened to him and felt him become vulnerable for me.

WE WENT UP the stairs, up and up and up, and he opened a window to the wavy winter night. I was all pure, luxuriant, rarely-in-a-lifetime, flying happiness as we lay together on the pristine bed. He seemed to have cut me and pushed back my skin and sinew so that he could directly touch my nerves. We listened to Palestrina; *Che meraviglia,* what a marvel, he said. What a marvel.

CHAPTER 26

Things like work, taking the subway, walking around, kept happening, generally without my noticing. Eating and sleeping mostly ceased. I drank smoothies so I wouldn't faint. I had always been so risk-averse, but I could tell you from the inside that, aside from scattered moments of total terror, none of it felt risky. It felt mandatory.

Patrick invited Nicola to the baby shower for his wife, Liana. The activity was glazing clay plates which would then be fired for Patrick and Liana to use.

"Should I come?" Nicola asked me.

"Do you have any plate-painting ideas?"

He seemed to be thinking about it.

"You should come," I said. Impossible to reject a chance to see him. "But don't wear a suit."

We met in front of Patrick's apartment. Nicola carried a gift bag and wore sweatpants and black sneakers and a sport coat. "Very informal," I said. "What did you get them?"

"A jack-in-the-box," he said.

"Is it demonic?"

"What do you take me for?" he said. "It's a bunny."

I was about to press the buzzer and he told me to wait.

He told me the previous night he'd gone to a bar at one of the Tribeca hotels and some girl had approached him, and her line had been, "Who *are* these people?" And they'd talked—he liked people, all people—and now we could *go out together,* which I'd like, he thought.

As always, when I saw his face, I had felt a roar of happiness, but quickly I began to get sad and confused. I'd thought I was the only one he would cheat on Iris with. Did he feel that now that he'd done one, doing more didn't add any harm?

I was thinking about how I would let him down. I looked at the line of buzzers on the doorframe, the scrawled handwriting of the tenants, Liana's block script. I looked down at the granite stoop, the little pot of decorative kale, chalky green and purple. "I'm not sure this is the right conversation to have before a baby shower," I said.

"This is *for* you," he said, as though I was being stupid. He was so burningly energetic. This was not at all what I liked, and not at all how I wanted to be pressed. I couldn't do it. This time he had me wrong.

"Are you okay?" he said. "What are you thinking about?"

He was so happy and I was going to disappoint him completely and then he would stop seeing me. I was not adventurous or strange or malleable. I just wanted kindness for as long as the center remained. "I don't know about this," I said, at last.

"Going to Liana's?" said a woman in a pom-pom beanie with a box of cupcakes.

"In a minute," I said.

Nicola seemed not to see her. "I'll just take her to the gallery first. She's nice, she doesn't know anything, she's younger than you. No stakes. You can follow behind us and watch." At that I whirled down, I couldn't help it. The truth was I was scared to say no. I was scared that he'd get tired of me, or that he'd see that he and I wanted different things. I didn't know how much things mattered to him. I didn't understand where his edges were. That gallery off the immense atrium, that silent fountain, his father rattling in the house, even his own physicality, the drifter, traveling everywhere with nothing of his own except, maybe, my heartbeat when I slumped against his cool hard belt. I had to rely on his sympathy as he pulled me deeper. I became skittish, spoiled, inconsistent. He showed me that personality had to do with circumstance, and I felt myself writhing into peculiar and unpleasant new forms.

"Is it too much too soon?" he said. It was awful; awful to hear his voice go gentle, to feel the need for that emotional management. In fact I loved that emotional management, but the second-order shame and guilt were so powerful—he put his hand on my shoulder, tried to pull me closer, but my skin was crawling.

"We have to go up," I said.

Liana's friends had laid out a plastic tablecloth with the bisque plates, rough and white, and little pots of glaze. The apartment was warm and humid and smelled like shampoo. Liana's friends were mostly public defenders, pediatricians, academics, women in pilled sweaters with their sleeves rolled up. Two of them had brought small children. Nicola had to take off his coat. It was strange to see his blue-tinted arms. Strange to see him in this context at all, the other women starting to look at him; even in hiding, there was a posture, or his trembling face, that made it all feel like some devious negotiation was about to take place. His T-shirt said JUNGFRAU SWITZERLAND with a mountain printed on it. "It's a famous summit," he said with a note of apology in his voice. Then he picked up a cupcake, looked at it from every side, and put the entire thing in his mouth at once. He struggled to chew it, breathing heavily. Everything he did made me laugh. "Have you ever had a cupcake?" I said. He pretended not to hear.

Patrick offered us tea. "I'm doing polka dots," he said, and showed us his plate, its glaze dry and pale.

"Nicola, you should also do polka dots," I said.

"You think I lack facility with a brush?" he said. I saw a few other women glance over, then look away. They thought we were together—we *were* together.

"I'm going to do an apple tree," I said.

"I'm going to do the Carracci."

He took it seriously. Even when the gift opening began and everyone left the table to crowd into the couch area, he was working on those lobed trees, trying to dot on the glaze, which kept sucking away into the plate. I kept going on my apple tree, too. It had to be at least as good as his. I added a circle border of squirrels (I hoped), and then red dots around the rim. I began to fill in a blue sky. It had been so long since I'd held a brush. Nicola stopped only when someone's toddler pulled up on his knee. "Hello there," he said to the little boy in his calm voice. "Aren't you accomplished." The child crawled away.

"Nicola, can we open this?" Patrick called.

Nicola assented and Patrick turned the crank and I could hear the plinks of the music box. Patrick turned slower and slower and then suddenly the bunny sprang out, wearing a little crown. Everyone laughed, applauded—Nicola leaned in close to my ear. "I think maybe I should cancel the gallery. But regardless. Can we hang out tomorrow or are you busy? It makes me extremely happy to see you."

I didn't say anything.

"I truly truly hate this feeling," he said. "The having pushed you too hard feeling. I will avoid it much more assiduously in the future."

Still throbbingly sad, I managed—"Who knows? I certainly don't know." I couldn't stop myself from minimizing, easing. I almost wanted to ask his forgiveness. With that thought, I began to regain some footing.

"If I didn't like you to the extent that I do . . ." he murmured, "I would be aroused at the thought of causing turmoil. However, our relation goes much further than would permit that."

My stomach dropped; it was a fear feeling. The feeling I got when I made a bad mistake and was scolded for it. It was identical to the feeling of him taking care of me.

Around the couch, everyone was laughing and applauding again. I looked over—it was a winter hat with a unicorn horn.

He continued, "I was disconcerted myself, because you make it feel untenable not to take art seriously. A totally separate thing I don't especially want to discuss now."

I thought about what to say. Something had changed. It was the space, the rabbit with the crown, the plate he'd labored over, now looking covered in white icing, hiding still how successful it would be. It was being surrounded by people who couldn't hear us but wished they could. It was how he'd continued—then I was no longer worried about letting him down or being unable to hit his goals because I could see how the pushing itself was part of it, for him.

He had wormed his way in, and I had been actually repulsed. And now shaking and steamrollered and just laughing. Euphoric. "Nicola."

"Yes?"

I couldn't think of what to say.

"Can we open this, Nora?" Liana shouted.

The baby was going to be a girl, so, in an attempt to get her something original, I'd bought a set of wooden construction equipment. A little saw, a little hammer. My parents had done the same for me, but despite their efforts I'd gravitated toward tutus.

"Isn't that nice," Liana called.

"We'll put her to work," Patrick said.

"You always do, Patrick," I said.

And Nicola was leaning in close to my ear, and my whole body was swelling and bowing like saturated wood. He said, "I am very excited for the day I am the reliable palliative, even if still the cause." He always knew.

This was what I could see in my mind's eye, though I didn't tell him—if you could bring the sunset closer and just smash it all over your face, that's how I felt. Like the eye doctor's yellow vertical beam.

IT WAS ALWAYS real with him. The next morning I woke up and took a shower not even realizing I hadn't had coffee. The lensing, glassy feel of the fine vapor in the fuzzy sunshine in my window. The happiest days of my life.

I made coffee and sat in the kitchen. I was thinking, in the fresh spinning morning, did I like him to be mean? Maybe. I knew from Federica that meanness was intimacy, and attention, and could be like a high.

I thought, if I have the choice to make an extreme intense connection and learn about huge, never before uncovered emotional landscapes, or to forgo it—well, it was impossible to forgo.

No, mean wasn't really the question. That was too simple. This process was not rational or transparent. Coercion of this kind felt like a rupture in experience. He was speaking to something over which I had no control.

He was such a perfect agent that there was no drama, nothing to improve. He was absolute. It wasn't really a love experience. It was a faith experience.

HE TOLD ME to meet him after work by the Delacorte.

Central Park was sublimely beautiful, ice hanging on the leaves and branches, ultralong shadows across snowy fields.

The world of inexpressible detail and opulence and glory, a feeling of total assimilation into the sky and landscape.

There he was, overcoat, dark suit, dark shoes. The park pulsed paranormally around us in silver and ultramarine. He asked me to tell him about yesterday and I told him I felt inadequate, left out, when I thought about adding in more lovers.

He said yes, he understood that all completely. He said that my being jealous was absurd—he'd known so many people and seen what they were like; they weren't like this. Only Iris, he said, was higher. I knew this, but it made me sad, and he saw that in my face.

"Nora," he said, "this is something I haven't done before. I've never done this. I'm falling for you." He looked questioningly at me. He wanted me to affirm something.

I told him, "It was going to happen, and it is happening."

"Okay," he said, as though there had been a decision we had settled. He kissed me in the park. He marveled—it was never like this with Iris, he said. He didn't want to protect her so.

He would bring that girl, Astrid, to the gallery by himself.

"I don't like that," I said. I'd thought the gallery was our place and now it seemed like just a stop on his normal route to bed with women other than me.

"Well then, I won't," he said.

"No," I said. "It's okay."

And so he carried on. He said if it all went well, then later this week sometime he would fuck her and I would watch, and then he would send her away and take me properly. I knew that if I wanted to go beyond myself, I had to lose my shame. I did not want another girl there, really, but I did want to go as far as he would pull me. I would keep my faith in him. I remembered a time when I never thought he'd hold my wrists so tightly that my hands would fade to cold, my veins full of his cold power.

CHAPTER 27

On the Astrid day we ate lunch at Peter's gallery in the embassy-size building with the fountain. Walking up, I listened to "Converse" from the *Shenandoah Harmony,* the most splendid of all nineteenth-century sacred songs, with a hobbled, spillover rhythm:

In midnight shades, on frosty ground,
I could attend the pleasing sound;
nor should I feel December cold,
nor think the seasons long.

My heart was pounding out of my chest. Ungodly bliss. Waiting outside, I stood next to a black dog, and there were tears in my eyes as I looked at its ears and nose, which quivered in exquisite reaction to all the movements of people, birds, and trees. There were so many kinds of life! It was too much for me.

Untenable not to take art seriously! I thought. You make it untenable not to take art seriously! So he'd said to me.

I watched him cross the street, effortlessly commanding and attracting attention. He beckoned me, and the passersby stole glances at him. Everyone wanted to know what was up with him. I ran to him just so we could take four additional steps together back to the gallery. Inside, we sat across from each other, and Peter the gallerist brought us apricot juice and sandwiches and to my surprise I couldn't even drink the juice.

"Did Patrick text you the plates?" he said.

"No!"

"The baby is going to love my plate," he said. He showed me a photo of the dozen or so fired plates. My apple tree looked sturdy, fine; his was a wash of green, the trees subtle. I zoomed in as far as I could on their feathery leaves. "I think I made the sky green by accident," he said.

He locked his phone. "Astrid," he said. He said it's important never to be mean. But know that only some people are worthwhile. The rest you can lie to, and seduce, and blow off, and never see again. Only some people follow the valuable and the good.

I told him I did not agree. There was too much arrogance to that view. And danger. Even derangement, to be so sure. He really thought he could judge. How did he have the experience to know? To that, he talked about how there are facts that are inaccessible through experience.

Despite all Nicola's interest in nuance, at his core he was as stark as an obelisk.

He said I was like him, intensely cultivating what I saw as good.

He was utterly sincere, that was what was so strange about him. It was an adolescent quality; he wanted to think about his values all the time.

He tried to get me to talk about writing. I lied and said that I wasn't sure what I subjects I wanted to write about. Because the subject I wanted was him. He told me about Eckhart, a medieval mystic he'd gotten obsessed with in high school. He read me some:

"As long as it has no reference point, the mind can only

wait as matter waits for form. And matter can never find rest except in form; so, too, the mind can never rest except in the essential truth which is locked up in it—the truth about everything." The words were vague and unfeeling, self-contradictory. I wanted to break into them, the way we'd broken into Palestrina, shattering that seamless song into emotion. *"Essence alone satisfies and God keeps on withdrawing, farther and farther away, to arouse the mind's zeal and lure it on to follow and finally grasp the true good that has no cause. Thus, contented with nothing, the mind clamors for the highest good of all."* As Nicola read I thought about how he split his life in two and so had maybe nothing in the center. I thought about how he'd lost his mother and sought to be good with me instead.

"What do you think?" he said. The light came in bright against the wood panels around the window, making his eyes look lit from within. Green eyes, black lashes. His face had so much in common with the paintings against the walls, the same stillness composed of a million disappearingly smooth strokes. The same beauty and composition that did not happen by chance, that was the result of practice, and focus, and intuition-building. He leaned forward and clasped his hands on the table.

I made him read it again: *The mind can only wait as matter waits for form.* He fetishized certainty. I uncertainty. Yet he was the one asking questions all the time. The ultimate questions, too vivid. He was responsive; that was his gift. And I was the one building things. I made real attempts, to paint, to write. I wrecked my life. I loved without an integral self, I was formless, everything falling apart around me, everything shaped by him; I loved without integrity. I was pure in a way he wasn't, certain of my commitment. "What did you like about it?"

"Eckhart is so enraged all the time," said Nicola. "Even

the happy parts are angry." He fought constantly for this impossible emptying. His writings were an upswelling: what comes, comes, and derives from the constant upsweeping surge. "This is why I wanted you to hear it," he said. "It seems to me like a very good way to approach writing." He only half looked at me.

I'd always thought that the reason for my writing was to find positions for unresolved but deeply felt moments, the sorts of moments that stitched the meaning into my life. The cigarette on the quay with Federica, the long nights painting—in fiction I could give these moments the proportion they deserved. But what Nicola was proposing felt to me like a column of light that throws off images as it goes. A fissioning, irregular beam, like a solar flare. The images were effects, not causes.

He said, the stronger a vision, the more it can include. Find the source that doesn't flag, and that will be the engine.

"If I wrote about you, would you be mad?" I said. A book about him, the sterile fruit of our impossible union.

"Don't worry," he said, "you could only plagiarize my middle essence."

Of course, I laughed.

We talked about the evening, during which I would watch him with another woman. I knew I'd find it confusing and repulsive—but repulsion was close to the feeling of the thrill.

He said what was good about Astrid was that she seemed tough and unfazeable. He'd told her "a female friend of mine to join." I was wearing a long-sleeved black silk midi dress. Nicola teased me, "That dress makes a statement, and the statement is, 'I am modest.'"

I smiled.

"Why don't you eat your sandwich?" he said.

"Where is Peter?"

"I sent him out," said Nicola. "Sometimes even discretion . . ."

He touched the side of his face. He said, "Do you want to see our new office?"

We walked across the atrium with the fountain, and he led me to a bronze-fronted elevator. Inside, the walls were hung with dark blue quilting. On the fifth floor, a smell of sawdust dried in the air. We walked around the circle of balcony, looking down into the atrium. The sound of the fountain was loud here. He pushed open each door, showing me the great wood-floored expanses of empty space, braced with white columns, burning with sun. He took my hand and led me into one of the vast empty rooms. Cold air came in through a tarped door; he pulled the tarp down and led me onto a stone balcony with griffins at its corners.

"Why can't you eat?" he asked. He leaned his forearms against the balustrade and looked at me slowly. I was so well acquainted with his frustration. Not this.

I was thinking about Astrid, and about my discomfort and my shame. I was thinking, violations were violations, whether or not there was some kind of verbal consent. And conversely—you could voluntarily and enthusiastically walk yourself into a pitch-black cave.

"I'm cold," I said. I led him back into the huge empty office with its incorrigible light. I stepped away from him through massive, weightless curtains of sunlight and darkness. He followed me, slow, a dark, calm shadow, drifting.

"I'm a bit worried about Astrid," I said. All agreement is backward-looking, I was thinking. I didn't want to ruin the immediacy of everything by layering on various understandings that would make something that was not a game for me into a game for him, a safe tidy game with its borders defined—impossible—and I didn't want him to shirk responsibility after he and I spoke thin words to each other.

"I promise that you won't feel thrown to the wolves," he said.

"I know," I said. But as was so often the case, I understood in the sense that I felt like he had dropped mines down to float in the darkness, tethered against the ocean floor. And later I would trigger them, and then see if I actually understood.

"Will you kiss me?" I said. He pulled me to him and kissed me. He was so moderate with his kisses; they were always a kind of special effect, like, in music, the recapitulation of the unadorned melody in a long and rich air varié.

AFTERWARD I WENT and sat in the park. The world was on a moving walkway past me. Solemn dog walkers, mothers with uniformed daughters on playdates, teen boys vaping, and tourists flowed gently by in the cold light. I felt drunk.

Patrick called. "Where are you, Nora?"

"I'm not feeling well," I said. I thought I'd written in, but I realized that I hadn't.

"Is there anything you need to tell me?"

"Just that," I said. "I'm sorry."

"Look," came his sigh. "I know you've been through rough times before."

Have I? I thought.

"It sounds like you're outside," he said. "Where are you?"

I was silent.

"I don't mean to alarm you, but I texted Leif, and he told me about the breakup."

"What?" I said.

"I was worried about you," he said. "You didn't tell me about it."

"I didn't tell you," I conceded.

"I don't want to put words to it like this, but if it's a substance thing, I can help you. You know I've been through it." I said nothing. "Or a guy, like Tad."

"What about Tad?" That was my college boyfriend.

"He didn't have a great reputation," Patrick said. Really what he meant was what he couldn't see—Federica. She was the one who taught me about debasement, frustration, and the thrill of invasion. She was the one who made me wish I had gone farther.

"I'm fine," I said. I was irritated, embarrassed. I felt weirdly caught, like when my father had cried at me about self-harm. Patrick didn't understand, and I couldn't talk to him about it. I would have to be more fastidious about faking transparency with him.

"When we first started working together, you were afraid of everything."

"I don't remember that."

"Fine, Nora," he said. "And for a time you really stood on your own feet. You can do it. I've seen it. You'll do it again."

"Leif and I weren't right for each other."

"He was upset that you haven't been in touch."

"That was his choice!"

"Is that true?" said Patrick.

I felt huffy, even though this was something of a compliment. Patrick was saying I had more power than I purported to. I felt stupid, small, anxious—that feeling from college, when I made everyone ask me three times before I'd consent to see them, and for which reason I had no friends.

NEAR SUNSET, NICOLA and I took a cab together south. We were going to a hotel in the West Village. He wanted me to see the room in advance, so that at least it would be known. We moved down Fifth Avenue in the lavender canyon light. His beautiful face and his rough-looking eyes, eyes that always seemed on the verge of tears, his bitten-down fingernails. I touched him through his shimmeringly thin wool trousers.

The cabdriver knew; all the pedestrians and passengers knew; my head dropped back. "Like a maenad," he said. We passed to the West Side and proceeded past low-budget windows filled with glittering outfits. The Garment District.

She might act like a porn star, or she might be quiet, he said. There's a huge range; it's unpredictable. Don't say it's my first time. Say, *I'll just watch for a bit*. He loved that he had no idea what would happen. It's so rare in life, he said, to have a situation of such complete uncertainty.

We were at the hotel. Bellhops in peaked caps stood to either side of the golden doors. He said, looking at his phone, that she hadn't texted him yet to confirm. She was late. "Is she going to cancel?" I said.

"I think so," he said. My first reaction was disappointment, after all that buildup. And imagining *his* disappointment.

We walked through the dim entryway. We went up forty stories so quickly that gravity compressed us at the end. It was a suite of several rooms with built-in seats and lights like flying saucers. The bedroom was on a corner and faced north and west toward a smoky blue view of the West Village and Midtown and the slick Hudson. The room was large but mostly window. The shadowy bed felt less real than the sky and the towers, many of which stood, as though caught in trances, beneath motionless columns of steam. A simple gold, smudgy sunset. My disappointment with her cancellation was shifting into relief. I confirmed with Nicola that the windows wouldn't break, since there was no way to be far from them. I knelt—he sat in a chair—in the last, setting sun.

"Your face," I laughed, touching it.

"What," he said.

"Your eyes aren't as open as usual," I said. He bit my mouth then.

"You can leave whenever," he said. "Absolute trust." He

was staring at me with wide pure rimless green eyes. "Also, it would break my heart if you left. Also, as close as we are now, you can assume we are three times closer, because I am already there," he said. "Eternal happiness, Nora."

And then she confirmed. She was coming.

He texted her that I was held up at work, because he knew I was too anxious to talk to her. He was going to take her out for a drink, and then he'd text me to come to the room. We took the elevator down forty floors. His face was so alive in the elevator, almost vibrating, his eyes moving like flames. He leaned against the wall, his dark soft curls on his forehead, and his attention seemed to pounce on me.

I WENT TO a bar and sat for an hour while the room filled, feeling, like in Italy, as though I didn't have a home. The freckled bartender comped my drink. That was the way it always was those days. The ginger cocktail stung my mouth and froze my hands.

At eight he texted me to come. When I stood I had trouble getting my footing. I collected myself in the bathroom and I exited. I waited to be alone in the elevator.

For a long time I stood in the hall. This was—I supposed, though I was wrong—this was the most intense moment of the night. I listened at the door. How I'd longed—I told Nicola later—for years, since I'd seen him kissing that girl at the magazine party, how I'd longed to know the sorts of things he did with women. How I'd longed to know what Dominique's smile had meant, and what secrets Nicola kept. Now I was permitted. I listened. They were quiet. I tried to imagine what might be going on behind the door. At least I could imagine some of the pieces—the very fine fuzz on the crest of her ear, and his rib cage swelling and diminishing. I could imagine the joints—how he invited her to the room, changing so eagerly between states, and how he went a long time without touching her at all. But then as I imagined the positions they might find themselves in, her crouching beneath him, or him lying back, or the two of them exerting themselves side by side, and the essential crudeness, I felt alienated from the moment. No matter how much I predicted it, the most experientially salient thing would be left out. Reality was so much harsher than imagination. There was no fuzziness to let desire creep in and shape it.

I looked both ways down the hall, at the empty room-service trays in still-life disarray, and the dark starlit city out the window at the end. I remembered the evening after the gondola lift, when I'd finally pushed through to Federica. I'd always felt I owed that moment to Nicola; his hand on me became my hand on her. In the hallway, though, I could see clearly the difference between his experience and mine on that day. I might have felt him directly guiding my kiss with Federica, but to him, he'd been just on his way from one Olympic sport to another, comforting a stranger the same way I sometimes gave tissues to crying people on the subway. It had been up to me to transform that into a moment with Federica. Tonight was different because I was taking his direction. I felt less chaotic, and I felt less proud. I knew he would handle everything. I had no agency here.

I waited, dared. I rounded on the door, put in the key card, and opened it.

Now I could hear the quiet sounds from the bed. The gold lamplight was brighter than the light Nicola fucked me in. I saw for a second in the mirror his head over her, his dark hair. I slipped behind the wall and unbuttoned and dropped my silk dress. Silent. I knew they must have heard the click of the door, but no other sound revealed me. I entered the bedroom and sat behind the little table. (In that moment, I told Nicola later, I felt like the biggest fool in the world. "I've never felt that way," he said.)

"Hello there," she said, in a gentle Swedish accent. "Come over here." She smiled in a dominating way.

I delivered my line: "I'll just watch—for a bit."

It was too graphic. Too strange. I wanted her to be happy. She kept her bralette on her small chest. At times I just looked at their smooth torsos to avoid the difficult parts: their faces. Her pale thin body, which he grabbed and maneuvered, was bendier than mine, and tilted up to receive him. I'd asked him to behave differently toward her, and it was different. I wondered if, when she let her head fall back, it was for my benefit or not: I wanted it to be real. She wore a long, clinking dagger pendent on a necklace.

Afterward Nicola held the dagger and said, "It's really sharp," and she said, "It's good to have a weapon on you." It came down to her belly.

When he went and flushed his condom, I said what I'd felt such an urge to say: "You look beautiful."

She said, silkily, it was a fantasy of hers to be watched.

Nicola came back and lay down on the bed, and we talked. He asked her about the Band-Aids on her toes, with *Frozen* cartoon characters. She said that they were preventative, for her servant who loved her feet. We looked out at the city. Everything was unreal. We rolled with it; we dropped our words into the quiet temporary relation that we'd formed in front of each other. There was an estranged, festive feeling. We were honest. So fun to be honest. We talked about how we met.

"He's an Italian nobleman," I said. "I met him during a panic attack at the Olympics."

"Is that true?" she said to him.

"It is," he said pleasantly.

I described how meeting him had led directly to my first kiss with my host sister. How it was my first public loss of control and how it produced both frustration and tenderness in Federica and then suddenly we could grip onto each other like gears. I told the story as though he had fated the whole thing, and felt a small pang for Federica, who would never have seen herself as a pawn of Nicola's, or my bridge to him.

"He cracked you," Astrid said.

Nicola and I just looked at each other. To Astrid, I was Iris, or Vittorio: she scrutinized our gaze. She asked what it was like between the two of us.

He said that there was no friction with us. I knew how meaningful this was to him, since he was the mediator: no buzz on the wire, no blemish in the glass.

She said, "Nothing Nora says is clear, which is why I keep asking questions." I found this astounding, that she considered me to be the one she was trying to understand.

"I'm comprehensible!" I protested. "I'm comprehensible."

"What are your families like?" she asked.

"Nora comes from distant nonconfrontational stock," he said.

"Nicola's father tortures him emotionally," I said, sitting with my elbows on the table, "and Nicola leaves his father in the cold, but even though they never speak directly, they love each other very much."

He smiled and tilted his head. I knew he would not punish me for this, and also, we would never talk about it.

"Neither family is close," he said.

"Nicola feels too much choice," I said, "but I'm the freer one. He's from the mountains and I'm from the sea."

"What sea?" she said.

"The Gulf of Mexico," he said.

She wanted to know what sex we liked. "I like everything," he said.

"And what do you like, Nora?" she said.

I looked at Nicola, so he would answer. "Nora likes a beautiful saint crowned in beautiful light, lifting her higher and higher, approaching but never reaching death," he said.

She gave a strained smile, looked down for a moment, gathered herself. She was jealous.

Astrid's view on me was precisely the opposite of anyone else's, since here we were in Nicola's inside-out world. I liked how serene he was. She put on her outfit, all layers of black chiffon. He put on his suit and walked her out. He wanted a cigarette. Now I was alone. It reminded me of first kissing him. Strange and unsettling. I felt so detached I knew I had been shaken.

CHAPTER 28

It took him a while to come back. When he did, I attempted: "You have to admit I chatted really well."

"It was too much chatting," he said. Though that
wasn't strictly a criticism of me, it catalyzed a mood
shift: I became energyless. I wanted to cry. I felt ruined. I felt I'd never be turned on again. I'd messed it up. So
the evening was the cab ride, the diner lunch, the lambent
before. Not the thing itself.

"Come here," he said. He turned out the lights. Manhattan rose up that instant, towering glitter. He showered
for two minutes. The shower had no walls; it was just a
vague area of the large, sleek bathroom. I was so tired I
dragged the chair over to sit. Then on the bed he pulled
back the sheets for the first time. We lay down on the surface that was as tight as a stretched canvas. He lay beside
me and picked up my hand, as though I was sick. Tears
came into my eyes. I turned my head away and swallowed
a sob.

He clasped his fingers around mine. With his thumb, he
stroked my palm. He said I'd seemed so nervous he could
barely stay present, he wanted it over with, wanted to send
her away: as soon as he kissed her he knew she wouldn't
break. I said I thought I'd done a good job. "But you didn't

like it," he said. This was the worst thing he could have said. I'd disappointed him.

He turned on his side and kissed my cheek. He dropped his fingers to my temple, then slowly dragged them through my hair, combing it back from my face. He pushed his fingertips against my scalp.

I'd thought we were at the end of the night. But we were in the center. Certainly it was related to how molten I was beforehand, the setting sun, kneeling beside him while he pressed perfectly on me. And it was related to how desperate I was for his generosity, how stretched out I was, how cantilevered, reaching for his positive opinion. I returned to him emotionally with no process, no shift. Black to white in an instant.

I'm going to strangle you, he said.

I'm worried it'll hurt, I said.

It won't hurt, he said. He had pulpy green eyes. Like lemon pulp.

I said okay.

The huge gem of the city behind him.

My head rushed. It didn't hurt, but it made my heart beat unnaturally. The animal part of me said fight back, escape. But my love of being overtaken was stronger.

When he reached that height, he rose over me, then he fell backward, arched backward and fell onto the bed.

We lay in silence for some time with Manhattan steaming below us. I lifted myself and ran my fingertips down his back and arms. Dopey, I kissed him against his sweet head. I felt overwhelmingly that we had done justice to the view. It was this, only this. My body had its own index and Nicola went ring-a-dinging at the top so of course he found himself among inhuman things, ancient trees and the cosmos.

For a while, we floated in the blue. I told him I was hungry and he told me to get dressed. He said, "I will never forget how you look."

We went down again. We were out in the West Village at one in the morning.

He mused about how he could lose his livelihood, his family's trust, everything, if anyone found out. I said I would say it was my fault. "That won't be needed, though I am glad to know you've wanted all of this," he said. It was true, wasn't it, that he always followed my desires. We found a late-night bodega with all that we needed: mango juice and steaming yellow rice in metal pans that bent in our hands. We sat on a bench. The park wasn't too cold.

He talked about how at times Iris shut him out completely. He used to try; now he left her alone. "That sounds right," I said. "People teach you how to treat them . . ." But he rejected that. "Not relevant here," he said.

When did she shut him out? When she thinks about growing older, he said, and losing her youth. But at those times, he would ask: "Have we wasted our youth? Have we not done enough? Is it over too soon?"

I nodded along and anticipated—"It's good to know you're living as you're meant to"—no, he rejected that too.

"The good days that happen," he said, "each one is a fuck you. We had this good day. You can never take it away. Tace, force of evil. This day can never be taken away." I knew he was speaking about his father.

On the walk back to the room, he held the ends of my hair, and I felt his slight distant pulling—"You have such nice hair"—and then he moved his hand up and began to touch my neck.

"You still have some left," he remarked. I said I was very tired. He said, "You don't have to do a thing. But I need you again."

Up in the room, the air was cold near the huge windows. Nicola was at home in midair. What was he thinking of, so far above me? There but not there, the intercessor of grace. All the ex-votos showed a violent but happy scene. You don't get one made unless the person survived the incident.

CHAPTER 29

He went home that night. "I have to," he said, and I knew it was for his father. So I slept alone and restlessly in the air in a hotel robe. The room was comfortable, with strange margins: the giant tumbling mat of the bed, the endless breeze of the cooling system I wasn't sure how to adjust, and the awareness that at some point in the morning the room would stop being mine. When I woke at seven, the city was covered in pink mist, and the Hudson was saturated with color and shining with the flips of the buildings on the far shore.

In the giant, cloudless mirror, I looked at the veins running in long parallel lines in my inner arms. I had red pinprick dots under my eyes. The shower, in one corner of the bathroom, was clad in black stone and had no walls. The water came down in an effervescent torrent. I used the tobacco-scented soap and shampoo, then put every miniature bottle into my bag.

I'd never slept overnight in Manhattan, and when I descended to the ground and entered the teeming streets, damp and clean and charged with secrets, I felt like an angel.

HE TEXTED ME that he was coming to the office later to meet Patrick. They were going to have dinner together.

He rang when he arrived. I felt a surge of excitement that

brought tears to my eyes. I rode to the ground floor to let him in and accompany him in the elevator. It was impossible to hold in mind what we'd experienced. "Just the two of you having dinner?" I said, hopefully.

"You're greedy," he said, and in a flash he struck me so hard across the cheek that my teeth hurt. I fell back against the elevator's metal wall. I was surprised he'd take such a risk. He had more at stake than I did. He wanted to use every moment we had together. I liked it.

"Compose yourself," he said, and we both laughed, as the elevator doors opened.

HE CALLED AFTER his dinner and said he'd found another girl for us.

I was silent for a time. I wondered if I'd disappointed him so much he wanted another try to get it right. I didn't want this to be a pattern. Again I felt that dropping feeling, I knew I was being inflexible, intransigent, demanding.

"I'll put her on hold," he said. He trounced me with deep patience and kindness, the kind I felt so strongly I must reject, the kind I felt must wear on him.

I protested. He said he'd come to my apartment. I heard him get in a cab.

I rushed to fix up my room. I'd never expected him to come over. I was ashamed of its cluttered frivolity.

Then he was there in his dark and slender suit. He was like a hologram amid the linoleum and roses.

I kissed him and listened directly to his heartbeat. He sat on my bed. "I've never felt a less comfortable bed," he said.

He caressed my face, lordly; I was his subject. He wanted to tell me about Astrid, but I was pumping with shame. I laid my head on his knee. He put his hands on my neck and choked me, watching me, said I should be less ashamed with him than I was with myself.

He told me to take off my clothes, he wanted to see me. He made me stand in front of him. He made me show myself to him, and turn around.

He kissed me, and let me take large drafts of his warm dark hair. With words, he brought me back to the gondola in the Alps, overlaying what he was doing, suspending me in two kinds of attention. First I would have touched only your shoulders. And Federica would have liked to watch you lose control, and to get treated with so little respect. Only I make you what you want to be. You would have made it easy for me, as easy as you always do. You can't even control yourself, you let yourself go, you don't think at all, it's too late for you . . . I felt myself opening uncontrollably for him, and came with dense shame.

I wanted to watch him. But when he was close, I failed to look at his face.

WE LAID TOGETHER. He told me he felt happier than he'd felt in years. "I love the way you live," he said. "I love being close to it." He'd drawn the sheets up over his chest.

"How do I live?" I said.

"I know there's pain everywhere," he said. "There's pain everywhere. But I think that your ethics uncage you somewhat." He kissed my ear and my temple. "Your honesty, I'd say."

I asked him what it felt like when he realized his father was *not a human,* which he'd said to me after we'd seen him listening to the singers. I imagined it must have been when his mother died, but maybe he didn't believe his father had done it, maybe he rationalized it away.

"I won't tell you what he did," Nicola said, heavy and long and pale in my bed, with his dark hair curling with perspiration.

This was frustrating. He only wanted to take risks in the areas he liked. "Just tell me what it *felt* like," I said.

He said he'd never had much awareness of his body, just as the seasons changing didn't thin out the layers of time the way they did for me, didn't allow the startlingly transparent evocation of memories from years ago.

At last, he said, "Sadness integrates you with the world. Certain things are sad and have value—grief can be positive."

As we lay there silently, I realized I wasn't sure I liked the way he'd inserted himself into the Federica memory. Not only because it minimized my agency—but also because it didn't mean anything to him. I remembered him rationalizing Gonfa SpA to me, telling me there was always friction when entering a new territory, but in the long term, it was good for the people. He was so sure he knew what was good and bad for other people, and I could see how that was the fine cutting edge of what someone might call evil.

I pictured him: a big dark meteor—a void meteor running black over the sky, the blacker black of sucking emptiness. Stars lensing around it. When it falls to the earth the only sound it makes—cannot be heard—like a very very soft kiss, the kind he gave me. Like getting choked, a meteor of draining calm, of ending struggle.

HE SLEPT OVER. His body was extremely warm, and I tried to move away from him, but even though he was asleep, he kept gripping me closer. A boy who'd lost his mother.

IN THE MORNING he sat in the kitchen, in the pearly sunlight, and I made him espresso in the moka pot, and then I made him toast. His hair was all askew. He was boyish and long-limbed in his undershirt. I buttered the pieces and they steamed. He said that the way I buttered, and the steam, and the music (a Haydn symphonic mass) were lightning, pure lightning.

"Does it remind you of growing up?" I said.

He said, "No, no one ever did this for me." We sat in lustrous French horn quietude and I watched him look at my mouth. He put his hand against my neck and then continued sipping his coffee.

"This might be too much to get into," he said. By now I knew he'd get into it anyway; he had poor impulse control, like I did. He looked me over with his dark-lashed eyes. "To what extent does it feel like falling in love?"

I shook my head as warmth unfurled around my heart.

"For me, a lot," he said. "But none of the bad. It's very intense, obsessive," he said, "but my personhood isn't at stake." This was not what I wanted and not what I expected. "I don't know how to say it. What I feel."

I was silent. "Let me go get dressed," I said. My personhood was at stake; that was the thing. It was, of course, love. But I had the good and the bad.

"Don't do that yet." He put his hand on my knee and I lit like a lamp. "You like the power imbalance," he said, as though he was being fair-minded.

"Yes, that's true," I managed. It was impossible for me to be demanding, because then I'd brush against the welder's flame of Iris. I knew going in that I had to be all right with every indignity. Still, I felt sad about his personhood.

He said, "It's a happy thing, Nora, what I said."

"Well, say the whole thing, then."

"I don't want to take advantage of you."

"It would be easy, though," I said.

"Maybe. Not really."

"Where's that ringing Nicola clarity?" I said.

"There are several tracks," he said.

"You have to plunge like an arrow into the heart of intensity!" I said. Upon this I stood up. I ran into my bedroom and shut the door. I felt his devious power: I was like the floor with the trapdoor slowly sawed in it, stroke by stroke. Even I had no idea how weak I was.

He knocked at the door. "Did I upset you?"

"No," I said.

"I'm sorry," he said. "Can I come in?"

"No," I said, but he opened the door. I backed up. "Why are you hiding from me?" he said. His face was so beautiful in the morning sunlight. His eyes were holy green. "You don't want to see me?"

He knew what my silence meant and circled me with his arms. I felt the hard beating current of his body. "You and I are very different," he said, "but we're alike in a way—we both care so very much." He directed me onto the bed and pulled a sheet over me. He laid down beside me. "I hate this bed," he said. "What do you want to do today, Nora?"

"Oh, what do you want to do?"

"I want you to choose."

He'd never asked me this before. I hadn't even imagined it. I was supposed to be the will-less one. "I want you to choose," I parroted.

"Stop," he said.

I flushed. Long minutes went by. "Okay, I want you to cook for me," I said.

"Ah, cooking," he said. "That's a good one."

"Are you going to do it?"

"I don't know why you doubt me so," he said.

"And something else," I said. "You know what I'd really like? It's not something you've offered."

"Now's the time," he said.

"I want to hear something about your mom."

He turned away. "What do you want me to cook?"

"A dinner," I said, sure he would say he had to leave.

Instead, he searched for butcher shops on his phone. "Oh, this one's Italian!" he said. He called them. In Italian, he asked, "Do you have duck? Only frozen?" He was already putting on his shoes. "Stay," he told me. "Do you have a microwave?"

I shook my head. Nicola left. I lay on the bed and texted Patrick for more photos of the plates. "Why do girls like Nicola so much?" Patrick wrote. "Everyone kept asking Liana about him."

I wrote "IDK" and changed the subject to doulas.

Nicola returned in an hour carrying a big box with a microwave, and a heavy oblong frozen duck wrapped in cream-colored plastic. "Fresh Duckling," it said on the plastic. He had to put the microwave on the floor because we didn't have counter space for it. "Unwrap the duck," he told me.

It was an oval upholstered in thick bumpy whitish-pink fat. And it was frozen solid as a log.

"I think it probably has a plastic bag inside," he said.

"No way," I said.

He microwaved the duck on low for five minutes, which made no difference. He groaned in disdain and put the time to thirty minutes.

"You can't microwave that for thirty minutes, it'll destroy it," I said.

When the duck was done in the microwave its fat was yellow and dry and crusted in places, and still pink and raw in others. Nicola began trying to palpate between its legs. "Don't watch," he said. But I stared in fascination. An edge of transparent plastic bag appeared. The legs were still frosty.

"Microwave it more," I said.

"Absolutely not," he said.

"Have you ever made this before?"

"It's the only thing I know how to make."

He began to try to wrench the bag out through the frozen hole. "You're clearly hurting your hand," I said. He ignored me. Pieces of the plastic ripped away, and as he forced his hand deeper, they got greasier and greasier, and his hands were sliding off them. Now I turned away. I tried to figure out if there was any way to get the microwave to fit on the counter. "Ah!" he said. He'd finally worked his hand all the way in. He pulled out the rest of the bag in one.

"What's in the bag?" I said.

"I don't know what it's called in English, nor do I care," he said, and threw it with a triumphant gesture into the trash. "We have to put something in the cavity," he said. "Got any oranges?"

"Apples?"

"Fine," he said. I got two out of the crisper. Wielding a carving knife like a sword, he hacked them in half and stuffed them in.

"Do you have any cooking twine?"

"Floss?" I said.

He shook his head. He opened all the drawers, found chopsticks, ripped them out of their paper covering and began snapping them into small pieces. I flinched. He stabbed them through the sides of the opening and pulled the fat together. "Now it bakes for three hours," he said.

"God," I said. "What will we do?"

He washed his hands, carefully cleaning under his nails. "I have to buy a few more things." He threw on his coat again and swept down the stairs and returned with a bag of parboiled rice and a bottle of something in a black bag.

Two hours left on the oven. He led me back to my bed, and pressed his forehead against my neck.

"You know what I've always wanted to ask you?" he said. "What did you fantasize about as a child?" I couldn't say anything. But he laid next to me, touching my hair, and asked and asked and asked. One of the film student roommates came home and texted me, "Smells great. What's with the microwave?"

Meantime Nicola was breathing in my ear, saying, "What were your errant, scurrying desires? What have you never told?"

"What did you?"

"I don't want to scare you," he said.

"Go ahead," I said.

He said he would tell if I did, and he pulled back my hair, a delectable, mothering feeling, but then he hit me on the face. I didn't tell him to stop.

I swallowed the bitter pillowy heat without letting him see it. I was drinking in his fierce attention. The taste of his attention, attention which was as flighty as it was powerful, which gave me this intense interest in life, which electrified me. If he paid attention to something, then it was alive for me and fascinating. He animated lifeless things with attention, his attention had the characters singing out from their paintings, the books fluttering like birds. No one got to keep his attention, not even Iris.

He asked me again to tell him what I used to fantasize about. He asked and asked and finally, with shame, I told him about how I'd wanted to be imprisoned, like Hansel and Gretel, and I'd wanted to be sick and cared for, and mostly how I'd loved watching the torture droid approach Leia in her lonely cell. "That's beautiful," he said. "*Star Wars,* why not." I felt the full force of how he liked people, all people. "What was it you liked? The pressure? The penetration? The resistance?"

I thought about it. Divulging, now that I'd broken into it, was not hard. I said I liked that she was trapped and good. I wanted to be forced into the things I wanted so I wouldn't have to deal with the shame of wanting them. "A pretty universal feeling, I'm sure," I added nervously. Why had I been so afraid to talk about this for so long? Maybe because, in a way, he was bleeding me dry. I thought about Patrick telling me I had a foot not in this world, telling me I was returning to fearfulness.

Of course, Nicola was safe, safe, safe. "That is just exactly right," he said.

He asked me about my first time. I sketched out the Egyptologist, Tad, who was now a corporate lawyer, his resin dragons, how, in the lead-up, I blew him in the library, how much it hurt to try, how before it happened I cried naked on the floor, and how he had liked that.

All this divulging, which was self-centered and self-indulgent in ways I generally strove to avoid, was in the service of closeness, trying to be as close as humanly possible.

Nicola said this virginity-losing story made him angry.

THE APARTMENT HAD filled with a warm, buttery scent. The sun was already setting. Soon he went to make the rice. The timer rang. He tried to pull the baking pan out using paper towels as hot pads and immediately burned both his hands. "Cold water, cold water!" I said. I got the hot pads and lifted the duck up onto the stove. It was a varnished-looking caramel brown now, and sizzling. The chopsticks were slightly burnt on the ends. The baking tray was full of liquid fat.

He said, "You want the rice plain, or soaked in fat?"

"Take a guess," I said.

He gave me a plate of random cuts of duck, some big wedges with the fat hanging off them, some small, torn-up pieces. A pile of pale yellow rice drenched in fat. And he brought us Sauternes in my mugs. "It should be drunk from a tiny fluted glass," he said, "but whatever." One mug had a Yellow Submarine handle and the scratched-up Beatles. The other said "Yep I'm from Sarasota Florida." The duck was mouth-coatingly decadent. It was like eating a violin. The Sauternes was rich and gold.

*

WE LAY IN my bed. "I hate this bed," he said.

"Sorry," I said.

I'd given him an ice pack for his hands. He was enjoying cooling his hands on it and sometimes suddenly putting one of his freezing hands on my leg or chest.

"So, a story about my mom," he said. I saw his eyelashes fluttering. The shine from the streetlight brightest on his eyes. "No, I can't do that. I could tell you more about my family, though."

"Okay," I said. I didn't understand how I felt. How could I have been offended?

"My family." He was silent again for a time. "Well, I have this aunt named Violetta. My mother's sister. I remember very clearly that she was terrible at games like chess and backgammon, and I was very competitive, so I was always sure to beat her. But still I was constantly asking to play with her. Even though it was too easy for me, barely fun for either of us. And she'd always play.

"She loved fortune tellers but she was so judgmental of them. 'Well, he doesn't seem to have the gift,' she would say. She used fortune tellers like I used her for my games. An unfair fight. No fortune teller ever wanted to predict her sister's death, but she was very sure it was going to happen."

"She was sure your mom would die?"

"That's right," he said. He pushed one arm under me and one over me and bumped his face into my neck. He reminded me of a child again. "Did you like the duck?"

"It was perfect," I said. "I told you about my childhood fantasies. And you?"

"Isn't this a bit extractive?"

"I'm just trying to level out." I kissed his cheek. "Have you forgotten?"

"I think we never really forget anything," he said. "I think it's all there underneath. And you tell me that your moods change for no reason, no correspondence. I think your moods *do* mean something. They're not random. You should think about that. You should think about your power."

"What was your childhood fantasy?"

He sighed. "I wanted to murder my father," he said. "I wanted to overtake weak people who liked the feeling despite themselves."

Confused, I became very warm.

Why did I feel that I had to be near death to be loved? For Federica to love me, I'd considered jumping off a balcony. Before her, I'd dreamed of being sick or captured. My compatibility with Nicola felt like the g-force giving way to weightlessness. Helplessness, total trusting slackness. Bare reality.

CHAPTER 30

He sent me a new mattress, which arrived, rolled up in a box, the day he told me Iris was coming to the city. I heaved the heavy roll onto my bedframe and slit its many tight plastic wrappings. It exhaled and fluffed up and when I lay on it I felt like I was floating in water.

I was afraid to ask how long Iris would be staying. It was January and I watched the snow sublime off the sidewalks.

On the phone, he dreamed of more combinations of me and other women. I said, "Don't you know I'm not a natural sybarite?"

"I want to put you side by side with someone who is," he said, "and see whose aesthetic wins out." I groaned and he laughed.

I felt our reciprocal daring, venturing deeper and deeper into the waves.

After I received the mattress but before Iris's arrival, he invited me to sit at the French restaurant where he was a regular.

My job was to pretend I didn't know him, and watch him. The maître d' gave me a wry look and a free drink. "Choose someone with dark hair," I said. I'd always found dark hair more exciting, because of Federica. I thought maybe I could feel more connected to the person if they looked like her. Federica still hadn't messaged me back; if she someday came to the city, I'd never try to absorb her into this life, but maybe she could come out for a drink with us.

"If she doesn't have dark hair, I'll make her dye it," he said.

I sipped my drink with one dark berry and witnessed Nicola sit down at the bar and get approached—he didn't even have to start any conversation—and unfold his wild and undeniable charisma.

I couldn't hear the conversations, but it didn't matter. He commanded effortless attention. He was curious, willful, selfish. I watched him question and laugh in his suit with its rumpled, skimming quality that made everyone else look costumed and stiff. For him, everyone was interesting, and easy. He lived in Virgil's golden age, honey from oak, grapes on briars, the world thronged and willing.

By the time I was done non-eating dinner, another woman who was open to joining had found him. From my distance, I could see her small fox face.

He took her number and after she left he came and sat next to me. Her name was Kara, he said.

When I asked, he said his effect was mostly from sensitivity and energy. "Don't keep asking me these things," he said. But I knew it was also his shamelessness. He would risk dominating people, and they acquiesced and decided to follow him, or they acquiesced and decided to hate him—or else, the most confident among them, like Patrick, and even dear Leif, realized that this was a man who, in Patrick's words, needed nothing from them.

He touched my neck and collarbone, and I sagged into him with desire, but he didn't go with me that night. Traveling home on the train, I was abject. Had I lost whatever it was that he'd found irresistible? I wanted to reenter the world only he could bring me to, the world stinging and alive, the real world.

*

IRIS WAS IN town, Patrick told me the next day. I didn't contact Nicola for a week. A week was short enough that I could manage. It helped that Nicola was plotting something. And it helped that Patrick and I talked endlessly about him. I pretended that I had seen him occasionally in the winter to discuss my writing. We talked about whether he was, as I termed it, an obelisk or an endlessly unfolding flower. We talked about future plans for Patrick's financial intelligence company, which was a way of talking about Nicola too, because Nicola had told Patrick to grow it. The most powerful stance is to make other people believe that their problems will become your problems, Nicola had told Patrick.

Nicola's power was how flexible, even slippery, responsive, he was, I said. "The Saracens, not the Franks."

"He's his own equilibrium," Patrick said. I knew he meant to tease me. I shook my head, but I was thinking of when Nicola had said, *I am very excited for the day I am the reliable palliative, even if still the cause.*

After four days I stopped whirring enough to sleep sometimes. I walked in the grayscale park, among the starlings pecking en masse in the dirty snow.

FINALLY, I TEXTED him, and he invited Patrick and me to a gathering with him and Iris.

I came an hour late. He fetched me at the door. My heart beat hard to encounter again his strangely stripling beauty.

I wore my long-sleeved black dress from the Astrid night, comforted by its modesty. I told him quietly, "Patrick and I really enjoy speculating about you. We must have the exact same personality."

"All kinds of people are obsessed with me." This made me laugh. "I missed you," he said.

A gathering, he had said, but already in the hall I could hear the hubbub and smell the humid fragrance of a crowded party: smoke, beeswax, roses. As we walked up the stairs the chatter grew louder, and we passed two tall people kissing on the landing. "Nicola, who is here?" I said.

"Iris's friends," he said.

We entered the second-floor living room. Now dozens of people gathered among its glowing ormolu and bar, attended by a silver-haired man, whom I was going to attempt not to make use of too quickly. It was strange not to have Leif around too. When I felt this anxious, I easily remembered how good he was.

Patrick wasn't here yet, and I knew no one, and no one was speaking English. They seemed to be speaking German and French. I watched them touch their glasses together. I looked at shining hair, and earrings like dropping golden flowers, and men in long slouched trousers. Many wore sneakers with neon accents, and thin cashmere sweaters. Nicola moved among the guests, but did not seem exactly like he was talking to friends. He was equal or superior, always.

Servers sleekly penetrated conversations with bottles of wine, and I felt closer to them than to the guests. They brought out oysters, pale and perverted-looking in their scaly shells. On a side table was a huge half-ruined still life of cheese, satsumas, matte black grapes, razor-slashed bread, and honeycomb. Next to that was a platter of shimmering white *lardo*. There were candles in the sconces and on the mantels, paperwhites, lilies on tall stems, and a record moving on the player, the disc slightly warped. I watched the needle climb and fall into the fine furrows, releasing scratchy jazz.

All I had to do was wait for Nicola. I was probably worse than average at keeping various things in mind at one time (where Nicola was far better than average), and so only when I wasn't facing the crowd, but just watching the precise hands of the bartender mixing me a gimlet, could I actually grip onto the knowledge that he had betrayed his wife with me. Why had he? Maybe because I was more besotted with him than she was. Maybe I was just newer and less known than she was. And that betrayal had opened the way for Astrid, and the girl from the bar, but they were to me what I was to Iris: nonthreatening.

The lime stung my fingers when I squeezed it. I embedded myself as deep as could be construed as unintentional into the olive velvet curtains and watched Iris talk with a large circle of women. Her flippy black hair was loose around her serene face. She wore a rigid black tweed jacket, black trousers, and a silk blouse. Grandmother clothes. Even Patrick's rich New York friends didn't dress this way. It pained me to think that what she had achieved was the female version of Nicola. Like his, her garments suggested the eccentricity of power.

But she wasn't really the same as her husband. Where Nicola could be, despite his sensitivity, uncouth and unbalanced, she was entirely sleek and poised. She had impenetrable, self-controlled, perfect loveliness which was unselfconscious because she'd been raised that way. I thought of Silvestre on Delacroix: *He holds himself prisoner within the worldliness of his education, which is perfect.* I could just see the maids in mobcaps folding down the sheet on her horsehair mattress, the bridge of the yacht where she would have stood in a pinafore and a plaited-straw hat. Rich people were permitted to live in the past.

Part of her appeal was her *latency*. She'd carried out graduate-level biochemistry experiments in high school and had achieved nothing since she'd found a dye that allowed MRIs to pick out more clearly certain flaws in the brain. I'd always thought young success must be devastating, but now I could tell it also suggested irrefutable potential, as though amazing future achievements were in process as she spoke, and aloofness of a sanctified and post-human kind: she'd seen what it was like to achieve hugely and publicly and had turned her back on that. Both combined into her aspect of all-knowing self-restraint.

Finally Patrick arrived, and I emerged from the drapes. He waved to me and came to get a drink. And then he took me with him to join a circle of guests. I felt something unusual standing there, because I was at Nicola's home, and I was his, simple, tangly-haired, surging inside with his beautiful energy. I couldn't be placed, not clearly a stranger or friend, rich or poor, awkward or deliberate.

Somehow Patrick had turned the conversation to great detectives of history. So that's what charms these people, I thought. He talked about Vidocq, the first private eye. He'd disguised himself so completely as a nun, while fleeing unrelated trouble, that he'd been assimilated by a group of nuns and had to learn the prayers on the fly.

"Everyone knows that spies are more trouble than they're worth," a tall man said. He had golden curls around his ears. "They get too caught up in double-crossing."

"Tell that to Gonfa SpA," one of the women said, with a look around. She wore a black dress with a wide white collar.

"I wouldn't depend on spies for facts," Patrick said, smiling at the woman, "but for the uncovering of networks, obviously."

Now Iris came to the circle. I wondered if she'd heard. The party stepped back to let her in, guiltily.

I wished I could be dazzled just by being able to talk to her. In college, on the literary magazine, I would have traced her path around a party with my heart beating faster. I also wished I could feel nothing but *energy*, as at the first party. But hatred flared up in me.

"Would you like to see the art?" she said to me.

I pointed at myself, surprised.

"Nicola told me you are a painter," she said.

"Not really," I said. At my side, Patrick was taking down the number of the woman with the wide white collar.

I followed Iris. We passed Nicola as we went out the door into the cool darkness. I could tell from the angle of his face that he saw us go out together. I wondered whether he was nervous to let me be alone with her. I wondered if he trusted me to be entirely discreet.

I wasn't interested in dominating her or putting doubt into her or having any kind of emotional impact on her, which would be inefficient, and possibly cruel, and anyway, people had always confused me and I was the opposite of Nicola and had no capacity for subtle emotional influence over others.

Rather what I wanted was: clues that in some small way I knew Nicola better than she did. Clues that in some way I gave him something she couldn't. I knew in most ways I was inferior to her, but I wanted to find one thing I could claim as my own. A characteristic, or mode of thought, or attitude I would know was mine.

I also wanted to learn whatever I could about Nicola, especially how his father was, and what had happened with his mother, and the evil he had inherited and maybe admired. Though the real mystery of Nicola had never been the family or the father or Iris or even the frequency, the coherence of our interactions—but the soul, which she would not speak about.

We walked up a flight of stairs and entered the third floor's long dark hall. My ears rang from the quiet. She pressed a button on one of those complicated light switches and turned on the picture lights and spotlights. The paintings were like the windows out.

On a plinth, spotlit, there was a Roman glass vial, rainbowed with age. On the wall, in tiny brackets, there was a fragment of an Etruscan vase, a black horse on red with a blaring white eye. There was a prato on parchment, an inky night with wild trees and dark-green foliage and a meadow of clawed red and blue flowers. She said it was by Buonaguida. A tangle of women, various portraits. The more recent art, the kinetic modernism and the fluffy little still life, interested me much less.

She told me the most significant object—and yes, I could tell immediately, she didn't even have to say—was the pointy-topped medieval painting, Madonna and Child, scrawny sophisticated Christ and his mother, who overlaid her mourning with a tight smile, on a gold ground.

I hated looking at this. It broke my remove: I was in love with their beautiful lives.

I blinked away tears. It was dark enough I didn't think she'd notice. "Whose taste is all this?" I said.

"Nicola's family's," she said. "It goes back." She had such a kind voice.

"Nicola never says much about his family."

She didn't respond. When I looked at her, as though to see if she'd heard me, she said, "Mmm."

"What are they like?" I wondered how much I could ask before I started to seem impolite. I let her silence go as long as I could. She defeated me. "Well, I love their taste in art," I said.

"Nicola likes art too," she said, "but you'd have to come to Italy to see what he's collected." This was a gesture of generosity.

"Nicola seems like a very—exciting person—to be married to," I said, trying to let my tone fall midway between enthusiastic and skeptical, so that she could choose a direction.

"We've known each other," she said, with deadening politesse, "quite a while."

I wondered if she knew about the gondola lift. I might have met him before she had. "And I would have liked to know him longer!" I said. I always tended to this sycophantic, coaxing conversation style. I disliked myself, but at least, acting like myself, I'd reduced the variables. "I'm glad my boss Patrick brought us together, I've really enjoyed talking to him about art."

She nodded. We were now at the end of the hall. I wanted to see what was behind each door but I knew I couldn't ask. I didn't know who made the last painting, and Iris didn't say. It was an inscrutable contemporary piece. It looked like a black lake of melting ice.

"How long do you plan to be in New York?" I said.

"We barely spoke while he was here without me," she said. First I was distracted by her tone, which was as mannered as it had been all evening. "All winter. It's very odd. If he doesn't talk to me—I'm worried," she said, "it's something with his father." Her voice was so very polite I wondered if there was some etiquette reason for telling me this. Then I felt a quick shot of danger. Was she confiding in me?

"What's with his father?" I asked, trying to assemble my face into simple, first-order concern.

She gave me a long look. She was clearly making some kind of calculation I didn't understand. "I'm worried it might be something with his father," she said.

Did she want to mention it to me because I was outside her social circle, a nonentity who could be as consoling as a priest? Was she envious of his father—as I was—in some way? For being in the center of his dark heart, the black hell-flames we couldn't help him with, we couldn't experience—or the shaping passion of his life?

Was she guessing that I was more interested in his father than my tone let on? Or was she using father as a stand-in for "another woman"? Or was she guessing that I—with my long loose hair, in my long loose black silk dress that was so unfortunately conductive of the room's chill, in my boys' oxfords, with a face I knew to be almost but not entirely guileless—was she guessing that I was the cause of his lack of communication?

"He has a difficult relationship with his father," she said.

"Oh," I said. "That's a shame."

"Nicola told me he was very sick," she said. "He said that starting on the Befana he had the flu and it lasted a few weeks. Did you know that?"

Now I knew why she was telling me this. She was trying to see if I could confirm his story. I was intensely aware of my face. I wished I could tell her that I knew he loved her most of all. He loved her more than anyone. I was envious of that love. She didn't have to worry. "That's a shame," I said again. He had never, of course, had the flu. He'd been in startling health as he'd taken a girl with a dagger necklace in front of me, and then made me senseless and struck my face.

"So, Nora," she said, "was he sick?" I couldn't believe she'd ask again so openly. Maybe she thought I was dense. Maybe she was just desperate for me to reassure her.

And despite the stakes, it was difficult to avow it. It was difficult to devote myself to the lie. I wanted her to know. But my answer had to banish all nuance. "My understanding is, he got very sick," I said.

Now she was uncomfortable. She'd gotten awfully close to the outer limit of a suggestion of an accusation, and she and I both knew that I was aware enough of it that she had to apologize or otherwise settle the emotional score. This is what I read in her nervous look. She had lost her sense of self and broken with her training, and owed me. For my part, I'd made great progress at being so embedded in a lie that I forgot I was lying.

She was blinking and suddenly the air felt hot and I had the sense I was intruding on something and even then it took me a moment to notice she was actually crying. Now

I realized how very concerned she must have been, about Nicola being out of touch. Had I been convincing in my lie? Or had I made her even more suspicious?

"I never cry," she said quickly, which made me feel pity— though also now I could see that she was a real person with the ability to break, which I'm sure Nicola loved. Her tears suggested the same turbulent passion that he'd described to me. He must have loved smashing down her walls. *Not in it for the kissing* . . . I imagined his hand on her lovely neck.

"I cry all the time," I said, trying to be sisterly and permissive. She wept silently for another minute. "You must have been extremely worried when you didn't hear from him," I ventured. I still had some hope of getting more out of her, about Nicola and his father and me.

"He has a lot of secrets."

"Okay, I don't know," I said.

"Don't you work in business intelligence?" She looked up at me, her face sharp again, her eyes ugly.

"I'm an admin," I said.

She walked away from me, back up the hall. "Do you know what's happening with Gonfa SpA?" Her voice was loud. I wondered what was behind the doors, if anyone could hear us. A dozen Matteo Cremas, waiting in their coats.

"No," I said. "I barely know what the company does."

"We're expanding," Iris said. "The infrastructure in your country is falling apart." She stepped back to the medieval painting. She ran her fingertips across the lower part of the frame, as if testing for dust. She adjusted the corner slightly. "I have to stop touching this. Vittorio alarmed it," she said.

"It's Nicola's dad's business?" I wondered if she would pretend not to hear me. "Do you work for Nicola's dad yourself?"

"We're all involved," Iris said. "Are you involved?"

"Of course not," I said.

"Nicola constantly speaks about wanting to kill his father," Iris said. "Kill his business, that is. I want you to know that that would be very disruptive and you would never see him again. His interest in revenge is very distressing to me."

"That's understandable," I said.

"I don't like that he seems to be using you to gather information for his takeover."

"Oh, Patrick is very good at not being used," I said. But this hurt. If Nicola was using us for business reasons, he was being very inefficient about it, but I wanted our relationship, as constrained as it was, to come from reckless sincerity.

"I don't appreciate you forcing me to speculate like this." She paused. "You and Patrick."

I felt relieved she'd added Patrick. "You're trying to prevent him from hanging out with us? Trust me, he's opaque," I said.

"He's probably lying to you," she said. "He's a liar." She lifted her face and then her eyes to mine. This gesture seemed to make a clashing sunk sound like the out-of-tune bells in the university belfry that I'd once learned to ring. "You're not married, are you?" she said.

I felt she was trying to figure out how old I was, and whether I was single because I didn't desire anyone, or because no one desired me. I shook my head.

"You'll see when you're married," she said, which struck me as delicately mean, "that most of the time, closeness comes from negotiating boundaries on your solitude." She looked back at the painting, giving me permission to examine the side of her beautiful face. "It's about learning to live with another limited person," she said. "You think the work is the joining. No, I can tell you. The work is the boundaries. It's what ends up consuming all your time, and your attention, and then, at a certain point, your interest."

She was digging up the volcano in the field. I felt the

opposite of the Federica feeling. I wanted to diminish what had driven her to speak this way, pedagogically, magniloquently, and I wanted to bury it down again. Was she attempting to tell me that she was always trying to free herself of Nicola? No—I knew she loved him. There was no one like him. I thought it was more likely that she was trying to free herself of *cares about* Nicola. Trying to free herself from worrying about the center and his relentless interest in other people, all people. Or maybe, by witnessing her tears, I'd hurt her pride, and she was trying to say that her crying over her husband's absence was what I myself would come to know when I was in her position, which was clearly the better position. She could also be communicating that she was trying to find herself again; maybe he'd dissolved her as he had dissolved me. Or maybe it was that she'd come up in a world where she had so much control over others, but Nicola was her equal, and maybe when she said solitude she just meant the state wherein she didn't have to answer to anyone. Whatever this speech meant to her, I could tell that the emotion behind it could destroy the only thing in my life that mattered. If she asked for more of him, he would go.

I told myself that she was hurt—she didn't know what she was saying. She *couldn't* know. She could suspect, but he was superhuman in his caution and would never tell.

CHAPTER 31

We returned to the party, descending from the dark chill of the third-floor gallery to the convivial world of the living room, which was hot now, scented with smoke and espresso. The little porcelain cups with their stained interiors stood all over the banquettes and mantles. The velvet curtains billowed back from the windows and the guests had formed smaller defined clusters after the evenly spaced tension of the party's first phase.

I immediately exited and locked myself in the bathroom. I sat on the heated floor.

What had I learned? Only that he had been inconsiderate of her, for a period, and more inconsiderate of her than she was used to, maybe more than she'd ever experienced, which meant that for a period which might now be past I had been his true focus, I had held his attention—completely.

And I learned that she feared him taking over the business. I wondered if she didn't trust Nicola to safely pull it off and feared Vittorio's wrath. I wondered if she feared Vittorio's violence. It was possible that she feared change, change that would take Nicola even further from her, if he became embroiled in a hostile takeover and had even less time for her. And in that case, as she said, I would never see him again. This affair required everything to stay in suspension, gravid with irresolution. I needed to be close to Nicola, but never close enough to see the evil that might cause me to flee or, more likely, plummet into self-destruction. Nicola needed to stick with his family and live in his father's house, never close enough to provoke the violence. I was his counterbalance of goodness, which allowed him to justify whatever he was up to, and he redeemed our relationship by keeping it suspended from all the life that threatened constantly at its walls.

He knocked on the door. I could tell it was his knock from its confidence. "Nora?" he said. "Nora?"

I didn't want to answer. I felt his whirling chaos, the golden storm of his intensity, the same gold as behind the Madonna and Child, the heaven they knew, that forced them out of their panel and into me, like incubi, and possessed me with desolation.

"Come out," he said. I unlocked the door, and in an instant he pushed it into me. In the split second it took me to realize that his arms carrying me, a sensation from decades ago, had caused this pressure on my chest and the dizzying motion, he'd already placed me down in a dim room and shut the door.

"What did Iris say to you?" he said. His eyes were foil.

I had no idea what she might have said to him, and so I didn't know how to bring him down from this chaotic urgency.

"She asked me if you got sick over the winter—"

"All I want to know is whether my father is angry with me. Because he doesn't communicate with me directly." I had my back against the wall, and he was close to me. I could feel and taste his heat.

"No, it was all about her feelings," I said, angry with her. "She started crying—"

"Did she mention my father?"

"I guess she thought he was preventing you from talking to her."

He gave a single bitter laugh. "What exactly did she say?"

"She said you had a difficult relationship. That's all—"

"Nothing about him knowing my plans?"

I shook my head. He was still so close to me, his body in that magnetized space where non-contact is still contact.

"Are you and your father not in touch?"

"Well, I've been busy," he said.

"With a takeover?"

"No," he said. "With you."

"I don't want to get between you and your father."

"Yes, you do," he said. "I'm just not sure how much he will allow."

"You're an adult," I said.

"Don't you love your parents?" he said.

But ever since they'd caught my self-harm, there had been shame and mortification in our always unspoken and modest love—a betrayal I could not repay, an incomprehensibility they could not right. The three of us lived in states of gentle distraction in the heat and hurricanes. "Of course I love them," I said. "I have to tell you, Iris thinks you were sick over the winter, and I said yes, you were sick."

He nodded. "You have to be extremely careful with her," he said. His voice was impossibly compelling.

"I think I was."

"You were." A wave of reassurance came over me, along with a pain that related to my expectation that he would now withdraw. The interrogation was over, and we would return to the party.

"She said"—I started. I was not going to say, *She said you were a liar.* "She said she doesn't like Patrick and me spending time with you."

"I see," he said, calmer now.

"Are you working with your father, or against him?" I said. "Because your wife wants you to stick with your dad, right?" Only in this heightened moment could I let my doubt take over like this. I did not like the way Iris had treated me.

"I think you were perfect," he said. "But you know you can't talk to me about those things."

"Remember that man who talked to me in the park?" I said. "Sometimes I see other men like him, I think. Does your dad send them to see what you're doing?" *Are you going to kill him? You used to want to. Patrick thinks you want to. Your wife thinks you want to. Are you going to kill him?*

He stepped back, releasing me. "No," he said. "Nora. My father has never cared to know what I do each day."

"How can that be true?" I said. But what I meant was, *Why do you sound sad about that? Don't you want his trust? Don't you want your independence?*

"You've never met anyone like my father," he said. "He is deadly confident. And people are always trailing us. Sometimes a whole flock of followers." When he talked to me I felt he'd punctured me with a long syringe and was very slowly pressing down the plunger. I turned to look at the dim room he'd brought me to. Something small and red glinted in the shadows. "Nora," he said, and I looked back to him.

I asked him to kiss me, and he did.

"Iris is skeptical of you," I said. "At the moment."

"I need to pay sole attention to her for a while," he said.

I knew he was right, but it hit me like an unforeseen tragedy. "Does she think that we are—" I started.

"No," he said. "She doesn't think that."

"Nicola," I said, "You told me you love intimacy but I am still confused all the time about how you feel."

"I don't feel that much," he said. And now he leaned over into me fully. "I need to be better with her, that's all," he said. "You did a good job, Nora. She likes you."

He spoke in and kissed my ear, controlling me in every way, hand and voice and body, legion. He covered my mouth with his.

He said that I had to accept the constraints on what we were doing together. He said that the constraints made it stranger, always unstable, never transactional, never enough. The public couldn't know about us, our friends couldn't know, the very closest people in the world couldn't know. It was just about each other. We could max out on all the available axes.

You make me happy, he said, so happy, so happy. Happy: so simple, but the word made me want to cry with its grandeur. He said I had to rejoin soon and tucked his shirt in carefully.

"What if I leave her, Nora?" he said.

"I can't believe you're saying that."

"I shouldn't," he said. "I may not be." He put his hand to his forehead. An expression of distress on his face. He shook his head and left the room.

I couldn't throw off the feeling that we were in the effervescent high, fast water before the cataract. I could hear the thunder and feel the vapor from that fall which we were being dragged toward in our happiness.

CHAPTER 32

I couldn't believe he'd suggested leaving her. The thought enraged me. It was, I thought, a manipulation, a way of getting more time and patience out of me. Because now he was out of touch, taking care of her.

I couldn't imagine being with him as his partner—a life of only joy.

The sadness affected my way of walking. I became slow and rigid. I didn't care to look at anything or to lift my head. This affair was not going to change. Stopping it could release me. Improve me, fix my ethics, allow me independence.

I added dozens of potential texts to my phone note, trying to offload my all-consuming desire to communicate with him.

I'd been in a period of total madness. How could I have lost touch so completely? I'd let him yank me away from myself.

I'd been kind and considerate and patient to try to ensure that he wouldn't get tired of me. The trick, I'd thought, was not to demand too much. No, no, no, being a mistress is no good. All you are is a pleasant padding to someone else's life.

I thought about him at every second and there was no chance that he was thinking of me. *The constraints make it stranger, always unstable, never transactional, never enough.* He'd said that. It now struck me as totally vacuous.

Enraged, I pictured myself as the woman falling over the railing in the ex-voto, or the woman with the sparks flying out from the stove. The saint's golden corner vacated. Without the saint it's just a scene of danger, and not worth celebrating. Without the saint it's just an evil little depiction of someone else's misfortune.

I wanted to write: "Your life would be so much better if I were dead." I wanted to correct it: "No, I don't even have that much impact." I imagined him writing, "Be fair, be reasonable, I have always treated you honorably, I know this is difficult but you've always known the limits." To that I would say: "If these feelings were mutable, if I could shift them along lines of *reasonable* and *fair*, then believe me, I would mutate them to not like you anymore." I imagined him responding, "I know how hard it is to be in your position, I admire your fortitude, and I miss you every day"— it would be very Nicola to inflect with kindness—"However, what would be best for you is for me to step back." And this I could not take.

I could have texted him but I refused to. For the first time I felt kinship with Federica during the time that she'd ignored me. Maybe I was like her: sullen, self-blocking. But there was no other way to preserve myself.

And I'd idiotically destroyed a relationship for this. I looked at Leif's Twitter, and looked at the profiles of the people whose tweets he'd liked. He was smart, and he was interacting with people I'd never heard of, and they were all being smart and living their productive lives of social impact. I knew that if it weren't for my actions I'd be in our high clean apartment instead of my flowery linoleum-floored isolation chamber, and I'd be in bed with him, not worried about money, listening to him breathe and feeling total safety and tranquility.

I dreamed nondimensional dreams where Nicola was

striding in and out, unable to hear me as I screamed and threw tantrums and begged for him to listen. He was running to take flights, in my dreams, to the farthest places on earth. Once I dreamed that he was present and attentive and I was asleep until I came, and when I woke up I sobbed with my face against my hands against the wall.

Three to five times a day I wished Iris dead, which wasn't that many, in my opinion.

Meantime the witch hazel was tasseling its branches in the park. I attempted to bury myself in work, and in Patrick, and in planning for his baby. Patrick was my new object of devotion. There was something disgusting about how mediated this kind of contact with Nicola was. I felt like a starving person holding a plastic fruit. I didn't mention Nicola to him. I wanted an opening.

Though eventually, at work, after the morning conference call, I asked him if he ever heard from Nicola and he said no. "Me neither," I said. "Why do you think he dropped away like that?"

"Sometimes, people just get busy," Patrick said. He didn't know how comforting he was. Out of touch with Patrick, too.

Was Nicola trying to give me space? Was he angry? Was he responding to Iris's paranoia, cutting off Patrick too so she wouldn't think they were plotting together? In any case, it meant life was not carrying on exactly as usual.

A NEW SET of emotions began to manifest. These emotions were all variations on worthlessness. There was no comfort in having been temporarily attractive to him. There were many, many women like that in his life. I'd expected to be able to take some lasting pleasure in having gotten him to commit adultery. But now it just made my pulling away more hopeless. I had never laid any track for this kind of relationship. What was its value? There were no norms I could expect him or myself to adhere to, and no norms against which I could measure our violations. I knew there was no reason for him to carry it forward, to be dependable, to treat me humanely.

It was good that it was over, because the things that he stirred up in me were too strong. The danger had come so near. The danger of losing my own life in some way, because of my own disproportionate and terrible decisions, or because of the closeness, the casual passing relationship with death in his own family, which made everything seem to happen on the edge of a grave. I could, I realized, make good on my longtime wish to jump off a balcony. I thought of my parents. I could never do that to them. Yet his mother had died—these things happened in his family. What did the Gonfalons care if their schemes killed other people? They had already lived the worst.

It was over. I repeated these words to myself, hoping to kill Nicola off, and I would cry to myself, *It's over, it's over,* the emotions passing over me in long, lapping strokes, like a solvent-heavy brush painting a sky. I didn't believe it was over. It would have been good to believe it was over.

FORSYTHIA. SNOWDROPS. I avoided Tribeca. I went to the park at sunset and saw a red-tailed hawk. High shoulder silhouette. A towering sunset over Belvedere castle. A nightmare about his mother dying, stiff and blue and moaning. Those pages in *Madame Bovary* were so revolting I had to skim them, and I could never open the book again.

There was a blizzard. The stores and streets might shut down but the parks just couldn't. I put on my down coat from the Alps—zipper broken now, candy from Federica walks still in the pockets—and I went into the white and discovered New York like Turin, that hadn't been seen and turned over and assimilated into common knowledge. Only a blizzard could have this effect, could dominate the city and force everyone inside, then drive everything to a halt.

What was he doing with Iris? Were they in town now, watching the blizzard come down around the conjoined house? Were they fucking on the bed in the room with the white carpet, were they out in the back garden among the white statues with their snow cloaks?

Snow blasted in under my AC and melted on my floor. Snow had blown all the way down onto the subway platforms. I'd never seen that before. I went to the park between the Brooklyn and Manhattan Bridges. Total solitude and the snow plummeting and plunging horizontally. Even in the city, you feel like this kind of weather can kill you.

I stared at the motionless carousel horses. Their eyes like the eye of the Etruscan horse on the fragment of pottery in his father's long hall. The snow was sharp in my eyes and mixed with my tears. Nicola had said: *Opening yourself to the vagaries of will-lessness.*

Sometimes the cold made everything fragile, and even the air would break. Other times, like in this blizzard, the cold made everything fleshy and sticky. The cold beat against me in great hard thwacks. I was about at the limit of misery and intensity, and I felt almost like myself. I was worried that my eyes would be permanently damaged from the flakes. The snow distracted me with its fury until at last I was subsumed. Only this killed my mulling on Iris and Nicola. The bridges were almost invisible halfway across the East River, and Manhattan was hidden in white.

The boardwalk of Brooklyn Bridge was immensely slippery. Because I was alone on the bridge, it was deprived of the squeak and rumble from many feet moving on the planks. The city was barely visible through the high cables. The East River was blackly eating up the snow. Careful, careful, careful, I whispered to myself. Halfway across the bridge I panicked for a moment that I would not be able to continue.

On the other side of the bridge I found a coffee shop that was open. Here the men in long dark coats reappeared, some looking at me, making me wonder. I felt I had nerve damage from the cold. I smelled like wet feathers and wool, like a chimera.

PATRICK HELPED ME choose photos for a dating app. I hated swiping, and he did it for me, amused, curious about being single in those days. He'd been married for years. We went out together to look at cribs and baby monitors. It was easy to be devoted to him; it only became ghostly if I looked at it too long.

Using an app, I went on a date at Monkey Bar with an architect who told me about walking through rooms he designed. I imagined how Nicola would talk about it—Nicola would be excited by experiencing conceptualization, design, and then realization in such elaborate physical ways. But the architect told me that walking through the rooms he'd designed was always (I held my breath) a letdown. That was all. A letdown. He wouldn't expand on it. I kept noticing the other people in the bar, who were all much more beautiful and happy than us.

Every part of the city begged to be conveyed to him—the woman I saw in a religious rapture, falling and lifted by many hands in the window of a second-floor church in Prospect Lefferts Gardens; the *brioche alla crema* with scent of almond and lemon that filled my head with the *giorni della merla* in Turin; the breeze from the south that brought forth the green fingers of daffodils; the attendant and the blind man at MoMA wearing gloves and slowly running their hands over the rough black surface of Picasso's bronze goat. I needed to tell him, tell him, make real all of this through him, who was the only satisfying witness and the creator of the real.

I looked up Meister Eckhart. *Essence alone satisfies and God keeps on withdrawing, farther and farther away, to arouse the mind's zeal and lure it on to follow and finally grasp the true good that has no cause.* It didn't mean much to me. It meant, be satisfied when you can't understand.

I dreamed of that tall red glass, the cursed goblet, Nicola had called it, filled with mulberry-colored poison, lightweight as alizarin crimson in the tube. Vittorio held it to the lips of his wife. What had she done? Did she defy him? Did she take Nicola from him? Did she like when he held her wrists until her hands were cold?

The snow kept coming down. I walked with my space heater to the bedroom, the kitchen, the shower. Then one day it was warm and rainy. My face was covered in rough pink scabs and I didn't know why. Everywhere I looked was hell.

So that had been Nicola.

DURING THIS PERIOD, Federica added me back as a friend on Facebook. I saw she'd messaged me. I opened it. "I've been wanting to check in on you," she'd written in Italian. My eyes darted over the message and took it all in at once like a thunderclap. "Sometimes I think about that year. I was thinking about that self-harm stuff you used to do, do you still do it? You seemed to really need it. I hope you are okay now."

My feeling of humiliation was so complete it felt like danger.

Then below that, she had written that she would be happy to speak on the phone any time. But no, I could never do that now. She wanted to press in close and scrutinize me and wake things that should be left lying.

CHAPTER 33

March. This time, for the first time, he broke our silence. When I saw the phone light up with the peasant in the field I dropped it. I let it ring through on the ground. What was I going to do with this? I stared out of my foggy windows at Skillman Street and he called twice more. I felt like a sword swallower, more blades widening my throat. Now what, now what. I told myself: Don't respond to this provocation. Don't go see him. What's the best that could happen? You've sunk the time into losing him. You want to throw away that hard work? Don't text him.

I texted him, "What do you want?"

He said he would see me later, if not tonight then tomorrow. Now at last the world began to open to me, though I still felt the aftershocks of desolation. Pink and teal sunset piled up then fell over Skillman Street.

He came over that night. I was asleep when he called.

It was three in the morning when he appeared on my stoop, dark and glittering on the still, empty street. I'd never received a visitor at this hour. Nicola always had some new physical limit, some challenge for me, and he did it without thinking, a product of his relentlessness, arrogance, and obsession. "Look how warm and sleepy you are," he said. "Are you feeling better?" I followed him up the hollow stairs.

"Please, Nicola," I said. My voice sounded choked up. I hadn't expected that.

"What's wrong?" he said, turning my face toward him.

I didn't want to pretend everything was free and easy and comfortable, because it wasn't. Yet I also didn't want to make him stop seeing me. I wanted him to understand the stakes of what I was giving to him—all my trust, all my shame, all my senses. After all this time, I was ceding again. It was a very sensitive edge I was asking for. I was asking to be overtaken.

"What is it?" he said, undressing. His belt clinked. He laid his shirt over a chair.

"I'm shy," I said.

"Stay there," he said, and went to wash. When he exited the room, my soul reentered my body. I began to cry.

Now he returned to me, it was amazing how everything about him could break, like re-breaking a poem, into kindness. "I am susceptible, you know. To missing you."

He came into bed and we lay in the silence for a time. I relaxed into his heat. He began to touch my cheek and hair. I stayed very quiet because I couldn't bear for him to stop.

Why do I want to hurt you? he said, in his genteel, hypnotic voice. My room was black and the walls rippled. But I do. He touched me scrupulously. He was preparing me.

Beg me to hit you. I was sinking with desire. Beg me to hit you. I did, and he struck me hard.

I gasped; there was a moment when it was too hard and everything heightened, like the volume was all the way up, the heat all the way on, and everything got extremely still.

Then he was sweet and a little high, his breath entering my ear, the tenderest touch. The sky began to lift.

I didn't feel I had imbibed his vicious attention. Rather it was a moment like when we'd slept together, and he'd clutched me tighter and tighter: I contained something of his that was unguarded.

I BLUNDERED INTO the kitchen. Restless, swarming predawn navy, and the beautiful, musical fall of the droplets in the sink.

I felt that the beads all lay scattered in a heap and he drew them up and showed that they were on an almost invisible line. The happy times were the times when I could remember the past without anguish. The feeling of morning blowing all the way in from Italy, the sound of Fede's footsteps on the quays. The fountain, the embassy. And even the banyan trees, the sugar skies and ocean of Sarasota. When the happy past moments still felt true, then I could be complete.

I loved the bright bottles in the fridge, the golden light on pink juice and berries and dill. I loved even the cold linoleum on my feet, I loved shivering. I loved fumbling for the golden doorknob and letting myself into the room where he was.

I brought him winter strawberries, overdark and over-seeded from their long trip, and I kissed him on the head and the ear and then lay next to him and drank in his beautiful profile, his endless charm. He lay close to the window with an arm behind his head. It was such a gift to have him here in my bed to talk to, and again I felt the drug of consorting with him, the feeling that he knew me so well that I couldn't possibly worry about how I appeared, or whether I was behaving correctly. Yet I couldn't dispel the terrible dark undernote, the timpani rumble. The morning was beauty and calm overlaying an endless sadness and loneliness. He was responsible for both. The palliative and the cause.

"You're so good," he said. "I used to think you were, but now I know you're blazingly good."

I asked why.

"You've taken this on so seamlessly," he said. "You're so

independent." He became warmer, softer. "I could never do this with anyone else. I trust you completely, with no qualifications."

This was exactly the impression I'd wanted to give him. I wanted to be dependable and self-contained. The constraints made it never transactional, never enough, he'd said. We could max out on all the available axes, he'd said. He knew I wouldn't call him in the middle of the night, or come knocking on his door rabid and sobbing, or tell Patrick, or write a first-person essay or anything like that. I'd succeeded. Still, his words wounded me. How could he truly believe it was seamless, and that I was independent? How was he unable to tell that I'd spent nights in agony remembering him and feeling, after I'd attempted to stop it, that I was inadequate and disgusting and stupid? But if I were honest about all that, he'd end it. He'd say, *I can't hurt you like that.*

He thought I had a confident, imperturbable core. I couldn't tell if he was incorrect, or justifying his own behavior, or correct. Now that I was with him it was correct. The saint was back to watch me.

The sky was royal blue now.

"I never want to see Kara," I said.

"Who's Kara?"

"That girl you picked up."

"You don't have to see her."

"I don't want to see anyone else with you."

"What do you want, Nora?"

"I want to meet your family," I said.

"My father?"

"Anyone," I said.

"Why?"

"I want to know you," I said.

"You will never meet my father," he said.

I remembered the old waiter in the French restaurant, almost stumbling from table to table in his suit.

"You could meet my aunt," he said finally. "My mother's sister."

"I would like that," I said.

"When she comes back to the US, we can do it," he said. "Her name is Violetta. The backgammon aunt, remember? She's bad at games and good at getting her fortune told. I think she dislikes my father nearly as much as I do."

I kissed his eyes. I asked him how Iris was. "She made me extremely angry," he said. "The angriest I've been in years. I'd forgotten what it felt like."

"What did she do?"

He shook his head. "My father got to Iris," Nicola said. "My father has always approved. I sort of need my dad's approval to do all things. I do respect him. I can't imagine who I would be without him. Maybe far better. Who knows."

She must have been trying to convince him to stick with his father's business. I still believed he was faithful to his father, even as he longed for independence, which would only be possible after his father's death. Iris must have demanded an end to his ambivalence. She was so spoiled, haranguing him on the path he was taking anyway. But he could also have hated the way she got so upset with his absence. I imagined he wanted to feel that he was making the right choices, even though he'd betrayed her. Maybe guilt had made him angry like this. Or maybe he disapproved of her questioning me in the hall, and crying to me.

I was pleased about their conflict.

"Did you—tell her about this?"

"Do you want me to?" he said.

I didn't react to that. I was thinking.

"It wouldn't destroy our marriage, you know." Immediately

I was sad. He turned onto his side, lifted himself to recline on one elbow. "Respond without fantasizing an insult," he said, and reached his hand inside my nightgown. His hand was cold. My heart began to beat. He touched me so gently. He always knew how to inflect. "I can tell her if it is important to you to be acknowledged, and reckoned with." He felt the form of my waist and ran his fingertips over my collarbone. What came to mind, in a dreamy way, were valves opening. Sea creatures unfurling their bioluminous, rainbow tendrils.

"No," I said, "I don't want you to." There was more power in the secret. "What did she do that made you so angry?" I said, from within the shelter of his exquisite touch.

"I can't get into it," he said. "I don't want to make her your enemy."

I wished I could make him massively angry the way that she had. This ferocious man, making him angry—can you imagine—with impunity because you know he'll always love you. Making him angry so he'll put the center on you.

Now the sky was glazed with light.

"She said you're a liar," I said.

"I love lying," he said. "Did I make that a secret?"

"When you said I reminded you of your own first love, who did you mean?" He'd told me that when we'd searched for Campari in the basement. "Was Iris your first love?"

"I don't remember saying that," he said. "I suppose I meant my mother."

"What was she like?" I said, barely breathing.

"I don't—" he started. He looked at my face. "She closed nothing off," he said. "When it came to me, at least. Oh, Nora, you'll make such a good mother someday. Once you forget about me."

I shook my head. "I'll never be in love with anyone else."

He put his hand against his eyes. "Please don't say that," he said.

"I just felt like saying it once." Because it was true.

He turned and pressed his lips to my temple.

"She died when you were little, right?" I said.

"I was ten," he said. "I used to imagine I could talk to her. I'd ask her for a sign, like a cup of water delivered to my bedtime table, and she would deliver it while I was sleeping. Of course it was my father. He used to move objects around in the house to encourage the delusion. He wanted me to believe she wasn't really gone."

"I'm so sorry," I said.

"You know, when you're in that state you'll take any sign at all," he said. "He meant well." All I did was uncertainly stroke his head and cheek as though he were a baby. It was clear to me now that Nicola did not think his father had committed the murder. "The problem with all that meaning well," he said with his eyes closed, "is that maybe it makes him a little random in his actions." We may have been asleep for a little while.

After a time, I said, "Federica messaged me."

"Saying what?" he said.

I explained I hadn't responded to the message yet because I was too anxious. He made me open it on my phone and we read it together. I was embarrassed to watch him read my cheery message, "Hello, my dear sister!" I had sent that when I was out of touch with him, and desperate to know why she had once said his father was evil. Then her comment on self-harm, and the invitation to speak to each other. I asked Nicola what he thought the tone was.

"Normal," he said. "Friendly."

"But we last spoke almost fifteen years ago, and she hated me."

He said, "You should definitely talk to her."

"Why?" I said, surprised. He was so decisive. "To understand what happened between us?" But I didn't want to know what Federica thought of my behavior on the day of the gondola lift.

"Because she liked you a lot," he said. "Be nice."

"Were you thinking that when you texted me in the summer?" I said. "'Be nice?'"

"Yes," he said. He took my phone and typed "Excellent, I'll schedule something soon," and sent it.

"Is that why you keep seeing me?"

"Of course not," he said. The sun had risen, and made a soft pink square on my wall. He drew the shades: a deep indulgence. In my room, it was night again. My walls were floral lungs.

"You believe it will give people purpose to follow you, and that they should follow you because your morals are the right ones." I said this with affection.

"That is what I inherited from my father," he said.

I asked him to tell me about his father. What his father had done, and why Nicola had called him "not a human."

"You've asked me that before," he said.

"Why don't you tell me?"

He gave me a long look. I was trying to show him that I would be receptive, that it would help him to tell me.

To my surprise, he answered. He spoke in Italian, and didn't explain why he'd switched. This was the second time we conversed in Italian. Hearing the language again was like swallowing a spiny thing—the discomfort, but the weird, uncontrollable bodily confidence. Each word came out unfamiliar, and then zapped me with recognition.

He said that he believed his father had—he paused—put out hits (he said just that part in English) on business rivals.

I said the first Italian phrase that came to mind, *"Che paura,"* how frightening.

"It is an immensely important part of his view, that life is unreliable. He made me learn this too."

Learn what? My mind filled. That his father had killed men himself? That his father had killed men in front of Nicola? "What does that mean?" I said. Partly because it was one of the only things I could remember how to say. *Cosa vuol dire?*

He responded that it was common in his father's industry. "Honor is important to him," said Nicola.

"I don't know," I said, trying to conceal my disgust. Another easy phrase to remember. But after I said it, he shifted, in irritation, I expected, and I wondered if I was being too judgmental. I'd opened this conversation because I wanted to care for him, I reminded myself. So be careful.

"People tend to think life is sacred, and that's why we don't kill," said Nicola. "However, my father thinks that people have gotten it precisely backward, and that his actions increase the sanctity of life."

"Did he make you participate?" Impossible to keep my voice even.

"In all things, always. As all fathers do."

I imagined Nicola as a boy. The back of his head, as he watched a coffin lower. As he watched a man fall. As he raised the gun himself.

"Are you saying you've killed people?"

He shrugged and said, "Certain things are inexpressible."

I did not like that phrase used here. I did not like it at all. Now it seemed very much like what a murderer would say to make himself feel better. Moral luck, too. Eckhart. His endlessly unfolding flower.

I said I was sorry.

He said that it made him who he was.

"No work is so important that people should die," I said.

He said indeed it was enjoyable, to have a father like this.

I couldn't prevent myself from staring at him. He lay still, looking upward.

I wondered what Patrick would think, and wondering this was an involuntary betrayal that suddenly introduced vast distance between me and Nicola. Patrick was so sure that Nicola was going to betray his father. Patrick was so sure that Nicola was obsessed with vengeance. Was it possible that Nicola was lying to me, bluffing? Was he lying very deeply to himself? Or was he truly dislocated, messed up in a way I could not even see the paths leading to and from? Part of Nicola's appeal was the sense that he could handle anything. Now I wondered if that was an illusion. His father shorted him out.

"I'm not going to let him carry on like this, Nora," he said. In English, he said, "You and Patrick keep wondering. There's nothing to wonder about."

He said it kindly. I realized what I'd done. I'd asked for this.

"I'm sorry," I said. I was shaky.

"It's fine," he said. I wanted to protest. It was only that there was always a duality to his words. As he said, *I'm not going to let him,* his tone, his face on the verge of tears, echoed back, *I love him and will never betray him.* "Everyone keeps wondering and wondering about whether I support my father," he said. "My father, my wife, Patrick. Everyone can tell I'm hiding something. But what I'm hiding is you. You who keep me good, despite everything. I am not in the end capable of perfect artificiality." It was the saddest I'd ever heard his voice.

For a very brief moment, he was flooded with light, and I could see the specificity, the shape underneath—his humanity, that was. His own uncertainty about what he had inherited, and the predicaments he found himself in, and the love that he had once convinced himself was unfaltering and un-deniable. I thought about how Iris wanted boundaries, how defining the boundaries took all her interest and time. I didn't want them. I wanted to know, I was engulfing and simple. I also chose to stay loyal to a powerful person and embrace the dictates that terrified me. For the first time, I thought, maybe he loves me because I am a witness. He wants someone to see him intimately. It was, I could tell, the first mature thought I had ever had in our affair; it carried the sadness and power of maturity. What Iris could not offer: Witness to his acting away from family. Witness to his straying into another life. In his single betrayal of them all, he wanted to be close.

He kissed me on my face and ear and neck. The sunlight through the blinds striped us and my eyes were dry with fatigue.

CHAPTER 34

I couldn't press him. But this is what he would have said: I love my father and I want to be like him. I don't know how else to be. My father believes that he is above other men. His purposes are worth others' lives. And how can I renounce that? I believe in moral luck, that you can change anyone's moral standing by putting a wire in their neck. Humans really are that slippery. Where else, beyond my father's world, are the stakes so high, the feelings private, raw, forbidden, unassimilated?

A FEW WEEKS later it was April, the star magnolias were just unfurling, and we were going to meet his aunt Violetta. In the late afternoon, I was sitting on the couch in the striped room in Nicola's house. He texted me that he'd come as soon as he could, but it might be an hour, and then we would go to a bar. A maid in a pearl gray dress let me in. I should read, he texted.

I sat on the couch. I was far too excited to read. My eyes slipped off the pages. Even my phone was boring. I kept finding myself staring at the mirrored box that held his father's Holy Annunciation badge. *Ordine Supremo della Santissima Annunziata.* I looked it up. The order began in 1362. I stood up—even standing up felt like a violation of Nicola's wishes—and walked over to the sideboard to look at the necklace. Nicola might come in at any moment, I reminded myself, though I was sure I'd hear the door opening.

The pendant was enormous and dented its blue cushion. Three ornate golden knots ringed the scene of Mary kneeling and Gabriel flying down to her. The figures were too small for me to discern their expressions. The Italian nobility was of unknown value. Nobles and royals were no longer recognized by the Republic. Were they a dysfunctional club of fading playboys? Or had they managed to maintain a sense of their history, which was filled with art and political maneuverings that even Patrick would have respected?

By now I was kneeling in front of the mirrored box. I wondered if the faces of Mary and Gabriel would look silly and vulgar to me, or if they were beautifully made. Nicola had certainly held this object; I was sure he'd scrutinized it closely. He would have passed judgment on whether it was interesting as a work of art. And maybe I could have the same discernment. Was there anything left to honor there? Any beauty? Did Nicola love the system, or did he reject it? Was it brave that he lived with his father? Was it appalling?

I just had to hold the badge in my hands and then I'd be able to feel its weight, and smell it, and hold it up to my eyes and examine it. I looked behind me. The room was empty. There were no shadows passing in front of the windows. I lifted the glass lid, reached down and touched the cool gold—

"*Eccomi!*" someone said loudly in the hall, which meant "Here I am." It was not Nicola's voice. I withdrew my hand as though from a flame.

My heart was racing. I darted around the couch and sat down and tried to make my posture look normal. I'd left the glass lid open, I realized.

"*Eccomi,*" he said from the hall.

There was no time to replace the lid. He passed in front

269

of the doorway, and I caught a glimpse of his dark suit and the way he held himself; it could be no one else but Vittorio, so much like Nicola, the same slim, centered body with its overarticulated, elegant hands and arms. A framework of antiquity around him. I didn't know if he'd seen me, or if he was talking to himself, or on the phone. I wondered whether he had some camera pointed toward his badge, or whether I'd tripped a wire touching it. I wanted to run into another room and hide, but I was too frightened to move. I heard him take two steps up the stairs. Then two more steps—but he'd come down; he was at the threshold.

He didn't look at me, but now I knew he'd seen me. "*Sono Vittorio,*" he said, "I am victory!," translating for no one, or for me. I caught the first glimpse of his face. For a moment I was surprised he didn't look just like Matteo Crema. I had begun to think of them as the same.

He took two steps into the room, then two steps back. Two steps forward, then two steps back. It wasn't quite a dance. My body had gone completely stiff, and I could feel a miserable sweat on my hands and neck.

There was no way for me to guess what he might do next. His behavior signaled that there were no limits. He might pull out a gun, or come over to me and hit me, or force me to talk about Nicola. I couldn't guess what sort of safety his family's generations of fortunes could have bought. He could have blackmail on the district attorney, diplomatic immunity. Or maybe he would calm down and play the host.

He took two steps into the room again, bending and bouncing on his knees, and now he lifted his arm and pointed directly at me. I looked him full in the face, which was startlingly young. He was as handsome as Nicola, and wearing a suit just like Nicola's. It was the same horror as turning over a piece of fruit and finding it frothing with ants or white with rot. Something sizzled in his eyes. "We've all

lost—well, nearly all—some of our decorum, haven't we?"
he said. He gestured in the direction of the necklace. He
stepped toward me.

I tried to smile.

"Answer me," he said.

"Yes," I said. "I'm sorry for invading your house, I'll—"

"You like my collar?" he said. "I'll tell you what it means
to me. It means a certain loss. You have to put on an entire
war, to make a point that once could have been made from
one man to another in a quiet room."

I followed his movements. My heart was pounding. Because of his tone, his grievance felt necessary to the point of
sympathetic. He was like Nicola, but he derived the power
not from intelligence and charm.

He walked to the sideboard from which Nicola had once
withdrawn bottles of water, when we'd sat here and listened
to the music and not yet touched. His mood had shifted again;
he opened the doors, behind which I could see glass bottles
and, farther back, something glittering. He muttered in Italian
about a little thing, where *cazzo* was the little thing.

"I have to go," I said. What was the thing, another item of
jewelry, a weapon? That ruby glass with the seahorse stem
was nowhere to be seen.

"Very kind of you," he said, still rummaging in the sideboard with his back to me. He opened each of the ten little
drawers, five on each side, yanking them out so that they
seemed about to fall, these delicate little boxes now splayed
open, each one disappointing him.

I stood up. "Kindly sit down," he said without turning
around. I sat. He began to walk around the room, running
his fingers down the long silk stripes on the walls. I lifted
up my phone. My hands trembled almost too much to press
the right buttons, but I managed to dial Nicola. I turned the
volume all the way down and put the phone against my leg.

I didn't know if he'd answered, and if he had, if he'd be able to hear.

Vittorio sat down in front of me, still looking for something in his mind. He crossed his legs, then crossed them in the other direction, tonguing the inside of his cheek. With a suddenness I recognized from Nicola, I felt his full force of mind startlingly on me, but his eyes hadn't moved; they still mindlessly scanned for whatever he was looking for. "What does Nicola say about me?" he said.

I thought desperately.

"Tell me," said Vittorio, the words falling almost inaudibly. There was a brutal pause, during which he looked over every inch of me.

Finally, I said, "I don't know."

"He talks about me," he said. Like Nicola, he was going to press his way to an answer.

"He said you like music a lot."

"That's what he said?" Vittorio smiled. The ghost of what, on Nicola, was an expression of kindness, passed over his face. As someone who loved Nicola, I could recognize Vittorio's love. No one got all of Nicola; no one got to keep him.

"He said you have musicians over to the house."

Vittorio was nodding. I couldn't take my eyes off of him. I felt slightly safer, now that he wasn't muttering and scanning. And with the feeling of safety came a prickling feeling of attraction. Maybe it was only because Patrick had called him a monster. "I love my son," he said, and sounded almost normal.

But then he stood again. "I'm sorry. I wasn't expecting a guest. I know I'm a bit"—his tongue was bumping against his cheek—"scattered. Would you like some music?" he said, and headed for the perimeter of the room. "Nothing *wrong* with a quiet *song*." Now he was going to ask me about the open box, and then he was going to realize something about me and my level of curiosity in him and his family, and he was going to threaten me.

What was I so afraid of? I tried to be calm. If I posed a danger to his business plans, he could harm me. More likely that he would insult me in some way that would cause me doubt for the rest of my life.

"I know who you are, Nora. My son's friend for many months. My colleague told me." And he touched both his eyebrows at the top, suggested the slits. What was worst of all, and most plausible, was that he could end the affair. He could tell Iris. If he wanted to, he could poison Nicola against me.

"Matteo Crema?" I said. I touched my eyebrows too.

"Is that his name?" Vittorio said.

"I thought you'd never spy on your own son," I said.

"It's something I find Nicola enjoys, being spied on," he said.

He stretched his hands and I saw his forearms flexing; he breathed in and tilted his head, and I felt a horrible dropping in my bowels and I realized I was, underneath those prosaic worries, afraid for my life. I had not wanted to seize onto this pulling, twisting rope of real fear. I always thought something would protect me. Modern mores. Patrick. My parents. Nicola. My own love of a certain kind of violence. But now the daylight was gone. Blackest night with Vittorio. He could act unilaterally. A death could be had in an instant.

A shadow crossed in front of the shades. I recognized that beautiful quick pace. I gasped in relief.

He entered the room in glorious green-eyed fury.

"Hi, Dad," he said. "You didn't tell me you were here."

Vittorio stood, speaking over him, "Crummy little stunt," cutting off the moment of salvation.

"It's a pity you can't behave," Nicola said in Italian,

"because you're one of the few people I would actually listen to." I'd never heard anyone compliment their own parent this way.

Vittorio smiled broadly and spread his arms as if to welcome Nicola into an embrace he knew his son would not accept. They looked at each other silently. Nicola's face had a tightness to it I'd never seen before, though he faintly smiled. I edged around the sofa toward the door. There was no affection on Vittorio's face, but no threat either.

Their shared look had the air of a conspiracy. I would have preferred disgust on Nicola's part, but I could see, and it made me shiver, that he did not actually hold the power.

Vittorio spoke in a lilting, silly tone. "So is this what you've been hiding from me? Throwing me off your tracks?"

"Sorry, Nora," said Nicola. "No, Dad, I'm not hiding her. As you can see, she's here in the house."

"She is your diversion," he said. "If I know about her, I know about everything."

"There's nothing," said Nicola stiffly.

"I have her here," said Vittorio. "I will have everything."

"We're going," Nicola said.

"Can we trust this girl?" Vittorio said.

"She's a friend," he said. "See you later, Dad," a final offering.

We were out the door. "Fast, fast, fast," Nicola whispered to me, and we turned the corner and walked south at top speed.

"I'm so sorry," I said.

"Well, you made his day," he said.

My face and hands were twitching. I could barely keep up with him. "Come on," he said. The panic was diminishing, and exhaustion rose up like a storm cell. He hailed a cab.

"He's a masterpiece, isn't he," Nicola said to me. I started to cry. Nicola would not come to me. He was lost in his own thoughts.

CHAPTER 35

We proceeded slowly in the twilight up the side of Manhattan, along the East River. The white and red taillights were bubbly stars in my wet eyes. I opened the window, inhaling spring air and fumes.

Vittorio had used me as bait. To them, in this interaction, I didn't matter at all. Maybe he'd known I was dialing Nicola, and he'd been glad at how docile I was. My mind conveyed images to me, one after another. The vultures in the Alps sunbathing upside-down with their wings out. The faces leavened by stones. Round and featureless as bread. The marble people in the secret garden behind his house, their bodies cold under the snow. The soldiers with tall pointed helmets with pennants on top, the suits of armor in the Met, empty and ancient and moving.

He touched my neck. His touch was medicinal.

"I never meant for you to meet," he said. "I made a mistake. Or did you? Did you touch any of the art?"

"I didn't do anything," I lied, thinking of the necklace.

"It's alarmed," Nicola said.

"Makes sense," I said.

"He never bothers to track my whereabouts like this," said Nicola.

I could see why Nicola didn't want to muddle up his

family life with me. I had pushed deeper and deeper and found something I did not want to see. With Nicola's hand warm and unrelenting on my neck I remembered how compromised Nicola had seemed; my being nothing more than an instrument; their dark truce, which from Nicola's end was more like martyrdom. And that last question, about whether they could trust me. Surely they didn't think I was a significant player, the kind you have to silence. Surely Nicola's words meant something. Maybe they forgave each other's weaknesses and kept each other's secrets: negative trust.

"Don't talk about Iris with Violetta," he said.

"What other instructions?" I said, feeling distant from him.

"It's important not to be totally silent."

I could feel his phone vibrate in his pocket. He took it out and looked at it. A string of numbers with an area code I didn't recognize. "Vittorio?" I said. The phone continued buzzing our whole way up to the Grill.

We walked up the stairs into the grand space. There was a long table full of fantastical cakes. Bronze rods hung over the immense bar like rain. Fine chains like necklaces shimmered pink-gold against the windows. The sun was just past setting, long bronze slits in navy. We sat on a low leather bench that was too narrow for three. The waitress had red lips and thick black glasses. People kept arriving up the stairs, orienting themselves to a space that was so expansive it didn't feel like New York.

He bought me a sour. "Drink it in one go," he said. He bought me another. He said, "The violence I feel toward you is very organic."

I said, "What's nice about you is that if I wanted to cancel the whole thing now, you'd say sure."

He said, "What's nice about you is that if I told you we should cancel, no matter your terror, you'd refuse." He kissed me softly on the forehead. I thought to myself: At some point, this intensity will only be accessible in flash-back. But I'm in it now. "That's courage, Nora," he said. "Those a lot less terrified have done very very much less. Not with fucking, but with the way you live, everything."

"Let's not talk about it," I said.

"All I have is sensitivity. I'm an overfitted curve, I think. I'm imprisoned, you're not." And I knew this was an apology, of a kind, about his father.

He carried on. He said he liked the idea of me talking to Violetta. He said she was a close friend, as well as a relative; she knew that I was a writer, and she was pleased to meet me, as she'd often felt he didn't have enough friends outside his family. "She takes up a lot of attention, you'll see," he said.

I said I didn't want his attention to be on her.

His energy had entirely returned; he was sparking. The drink in me was warm and resonant. He was addicted to the stepping away from normal life. The remove, yet it feels like how life always *actually* is.

Violetta arrived and he waved her over. She was younger than I expected, perhaps fifty, tan, with a wrinkled, reptil-ian face and silky near-black hair, and black liquid eyeliner in points. She wore a black outfit and had a large necklace and earrings, but I didn't bother to engage with her outfit or jewelry—the controllable aspects of her self-presentation washed over me and left no impression.

She took the least comfortable seat, a little round stool. She said hello to him and then turned her gaze to me. She said she was glad to meet me. "I heard you are very intensely committed to only a few things," she said, her vowels laden with Italian. This was Nicola's doing. He'd framed me to her in this way. Toiling over my many pots. "That is the most admirable way to live," she continued. She had a slightly af-fected, knowing posture, which was unbecoming on a woman who could almost have been my mother. But if she needed a touch of affectation to bypass small talk, I didn't mind. What I minded was her posture toward me: submissive, as though this cavernous bar were mine. I wanted to overthrow this and retreat to my habitual position, the overtaken. "I don't know anyone like that," she said. Her hair swished as she spoke, punctuating her quick little movements. "All my friends are so busy, we start projects and never finish them. How do you choose what to be committed to?"

Speechless, I turned to Nicola. I remembered Nicola's duality during our first day in the park, when I asked him to explain himself, and everything he said suggested another answer. I understood now the vulgarity of speaking directly about things.

"She's bashful," Violetta said to Nicola.

"No," he said, "she's very, very amused."

I realized, with a feeling of distress, that they were flirting. I saw how they were ungainly. Violetta was insubstantial. She wanted to be self-aware and she also wanted to be naive. I felt contemptuous.

She spent a long time looking at the stiff leather drinks menu, and wouldn't give it back to the waiter. She was so curious, surprised to find that I was—I knew roughly how I came off—this timid, critical person, surprised to find me next to Nicola with his graceful charisma, eager to move farther down toward him, to try to understand the nature of our friendship. I wondered about the quality of her care for him. She was the closest thing he had to his mother. When he looked at her full on, she looked away. His face was brutal from the front. She wanted to hide from it. And when he looked away she stared at his tender profile, the sylvan gentleness of his dark curls and long lashes.

So this was the woman who played with Nicola even though he always beat her. There was so little gentleness in his life.

She said he was vain, with his haircut, and his bar. "This suit of his," she said, as though she and I were collaborating. "Doesn't he create quite the picture!" She was knowing, flirtatious, and wrong.

I said, "No, he's not enamored of himself in a suit—" It didn't matter how distant I'd felt in the cab. I was roused into his defense.

"He is a performer," she said. At that, I wanted to stab her.

"Oh, he's real," I said.

"Does Iris know about the two of you?"

"Of course she knows," said Nicola. "That we are friends. I've learned a lot from this friendship. Nora is so single-minded about things, where I have no coherent tendencies," he told her.

"And Nora's the writer," she said.

"Nora's the writer," he said.

She said, "You two are making everything up."

"Believe what you want," I said.

This conversation counted out time like a clock. I realized how well Nicola and I had come to know each other. We had never tested ourselves this way, because we'd always been isolated and secretive. Now it was plain: we were very good friends.

WE WERE THERE for a long time. I saw him check his phone. He had seventy-eight missed calls from the same number. When she excused herself, he gripped the back of my neck, and touched me under my skirt. It was deeply unsatisfying, and the night changed texture.

When she returned I admired her snaky face and narrow neck. As the conversation lengthened she had solidified into something voluptuary and laid-back, the way that Nicola and I weren't.

She said, "He became the person he is when he was twelve."

"What happened then?"

"A face in the snow," he said. "The first time I saw death."

"The second," she corrected. He raised his drink.

Violetta said he went with the ski patrol after an avalanche in the Alps. They conducted an avalanche probe line, which was just as good as dogs. A line of skiers, each with a pole, pressing it down into the snow, hoping to feel someone. First they probed shallow and coarse, looking for rescue. Then they probed slow and deep, looking for recovery. And Nicola recovered a dead man. And then, when he returned, Vittorio punished him so much.

What kind of punishment, I wondered.

"He didn't want me to go out," said Nicola. "He didn't want me to be comforted by other men. He wanted me to see it how he sees it. Honorable, you know, meaningful. Remember when we met in the ski lift? You reminded me of myself that day. I wondered if you'd been doing recovery."

No. Although I could imagine with startling clarity the pole sinking into the snow and making contact with something soft deep below, the truth was that Federica and I had used our poles only to pull each other along the surface.

Violetta said, "I think your father would have loved to have been rescued by you."

"You think so?"

"Not in a way he could express," she said. She was a bit too clever. There was something far too sparking and unresolved about their interaction.

A performer? I hoped that, like me, she believed he was a medium more than anything. A seeker, a mediator. He didn't want to state things outright since they couldn't be completely correct. Surely not the same as a performer?

She was figuring out something about me. I just wasn't sure what it was.

We were very drunk when Violetta said, "Did you ever tell Nora about that fortune teller?"

He said no. He was looser than I'd ever seen him, almost falling apart with ease. "She predicted I'd kill my father. In a way, she gave me the idea."

"Funny how that works," said Violetta. "My, my, my, what a little infinity."

"Violetta is going to help me kill my father," he continued. She laughed.

"I don't think you should be telling me that," I said.

"What are you going to do about it?" he said.

But my fear was what Vittorio could do to me, to both of us.

"Oh, Nicola," she said, in a scolding tone. To me, she said, "He's been talking about this for years, and you see, Vittorio is still alive."

"Nora, you're the one who wanted to come out and meet my family," he said. Then he looked at Violetta. "It makes Nora a bit less effective as an uncompromised world apart— which is how I like her best."

I always did want real heat, and now I was seeing it and it was punishing. I was tired of pretending to be confident and pretending to be who they wanted me to be. This evening had been all about position, her envy, then mine; my humiliation as she knew him so much better than I did. I was losing track of what was performance, light, fine, and normal, and what was not. This evening, I thought, was too much Vittorio, too much disembodied power. I wanted to be with Nicola and let him force all this anxiety down and make me into just a sensibility.

WE WENT DOWN to the street, and he kissed her cheeks and hailed her a cab. Then we went to a hotel nearby. The corner view south and east, the huge, beseeching Chrysler Building and Empire State Building, the monumental bed. He opened the small bottle of champagne.

We repaired to the dark-paneled sitting room. It was cold and we were drunk. Nicola turned on a lamp and found two blankets. He wore his undershirt and navy boxers, hair ragged, cheeks and lips pink. For a while, I floated near the floor. He smoked even though it was a nonsmoking room. We listened to Palestrina, both tilting our heads ecstatically.

I had changed. Like raindrops on a sheet, first the changes were discrete, and now vast swaths of me were different. In truth I was all adrenaline, and my thoughts weren't measurable. I wasn't anxious. The feeling wasn't arousal. It was closer to gratitude, after that time with Vittorio and Violetta. *It's something I find Nicola enjoys, being spied on.* He was letting me in, and exposing himself. There was so much loneliness in this self-emptying he did.

I went back into the bedroom and lay down. It was three in the morning.

Nicola told me to come lie down by him, and so I did. He choked me for one second, restoring vivid color to the world. He whispered, "I love you."

"That was too long with Violetta," I said. (Afterward I hated myself for not saying "I love you" back.)

"Take your clothes off," he said, but I didn't want to.

He placed quick hard kisses on my neck. His breath like a candle flame.

He yanked on my dress until it began to come off. He pulled down my tights and underwear. Then he touched me softly, teasingly. He ran his hands over my jawbone and my temples, and brushed my hair away from my face. I couldn't see the city. I filled my eyes with his sensitive unrelenting face.

He touched me for a long time, it was past the point of polite, past the point where I could worry that he was tired of it, we had swept out into the sweet fields of the voluntary.

Several hours, it could have been. I'd been hurt by Violetta's presence, I'd gathered up my frustration all evening, waiting for her to go, and now, with that lump in my throat, I threw it all away. Gone, done. Something else would happen now. You wanted this, he said, you like this, you asked for this, this was your idea. Right, Nora? Isn't that right? Disobedience flew away from me, along with exhaustion and shame: the dark screaming seabirds. Under his touch I became entirely pliant. I was pure as crystal with desire. All that mattered was that he continue, and meanwhile he spoke to me, calling me names for being so easy and eager and desperate for him. Oh, it's fine, it's fine, I whispered as he touched me. It's okay, he said. I got calmer and calmer like that. Day colors occurred to me, spontaneous phrase, but there they were, lucent and glorious turquoise, fuchsia, cerulean blue, out past the border.

He sat back, and touched down my cheek so kindly. Then like a striking snake he hit me on the side of my face. I lay in an animal state and after he landed a blow he reached down and touched between my legs, for just a second, and I caved with pleasure.

"Turn to the side, Nora." He turned me. Grabbed my shoulder and held it. Pressed his forearm on me. He told me to be quiet, and balled up a piece of the comforter, pulled my hair back till my head lifted, and stuffed it in my mouth. Then he gored me. I had no feeling of catharsis—the feeling was of coarseness, rubbing against a brick wall, panting on an icy day. Soundless, it was easier to give in. I could feel my hot tears seeping into the fabric against which he pressed my face. But I accepted it. I had a vision of his father, Vittorio. His father looking on—proud of his son but envious, envious of me.

I was on my hands and knees, and, both of us completely silent, he grabbed my hair and pulled it back. I was a bow and arrow and he used all his trembling strength to pull the string. The feelings then had nothing to do with the world. Trapped and treated, caught and helpless, I was alone with him, and everything was juddering lightning. One huge swoon, a dream, and a roaring in my head. He hit my face, his hand like a whip. I could barely feel it except that I seemed to rise off the bed. He carried on until I was beating like a heart, then he mashed his hand into my face, his fingers in my mouth, then he fed me himself once more and I came in an emergency with nothing to temper or support me. Coming was like a channel of water that's always running—as though I just put my hand in it for a moment. It was a state that was always there, that I adjoined. And the shame at my spoiled self-indulgence went off like a bomb as soon as I could open my eyes.

My hand was clenched up, my right hand.

I curled up and shut my eyes.

"Maybe I should be with you," he said.

"Maybe you should be with me," I said back, my voice so slurred and unfamiliar.

"Look, I want my father out of the way, and then who knows. I can't see the future anymore. It could very well resolve in your favor."

I wanted to say, don't abandon your wife for me. Don't you come from a tradition of people destroying their wives? But I didn't feel it. Go ahead and kill your dad, kill your wife. Then come home and be with me.

When he took his definitive leave, this was the evening that most easily prompted fantasies. It was the seed, not the fruit. I meant a wild seed, not a cultivated one. A hard rich armored thing.

For a long time I lay there—he stood, and left, and returned—and then I called him baby and he liked that so much he made me say it again. What a special thing we have, he said, as I kissed him and pistoned him, devotional, devotional.

And then I was as happy as a bird darting through the room naked.

Then I was laughing. You're the devil, Lucifer, Satan, I said.

"IT'S RAINING," HE said, pointing, and buttoned up his shirt.

I hadn't noticed. "We're up too high for rain," I said. But there it was, pulling low faraway Manhattan against the windowpane into clinging strips of light.

He went to the window. He unlatched it and spun the mechanism. The window opened on a vertical axis with a suction sound.

"Be careful," I said.

"Are you afraid of heights?" he said.

Any reasonable person would be afraid of that height. We were on the fortieth floor. He returned to me. He stood over me, touching my face, considering. "Come on, stand up," he said. "Come on, come on." He held my neck and brought me over to the window.

"I don't like being so close," I said.

"It doesn't go any wider than that," he said. He'd opened the window about a foot. He pressed his hand against the pane, testing it. It went wider. "I'll hold you."

"What do you want?" I said.

"I want you to get rained on."

He put his arms around me and pulled me closer to the window. I looked down. There were no people out at this hour. Just sparse cabs, and the green and red ovals from the lights. I imagined the glass of the window above falling, decapitating me; I imagined the side of the building sheering off. I was nauseated. A strange perfume came in the window, a warm scent like stones. He held my waist. He didn't worry about the glass breaking. He didn't tell himself a lot of myths about the world.

I leaned closer and closer to the dark opening, and finally I began to inch my head out. "Good," he said. The rain against my hair was dirty little psychological pinpricks. I leaned half my shoulder out—now my whole head was in this other space, in the night, floating. His warm arms were around me, back in the other realm. I was in the center, the exact center, a place I didn't belong, this was not a human domain. At last in the cloud or aureola, suspended above the city, with the rain soaking into my hair—I tilted my head—the rain trickled into my ear—and I twisted myself to look skyward, where the rain fell down (I'd never opened my eyes to it before) in a star pattern, from the black of outer space down in these long-limbed slow stars centered around my head. The rain was always this way; you just had to recover it.

He didn't speak to me, though I could feel his fine shirt like paper crushed around me, the lavish warmth of his body that would never be mine. I wasn't nervous at all. My crying streamed upward into the rain. He knew what I loved.

WHEN I CAME back, he toweled off my head for me.

The rain dulled out. The sky was rising. In the cab, he said, "I'm worried you'll leave me. I'm worried you'll kick me to the curb."

"Really?"

"Sometimes," he said.

I wanted him to explain why Violetta was so tentative at first. He said it was probably because she was vain and worried about it. He said, "You don't make it a problem that you like what you like. So it gets realer." I knew that his faith was the source of his power. I felt his faith in me and became better.

The smooth ramps were so beautiful, exactly the right tilt and pace. The expressway down Manhattan's east side, and the buildings I didn't recognize. To my nearsight, tall shardlike buildings.

"You know," I said, into the quiet air, "your dad did send that man to spy on you."

"He did?" Nicola said. His voice was a strange drawl. From his eyes, which were characteristically always on the verge of tears, real tears seemed about to fall.

"Oh," I said, "and he said he loves you."

But then he only asked who in whose lap, then he put his heavy noble head down in mine. I stroked his hair gently and I fell asleep too.

It was dawn when we reached my apartment. The brick buildings of the project were blazing red, and the sky was low and black.

He let down the blinds. Since that day I never again let down the blinds. He was the only one allowed to do that. We fell asleep with our clothes all over the floor.

CHAPTER 36

I always thought he'd get tired of me. But in the end what divided us was harder than that.

When we woke at two in the afternoon he said he had to go immediately, and the anguish of that almost wiped out the goodness of the preceeding day. He didn't even let me make him coffee. I pulled up the blinds and the livid spring afternoon came blasting in. He buttoned up his shirt, tucked it into his trousers, slipped on his suit jacket, and was gone, then I was alone in bed with his fading warmth.

When I put my silk dress in the laundry bin I found the little rings of his tears on the lap.

I lay around, showered, and returned to bed. Everything had a sweetness and a lilt to it. I texted him and he said he couldn't stop thinking about it. Thinking about what? About being there after Violetta and what I sounded like. What did I sound like? "So open, so possessed by it," he wrote. I said I was going crazy. He said he had been thinking about it all day. He marveled at it. He was just pure energy, he said. Oh yes, I said, I'm exactly the same. He said he was surprised how quickly I'd managed to subdue Violetta. "You are high velocity," he wrote. This offended me. I wanted him to see it wasn't easy and I wanted to be coherent. But when he changed my context he changed me. Like two examples of moral luck, we kept drifting through possible worlds.

THAT EVENING PATRICK emailed the office that his wife had gone into labor. I could barely sleep, I was so excited for him. The following day the baby was born. So we'd have a month without Patrick in the office. Nicola sent Patrick a huge bouquet of white roses. He texted me that he had moved into a hotel and was not in contact with his father. I should let him know when I was free, he wrote.

Though I'd been afraid of how work would be without Patrick, during that first week, everything was easy, effortless dominance. All the symbols in the world were comprehensible. No longer shadows in mirrors. I was no longer swinging through uncertain space, I was pressed, like Nicola's pressure on me as I came, with awareness. Yes, reality felt like pressure, like close abundance. If you think about things you can understand them! Easy to manage complex procedures, easy to explain complex thoughts, easy to understand what people wanted, their pride, their self-consciousness, their inherent goodness. Sudden insight, offerings made to me freely, everyone watching me, waiting for my word. In the past, I'd felt that people were like suns, and I couldn't look at them full on, but Nicola did. He was constantly kind; he recognized people as agents in their own lives. Now that my blood was up as high as it could go, I was just like Nicola. If you combine energy and extreme responsiveness and some kind of moral authority people will simply follow you. It was a beautiful golden week, the last week.

Then finally I texted him, "Can I see you tonight?"

I HEARD HIS voice before he came in. He was on the phone with someone. The pitch of his voice was indistinct, so

I could only tell it was him by the emphasis, which was assured, rhythmic. No one else on Skillman Street had such an assured voice. Then he called me. He was on my doorstep, then up my hollow stairs. I'd never seen anyone like him.

I was shy against the door. "What a feast for the senses, Nora," he said. The tenderness with which he took my head and my chin. I knelt before him. "Take off your clothes," he said.

"Not yet," I said.

"Do what I say," he said, almost curious. I was pressed against the wall, groped and choked into stars. He gathered my neck, chest, ribs, stomach, then turned me and held me with my back against him and squeezed my neck in the crook of his arm, harder and harder. Then he owned my whole form.

The way in which it would unfold was not yet clear.

Then his phone started to ring. I handed it to him—unknown number, which meant abroad—"I don't mind at all," I said. "You can take it."

"No, no," he said.

He returned. The person called again. "Just take it, I don't mind, take it, I don't mind," I said.

On the third ring, he took it. "Iris," he said.

It was quiet and at first he didn't say anything, just thinking. There was no gasp or exclamation. But when he said it to me, I repeated back, "In the hospital?," and my voice was low like I was trying to do a man's movie trailer voice-over voice. "He's alive?"

His father had been attacked in Turin. He was currently unresponsive.

He stood. I pulled on a nightgown. "What happened?" I said.

He called Iris and said, in Italian, "What happened?" Like

he hadn't thought to ask until I asked. A young man, he said, repeating to her. A protester? A rival? No one knew.

"I'm going to the airport," he said.

He put on his clothes.

I wondered if he had to go because his dad was still alive.

I felt I was watching him from my deathbed. He got to hold on to the vivid world. I was dying but not detached. I had watched my grandmother die. She stopped being able to move or eat. She didn't like dying. She knew what she was losing.

I wanted to ask if he loved me. But it wasn't appropriate.

He kissed me on the head. "Goodbye, Nora."

Then what I noticed was his clumsiness. Clumsiness as he put on his socks and his coat, and clumsiness particularly as he fell down the stairs. I turned on the light after he'd already tripped to the bottom. The chime on his phone meant his car was approaching.

"Just go," I said ridiculously. "I'll lock up."

I thought he was calling Iris again, but he was calling Violetta. I heard him speak her name on my stoop. Though I knew it would hurt me, like Orpheus I looked out at him, my last look, his gorgeous frame, his dark beloved head. He bent into the back seat of the car.

I was thinking, it's going to be a long long ride over the ocean. A long long night until he knows what's going on. I wouldn't have cared about his father, but for his jerking and wheeling through the world with a whole different voice.

I lay on my bed in the worst night of my life. I had the full-body shakes.

I remembered watching his naked body while he talked to Iris.

"I'm thinking of you," I texted him. "You don't have to think about me, but let me know if you have any news."

His father would be fine, or he deserved to die. But I knew what was gone was Nicola putting me in the center. It had been borrowed time all along.

An hour later he wrote, "The plane is taking off. Thank you, Nora. It's painful to write this, but please don't contact me. Don't wait for me. I don't think I'll be back."

CHAPTER 37

Though it was one in the morning, and he had an infant daughter, I called Patrick. He picked up. "Patrick," I said, "I'm sorry to bother you."

"What is it, Nora?" He sounded tired.

Then I began crying so hard I hung up the phone. What was I doing? What could I say to Patrick? I just couldn't explain, nothing would be the right degree of horrifying, and I needed *desperately* for him to understand, I was totally, totally alone, and I needed to confess, to match the horror of the moment, to make it an offering.

But I couldn't confess. I couldn't. Maybe I owed Nicola nothing, and would never see him again. But out of love for him, which clung like an incubus to my chest, I could not tell the secret.

He called me back. "Did something happen?" he said.

I said I was sorry. I asked how the baby was.

"Fine, fine," he said. "What happened?"

"I just heard from Nicola."

"Just now?" I imagined Patrick deciding how inappropriate this was, reckoning up why Nicola would call me this late. I was so glad for him to know—to know just this much, that we were very close. The gladness overwhelmed me to the point where I stopped crying.

"Something terrible happened with his father," I said,

"and he was telling me he was going to leave the country and never come back."

I'd wanted Patrick to question the "never," to tell me that was unlikely, but he was silent.

"Or not come back on any conceivable timeline," I said.

"What exactly did he say?" Patrick said, though his tone implied, *Why did he tell you?*

"His father was attacked," I said.

"A hit," said Patrick immediately.

"What?"

"He called in a hit on his father."

"No," I said. "It was a young man. Could be anyone. You know that his father used to kill business rivals?"

"Is that what he told you?"

"Yes."

"It was Nicola's hit," said Patrick.

"You said he had a moral core." If it was a hit, it meant he'd planned it out, he'd been lying to me, and he'd intended to leave me.

"When I say moral core, I mean going against Vittorio, Nora. Why did he tell you?"

"We talk about a lot of things." Hot phone against my face. I paced blindly around my room.

"He told you because he wanted the business world to know," Patrick said, working it out as he spoke. "He knew you'd tell me. So he wanted to signal that he's not coming back for a while. What he's going to do is put a hold on his expansion plans and take over the European business now."

"This has—" I started.

Patrick had switched into his full-speed mode. "Is he doing me a favor? Maybe, yeah, and in exchange—he wants a good story out. It's a good story that it's an urgent family problem that led to this move, not a failure with investors."

"This had nothing to do with business," I said.

"I suppose he had the family cruelty in him," said Patrick. "He must not have gotten enough going here to accomplish the patricide by financial means. Well, yes, he's principled."

"He would never kill his father," I said. "You think Vittorio is going to die?" I didn't want Vittorio to die. If Vittorio died, the Nicola I knew would be gone forever. He'd told me, *I could use a little goodness.* I was his counterbalance to Vittorio, and now the scale had fallen over.

"The principle being win-at-all-costs power hunger," Patrick continued.

"I promise you, Patrick, you've got him wrong," I said. I didn't even want to take the time to plug in my headphones. My phone screen was slimy and salty.

"The principle, then, is vengeance for the mother," said Patrick.

"He loved his father," I said. "He wanted him to live. You think he'll die?"

"I know less than you do about it."

"There's no way he tried and failed to get business here," I said. "He was never doing that. He was always helping his father. He told me that. And I saw him with his father, too. They loved each other."

Again Patrick was silent. Considering me in a new way, for this friendship that had gone deeper than he supposed.

"Also, Iris didn't want him to split from his father." Then I felt I was beginning to understand what the attack on Vittorio really was.

"Why didn't you tell me about this before?" said Patrick. He answered himself. "You're very loyal, aren't you. Loyalty—so that's what you think. You see what you think is Nicola's loyalty, and you behave that way yourself. I always found your intuitions quite solid, Nora. And your behavior, too . . ." I could hear in his voice the friction of him taking an idea seriously. Yes, loyalty, family, self-abnegation, martyrdom—

these were Nicola's values. The only values with gravity in a world he saw as utter filth. I liked hearing Patrick start to realize it. I liked his vision of Nicola suddenly becoming much stranger than he had ever thought. Yes, Patrick, some people are depthless. Your understanding has to peter out.

"Patrick, you know what I think it is?"

"Yes?"

"Vittorio called in a hit on himself."

"Huh!" said Patrick. And with that word the gap between us widened again. Patrick puzzled over Nicola from a distance.

"Vittorio got someone to attack him, or maybe just to fake-attack him. Nicola only heard about it from Iris, so who knows. Vittorio wanted his son back, that's all."

I held my breath. My heart was pounding.

"Would be a shitty thing to do," Patrick said. Which meant that even if he didn't agree, he understood the possibility.

For my part, I could see it all. How Iris had used me to communicate with Nicola when she'd shown me the art and cried—getting his attention with disloyalty. How Vittorio had used me, dancing around in the striped room, knowing I'd call his son. Both of them wanted his attention so badly. I was a conduit, but even as they used me they knew that I mattered to Nicola. Vittorio attacking himself, one way or another—I knew exactly how he must have felt. I knew all about self-harm. I'd once felt the same way. What will provoke Nicola's attention? What will bring him back? What will prove once and for all that he loves me?

In the background of Patrick's phone, I heard the baby start to cry.

"Is she sleeping well?" I said.

"Not really," Patrick said. He said he had to go. "Now I have some things to think about," he said.

"Yeah," I said.

"Are you okay about it?" Patrick said. "You were upset when you first called."

"I'm okay."

"Was Nicola always nice to you?" said Patrick. "Did he hurt you somehow?"

"I was only crying because he was always nice."

I hated leaving this conversation, which was as close as I could get to talking to Nicola. Patrick hung up. Now I was alone. I cried agonizingly, as I hadn't cried in years.

PART III

CHAPTER 38

Patrick scheduled a conference call—"From paternity leave, just one note," he wrote the investors. On the call he said that Nicola was not going to be taking over the company and bringing it international. "Between us, his father's health problems may have caused him to return," said Patrick. That was Patrick trying to obey Nicola's wishes. "In any case, he's not leaving Italy now," Patrick said. "He's loyal." And that was my read.

For the first time, I sensed that Patrick truly trusted my view. And I got pleasure from the fact that we got to publicize Nicola's values, which made no sense, no market sense nor ethical sense, if you knew that his father was a criminal and had abused his own family. Yet Nicola was always answering to a higher power. He couldn't be pinned down. We'd thought we had something on him, and he'd broken our hearts.

NOW WHAT? IT had only been a week since Nicola left. I gazed in surprise at the kinetic shadows on the sidewalks from the new leaves on the trees. No one could say it was winter anymore.

On Facebook I messaged Federica. The last she'd written was about how I loved self-harm, and then there was Nicola's friendly "Excellent!" Now I wrote, "Just thinking of you—are you around for that call?"

I WAS NAUSEOUS with nerves while I waited for her WhatsApp call, propped up with pillows on my bed. I was there mostly to connect to Nicola in some way, of course. But also to be released by her from my childhood of desire. Maybe she could untie the knot that held the shuddering kite that was Nicola.

I wanted her to tell me that our kiss, the day of the gondola lift, was nothing: that I hadn't taken advantage of her, nor she of me; that she didn't think about it; that it was one of those commonplace unfraught random childhood occurrences, not shattering, not shaping. If she could diminish my kissing her, then she would dissolve the power Nicola had given me in the gondola.

I was asking for an old magic to be made mundane. This was a tragic thing to ask. But I needed to be able to control my life again. Control was mundane to me.

We spoke Italian. I could only speak with incredible difficulty, but I understood her voice so well. The voice I came up on.

We talked loosely about how we were doing. She'd gotten married, she said, to Gian, who did Slow Food. They lived near Piazza Solferino. They wanted to have kids. She wasn't too interested in my life, and her disinterest was exacerbated by how difficult it was for me to talk. I couldn't really picture her. It was like talking to a grandparent, or I was the grandparent, awkward, a bit senile because of my language loss. Finally, I asked about Nicola. "Nicola Gonfalon," I said. "I used to see him in New York sometimes."

A long pause whispery with static.

"You see Nicola Gonfalon?" Her tone was astonishment.

"We met him on the gondola lift," I said. The *ovovia*—I

remembered the term. I didn't remember how to say "bob-sled race."

She didn't react to this.

"I think he's back in Italy for a while," I ventured.

"His father was attacked," she said. "He almost died."

"I'm sorry," I said. "What happened?"

"Everyone says that it was Nicola," said Federica.

"How could it be Nicola?"

"That's what they say in Turin," she said impatiently.

"So Nicola is quite famous around Turin," I said.

"Of course he is," said Federica. "He's one of the richest men in Italy."

"You know, some people say he's evil," I ventured. "Have you heard that?"

"Yes," she said.

"Why do you think?"

"He tried to murder his father," Federica said.

"Is that a rumor? Is it verified?"

"It is a rumor," she said. "It is verified." Her tone was easy, shrugging. "Everyone knows it." I wondered if she intended the delicacy with which she added, "Everyone likes Nicola, though."

"I hope he'll come back to New York sometime," I said.

She said nothing. I could hear crunching. I wondered if she was eating grissini with Nutella.

"Don't you remember meeting him with me in the gon-dola lift?" I said. "Don't you remember?" I asked again. I was pleading with her, I realized, and now I could imagine her beautiful face. The strong-willed animal trainer, the girl who saw me naked in the shower and then shut me out completely all spring. Patrick would have called her "prin-cipled."

"Of course I remember," she said. "You got sick."

I wanted to say, *And do you remember the night that*

followed? But I didn't need to ask. I knew she was remembering it.

"You always seemed so free," she said. "I was jealous of you. But now I'm married, and you haven't done much."

"I write," I said. "I have a good job."

"You'll never find a person to be with," she said. "Which was what you wanted so much when we were little."

"People like me best when I'm the second choice," I said.

She didn't accept this. She wanted my agency to be a part of it. She said something I didn't understand. I made her repeat it. "I don't think it's possible for you to give yourself over," she said. "I knew it. You're going to spend your life alone."

I couldn't understand her bitter tone. I asked why.

"You're just a loner. You could never be dedicated to another person."

"I'm not so much of a loner," I said, "anymore."

"You are very walled off. You don't know what closeness is. You are so removed."

"You can't tell me that," I said, because my Italian was clumsy. I meant to say, you can't believe that, or how can you tell me that? The words felt thick and stupid in my mouth.

"Remember how you ignored me?" she said. Was this how she'd read our failed connection in Italy? She'd thought I had been too walled off? But she was the one who had withdrawn. All those lonely walks without her had been a means of coping with *her* ignoring *me*. I cared so much that I pulled away. Didn't she know how fervently I'd avoided begging?

She sounded tearful. "I'm sorry," she said. "I'm stressed. Gian is about to come back and I can't talk in front of him. Come see me when you're in Turin. Someday you'll be back here." With those words I realized I hadn't attempted to imagine her life. She had been living a life with its own colors and memories I'd never seen.

"You're right," I said. "I should come." I imagined once again a sisterhood—an end to the loneliness. I wanted to know why she couldn't talk in front of her husband. A tiny opening of curiosity for something that wasn't Nicola. And I wanted to show her, I am not so walled off anymore.

Soon we said goodbye, and I entered a mood that would not move. I slowed down to nothing. This mood lasted for months, and I could not feel the summer. I was cold.

I'D SOUGHT ABSOLUTION from her. Instead she'd shown me I'd never recover from Nicola.

He had, and I came to see it more each day, attempted to kill his father. Everyone had always told me that and now I saw it too.

He had never denied it. Only changed the subject or said *What do you take me for? Certain things are inexpressible,* he said, never really lying. I imagined what I would tell him, if I saw him, what I would scream at him: there was the speech part and then everything below it. He acted as though by keeping the speech part clean, all the rest was clean too, he could be "good" with me. He hid from me and from himself, pretending that everything was so very much more complicated than it was. Everyone saw that he'd attempted to kill his father. The only strange thing was that he hadn't succeeded. I supposed he'd been using me as a distraction for himself, or even a smokescreen for his father and his father's spies, while Violetta or someone else handled the part the anticipation of which made him cry onto my lap.

Not an illusionist, he was real, and obsessed with vengeance, that was it. My love for him was a horror story.

The constraints—his constraints—made it possible to give in, he'd said. He could consume me.

What Federica was saying was that I must have wanted it that way.

I liked him as a killer, I liked him killing me too.

There would never be such a thing as Nicola but available. She would say that I desired him because of his un-availability, but that was ridiculous. Or she would say that I allowed myself to desire him because I knew he wouldn't penetrate my loneliness. But he *had* penetrated it. I had let him in. I had. How was it possible that I was even questioning it? But I was.

He was an endlessly unfolding flower, and now that I was apart from him he was deathly still, and that lack of movement killed everything we'd experienced together. What we'd experienced together was, in its essential quality, an experience of present change. There was no possible world in which it was static or calm. It couldn't become memory without changing so profoundly that it simply was no more. The entire experience with Nicola was reaction and fear and groping at him for mercy, his responsiveness to my responsiveness that rocketed us upward, it was shapes made out of sand and hail and other projectiles and clouds. Had he ever brought me into and out of panic? Had he breathed into me and forced my wretched body at last into pure grace? I wished I'd done something so extremely deranged with him that I could always point to it as a memorial of our connection, of being lost in and because of him. I wished that I'd gotten him to stab me, scar me. I wanted to know that I mattered enduringly to him. What was the good of an *enduring* connection? Why did it feel so critical? Why couldn't I be happy that there was *once* a connection? But he had filled me with electricity. He had forced me to think and read and push into life as it always *actually* was.

It was not true that everyone was the same. (This took me years to realize, and I was sorry that I ever did.) This was heartbreak's foul rotting core. It was not true that most people were good. That most people could teach you something worthwhile. That you could pursue reading and art in any setting at all with equal avidity. Rather: There were differences in the world. Certain things mattered more than others. Certain times of life were happy and certain times of life were sad. Getting older was sad. The passage of time clouded emotions that were once consciousness-altering. Only some people searched for and took action on behalf of the good. He was the love of my life. We were never going to get to see what happened after the first phase. He didn't like me quite enough for that.

I wished I had the self-respect, the dumb self-respect, the strict, unbudging, stupid, moral self-respect, to turn away. To say, he doesn't like you enough, so turn your back on all of this.

But I had no self-respect. Curiosity and totalizing craving—those were the drivers of my life, as it turned out. A compass that spun to point just to the one person I loved most. And I admired him so much that I understood why he would never want to be with me. I was not a match for him. Of course not.

Federica did have me wrong. It had always been doomed but not because I wanted constraints. It was doomed just because Nicola was a god. If you met him you would think so too. He would possess you. He would read your mind. He would live with Iris, forever in the sky.

CHAPTER 39

What surprised me about the sadness was how disgusting it felt. Squalid, disgusting, narrow sadness. Abhorrent. It wasn't feathery and black. It was corrosive like hatred. It was obsessive, and I had to stare at my face in every mirrored surface just to reaffirm, again and again, how ugly I was.

For the first month, before and after the Federica conversation, I kept thinking he might text or call. In the second month I was less vividly hopeful. In the following months the hope faded but not the sadness. Sadness like what we're taught to look for in a breast cancer self-exam: the lump that won't move. Thinking of my college self, I went to draw nude models in Gowanus, and cried and had to stop. The art at the Met bored me out of my skull. Music was boring. Food was pointless. The changing seasons, up with the roses, up with the poppies, oh look here come the coneflowers, felt as uninteresting as Violetta's jewelry—just layers on top of an unchanging structure. Palestrina or really any music with singing was unlistenably sad, Central Park was unwalkably sad, noncontemporary fiction was unreadably sad, and everything else was pretty much dead boring.

You can't take it with you when you go. You can't! You can't take it with you. (Iris could; not me.) Crying made me feel like he might call me, and also like I might realize something. But there was nothing to realize. It was the plainest thing in the world.

I couldn't wait to be apart from people so that I could focus on my self-loathing. I loved a man who loved vengeance and that was it. I did no work at all. I was amazed by the kindness of my coworkers, but only in a distant way that was also deeply boring. I kept telling them I was having mental health problems and they let me say it and not work. When I bothered to go into the office, I closed the huddle-room door and taped paper over its window and slept.

Tace, force of evil, I tried, and failed.

It became clear to me that I had never actually been sad in my whole life until now. The other periods of Nicola's absence, I could now see, had been leavened by the fact that I'd set the terms, that I'd been the one with the power to text him.

I went back to the North Woods. I would have done anything to see Matteo Crema, or anyone else from Nicola's life, Peter the gallerist, even one of Iris's beautiful friends, anyone coming up behind me: "Excuse me, do you know Nicola Gonfalon?" I would have embraced Matteo Crema. Asked him for a drink. Brought him home.

This was real hell. Not trailing my hand in a lake in a melancholy but meditative way—a silver cascade of tears—no. What I had was extreme self-consciousness, invasive, endless criticism of my body, a feeling of aging. Body hatred and no energy. I used to love eating peaches and nectarines but I was actually too sad to eat any during the whole summer, the prospect of (a) all that bounteous, dynamic juice and (b) having to rinse my hands and chin after was too much, too much to attempt. I spent enormous quantities of time scrutinizing my objectively loathsome, veiny, bumpy, oily, spotted, and stiff body. A bad taste in my mouth and a cloudy head. A feeling of trying everyone's patience.

Everything was boring without him, including people. Dull, impossible, empty. The subway seats weren't high-backed enough to support me. It was painful to hold my own spine up.

And I was so hallucinatingly sad that everything took on its own soul and everything was damaged. I hated slicing bread; I felt sorry for the bread and for the knife. I wept over the soles of my shoes that had to get worn down each day. My shoes, sitting at the door for me, were alive and obedient and willing and crushed over and over and over again. My filthy room was alive. The walls fluttered and tried to comfort me, and I disappointed them, my scattered, ignored possessions sighed for me, lonely and confused and helpless.

Now came the days that were one full revolution from the time we'd spent together. The exact day that Leif and I had gone walking in Dumbo and watched the sky turn gold. The exact day that Patrick and I had looked at Nicola's wedding photos . . . The day of our first walk in the park. The ivy on the community garden chain-link fence waved in the black September air, as I sobbed too hard to see if anyone was watching from the stoops, and couldn't tell who was a human and who was a fixture or shrub. The plants were grayish black. I was borne along in a tunnel. The normal sirens were extremely loud. It was amazing to be this sad—a state of childhood, when perception of space was wrong.

The subways were so loud and fast coming into the stations. A burst of brightness and a strong wind in my hair. Everyone stepped back from the yellow edge. I was so sick of all of it.

I decided to go to the embassy building, where Peter had his gallery. I wasn't sure whether I would be able to enter, whether the door would still be unguarded for me, or even if I wanted to see again that fountain with its marble child beneath the disorienting skylight. And what would Peter say if he saw me; was he another of Vittorio's spies, or would he convey Nicola a message?

I seemed to have turned down the wrong street, and couldn't find the white stone steps, and that facade with its fire-breathing salamanders and its crowns.

I walked a few blocks toward the park, then north, east, south again, hot, exhausted, angry with confusion. Once I found the building, I'd demand to be let in, I didn't care anymore about decorum. I would let myself kiss Peter's paintings, in that dark-paneled room with its must and espresso scent.

Finally I asked a doorman under his green awning, describing that facade of follies, and he said, "They're building a tower where that old building used to be." And he pointed to the green-painted plywood around a vacant lot. With tears in my eyes, I rushed over to look through the Plexiglas windows. There was a deep pit of rubble, nothing else.

I texted Leif and he said he was sorry but too busy now. I texted the architect and he didn't respond.

I could barely lift my head. I threw away my bride and groom candles. I visited Patrick's baby. I hadn't realized that babies had such perfect skin. This baby was so flawless it looked like vinyl. It slept in its barren crib. It was quickly boring to look at; I wanted to shake it until it woke up. But I also wanted it to stay asleep so that I wouldn't have to watch Patrick take care of it. Patrick said, "I miss seeing you happy, Nora." I coughed to disguise that I was crying.

Nights were the worst. One night I was so agitated and aching and helpless that I went and got a paring knife and tried it against my upper thighs, exactly the behavior that had gotten me sent to Italy in the first place. It had been fifteen years. My skin, which was very soft on my upper thighs, was surprisingly like a hide. It wasn't easy to cut deeply and it hurt. I felt slightly calmer afterward. The activity had given me something to do.

I went on dates. I had no way to describe them but extremely fucking sad.

IT WAS ALWAYS going to be limited with Nicola, but I obsessed over the idea that I may not have needed to *see* the limits like this. Only the margin could have been different, so the margin was where I stuck. Some reckonings never come—does that falsify the entire experience that one might have reckoned about? I read that if I watched you fall into a black hole, from my point of view, because of the way the black hole prevents light from escaping, you would seem to be waiting for a time approaching infinity on the edge. I supposed that was the most I could have wished for with Nicola. A trick of point of view so that it would seem to me endless.

Heliotropism. All golden threads straining and straining in one direction and not reaching it. The gondola lift that never reaches the ground, that orbits forever like a moon. Nico, don't you know not every phenomenon is linear? There are cycles, ellipses, a spiral too I would accept.

Everyone dies, it's okay. It was just a more extreme version of a normal life process that we lived together.

No, in fact it was real life. He was an unveiling person. In the end he unveiled and then when he was gone I veiled back up. Veiling was a mixing-in of white.

Wittgenstein: *But what kind of a proposition is that, that blending in white removes the coloredness from the color? As I mean it, it can't be a proposition of physics. Here the temptation to believe in a phenomenology, something midway between science and logic, is very great.*

Eckhart: *Essence alone satisfies and God keeps on withdrawing, farther and farther away, to arouse the mind's zeal and lure it on to follow and finally grasp the true good that has no cause.*

He was a dynamic more than a person. He was the gold ground. He said, come, here you are in the center of the world. What does that make you? You get to inhabit yourself completely and have the pressure of maximal import and justify yourself to yourself.

His pure responsiveness was brutal. Walk up to him, he delivers you to who you are. And then—you won't change him, he won't be confused, it won't turn out differently. He'll walk away.

The weather cooled off and I barely noticed. Leaves green but just slightly crinkly in the canopy. Then leaves all over the sidewalks; I noticed the smell more than anything. One moment later all the leaves were gone.

CHAPTER 40

I didn't hear from him for nine months.

I was dating again. Dating a man who liked bird-watching. I was thirty. It had taken me months to find someone who liked bird-watching. This was what I wanted, right? He also liked rock climbing. He said rock climbing made him more anxious, which was good for him, while it seemed to him that I needed an activity that would make me less anxious. This was what I wanted, right? He scolded me for using my phone too much, a criticism I agreed with. We were going to camp in the Catskills.

FEBRUARY, I WAS on the subway platform at Jay Street–MetroTech. Unknown number. It was Nicola. When I heard his voice—it's not too much to say I had a heart attack and died. The first thing I felt was fury. The station was strobing. I bent double, gasping. The train was arriving and I pressed the phone into my face and heard what he was saying. Come to Italy tonight, he said. Iris wanted to go to Switzerland with my father to do business. She might be gone a short or long while. I don't know. Fly into Milan. He said, take the first plane out. I'll pay for your ticket. Get first class.

On the platform, I rushed to buy an economy class ticket for a plane that night. I couldn't question going—I was going—I had to go—but at least I could try, on the way, to remember who I was.

I told Patrick I had something to do for a little while. I thought he might fire me. But part of him knew. He told me to be safe.

I PACKED IN ten minutes at home. I put a toothbrush and a shirt in my backpack. I didn't know how long I'd be in Italy. I knew I'd be there less time than I wanted, so why pack a hopeful bag? I might be there one night. I had no idea what would happen to me. I had never been less certain of anything in my life. All my past selves had folded in on themselves like a curtain thrown open. Densely collapsed into shadow.

I called a cab. I checked in. I hadn't eaten anything all day, I realized.

In the security line I was forced to stand still for the first time since the morning and I thought about the other person I knew in Turin. I knew I might regret any obstacle between Nicola and me. But it would be reassuring to touch against the person I used to be. Then if he stood me up—which was a real possibility—I wouldn't be completely alone. Or maybe I just missed her. I wanted another shot at talking to her.

I messaged Federica. "*Cara* Fede, I'm coming to Turin last-minute for a work thing! Want to meet up for an hour tomorrow morning?"

As soon as I texted her, I felt sure that Nicola would not stand me up. My sense of the future kept switching back and forth.

On the plane I was surging with pure energy. Every sensing part of me, every nerve, was twinkling. Constant, uncontrollable, exquisite motion, even as I sat perfectly still in my chair with my head against the cold dark glass far above the black Atlantic. I spent the whole flight listening to masses and madrigals. The music very slowly dismembered me and suspended all my body parts on golden cords.

Milan. I connected my phone and Federica had responded. Yes, we could go to Fiorio today.

Nicola was wrong when he said that she controlled me. It was my own body that controlled us both with its wild needs . . . I remembered thinking my body was disobedient, but that just meant I had to follow it.

At the airport, I had a cappuccino as mild as dawn. A light taste, totally unaffected, an airy foam. I found the bus to the train station. The bus driver wore a tight tailored blue uniform. Everyone was smoking. It was cold outside, February, but so much more fragrant than New York. Nothing had ever smelled this good. The air smelled like cigarettes and sage and bitter orange. I surely had never breathed before. My eyes were tense with tears and every time I blinked I scattered them over my cheeks.

On the bus ride through Milan's captivating suburbs, I told myself he wouldn't be there when I got to Turin. He wouldn't be there. There was nothing to worry about so long as I believed he wouldn't be there in Piazza Vittorio Veneto where he said he would meet me. There was no chance he would really be there and able to see me. Iris would stop him or Vittorio would stop him. He'd get in a car wreck. Patrick thought he had a moral core. Maybe he did, maybe his morals would stop him, he'd realize he couldn't see me. For my own good. What this was, I told myself, was a quick tourist trip to Italy, to remember it. I could see Federica and look at the ex-votos and walk through the park where Nietzsche had lost his mind. I couldn't let this be a trip for Nicola.

But my body was roiling, roiling, far ahead of me.

It was too late for me.

In Milano Centrale I bought a *brioche alla marmellata*. A

small, soft, squashy pillow with a jammy apricot core. Again, so simple, I'd forgotten. Taken for granted, that was what made it so lovely. Everyone around me spoke Italian so beautifully. The words were as taut as ships' rigging. I closed my eyes and listened to the *caffé*, the heavy porcelain cups ringingly stacked on the bar, the steamy bursts of the espresso machine. The businessmen came in and placed their orders and took their shots and left. The Milan train station had a lofty steel canopy and birds flew under it. Trains to Zurich, Marseilles, Munich. Alpini in their feathered caps. All of this was his.

The train to Turin cost eleven euros. Totally ill, out of my mind, I passed Magenta. Novara. Vercelli. Chivasso. Snow on the fields. These names poured straight into my heart. I could now see that my entire life, and everything I had experienced, had been tracing one enormous circle. And just now the point where I had begun was coming into view.

Ten a.m. in Turin. The buildings looked steeped in tea. I walked by the old apartment where the host family had lived, and the school. The arcades' paint was peeling again, like the men who had painted them for the Olympics had come by and chipped at them.

I walked down Via Roma to Via Po and through Fiorio's cream-colored entrance into the back room, so perfectly elegant it preserved even the lower standards of comfort from the past, the stiff worn velvet banquettes, the dim mirrored interior. Brioches under domes on silver stands, cream puffs on gold doilies, baristas in white with gold epaulets. The elegance was like island gigantism, evolution cut off from the world. They'd kept on their lonely way.

I ordered an espresso. Then Federica was coming toward me, nearly unrecognizable. She looked like my host mother, Carla. It was shocking how old she looked. I remembered the rapture of spotting Nicola at that college party after five years, how different that felt from this. Her face was tight on her cheekbones and forehead, but oddly slack in her cheeks, with a mottled, grayish tone to it. Beauty is orthogonal to moral worth, but I felt she must have conducted herself badly in life to have lost her vitality this way. Maybe this self-inflected effect came from her outfit, which looked chosen for its ugliness. Her pointed boots and black jeans with white seams and burn-out shirt. As a teenager, she would have liked to wear a soccer uniform all the time, and I couldn't imagine she'd changed much.

When she smiled, lifting the skin on her cheeks into many small wrinkles, I felt so much pity it curdled into scorn.

We greeted each other with cheek kisses, and sat.

We began by talking about my flight. "All easy," I said. I was on edge. Last time we'd spoken, on the phone, she'd tried to tell me how alone I would be, forever. I wondered if she would bring that up again. She had seemed to want to take shots at me. Now she acted like she had forgotten that conversation. Maybe she was that disagreeable with everyone all the time.

"Are you hungry? Let me buy you something," she said. She ordered two cream puffs. She directed the waiter to set one down in front of me.

"Are you here for work?" she said. "No, your cheeks are too red."

"They are?"

"You seem like you are on drugs."

I flushed and, breaking my rules about effective lying, admitted I was there to meet a man.

Her mouth fell open and her face transformed. There she was, herself, young again.

"I see," she said finally. "I'm sensitive to the drugs thing because that was Gian's problem."

"How's it going with Gian?"

"I got a divorce," she said.

I felt my eyes widen at that. I imagined the judgment from her Catholic parents. "That's completely terrible, I'm so sorry, Fede," I said.

"You don't need to be that sorry. You make it sound like the worst thing that could happen." We sat in silence as she lifted her macchiato cup. I wasn't sure I understood every single word but this was the voice I had come up on, the first voice that made me desperate to understand Italian.

"I'm sorry," I repeated automatically.

"Meeting a man," she said, inspecting me, in my crumpled black traveling clothes. I felt unimaginably disheveled and regretted telling her.

She said something like, "Maybe you're scared that what happened to me could happen to you." The sentence was a twist of grammar; I wasn't sure I caught it.

"*Forse,*" I said. I hoped this was the right word for *maybe*. I remembered how she had separated herself from me at age sixteen. She'd struck me as less than human because of the way she turned away from passion. Something I could never do.

She became frank, determined, pushing. "I have the feeling, if you came here last-minute to see a man, and you look, forgive me, crazy, that not all is well with you. So I will tell you what I would have told myself: You are your own person. Learn to value yourself," she said, and I thought, what a ridiculous sentiment, it sounds like she read it in loopy cursive over a photo of a beach sunset. "You can be responsible for your own life. You can seek to be responsible."

I stifled a giggle.

She ignored that and sloppily bit the side off her cream puff. She chewed it openly and unselfconsciously, looking at me.

"What are you thinking?" she asked. Where was the

Federica who let me set the terms? She spoke like how she skied. So much faster than I.

I remembered I had mentioned Nicola on the last call. I had a terrible feeling that I wasn't as good at hiding the secret as I thought. Whom else could I possibly be meeting here? She understood. She saw. I blushed.

"I don't know," I said, with an attempt at a casual shrug. It was hard to say anything substantive in Italian. With a burst of inspiration, I added, "Certain things are inexpressible."

"You're good at language!" she said. "Certain things are clear."

She ate the rest of her cream puff.

"Have mine," I said.

"Try to eat it," she said. She turned her macchiato cup this way and that, rolling the last drop of coffee over the porcelain. "Are you doing your art?"

"What art?"

"Your writing," she said.

"How do you know about that?"

"You told me on the phone," she said. "I'm going to say something, Nora." She gestured at my cream puff with her fork and I thought for a moment she was going to try to feed it to me. "You're a creative person who's forgotten about the creation part. You stop short. You don't grow." She said something I didn't quite understand. Maybe it was that I was losing myself, not finding myself. *Perduta. Trovata.*

I noticed the drops on the little round travertine table before I even felt them falling from my eyes. I brought the napkin up to my face and my eyes made it wet. My whole head seemed to be numb.

"Have a bite," she said, the dog trainer.

I lifted the cap of pate a choux off the cream puff. With a sip of sparkling water, I swallowed it like a pill.

"The cream is easier," she said encouragingly. "So? What are you thinking?"

"I don't know what I want to do anymore," I said. "I don't know what my intentions are." (*Intenzioni,* easy enough to guess.) "I do all these things. I don't know why." This felt too broad, giving her too much, so I narrowed—"I don't know what I intend to do in my writing."

"You can only really intend a few things at a time," she said.

How had I never thought of that before.

"I'm just telling you what I learned when I was breaking up with my husband. I don't mean to presume. I've just been thinking about you since our phone call. I was at a low point then and have only become just the slightest bit wiser."

I laid my head on the table. I saw the sparkling water in the glass next to my eyes was shaking.

I don't know how long she watched me. At some point, she paid the check. "Want to go to Siculo?" she said.

Where we got the mulberry granita.

I imagined going with her. We would fall into step beside each other, like in the earliest days. Nicola would pause in the square, let five minutes go by, ten minutes, but surely no longer than that. He would signal to the driver, and they would carry on up to the hills. And Federica and I would be walking away together. Maybe she would be the first person I would tell the truth.

I checked my watch. Twenty minutes. It was hard to breathe. I clenched and unclenched my toes.

I remembered waiting in the halls to enter the rooms, the room of paintings, of singers, of Astrid, rooms of dares, and fear, and things I could not imagine. Relinquishing him would be an act of destruction, and going to find him was creativity itself. I didn't know how I could turn away from the very best thing in my life.

I felt something like panic in having to tell her no. There was a nauseated pulsing feeling in my chest. But Nicola could fix my panic too. That was how we'd met. "No, I'm going to Piazza Vittorio," I said.

"Okay, Nora," she said. And then instead of saying ciao she used the more formal goodbye, *arrivederci*. Until we meet again. She left me at the table.

Maybe she could tell that I thought I'd never see her again in my life.

I stood. I seemed to have forgotten how to walk. I stumbled down the red runner and out through the bar with its gilded mirrors. An old man in a flat cap held the door for me as I exited. I turned right. I walked under the grand arcades, slipping among the silent crowds.

I was angry with her for disordering my reunion with Nicola. I knew that, reeling from divorce, she had a particular view she was invested in, vaunting the benefits of lovelessness. I didn't want her to prove anything to herself by changing me. I didn't want her to treat me like she treated herself. Stop transgressing, that was her idea, stop dissolving, define the boundaries, try writing about it. She thought I was losing myself, not finding myself. She thought I was stopping short of self-knowledge. But I didn't want straightforward things that felt good, simple expressible things. I did not believe in intensity without pain, because pain was the feeling of bare reality. Pain was the feeling of being unprotected and open to the other. Nicola transformed me into something else, and I wanted that.

IN THOSE MOMENTS I did imagine turning around, catching up to her, and telling her yes, we were the same. But she had already gone.

I would have to text her again. I was too proud.

I took gasping breaths of old books, coffee, the water

in the bull's-head fountains straight from the Alps. Via Po faced the river and the Collina, the hill past the river where I had never tried to go. It was like a matte painting of a hill, and the world didn't render beyond it.

With each step I took I felt farther than everything Federica had said. Her words unwrapped from around me and dissolved in the air. It was like walking into infinity. The pure attention I experienced then didn't feel like attention, it felt like hyperdrive, a feel of apprehending everything at once, where each sensation and movement was as loaded with plain meaning as words. The drops gathered up, paused, and tumbled. I remembered how his shoulder blades looked like flapping wings. Nicola was hidden in a painted forest of porcupine and boar and juniper berry, turning leaves, castle sinking in vines, roses growing out of the walls, the spikes lengthening. I loved the challenge he gave me, moving together ever more quickly into an unsafe element, the sea, the snow, out past the forbidden border. Push me, talk to me, take the daylights out of me. Suspend me in the rain where I can see the full circle of the rainbow around me. Reach down from your heaven above me and touch my frozen face. I imagined his basement, the room with the rug against my back, and falling all around us, dead, staring, the coat-clad corpses of his adversaries.

At the edge of Piazza Vittorio I looked at the slow green Po. The cypresses were like fingers. I watched the wind-intoxicated birds rise and fall. Men in red caps were out on their long boats. "How beautiful," I whispered to myself, and my voice was lost immediately in the wind.

A black car by the bridge, creeping along. I ran across the cobblestones, Turin's foggy sunlight bearing down on my shoulders. The door with the blinding sun in the black glass. As I reached for it, I saw the small distant figure reflected behind me and I turned; Federica had followed me to the neck of the piazza. And she waved, as though it were possible to grow up and bridge the silence that could have been more of an adolescent phase than eternal truth, as though the form could change, our minds could change, she could be not my abandoner but a human who was also trying to understand how to live, a person of ambivalence, passion, and self-harm all her own, a shy person and my truest friend. Her mouth was open but I could not hear her. She was only an image now and soon she would be only a memory. We would not again come together, the three of us, as we had in the gondola lift.

She had always seemed so transparent to me. And Nicola was so muddy. I could not see the borders or what was below. I wasn't finished trying.

I turned away. The thick silver handle moved in my hand. The rubber seal opened and released out the air he breathed. The beautiful scent I never thought I'd experience again in my life. Exactly like a dead dear one come back to life. I looked out as I closed it, and she had stopped waving. I was certain we were too far for her to see the shadowy splendor of the interior and there, in the backseat, Nicola.

"Hello," he said. I felt I'd blasted him back against his seat with my rabid larky joy.

"Where are we going?"

"Up into the hills," he said.

No time seemed to have passed at all. I joined him and he pulled the black partition shut.

He reached out and took my throat. He squeezed and released. I've always wanted, he said, to choke you until you pass out.

Yes, I said.

When you wake up, we'll be closer, he said.

ACKNOWLEDGMENTS

Thank you to Jessica Vestuto, whose brilliant reading and incisive editing transformed the book, and whose generosity and kindness created the best possible environment for creative experimentation and collaboration. And thank you to PJ Mark, for whose support, guidance, and incredible knowledge I thank my lucky stars. Thank you to Ian Bonaparte, Kerry-Ann Bentley, Madeline Ticknor, Will Watkins, and everyone at Janklow and Nesbit, and to Kate Nintzel, Laura Brady, Beatrice Jason, Tavia Kowalchuk, Sarah Falter, Eliza Rosenberry, Brittani Hilles, Yeon Kim, and the whole team at Mariner.

I am also extremely grateful to the institutions that supported this book in its earliest stages: Harvard's Office for the Arts, Shaw Fellowship, and English Department provided invaluable funding for research and travel. The Sewanee Writers' Conference Dakin fellowship program and Shakespeare and Company in Paris gave me community in Tennessee and the Left Bank respectively.

I am as always indebted to my teachers—Amy Hempel, Bret Johnston, Joshua Henkin, Dinaw Mengestu, Matt Saunders—and the Brooklyn College Fiction MFA program. At Sewanee, Jill McCorkle and Tony Earley provided galvanizing feedback on early chapters of this book. I am infinitely grateful to Eve Gleichman, David S. Wallace, and

Mark Chiusano for reading all kinds of early drafts of all kinds of things, and to Nasir Husain, Cora Frazier, and Sofia Groopman for their wisdom in our writing group. Thank you to Julian Gewirtz, Lu Zhang, Herb Tam, Phillip John Velasco Gabriel, and Ceramics Club for their constant inspiration from other regions of art.

Thank you to my parents, Nancy and Dan, for letting me go to Italy at fifteen and for not judging the contents of this novel. Thank you to Katie, Charlie, and Trevor.

And thank you to Trisha Baga for all the most liberating ideas.